301305036376 41

Please return this book on or before the date shown above.
To renew go to:
Website: www.slough.gov.uk/libraries
Phone: 01753 535166

Slough
Borough Council
www.slough.gov.uk

KT-426-944

Slough Library Services

Lindwood Barclay is married with two children and lives near Toronto. A former columnist for the *Toronto Star*, he was featured on the Richard & Judy 2008 Summer Reading List with his No. 1 bestseller, *No Time for Goodbye*.

You can discover more about the author at www.linwoodbarclay.com

A TAP ON THE WINDOW

Cal Weaver reluctantly agrees to give a lift to a bedraggled-looking girl one rainy night, though he's aware that inviting a teenaged girl into his car may not be the smartest move. During their short journey, Cal discovers that Claire Sanders is not all she seems. But nothing prepares him for the consequences of trying to help her out. The next morning he finds he's gone from Good Samaritan to murder suspect, and with one girl dead and another missing, he's suddenly at the centre of a deadly puzzle that reaches right through the small town of Griffon — from its bullying police force to its strangely furtive mayor — and finally to one family's shocking secret.

Books by Linwood Barclay
Published by The House of Ulverscroft:

NO TIME FOR GOODBYE
TOO CLOSE TO HOME
FEAR THE WORST
NEVER LOOK AWAY
THE ACCIDENT
NEVER SAW IT COMING

LINWOOD BARCLAY

---◆---

A TAP ON
THE WINDOW

Complete and Unabridged

CHARNWOOD
Leicester

First published in Great Britain in 2013 by
The Orion Publishing Group Ltd
London

First Charnwood Edition
published 2015
by arrangement with
The Orion Publishing Group Ltd
An Hachette UK Company
London

The moral right of the author has been asserted

A catalogue record for this book is available
from the British Library.

ISBN 978–1–4448–2342–4

Published by
F. A. Thorpe (Publishing)
Anstey, Leicestershire

Set by Words & Graphics Ltd.
Anstey, Leicestershire
Printed and bound in Great Britain by
T. J. International Ltd., Padstow, Cornwall

This book is printed on acid-free paper

For Neetha

'Can you swim?'

'Man, you're crazy! Let me go!'

'Because even if you can, I don't like your chances. We're so close to the falls, the current's unbelievably fierce. Before you know it, you're swept over. And it's a long way down.'

'Let me go!'

'You might grab onto one of the rocks just before the top, but the thing is, if you hit one, it'll probably kill you. Like driving into a wall at a hundred miles per hour. If you were in a barrel, like some of those daredevils who've tried going over in one, you might have one chance in a hundred, which is pretty good odds, when you think about it.'

'I'm tellin' you, mister, swear to God, it wasn't me.'

'I don't believe you. But if you're honest with me, if you admit what you did, I won't throw you over.'

'It wasn't me! I swear!'

'If it wasn't you, who was it?'

'I don't know! If I had a name I'd give it to you. Please, please, I'm begging you, man.'

'You know what I think? I think when you go over, it'll feel like flying.'

1

A middle-aged guy would have to be a total fool to pick up a teenage girl standing outside a bar with her thumb sticking out. Not that bright on her part, either, when you think about it. But right now, we're talking about my stupidity, not hers.

She was standing there at the curb, her stringy blond, rain-soaked hair hanging in her face, the neon glow from the COORS sign in the window of Patchett's Bar bathing her in an eerie light. Her shoulders were hunched up against the drizzle, as if that would somehow keep her warm and dry.

It was hard to tell her age, exactly. Old enough to drive legally and maybe even vote, but not likely old enough to drink. Certainly not here in Griffon, in New York State. The other side of the Lewiston-Queenston Bridge, maybe, in Canada, where the drinking age is nineteen and not twenty-one. But that didn't mean she couldn't have had a few beers at Patchett's. It was generally known your ID was not put through a rigorous examination here. If yours had a picture of Nicole Kidman on it and you looked more like Penelope Cruz, well, that was good enough for them. Their policy was 'Park your butt. What can we getcha?'

The girl, the strap of an oversized red purse slung over her shoulder, had her thumb sticking out, and she was looking at my car as I rolled up

3

to the stop sign at the corner.

Not a chance, I thought. Picking up a male hitchhiker was a bad enough idea, but picking up a teenage girl was monumentally dumb. Guy in his early forties gives a lift to a girl less than half his age on a dark, rainy night. There were more ways for that to go wrong than I could count. So I kept my eyes straight ahead as I put my foot on the brake. I was about to give the Accord some gas when I heard a tapping on the passenger window.

I glanced over, saw her there, bending over, looking at me. I shook my head but she kept on rapping.

I powered down the window far enough to see her eyes and the top half of her nose. 'Sorry,' I said, 'I can't — '

'I just need a lift home, mister,' she said. 'It's not that far. There's some sketchy guy in that pickup over there. He's been giving me the eye and — ' Her eyes popped. 'Shit, aren't you Scott Weaver's dad?'

And then everything changed.

'Yeah,' I said. I had been.

'Thought I recognized you. You probably wouldn't even know me, but, like, I've seen you pick up Scott at school and stuff. Look, I'm sorry. I'm letting rain get into your car. I'll see if I can get a — '

I didn't see how I could leave one of Scott's friends standing there in the rain.

'Get in,' I said.

'You're sure?'

'Yeah.' I paused, allowed myself one more

4

second to get out of this. Then: 'It's okay.'

'God, thanks!' she said, opened the door and slid into the seat, moving a cell phone from one hand to the other, slipping the purse off her shoulder and tucking it down by her feet. The dome light was a lightning flash, on and off in a second. 'Jeez, I'm soaked. Sorry about your seat.'

She was wet. I didn't know how long she'd been there, but it had been long enough for rivulets of water to be running down her hair and onto her jacket and jeans. The tops of her thighs looked wet, making me wonder whether someone driving by had splashed her.

'Don't worry about it,' I said as she buckled her seat belt. I was still stopped, waiting for directions. 'I go straight, or turn, or what?'

'Oh yeah.' She laughed nervously, then shook her head from side to side, flinging droplets of water like a spaniel coming out of a lake. 'Like, you're supposed to know where I live. Duh. Just keep going straight.'

I glanced left and right, then proceeded through the intersection.

'So you were a friend of Scott's?' I asked.

She nodded, smiled, then grimaced. 'Yeah, he was a good guy.'

'What's your name?'

'Claire.'

'Claire?' I stretched the name out, inviting her to provide a last name. I was wondering if she was someone I'd already checked out online. I really hadn't had a good look at her face yet.

'Yep,' she said. 'Like Chocolate *E*. Claire.' She

5

laughed nervously. She moved the cell phone from her left to right hand, then rested the empty hand on her left knee. There was a bad scratch on the back, just below the knuckles, about an inch long, the skin freshly grazed and raw, just this side of bleeding.

'You hurt yourself, Claire?' I asked, nodding downward.

The girl looked at her hand. 'Oh shit, I hadn't even noticed that. Some idiot staggering around Patchett's bumped into me and I caught my hand on the corner of a table. Kinda smarts.' She brought her hand up to her face and blew on the wound. 'Guess I'll live,' she said.

'You don't quite look old enough to be a customer,' I said, giving her a reproachful look mixed with a smirk.

She caught the look and rolled her eyes. 'Yeah, well.'

Neither of us said anything for half a mile or so. The cell phone, as best I could see in the light from my dash, was trapped screen down beneath her hand on her right thigh. She leaned forward to look into the mirror mounted on the passenger door.

'That guy's really riding your bumper,' she said.

Headlight glare reflected off my rearview mirror. The vehicle behind us was an SUV or truck, with lights mounted high enough to shine in through my back window. I tapped the brakes just enough to make my taillights pop red, and the driver backed off. Claire kept glancing in the mirror. She seemed to be taking a lot of interest in a tailgater.

'You okay, Claire?' I asked.

'Hmm? Yeah, I'm cool, yeah.'

'You seem kind of on edge.'

She shook her head a little too aggressively.

'You're sure?' I asked, and as I turned to look at her she caught my eye.

'Positive,' she said.

She wasn't a very good liar.

We were on Danbury, a four-lane road, with a fifth down the center for left turns, that was lined with fast-food joints and a Home Depot and a Walmart and a Target and half a dozen other ubiquitous outlets that make it hard to know whether you're in Tucson or Tallahassee.

'So,' I said, 'how'd you know Scott?'

Claire shrugged. 'Just, you know, school. We didn't really hang out that much or anything, but I knew him. I was real sad about what happened to him.'

I didn't say anything.

'I mean, like, all kids do dumb shit, right? But most of us, nothing really bad ever happens.'

'Yeah,' I said.

'When was it, again?' she asked. ''Cause, like, it seems like it was only a few weeks ago.'

'It'll be two months tomorrow,' I said. 'August twenty-fifth.'

'Wow,' she said. 'But, yeah, now that I think of it, there was no school at the time. 'Cause usually everyone would be talking about it in class and in the halls and stuff, but that never happened. By the time we got back, everyone

7

had sort of forgotten.' She put her left hand to her mouth and glanced apologetically at me. 'I didn't mean it like that.'

'That's okay.'

There were a lot of things I wanted to ask her. But the questions would seem heavy-handed, and I'd known her less than five minutes. I didn't want to come on like someone from Homeland Security. I'd used Scott's list of Facebook friends as something of a guide since the incident, and while I'd probably seen this girl on it, I couldn't quite place her yet. But I also knew that 'friendship' on Facebook meant very little. Scott had friended plenty of people he really didn't know at all, including well-known graphic novel artists and other minor celebrities who still handled their own FB pages.

I could figure out who this girl was later. Another time maybe she'd answer a few questions about Scott for me. Giving her a lift in the rain might buy me some future goodwill. She might know something that didn't seem important to her that could be very helpful to me.

Like she could read my mind, she said, 'They talk about you.'

'Huh?'

'Like, you know, kids at school.'

'About me?'

'A little. They already knew what you do. Like, your job. And they know what you've been doing lately.'

I suppose I shouldn't have been surprised.

She added, 'I don't know anything, so there's

8

no point in asking.'

I took my eyes off the rain-soaked road a second to look at her, but said nothing.

The corner of her mouth went up. 'I could tell you were thinking about it.' She seemed to be reflecting on something, then said, 'Not that I blame you or anything, for what you've been doing. My dad, he'd probably do the same. He can be pretty righteous and principled about some things, although not *everything*.' She turned slightly in her seat to face me. 'I think it's wrong to judge people until you know everything about them. Don't you? I mean, you have to understand that there may be things in their background that make them see the world differently. Like, my grandmother — she's dead now — but she was always saving money, right up until she died at, like, ninety years old, because she'd been through the Depression, which I'd never even heard of, but then I looked it up. You probably know about the Depression, right?'

'I know about the Depression. But believe it or not, I did not live through it.'

'Anyway,' Claire said, 'we always thought Grandma was cheap, but the thing was, she just wanted to be ready in case things got really bad again. Could you pull into Iggy's for a second?'

'What?'

'Up there.' She pointed through the windshield.

I knew Iggy's. I just didn't understand why she wanted me to pull into Griffon's landmark ice cream and burger place. It had been here for more than fifty years, or so the locals told me, and even hung in after McDonald's put up its golden arches half a mile down the street. Folks around here who liked a Big Mac over all other burgers would still swing by here for Iggy's signature hand-cut, sea-salted french fries and real ice cream milk shakes.

I'd committed myself to giving this girl a ride home, but a spin through the Iggy's drive-through window seemed a bit much.

Before I could object, she said, 'Not for, like, food. My stomach feels a bit weird all of a sudden — beer doesn't always agree with me, you know — and it's bad enough I've got your car wet. I wouldn't want to puke in it, too.'

I hit the blinker and pulled up to the restaurant, headlights bouncing off the glass and into my eyes. Iggy's lacked some of the spit and polish of a McDonald's or Burger King — its menu boards still featured black plastic letters fitted into grooved white panels — but it had a decent-sized eating area, and even at this time of night there were customers. A disheveled man with an oversize backpack, who gave every indication of being a homeless person looking for a place to get in out of the rain, was drinking a coffee. A couple of tables over, a woman was divvying up french fries between two girls, both in pink pajamas, neither of whom could have been older than five. What was the story there? I came up with one that involved an abusive father who'd had too much to drink. They'd come here until they were sure he'd passed out and it was safe to go home.

Before I'd come to a stop, Claire was looping

the strap of her purse around her wrist, gathering everything together like she was planning a fast getaway.

'You sure you're okay?' I asked, putting the car in park. 'I mean, other than feeling sick?'

'Yeah — yeah, sure.' She forced a short laugh. I was aware of some headlights swinging past me as Claire pulled on the door handle. 'Be right back.' She leapt out and slammed the door.

She raised her purse in front of her face as a shield against the rain as she ran for the door. She disappeared into the back, where the restrooms were located. I glanced over at a black pickup, its windows tinted so heavily I couldn't make out who was driving, that had pulled in half a dozen spots over.

My eyes went back to the restaurant. Here I was, late at night, waiting for a girl I hardly knew — a teenage girl at that — to finish throwing up after an evening of underage drinking. I knew better than to have allowed myself to get into this position. But after she'd mentioned that some guy in a pickup was putting the moves —

Pickup?

I glanced again at the black truck, which actually might have been dark blue or gray — hard to tell in the rain. If anyone had gotten out of it and entered Iggy's, I hadn't noticed.

What I should have done, before she'd gotten into my car, was tell Claire to call her own parents. Let them come get her.

But then she'd gone and mentioned Scott.

I got out my cell, checked to see whether I had

any e-mails. I didn't, but the effort helped kill ten seconds. I hit 88.7 on the radio presets, the NPR station out of Buffalo, but couldn't concentrate on anything anyone was saying.

The girl had been in there five minutes. How long did it take to toss your cookies? You went in, you did your thing, splashed some water on your face, and came back out.

Maybe Claire was sicker than she'd realized. It was possible she'd made a mess of herself and needed extra time to clean up.

Great.

I rested my hand on the ignition key, wanting to turn it. *You could just go.* She had a cell phone. She could call someone else to come and get her. I could head home. This girl wasn't my responsibility.

Except that wasn't true. Once I'd agreed to give her a ride, to see that she got home safely, I'd made her my responsibility.

I took another look at the pickup. Just sitting there.

I scanned the inside of the restaurant again. The homeless guy, the woman with the two girls. Now, a boy and girl in their late teens sitting in a booth by the window, sharing a Coke and some chicken fingers. And a man with jet-black hair, in a brown leather jacket, was standing at the counter, his back to me, placing an order.

Seven minutes.

How would it look, I wondered, if this girl's parents showed up now, trying to find her? And discovered me, local snoop-for-hire Cal Weaver, waiting here for her? Would they believe I was

12

just driving her home? That I'd agreed to give her a ride because she knew my son? That my motives were pure?

If I were them, I wouldn't have bought it. And my motives hadn't been entirely pure. I had been wondering whether to try and get some information about Scott out of her, although I'd quickly abandoned that idea.

The hope of getting her to answer some questions wasn't what kept me here now. I just couldn't abandon a young girl out on this strip, at this time of night. Certainly not without telling her I was leaving.

I decided to go in and find her, make certain she was okay, then tell her to find her way home from here. Give her cab fare if she didn't have anyone else she could call. I got out of the Honda, went into the restaurant, scanned the seats I hadn't been able to see from my outdoor vantage point, just in case Claire was sitting down for a moment. When I didn't find her at any of the tables, I approached the restroom doors at the back, which were steps away from another glass door that led outside.

I hesitated outside the door marked WOMEN, screwed up my nerve, then pushed the door open half an inch.

'Claire? Claire, you okay?'

There was no answer.

'It's me. Mr. Weaver.'

Nothing. Not from Claire or anyone else. So I pushed the door open a good foot, cast my eye across the room. A couple of sinks, wall-mounted hand dryer, three stalls. The doors, all

13

closed, were painted a dull tan and bubbling with rust at the hinges. They stopped a foot from the floor, and I didn't notice any feet beneath any of them.

I took a couple of steps, extended an arm and gently touched the door of the first stall. The door, not locked, swung open lazily. I don't know what the hell I was expecting to find. I could tell before I'd opened the door there was no one in there. And then the thought flashed across my mind: what if someone *had* been in there? Claire, or someone else?

This was not a smart place for me to be hanging around.

I exited the bathroom, strode quickly through the restaurant, looking for her. Homeless guy, woman with kids —

The man in the brown leather jacket, the one who'd been ordering food last time I saw him, was gone.

'Son of a bitch,' I said.

When I got outside, the first thing I noticed was an empty parking space where the black pickup used to be. Then I saw it. Turning back onto Danbury, flicker on, waiting for a break in the traffic. It wasn't possible to tell, with those tinted windows, whether anyone was in the car besides the driver.

The truck found an opening and took off south, in the direction of Niagara Falls, the engine roaring, back tires spinning on wet pavement.

Could this have been the truck Claire'd been referring to when I allowed her to jump in at

Patchett's? If it was, had we been followed? Was the driver the man in the leather jacket? Had he grabbed Claire and taken her with him? Or had she decided he was less threatening than she'd originally thought, and now was going to favor him with the opportunity to drive her home?

Goddamn it.

My heart pounded. I'd lost Claire. I hadn't wanted her in the first place, but I was panicked now that I didn't know where she was. My mind raced while I worked out a plan. Follow the truck? Call the police? Forget the whole damn thing ever happened?

Follow the truck.

Yeah, that seemed the most logical thing. Catch up to it, come up alongside, see if I could catch a glimpse of the girl, make sure she was —

There she was.

Sitting in my car. In the passenger seat, shoulder strap already in place. Blond hair hanging over her eyes.

Waiting for me.

I took a couple of breaths, walked over, got in, slammed the door. 'Where the hell were you?' I asked as I dropped into the seat, the interior lights on for three seconds tops. 'You were in there so long I was starting to worry.'

She stared out the passenger window, her body leaning away from me. 'Came out the side door I guess when you were going in.' Almost muttering, her voice rougher than before. Throwing up must have taken a toll on her throat.

'You gave me a hell of a start,' I said. But there didn't seem much point in reprimanding her.

15

She wasn't my kid, and in a few minutes she'd be home.

I backed the car out, then continued heading south on Danbury.

She kept leaning up against her door, like she was trying to stay as far away from me as possible. If she was wary of me now, why hadn't she been before she'd gone into Iggy's? I couldn't think of anything I'd done to make her fearful. Was it because I'd run into the restaurant looking for her? Had I crossed some kind of line?

There was something else niggling at me, something other than what I might have done. It was something I'd seen, when the light came on inside the car for those five seconds while my door was open.

Things that were only now registering.

First, her clothes.

They were dry. Her jeans weren't darkened with dampness. It wasn't like I could reach over now and touch her knee to see whether it was wet, but I was pretty sure. She couldn't have stripped down in the bathroom and held her jeans up to the hot-air hand dryer, could she? I could barely get those things to blow the water off my hands. Surely they couldn't dry out denim.

But there was more. More disconcerting than the dry clothes. Maybe what I'd thought I'd seen I hadn't seen at all. After all, the light was on for only those few seconds.

I needed to turn it back on to be certain.

I fingered the dial by the steering column that

16

flicked on the dome light. 'Sorry,' I said. 'Just had this thought I left my sunglasses at the Home Depot.' I fumbled with my right hand in the small storage area at the head of the console. 'Oh yeah, there they are.'

And I turned the light back off. It was on long enough for me to be sure.

Her left hand. It was uninjured.

There was no cut.

2

I'd seen that wound on Claire's hand, the ragged bits of skin, the tiny bubbles of blood just below the surface, waiting to come out. She'd suffered that injury — small as it was — only a few minutes before she'd gotten into my car at Patchett's.

Unless Claire was one of the X-Men team, and had super healing powers, the girl sitting next to me now was not the same girl who had been sitting next to me when we pulled into Iggy's.

I had a surreal feeling as we continued along Danbury, like I'd stumbled into a *Twilight Zone* episode. But this was real, and there had to be some kind of rational explanation.

I tried to think it through.

This girl was dressed pretty much identically to Claire. Blue jeans and a short dark blue jacket. The same long blond hair. But, glancing over, I noticed that this girl's hair, like her jeans, was not nearly as wet as Claire's had been. And there was something slightly off about it, like her entire head was askew. I was pretty sure I was looking at a wig.

I broke the silence. 'Do I make a turn soon or anything?'

The girl nodded, pointed. 'Two lights up. Go left.'

'Okay.' I paused. 'You feeling better now?'

18

A nod.

'When you were gone so long, I wondered if you were even sicker than you'd first thought.'

'I'm okay now,' she said quietly.

There was a sudden glare coming from my rearview mirror, even with the night setting. Raised headlights again.

'You were telling me before,' I said, 'about how you met my son.'

'Hmm?' the girl said.

'I was just wondering where it was that thing happened, where he spilled an ice cream cone on you.'

'Oh,' she said, not staring out her window, but still down and to the right, so that the side of her face was still shrouded by the wig. 'Yeah, that was pretty funny. It was at the Galleria Mall. I ran into him at the food court. Like, literally. He was eating this cone and the ice cream fell off the top and landed on my top.'

'Really,' I said. We were sitting at the light where I was supposed to turn left. The truck that had been behind us was to our right, waiting to go straight. It was an SUV, not a pickup, like the vehicle I'd seen at Iggy's.

Before the light turned green, I said calmly, 'How long do you want to do this?'

'Huh?' She almost turned her head to look at me, but resisted.

'This act. How long do you want to go on like I don't know you're not Claire?'

Now she looked at me, and her fear was instantly palpable. She didn't say anything.

'It was a nice try,' I said. 'The hair, the clothes,

it's all pretty convincing. But Claire had a cut on her left hand. She'd just got it, at Patchett's.'

'The cut doesn't matter,' the girl said quietly. 'It just has to work from a distance. It wasn't meant to work close up.'

'What are you talking about?'

She bit her lower lip. 'Just make like you think I'm Claire, okay? Don't do anything weird.'

'Why? You think someone's watching us?' I raised one hand, a gesture to the world around us. 'Someone tracking us on satellite?'

'There was that truck a while ago. Maybe him. I don't know. Could be a different guy.'

I could see why they thought they could pull it off. Judging from the oversized purse she had down by her feet, she'd come out to the car with a similar red bag. It might have been the same one.

This girl's skin tone was about the same as Claire's, almost porcelain. Her facial features were only slightly different. Maybe slightly more oval, but Claire's nose was a little shorter, I thought, even though I'd never gotten a really good look at her. But they were about the same height and build. Skinny, about five six. It would be easy enough for them to pass themselves off as each other on a dark, rainy night, from a distance, especially with the wig, similar clothes, a nearly identical bag. If they'd said they were sisters, I'd have believed it. So I asked.

'You two sisters?'

'What? No.'

'You look it,' I said. 'Although you need to work on the hair. It's a bit crooked.'

'What?'

'The wig. It's off-kilter.' She fiddled around with it. 'That's better. Pretty darn close to Claire's. Not bad.'

'She got this at a Halloween place in Buffalo,' she said. 'Please, just drive me to Claire's house, like you were going to do. It's not far.'

'I'm trying to figure it out. You must have been waiting for her in the bathroom. She goes in, you come out, wearing pretty much the same clothes. You went out the side door as I was going in. I popped into the ladies' washroom.' The girl gave me a startled look. 'Was Claire hiding in there until the two of us drove off?' I could picture her perched on the toilet in the second or third stall, so her legs wouldn't show. I should have kept going after I'd pushed open that first door.

'I guess,' she said sullenly.

'So the idea was, whoever's following her will start following you? And now Claire's free to run off and do whatever it is she wants to do without whoever's following her knowing about it.'

'Wow,' she said. 'You're like a genius.'

'Boyfriend stuff?' I asked.

'Huh?'

'Is some boy stalking Claire? She wants to ditch him and meet up with a new guy?'

The girl made a soft snorting noise. 'Yeah, sure, that's what it's all about.'

'But you said it could be a different guy. Has she got more than one guy stalking her?'

'I said that? I don't remember.'

'What's your name?'

'It doesn't matter.'

21

'Okay, forget your name. If it's not a boyfriend thing, what the hell is it?'

'Look, don't worry about it. It's got nothing to do with me, and it's sure got nothing to do with you.'

'Is Claire in some kind of trouble?'

'Listen, mister — it's Mr. Weaver, right? Claire said you're Scott's dad.'

I nodded. 'You knew Scott, too?'

'Yeah, sure. Everyone kinda knew who he was.'

'Did you know him well?'

'A little. Look, like, I don't know anything. Okay? Just let me out. Anywhere. Right here. Forget any of this ever happened. It's none of your business.'

I watched the wipers repeat their rhythmic swipes across the glass. 'It is my business. You and Claire've involved me.'

'We didn't mean to, okay?'

'Was someone else supposed to pick Claire up at Patchett's? They didn't show so she grabbed a ride with me? Who picked her up at Iggy's?'

'Stop the car.'

'Come on. I can't let you out here. This is the middle of nowhere.'

She unbuckled her seat belt and grabbed for the door handle. The car was doing about thirty. I didn't think she'd actually open it, but she did. Just an inch or so, enough to cause a huge rush of air.

'Jesus!' I shouted, reaching across her and scrambling for the handle. I couldn't reach it and shouted, 'Close it!' She did. 'You out of your goddamn mind?'

'I want to get out!' she screamed, loud enough to make my ears ring. 'It doesn't matter now, anyway! Claire's gotten away.'

'Gotten away from what?'

'Stop the car and let me out! This is kidnapping!'

I hit the brakes and swung the car over to the curb. We were in an area where residential met commercial, where old homes sat cheek by jowl with furniture-stripping and electrical-supply stores. There was a cross street just ahead where a suspended traffic light lazily turned from yellow to red to green and then did it all over again.

'Look, I can take you wherever you want,' I said. 'You don't have to get out. It's pouring. Just — '

She threw open the door, swung her legs out, and bolted from the car, snatching her purse at the last second. She stumbled, went down onto one knee on the grass, yanked the wig from her head, and threw it by some bushes. Her own hair was blond, too, but it only fell to her shoulders, about half the length of Claire's.

I couldn't reach the passenger door from where I sat, so I got out, engine running, went around the vehicle, and slammed it shut.

'Stop!' I shouted. 'Come on! No more questions! Let me drive you home!'

She looked back, just for a second, and waved her hand in the air. It looked like she was holding a cell phone. Telling me not to worry, she'd get someone to pick her up.

Her feet splashed through the puddles, and as

she got to the corner, she turned right, disappearing down the far side of a television repair shop that looked as though it had gone out of business years ago.

I felt a sense of unease as she vanished from view. Rainwater filled my eyes, dripped into my ears.

I tried to convince myself she was right. This wasn't about me. This wasn't my problem.

I got back in my car, did a U-turn.

Drove past a black pickup parked on the other side, lights out. I hadn't remembered seeing it there before hitting the brakes to keep the girl from jumping out of the car.

I drove on another half a mile, that damn truck niggling at me. Finally, I pulled over to the shoulder, checked my mirrors, and swung the car around. In a minute I was back to the spot where I'd seen the truck.

It was gone.

I let the car roll to a stop at the light, looked ahead, to the left and then the right. I didn't see any sign of the truck, or the girl.

So I turned around again and headed for home.

3

Used to be, when I'd get home after something crazy like that, the first thing I'd have said would have been 'You're not going to believe what just happened.'

But that was then, and this was now.

It was nearly half past ten when I came in, and even though Donna would almost always be upstairs in bed by now, there was a time when she'd have come down to meet me the moment she heard the front door open and close.

At the very least, she would have shouted down, 'Hey!'

And I would have said, 'Hey!'

But now, there was no 'Hey!' Not from her, and not from me.

I dropped my coat on the bench by the front door and ambled into the kitchen. I'd missed dinner, as I often did, but I hadn't had much of an appetite the last couple of months. I'd gone in two notches on my belt to keep my pants up, and on those rare occasions when I wore a tie, I could get a couple of fingers inside a buttoned collar.

Last time I'd had anything to eat was around six, sitting in the car, watching the back door of a butcher shop in Tonawanda. A bag of Wise potato chips. The owner suspected someone on his staff was stealing from him. Product, not cash. He was running out of pot roasts and

25

T-bones sooner than anticipated, and figured either his supplier was cheating him or someone under his nose was ripping him off.

I asked him for the hours when he left the shop in charge of his employees, and those were the periods when I staked out the back entry, positioning my Accord down an alley that still afforded a good view of comings and goings.

Didn't take long.

Late this afternoon, around dusk, the wife of one of the butchers drove up to the back, sent a text. Then seconds later the door opened and her husband ran up to her window with a garbage bag wound tightly at the top. She took the bag, threw it onto the passenger seat, and drove off like she'd just robbed a liquor store.

I took pictures using the telephoto, then followed her home. Watched her take the bag into the house. Would have been even better if I could have crept up to a window and snapped some shots of her putting a pork roast into the oven, but there are limits to what I can do. I am called upon, in my line of work, to be something of a Peeping Tom at times, but it didn't seem necessary in this circumstance. I didn't have to prove she'd slept with dinner.

So maybe I wasn't on the trail of the Maltese Falcon or some missing plutonium. In the real world of private investigation, it was food, or building materials, or gas, or cars, or trucks that got ripped off. A while back, I cracked the case of some stolen cedar shrubs that kept going missing every time the homeowner replanted.

When someone stole from you, you not only

wanted your stuff back — you wanted to know who did it. Police are too busy and shorthanded to solve crimes like these. A random theft, a one-shot kind of thing, well, that was pretty hard for me to solve, too, but if there was a pattern, if you were the victim of a serial pain-in-the-ass offender, chances were I could help you out, because I had the time to wait until the son of a bitch who was preying on you did it again.

It wasn't rocket science. It was sitting around and staying awake.

Finding people wasn't all that much different. Husbands and wives and sons and daughters went missing as often as steak and lumber and fuel and Toyotas, although it had been my experience *things* were often more missed than *people*. Someone stole your truck, there was no question you wanted it recovered. But if your two-timing, fist-swinging, scotch-drinking husband failed to come home one night, you had to ask yourself whether good fortune had smiled upon you.

It hadn't been smiling much on us lately.

I opened the fridge, took out a beer, then went into the family room, where I dropped myself like a bag of sand into a leather recliner. On the coffee table lay several sheets of paper torn from an art pad, each one a sketch of Scott. One profile, a three-quarter, and a third, straight on, like a passport shot. Alongside the sketches, half a dozen sharpened charcoal pencils, some soft, some hard, and a small container of fixative spray, about the size of a shaving cream dispenser you'd toss into your travel bag. When

Donna had taken a sketch as far as she could — she never really finished one because she always found something wrong with it — she sprayed it to keep the charcoal from smearing. Even drawings she felt failed to capture our son she kept for reference, to copy those parts she believed she'd gotten right. There was a chemical whiff in the room, which told me she'd been using the fixative earlier. The stuff could take your breath away.

This was Donna's coping strategy. Drawing pictures of our son, some from memory, others copied from photos. I found them all over the house. Here, in the kitchen, next to her bed, in her car. There was one taped to the bathroom mirror for a couple of days that she kept looking at as she put on her makeup. I thought it was a near-perfect likeness, and she must have been thinking the same, but finally she took it down and tucked it in the folder with her other rejects.

'I thought that was a good one,' I said.

'Ears were wrong,' she said.

It was, for us these days, an extended conversation.

I had doubts whether this obsession of hers to capture the perfect image of our boy was healthy. For her, or for me. I suppose that if she'd been so inclined to sit at the computer and work through her grief writing poems and recollections, I might not have felt the same. That method of coming to grips with what had happened to us would have been more private, would not have drawn me in, unless she invited me to read what she'd written. But the sketches involved me. I couldn't avoid them. They might have been therapeutic for her, but for me they were a constant reminder of our loss, and of our failure. And the fact that so many were unfinished, and imperfect, underscored how troubled Scott had been.

Of course, Donna wasn't that crazy about how I was dealing with things, either.

I found the remote under a drawing of Scott with one eye unfinished, turned on the flat-screen, kept the volume low and my thumb on the channel changer. So many of them now. Channels with nothing but food, or golf, or decades-old sitcoms. Even one for poker. People sitting around, playing cards. That was a channel. What would be next? The Parcheesi Channel? I clicked through a couple of hundred of them in under five minutes, then did them all again.

I found it increasingly difficult to concentrate. I had diagnosed myself with something I'd coined PT-ADD. Post-traumatic attention deficit disorder. I couldn't focus because there was always just one thing on my mind. I managed to do my job, more or less, but it was always there, white noise in the background.

Finally, I settled on some news out of one of the Buffalo stations.

Three people were mugged outside a liquor store in Kenmore. A West Seneca man ordered his pit bull to attack a woman, who'd required thirty stitches. The dog's owner told police she had 'looked at him funny.' There was a 'pedal-by' shooting in Cheektowaga. A man on a bicycle fired three times at a house, hitting the shoulder of a man who'd been sitting on his couch watching an old episode of *Everybody Loves Raymond*. Two men were rushed to Erie County Medical Center after getting shot coming out of a bar. A credit union on Main Street was robbed by a man who'd handed the teller a note saying he had a gun, although none was seen. As if all that weren't enough, Buffalo police were looking for three teens who, after stabbing a fourteen-year-old boy behind a house on LaSalle Avenue, poured gasoline on him and then tossed a match. The kid was in the hospital, still alive, but no one expected him to last long.

And that was just tonight.

I turned off the set and scanned that day's *Buffalo News*, which had been tucked into the wicker magazine holder next to the chair, the thin sections already pulled apart by Donna earlier in the day. On the page dedicated to smaller towns outside the city, there was a piece on whether our local police had overreacted at the Griffon Jazz Festival in August. When half a dozen young thugs from out of town crashed the event and started stealing refreshments from the beer tent, it was alleged that some of Griffon's finest, rather than arresting and charging them, tossed them into a couple of cars, took them out past the town's water tower, and liberated them from enough of their own teeth to make a nice necklace.

The mayor, a guy by the name of Bert Sanders, had made bringing the cops in line his number one issue, but he wasn't getting much support from the rest of the council, or the good people of Griffon, who didn't care how many teeth out-of-town troublemakers lost so long as this town didn't turn into Buffalo.

That city was less than an hour away, but it was another planet compared to Griffon, a town of some eight thousand that ballooned to three or four times that in the summer when tourists came here to launch their boats and fish in the Niagara River, attend the various weekend festivals like that jazz event, or shop in the quaint gift shops downtown that struggled to hold on to customers who were being lured away to the Costcos and Walmarts and Targets of western New York.

It was late October now, so Griffon was back to its generally sleepy self. There wasn't that much crime to worry about here. People locked their doors — we weren't stupid — but there were no parts of town you feared going into after dark. Shopkeepers didn't draw metal doors down over their storefronts at the close of business. We didn't have helicopters with searchlights hovering over the neighborhood at three in the morning. But there remained a sense of unease, given our proximity to Buffalo, where the violent crime rate was roughly three times the national average, a city that regularly placed in the top twenty most dangerous American cities. There was a fear that at any moment, unruly hordes would surge northward like marauding zombies, putting an end to our more or less tranquil lifestyle.

So folks in Griffon gave their police some

31

leeway. The head of the business association was encouraging everyone to sign their names to a pledge of support for the local police force. Downtown shops were urged to carry a form headlined OUR GRIFFON COPS ARE TOPS! and all who put their names to it would not only feel good about themselves but get a five percent discount on their purchases. A little way to say thank you for keeping our town safe.

Not that bad things didn't happen in Griffon. We had our share of problems. Griffon wasn't Mayberry.

There were no Mayberrys anymore.

I looked at a framed photo on the bookshelf across the room. Donna and me, Scott in the middle. Taken when he was thirteen. About the time he was entering high school.

Before the storm.

Smiling, but careful not to show his teeth, since he'd had braces put on only a couple of weeks earlier and was feeling self-conscious. Looking awkward, embarrassed maybe, trapped in his parents' arms. The thing was, at that age, what didn't make you feel uncomfortable? Parents, school, girls. The need to belong, to fit in, was a much greater driving force than the desire to ace a math test.

He'd always been looking for a way to fit in, yet couldn't turn himself into somebody he wasn't to do it.

He was an eccentric kid, more likely to have Beethoven than Bieber on his iPod. Loved almost anything that was deemed classic, in music, in movies, even cars. That aforementioned Maltese

Falcon was a poster on his wall, and there was a model of a '57 Chevy on his bookshelf. He drew the line at classics of literature. He wasn't one to stick his nose into a four-hundred-page novel, a trait the doctors had said might be linked to attention deficit disorder — a more clinical diagnosis than the one I'd assigned to myself — although I was never sure I bought any of that stuff. But he did have all the graphic novel classics. *Black Hole, Waltz with Bashir, The Dark Knight Returns, Maus, Watchmen.*

With the possible exception of those graphic novels, he shared few interests with other kids his age. He didn't care about the Bills — something of a religion in these parts — and he'd rather put sticks in his eyes than watch the adventures of Jersey Shore nitwits, spoiled housewives, mentally disturbed hoarders, or any of the other reality shows his friends were addicted to. He did like that comedy about the four nerdy young scientists — even took some comfort in it, I think. It gave him hope that you could be uncool, and cool, at the same time.

So as much as he wanted friends, he wasn't about to feign interest in things he cared nothing about to acquire them. But then, summer before last, at another Griffon concert, this one featuring several alternative bands, Scott connected with a couple of Cleveland-area kids, vacationing here for the summer, whose contempt for much of popular culture provided an initial bond. These new friends found that mocking the world around them was easier when you softened the edges of it, and they

33

accomplished that with booze and marijuana. They weren't exactly the first.

No question, Scott'd had opportunities before to try alcohol and drugs — show me a parent who thinks his kid lives in a neighborhood where this stuff isn't available and I'll show you a parent with his head up his ass — but up to now he had, as best we could tell, given them a wave. He'd been at that age where pleasing his parents was important, but now was moving out of it. Having friends trumped making Mommy and Daddy happy.

Not exactly an unfamiliar tale.

There were changes in his behavior. Small things at first. An increased fondness for secrecy, but hey, what kid, moving further into his teens, didn't want privacy? But then came trust issues. We'd give him cash to pick up a few items at Walgreens, and he'd return home with only half the items but no money. He forgot things. His grades started to slip. He'd claim to have no homework, but then we'd get notices from the school that he wasn't turning in assignments. Or that he'd skipped classes altogether. Values he once held dear — being straight with us, keeping his word, honoring his curfew — no longer seemed to matter.

I never blamed drinking and pot for all of this. I didn't have a *Reefer Madness* moment, convinced that marijuana had warped our son's mind, turned him against us. Part of it was his age. Part of it was wanting to belong. Scott had bonded with the kids who made getting drunk and high part of his life, and when they went

34

back to Ohio at the end of that summer, our boy's new habits were well established.

We prayed it was a phase. All kids experimented, right? Who didn't have a few too many beers, smoke a few too many joints? Still, we had the talk — lots of them — about making *smart choices*. Jesus, what a load of bullshit. What the kid could have used was a swift kick in the ass, and to be locked in his room till he was twenty.

Maybe, if we'd been smart enough to figure out that he would move on to something stronger, that's what we would have done.

Because it wasn't beer and pot they found in his bloodstream when they did the autopsy.

Donna and I talked — endlessly — about getting help for him. Counseling. Enrollment in a program. We sat up nights, searching for answers on the Internet, reading other parents' stories, finding out we weren't alone, but taking little comfort in that fact. We still didn't know the best course to follow. We tried the usual things, to varying degrees, but with a consistent lack of success. Yelling. Grounding. Emotional blackmail. Rewards for improved behavior. '*Pass that math test and I'll get you a new iPod.*' Instilling guilt. I told him what he was doing was killing his mother. Donna told him what he was doing was killing his father.

But there must have been part of us that thought — I know this was true of myself — that while things were bad, they weren't *that* bad. Millions of kids got into trouble in their teenage years and came out the other side. I wasn't high much when I was in my teens, but getting shit-faced was a weekly ambition. Somehow I'd survived.

We deluded ourselves.

We were stupid.

We should have done more, and we should have done it sooner. It ate at me every day, and I knew it ate at Donna, too. We blamed ourselves, and there were moments when we blamed each other.

Why didn't you do something?

Me? Why didn't you do something?

In my heart, I believed I deserved more of the blame. He was a boy. I was his father. Shouldn't I have been able to get through to him? Shouldn't I have been able to connect in ways Donna could not? Shouldn't I have been able to use some of the smarts I'd acquired in my former career to knock some sense into him?

Reading the paper without really taking it in, staring at the TV without any idea of what I was watching, finishing my beer and going back into the kitchen for another, and repeating the whole process again, took up the better part of two hours. I figured by that time Donna really would be asleep and wouldn't have to pretend.

I was right.

When I went upstairs the only light on was in the bathroom off our bedroom. If I'd come up earlier, Donna's eyes still would have been closed, but she'd have been faking it. You don't spend twenty years with someone and not know when they're really sleeping, and when they're trying to put one over on you. But never mind. It wasn't like I'd ever call her on it. It was a game we played now. *I'll pretend to be sleeping so you don't have to feel weird not talking to me.*

I stripped down in the bathroom, brushed my teeth, killed the light, and quietly slipped under the covers next to her, my back to hers. I wondered how long this would go on, how it would end, what could help us move forward.

I still loved her. As much now as the day we met.

But we weren't talking. We couldn't find the words. There was nothing to be said because there was only one thing either of us was thinking, and it hurt too much to talk about.

I imagined making the first move. Turning over, edging closer, slipping my arm around her. Not saying a thing, at least not at first. I imagined the warmth of her body as I held her. Felt her hair on my face.

Imagined it so perfectly, it was as though it was happening.

I lay awake for some time, staring at the ceiling, or the digital clock on the bedside table. One in the morning, then two.

It wasn't all our fault.

Not everything.

Some of it, of course, was Scott's. Sure, he was a kid, but he was old enough to know better.

But there was someone else. Not the kids from Cleveland. Not the kids from Griffon who might have sold Scott marijuana and liquor.

I wanted to find the one who gave him 3,4-methylenedioxymethamphetamine. What the rest of the world knows as ecstasy.

That's what the toxicology report turned up.

That's the stuff that evidently made Scott believe he could fly.

I was going to track down the guy who provided that final, fatal dose.

We all had a lot to answer for, but that son of a bitch, as far as I was concerned, was the one who'd pulled the trigger.

4

In the morning, the woman comes into the bedroom bearing a tray.

'Hey,' she says to the man, who is still under the covers.

He raises himself up on his elbows, surveys the breakfast as the woman sets it down on the bedside table.

'Scrambled,' he says, looking at the eggs almost suspiciously.

'Just the way you like them,' she says. 'Well cooked. You should eat them before they get cold.'

He gets his legs out from under the covers, sits up on the edge of the bed. He is wearing a pair of faded white flannel pajamas with blue pinstripes. They are threadbare at the knees.

'How'd you sleep?' the woman asks.

'Okay,' he says, reaching for the napkin and spreading it on his lap. 'I didn't hear you get up.'

'I got up around six, but I tiptoed around the kitchen so I wouldn't disturb you. You given up your hobby?'

'What? What do you mean?'

'Where's your little book? It's usually right there.' She points to the bedside table.

'I write in it after you leave,' he says, setting the plate atop the napkin, resting it on his knees, taking his first bite. 'Good eggs.' The woman says nothing. 'You want to sit down?'

'No. I have to go to work.'

He picks up a strip of bacon, bites into it with a crunch. 'You want some help?'

'Help with what?'

'At work. I could come and help you.' He chews the bacon, swallows.

'You're confused,' she says. 'You don't come to work.'

'I used to,' he says.

'You just enjoy your breakfast.'

'I could help, I really could. You know I'm good at doing the books. I catch everything.'

The woman sighs. How many times has she had this conversation? 'No,' she says.

The man frowns. 'I'd like things to be the way they used to be.'

'Who wouldn't?' the woman says. 'I'd like to be twenty-one again, but wishing don't make it happen.'

He blows on his coffee, has a sip. 'What's it like out today?'

'Nice, I think. Rained last night.'

'I'd like to go out, even in the rain,' the man says.

She's had enough. 'Eat your breakfast. I'll be back for the tray before I go.'

5

I'd arranged to meet Fritz Brott, owner of Brott's Brats, the Tonawanda meat business I'd been watching for a couple of days, at his shop. He had an office in the back where we could talk privately.

Brott had been a fixture in the community for more than twenty years. He'd emigrated from Germany in the seventies with his wife and infant daughter. He found work behind the deli counters at several different grocery stores over the years, but his dream had always been to have a shop of his own. In the early nineties he learned that the elderly owner of an existing butcher shop wanted to retire. He'd hoped his son would follow him in the family business, but before the boy had even hit his twenties it was clear he was more interested in computers than red meat. So the father continued to run the business on his own for another two decades, but with no one to pass it on to, he decided to sell.

Fritz didn't just know meat. He was a great cook, and had a recipe for bratwurst that had been handed down through several generations. That, he told his wife, would be the store specialty. It also provided the shop a new name.

Fritz's wife, while an integral part of the business, wasn't in the shop every day. From home, she handled the paperwork, paid the bills, did the payroll, all so Fritz could concentrate on making his bratwurst and selling his thick, beautifully marbled steaks. It was his wife who noticed things had not been adding up in recent weeks. They were making less money. The sides of beef hanging in the freezer were not turning out the same number of steaks and roasts as they used to.

Something was up.

Fritz employed three men. Clayton Mills, in his late sixties, had worked for the previous owner, and lived alone now that his wife of thirty-two years, Molly, had passed away. He lived frugally, and he never struck me as a viable suspect. Nor did Joseph Calvelli, about ten years younger than Clayton, with a wife and a grown son who ran an investment firm.

Very quickly, I zeroed in on Tony Fisk, twenty-seven, married, with two kids, aged five and two. It was his wife, Sandy, I'd seen drive up to the back door and wait for Tony to pop out with a green bag that he pushed through her window before running back into the store. This had happened at a time when Fritz was not in the shop.

'What have you got for me?' Fritz asked as he settled his nearly three hundred pounds into the chair at his desk in the tiny office.

I'd brought along a small laptop, onto which I had transferred some photos, and video.

'Mr. Brott, I watched your place for two days and based on what I've seen, you don't have anything to worry about where Mr. Mills and Mr. Calvelli are concerned.'

He waited. He knew where I was going.

'Tony,' he said, pursing his lips. 'The son of a bitch.'

I opened the laptop and set it on his desk. 'This is yesterday afternoon. Just before five o'clock.'

His eyes narrowed. 'When I was out. Getting my truck fixed.'

'That's right.' I had clicked on PLAY to start the video. 'You see this car pulling up here?'

Fritz nodded.

'I checked the plate to confirm. This car is registered to Anthony Fisk. Behind the wheel is his wife, Sandra. They call her Sandy.'

'Yeah, I know her. I know that car.'

'You can't quite tell in the photo here, but there are two children's safety seats in the back. I believe, although I can't confirm, that she had their two children with her in the vehicle.'

Fritz was stone-faced. 'Okay.'

'She stops the car right by the back door. She's got her phone out now, and she's using her thumbs, so it looks to me like she's sending someone a text. Now she waits a few seconds . . .'

Fritz's jaw tightened as his eyes stared at the screen.

'And out comes Tony, with the garbage bag. Hands it off to her and runs back into the shop. She takes off.'

'Go back.'

'Hmm?'

'You can go back and frame-freeze this?'

'Freeze-frame, sure.' I fiddled around with the mouse pad, took the video back about fifteen

43

seconds, then started advancing it again.

'There. Stop it there.'

I had to go back a fraction of a second. Fritz wanted to get a look at the bag. He appeared to be studying the shape of what was inside, tracing its outline with his finger, half an inch from the screen.

'Can you blow that up?' he asked me.

'Sure.' I moved my finger on the mouse pad, clicked. 'There you go.'

'Shoulder roast,' he said.

I smiled. 'I guess you would know.'

'The son of a bitch,' he said.

'I can try to get hold of the text message his wife sent him. But all it would probably say is she's there. It's not likely she'd type out 'bring out the meat' or anything. If you're going to bring the police in and have him charged, they can probably get the transcript.'

'You think I should call them?'

'That's up to you. You asked me to find out if someone was stealing from you, and I believe this answers your question. What happens next is your decision. Is he a good employee?'

Fritz nodded sadly. 'He's worked three years for me. Does his job. Does what I tell him. I treat him good. Why would he steal from me?'

'He's maxed out on his credit cards. And his wife just got cut from four days a week to three at Walmart.'

The sorrow that had washed over Fritz's face a moment ago was transforming into something else. 'There were days I didn't think I'd be able to keep a roof over my head, back when I first

44

came to this country, but I never stole from anybody.' He pointed his finger into the air. 'Not once.'

He stared down at the top of his desk, shook his head, then trained his eyes on the closed metal door like it was made of glass and he could see Tony right through it.

'I went to his kid's christening,' Fritz said.

'It happens,' I said.

'I let him stay, what's it say to the others? It says 'Hey, you steal from Fritz, he'll forget about it. He's a softie.' That's what they'll think.'

'Like I said, it's your call. I'll write you up a formal report of my investigation, my hours, what — '

Fritz waved his hand. 'Fuck that. I know.' He pointed to the laptop, the frozen image of Tony clutching the bag of meat. 'I've seen it with my own eyes.'

'You'll get a report, just the same,' I said, 'when I invoice you.'

His eyes were still boring into that door. I had a pretty good idea what he was thinking, and what he was going to do next, but hoped I was wrong.

'Tony!' he bellowed. I was right. In the tiny office, it was like a cannon going off.

I'd have preferred that Fritz waited until I was gone before he acted on what I'd found out for him. I gathered information. I didn't hang around to mete out sentences. I could handle the confrontations if they developed, but they weren't what I was paid to deal with. I wasn't a counselor, God knows. I just found stuff out.

45

This was never more true than when I handled cases involving cheating spouses. You watch TV detective shows, especially back in the sixties and seventies, you'd think a lot of investigators are above that kind of work. In the real world, those kinds of detectives have to rely on food stamps. When you worked in private investigations, saying no to divorce work was like opening a donut shop and refusing to sell coffee. When I found out a husband was sleeping with his secretary, I didn't tell his wife she should kick the guy out, pour gasoline all over his Porsche and light a match, drill a hole in the bottom of his boat. If she wanted to forgive him, look the other way, didn't matter to me one bit.

I didn't care what Fritz did with Tony, just so long as he did it without my being there.

Wasn't working out that way.

The door swung open and there stood Tony in a bloodied apron, a blood-smeared cleaver in his right hand. He looked like he'd just stepped off the set of a horror movie. All that was missing was the severed head grasped by the hair with his other hand.

'Yeah, Fritz?' he said.

'How long?'

'What?' A look of puzzlement. Feigned, no doubt, but it looked genuine.

'How long you been stealing from me?'

I'd never taken any employee relations course, but there had to be a rule somewhere that you shouldn't accuse one of your people of theft when they're wielding a meat cleaver. If Fritz was worried about it, he gave no sign.

He planted his hands on the arm of the chair and pushed his considerable bulk to a standing position, then came around the desk on the far side from where I'd been sitting. But now I was on my feet, too, and the three of us had formed a little triangle.

'I don't know what you're talking about,' Tony said.

'Don't lie to me,' Fritz said. 'I know what you've done.'

I kept my eyes on the cleaver. The thing looked like it weighed ten pounds if it weighed an ounce. And Tony's arms were evidence that in his hands the tool was light as a feather.

'What?' he persisted. 'What the hell are you talking about?'

Fritz swung the laptop around, pointed to the screen, the paused video of Tony running out to his wife's car. Said nothing.

Tony blinked a couple of times, looking at it. 'What's that?'

'That's a thief,' Fritz said. 'And that's a thief's wife.'

Tony, his mouth tight, shot me a menacing look. He'd put it all together in a second.

'Get out,' Fritz said to him. 'Get out and don't come back. I'll mail you your last check.'

Tony took his eyes off me and focused them on his former boss. 'You docked me,' he said.

'What?'

'The day my kid was sick. She had that fever, a hunnert and four, we thought she was gonna die, we took her to the hospital. I couldn't come in and you docked me a day's pay.' Tony shook his head. 'I'm just paying back what you owe me.'

And he raised the cleaver over his right shoulder, getting ready to put some power into it.

'Don't even think about it,' I said, my voice firm but calm.

Tony glanced my way. A lot had happened in the few seconds since he'd last looked at me. I had a pistol in my hands now, the Glock 19 for which I had a concealed carry permit. The weapon was pointed directly at Tony's chest.

'Don't be a part of history,' I said.

'Huh?'

'I've never shot anyone before. You'd be a first.' We sized each other up for a full five seconds. Finally, I said, 'We all need to catch our breath.'

His arms frozen, he stared straight into the barrel. Out of the corner of my eye I saw Fritz retreat a couple of steps.

'Put the cleaver down,' I said.

Tony nodded at me with his eyes, telling me he was going to do what I asked. But he brought that cleaver down a hell of a lot faster than I was expecting, driving the blade into the top of Fritz's desk. When Tony took his hand off the handle, the cleaver was still standing.

Tony looked at me and said, 'I don't forget.' Then he turned and walked out of the room, his hands going around his back to undo the knotted apron strings.

Fritz was dumbfounded, his mouth hanging open so wide I could have shoved a pot roast in there. His eyes went from my gun to the door and back to the gun. He'd just had the shit scared out of him.

I was feeling a little rattled myself. I holstered my weapon.

'I thought it was bullshit,' he said, his voice cracking. 'About his girl being sick. I thought he was making it up.'

★ ★ ★

I had a hell of headache on the drive home. Tension, most likely. I usually have some pain reliever in the glove box, but there was nothing there, so as I was coming into Griffon I wheeled into a gas station that was also a convenience store and went inside.

They had small bottles of Tylenol, so I grabbed one of those, along with a bottle of water, and reached into my back pocket for my wallet as I approached the counter.

'Hey, how ya doin' ,' the kid at the cash register said, not really asking, just saying what he felt he had to say to everyone. He was about Scott's age, fifteen to seventeen. Face ravaged by acne, hair hanging over one eye that he brushed away every three seconds.

'Great,' I mumbled. I handed him a ten and he rang up the two items.

'Bag?'

'Hmm?'

'You want a bag?'

'No.' I glanced at the counter. There was a clipboard there, with what looked like a petition attached to it, as well as a pen on a string.

But the people who had signed, a considerable number, were not opposed to something, but in support. It was headlined: OUR GRIFFON COPS ARE TOPS.

'You can sign it if you want,' the kid said without enthusiasm. 'Manager says I'm supposed to ask everyone.'

I worked my nail under the plastic wrapping that hugged the top of the pill container as I scanned the form's preamble, which sat below the headline, and above the names. It read: 'We the undersigned are 100 percent behind the good men and women of the Griffon Police Force and appreciate the terrific job they do! Our cops are tops!'

I peeled away the plastic, popped the lid, struggled to remove the cotton. If I'd had only ten seconds to live, and one of these pills could have saved me, I'd have been a goner. Getting the cotton out of the way took the better part of half a minute. Then I shook out three red pills, cracked the cap on the water bottle, and washed them down.

'You must have some headache,' the boy said.

Holding the clipboard, I looked over the names of those who'd signed the top sheet, which was about half full, but didn't see any I immediately recognized. There was a spot, alongside an individual's name, where people were supposed to write down their home and/or their e-mail addresses. Not everyone had included this information.

I flipped to the second page, which was full, as were the three behind it. About seventy percent had put down information other than their names, thereby making it easier for someone to authenticate the signatures, should they want to.

'How many people who come in sign this?' I asked.

The boy shrugged. 'I don't know. It's mostly just the old people, anyway.'

I smiled. 'People like me.'

'No offense,' he said. 'When you're my age, cops around here stop you all the time for doing nothing.'

Scott had said the same thing, the last year or so. Not more than a week before we lost him, he'd come home telling us he'd seen a Griffon cop doing a pat-down body search of a girl behind Patchett's. 'She hadn't done anything wrong,' he'd said. 'Cop just wanted to feel her up.'

I'd asked Scott at the time whether the girl was going to make a complaint. 'She won't do anything,' he'd said. 'You can't do anything about these guys. I don't think he thought anyone saw him, so I shouted, 'I know who you are, dickface.' Scared him pretty bad. And then I ran like hell.'

'You gonna sign it or what?' the kid behind the counter asked, bringing me back to the present.

I saw a signature I recognized. 'Donna Weaver.' I studied it a moment, even ran my finger along the page where my wife had taken this pen and signed her name.

'No need,' I said.

'You know what I think?' the kid asked.

'Tell me.'

'I think the cops are collecting these, and checking the names and the addresses, and figuring out which people who live here have signed and which ones haven't.'

'You don't say.'

He nodded wisely. 'Oh yeah. That's how they work.'

'So I guess you've signed it, too? Just to be safe?'

He grinned and shook his head. 'Manager told me to, and watched me when I did it. But I wrote down 'Dougie Douche.' No way I'd ever sign something supporting these clowns.'

'You're not a fan?'

'You ever had someone spray paint down your throat?'

'Excuse me?'

'I wasn't even the one doing the tagging. It was my friend, but he took off, leaving me with the spray cans, when the local cops showed up. One of them decided to do some graffiti in my throat.'

'That could have killed you,' I said.

'Yeah, well, she just did a couple quick shots. Lost my breath for a few seconds. My teeth and lips were yellow.'

'She?'

Someone else came in to pay for gas. The kid grabbed the clipboard, told me to have a nice day, and turned his attention to the new customer.

★　★　★

52

I got back in the Honda, drank half the bottle of water, then put the car in drive.

It was only three or four minutes to home from there, but the pulsing in my temples and above my eyes was already starting to fade when I turned down our street.

And then, just like that, the headache was back.

It probably had something to do with the fact that a Griffon police cruiser was parked across the end of our driveway.

I was thinking they'd find out pretty damn fast that I hadn't signed the petition.

6

It was almost five.

Donna usually got home around four thirty from her job at Griffon Police Service. They changed the name on the building a few years back. No longer was it the Griffon Police Force. That sounded a bit too, well, forceful. Too close to the truth, actually. So they changed it to 'Service,' which made it sound more like they were gun-toting caterers. The powers that be must have decided that if they sounded gentler, they'd somehow be perceived that way.

Didn't happen.

And while Donna did work there, she didn't carry a gun, or ride in a cruiser, or work weekends and nights. She went in Monday to Friday, nine to four, got all the statutory holidays off, and didn't have to wear a uniform. That's because she wasn't a cop. She worked in payroll and admin, making sure everyone's monthly paychecks got deposited to the financial institution of their choice, sorted out overtime disputes, and remembered to pay the department's bills so that when a Griffon resident dialed 911, somebody answered.

So it was possible that a Griffon cruiser parked in front of our house was not a cause for worry the way it might be for anyone else. Donna knew every member of the force, if not personally, at least by name and Social Security number. She had been known, on occasion, to bring in baked goods and share them with anyone who walked past her desk. An officer could have been dropping by to return the favor. Donna and one of the town's two female police officers — Kate Ramsey — sometimes went to the movies together, although not lately. Neither Donna nor I had been particularly social with anyone lately.

But still, I didn't have a good feeling about this.

Only half a block from home, my cell, sitting on the seat next to me, rang. I glanced down and saw the word HOME. Used to be, Donna called me at least a couple of times during the day. Usually nothing important. Just calling to chat. She'd know there was a good chance I wouldn't answer, but that it was still safe to try, since I'd have my phone muted if I was someplace where I didn't want to make my presence known.

I snatched up the phone.

'Yeah,' I said.

'The police are here,' she said.

'I'm just coming down the street,' I said. 'I thought maybe it was Kate.'

'No. It's Haines and Brindle.'

'Haines,' I said solemnly. One of the younger cops on the force, although he still had more than a decade in. He'd been the one who came to us with the news, in August. 'I don't know Brindle.'

'You're in for a treat, then,' she said.

'What's going on?'

'They're not saying. They want to talk to you. At first I thought maybe they'd found out who

55

sold him the drugs, had come to tell us.' Donna could draw pictures of Scott all day, but it was hard for her to write his name out, or say it aloud. 'But I think they'd have been willing to talk to me about that.'

I'd have been surprised to learn that tracking down who provided Scott with ecstasy was still a priority for the Griffon Police Service, if it ever was. Not that the cops around here weren't concerned about keeping the peace. They just went about it differently. If they thought you were a drug dealer, particularly one from out of town, they took you out back of a Griffon snowplow shed, beat the living shit out of you, then gave you a lift down to Niagara Falls and dropped you off in front of some abandoned industry on Buffalo Avenue.

There'd long been stories about excessive force around here, which explained Scott's take on that officer patting down the girl behind Patchett's. He'd said there was no reason for it, but for all I knew, the officer had a legitimate suspicion she was up to something. I'd learned long ago, during my stint with a police department, that when you gave someone — male or female — the benefit of the doubt, you reduced the odds that you'd be going home at the end of your shift.

For the most part, no one around here was troubled by rumors of police overstepping their bounds. The citizens of Griffon felt safe in their homes. As long as that sense of security continued, they didn't need to know the details.

When I was honest with myself, I had to admit

56

that was my attitude, too. I knew that if and when I found the one who sold Scott XTC, X, E — whatever they were calling it on the street these days — I'd handle the matter myself.

'Talk to you later,' I told Donna, and ended the call. I pulled up alongside the police car, saw the two male officers inside. I pulled over to the curb ahead of the cruiser, got out, glanced at the house and saw Donna watching through the living room sheers.

Ricky Haines, the younger of the two, got out on the passenger side and nodded. Early thirties, black hair and moustache, all neatly trimmed. In shape, too. He had the look of someone who might have played football at some point, although he was a little shy of the necessary bulk. Hockey, maybe, although bulk had its pluses there, too.

'Mr. Weaver,' he said, touching his index finger to his forehead in a mini salute.

'Officer Haines.'

'Good memory,' he said.

It's hard to forget the name of the man who told you your son was dead.

The other door opened. This cop looked to be in his late thirties, and if he'd ever played a sport, he'd long since given it up. I was guessing he weighed two-eighty, and he was carrying a good chunk of it around the middle. There was more hair above his lip than on his head.

'This is Officer Hank Brindle,' Haines said.

I nodded. 'Hey.'

'So you're Donna's husband,' he said. His voice was low and gravelly.

'That's right.'

He nodded, thought about that for a second, then said, 'Wonder if you might be able to help us out with something.'

'I'll give it a try.'

Brindle pointed to my Honda Accord. 'This car's registered to you?'

'Yes.'

'Were you driving around in this vehicle last night?' Brindle asked.

'Yes.'

'Can you tell us where you were?'

'It would depend on the time,' I said.

'Say around ten.'

'I was on my way home.'

Brindle nodded. 'On your way home from where?'

'I'd been doing some work in Tonawanda.'

Brindle's head kept nodding. 'Ricky here tells me you're a private investigator. That right?'

I nodded, waiting. I could've asked what this was about, but cops had a way of getting to things in their own sweet time, and didn't like to answer questions. I knew the drill.

Brindle nodded thoughtfully again, then glanced over at his younger partner. 'I guess I'll let you take it from here. You're more up to speed on this.' I thought I heard a hint of resentment.

I turned my attention to Haines. 'Up to speed on what?'

'We're looking for a girl,' Haines said. 'A teenager.'

I waited.

'Her name's Claire Sanders. Seventeen. Blond

58

hair, about five five. Hundred and fifteen pounds or so.'

'Why you looking for her? She done something?'

'It's important that we find her,' Haines said, sidestepping the question.

I persisted. 'Because she's done something, or because she's missing?'

Haines cleared his throat. 'She's unaccounted for. We'd be grateful for your cooperation here, Mr. Weaver. This is kind of an unofficial inquiry, to be honest. Considering who Claire's father is, we've opted to handle this with discretion.'

I had to think a second. Claire Sanders? 'This girl is Bertram Sanders' daughter? She's the mayor's kid?'

'I can see why you're a detective,' said Brindle.

'Our information,' Haines said, 'suggests you may have encountered Claire last night.'

'You have a picture of her?'

Haines got out his phone, tapped it a couple of times, and approached me. He held the phone close enough that I could see the screen, but didn't hand it to me. The photo looked like it had been taken at a party. The girl was laughing, her head tilted back, a martini glass in her hand. I was guessing it was off Facebook.

'I gave that girl a ride last night,' I said. 'But I'm guessing you already know that.'

Haines nodded. 'You picked her up at Patchett's.'

No sense denying it. 'Yeah. I get picked up on closed-circuit?'

Haines hesitated, then said, 'Yup.'

59

'That something you do a lot, Mr. Weaver?' Brindle asked. 'Pick up teenage girls?'

'She tapped on my window when I was stopped at the sign. Asked for a lift home.'

'And you gave her one.'

'Yes.'

'So you already know Claire Sanders?' the older cop asked.

'No,' I said.

'Hmm,' Brindle said. 'If it was me, and some young girl asked me for a lift — assuming I was in my own car and not the cruiser — I'd feel a bit odd about that. Like maybe it wasn't the smartest thing in the world to do.'

'She recognized me. She said she'd known my son, Scott.' I looked at Officer Haines at that point.

Hank Brindle cocked his head like a dog hearing a whistle. 'That's the one that died, right?'

I felt warm under my collar. 'Yes.'

'Got stoned and went flying off the roof of Ravelson Furniture a couple months back,' Brindle said, like we were just reminiscing. 'I got that right?'

'Yeah.'

'You got that call, didn't you, Ricky?' he asked Haines.

'Yeah.' His face flushed. 'I had to deliver the news to Mr. and Mrs. Weaver.' I sensed discomfort.

'I remember that,' Brindle continued. 'That was the week I didn't get any of the overtime I was due in my pay slip. 'Cause your wife had taken some time off and didn't put it through.'

60

Now my neck was feeling hot. I made fists, not because I was planning on taking a swing at anyone, but to channel the tension. I kept my hands down so Brindle wouldn't think I was about to hit him in the nose, much as I wanted to. 'On her behalf, allow me to apologize for the inconvenience,' I said.

Brindle waved a hand. 'No biggie.' He cleared his throat. 'So you gave this girl a ride because she knew your son?'

'It seemed wrong, at that point, to leave her standing in the rain. I told her to get in. She asked for a ride home.'

'Did she tell you her name?' Brindle asked.

'Just Claire.'

'So you dropped her off at her home?' Haines asked.

They were both looking at me intently. I had a bad feeling about the way this was going, because the story I felt it was inevitable I'd have to tell stretched the limits of credibility.

'No, I didn't drop her at home. We stopped at Iggy's, out on Danbury. Claire said she felt like she was going to be sick.'

'You could have pulled over to the side of the road for that,' Brindle said.

'She asked to go to the restaurant, so I pulled in and waited in the car. She was in there for quite a while, so I went in looking for her, couldn't find her, but when I got back outside there was a girl sitting in my car.'

'What do you mean, 'a girl'?' Haines asked. 'You mean Claire.'

I shook my head. 'I thought it was her, at first.

This girl wanted me to think she was Claire — she was wearing a wig to make her look like Claire, and her clothes were similar — but there were differences you could spot up close. For one, Claire had a cut on the back of her left hand, but this girl didn't.'

'Whoa, whoa,' Brindle said. 'You're saying Claire Sanders went into Iggy's, but it was a different girl that came out.'

'That's what I'm saying.'

'What the hell happened to Claire?'

'I don't know.'

'Who was the second girl?' Haines asked.

'No idea. A friend of Claire's, obviously, but she wouldn't tell me her name. Once we were down the road a short stretch, and I realized she wasn't Claire and called her on it, she told me to keep acting like I thought it was her. In case anyone was watching.'

Brindle made another snorting noise. 'This is the craziest story I ever heard.'

'No, wait,' Haines said. 'If Claire was being, you know, stalked or something, and wanted to lose that person, that'd be a way to do it.'

'That was what I was thinking,' I offered.

Brindle was shaking his head. 'This is horseshit.'

'She demanded to get out of the car around Castleton and Berkeley,' I said. 'I let her out.'

The cops exchanged looks. Then Haines said, 'Did Claire say anything, before she went into Iggy's? That suggested she was about to switch places with someone else?'

'No. If I'd known what they were planning, I

62

wouldn't have gone along with it.'

'She say anything about where she might be going?'

'Just home,' I said.

'That's probably what it was,' Haines said.

'Huh?' said Brindle.

'Some stalker — and not the creepy killer kind, but an ex-boyfriend or something — was bugging her and she needed to get away. Maybe to see a different boy. So she set her friend up as a decoy.' He smiled and shook his head in admiration. 'Pretty damn clever when you think about it.'

Brindle looked unconvinced.

I said, 'Except where's Claire now?'

'My bet,' Haines said, 'is she's with the boy she really wants to be with. Gettin' it on somewhere. That's probably what happened.'

I said, to both of them, 'How did you know to check Patchett's?'

Brindle pointed his thumb at Haines, who said, 'She was known to go there, so it was kind of a starting point.'

'Let me ask you again,' I said. 'Are you looking for Claire because she's done something, or is she missing? Have you some reason to be concerned for her?'

Haines rubbed his chin, an awkward gesture designed to fill time. 'I guess there's always reason to be concerned about somebody when you can't find them.' He clapped his hands together, rubbed them. 'I guess we're done here, Mr. Weaver. We'll get out of your hair now.'

'I hope you find her soon,' I said as the two of

them started getting back into their car.

Brindle locked eyes on me. 'With a fishy story like the one you just told us, about some look-alike girl getting in your car, you better hope we do.'

7

I watched as the cruiser did a three-point turn in the street and rolled back up to the corner, turned left, and disappeared. When I got into the house, Donna was standing there.

'What's going on?'

'It's okay,' I said.

'I didn't ask if everything was okay. I asked what's going on.'

'I gave one of Scott's friends a ride last night. They're trying to find her.'

'Her?'

'Yeah. Girl named Claire.'

'You picked up a girl hitchhiking?'

'Not . . . hitchhiking. She was out front of Patchett's, asked for a lift. She recognized me, said she knew Scott.'

'How would she recognize you?'

'She said something about seeing me drop him off at school. It was raining. Look, if you'd been there, you'd have given her a ride, too.'

'I might,' she said. 'You don't see the difference between my doing it and you doing it?'

'Of course I do.'

'I could do it without exposing myself to as much risk,' she said. 'But you, picking up a young girl, late at night? That seemed like a good idea?'

'I told you why I did it.'

Her mouth opened slightly as something dawned on her. 'I know why you did it. You thought she might *know* something. You think everyone may *know* something. You keep interrogating everyone under twenty in this town, you're going to put your foot in it sooner or later. You'll push someone too far, get yourself in trouble.'

She didn't know the half of it.

'That wasn't why I picked her up. But yeah, I'd probably have gotten around to asking her some things, but she cut me off before I had a chance. Said she didn't know anything.'

'They're all wary of you.'

'Maybe they should be,' I snapped.

Donna didn't flinch. 'You're obsessed.'

'I'm obsessed? Do I have a sketchbook this thick?' I held my thumb and index finger an inch apart.

This time a microscopic twitch. I'd wounded her. Trying to soften my voice, I said, 'I'd have thought you wanted answers, too.'

She lightly touched the closest wall, as though bracing herself. 'Would that make everything better for you? Finding out where he got the stuff? Who gave it to him or sold it to him? Then you'd have your culprit. Then you'd be off the hook. Would I be, too? Would I be exonerated as well? Could you stop blaming me as much as you blame yourself?' She lowered her head and touched her fingers to her forehead, massaged it, then said, 'Let's say you find whoever it is. Let's say you could even get him to confess. Then what'll you do? Turn him in? Mete out some kind of frontier justice of your own?'

66

'I can't talk about this now,' I said.

'And the thing is, whoever it is, if it hadn't been that person, it would have been somebody else. What you don't get is, *who* has never been the issue. The issue is *why*. Why'd he take the stuff in the first place? What was wrong with his life that he thought getting high could fix?'

'I told you, I can't do this now.'

'Of course you can't,' Donna said with mock acquiescence. 'When would be a better time? Maybe I could make an appointment.'

'I'm worried about this girl,' I said. 'I don't think she disappeared because of some stalker boyfriend. I don't think she'd have gone to all that trouble, to have another girl dress up like her, just to ditch some guy.'

'I have no idea what you're talking about,' Donna said. 'Are you talking to me, or are you talking to yourself?'

I gave my head a shake. 'I guess to myself.'

'There's your problem,' she said, turned and walked away.

★ ★ ★

I wasn't able to just let it go. I couldn't go about my own business while the Griffon police looked for Claire Sanders. I'd meant what I said when I told the girl who'd pretended to be her that, even if the two of them never intended to, they had involved me.

Now that I knew the girl was missing, nearly a day after I'd given her a lift, I was reevaluating everything I'd done the night before. I shouldn't have let the second girl get away. I should, at the very least, have gotten her name. I should have followed her when she bolted from the car. I should have asked Claire more questions. Was there really a guy in some pickup watching her? If so, who did she think it was?

Woulda coulda shoulda.

I didn't much care for Officer Brindle's parting shot, that I'd better hope they found her soon. But there was some truth in it. If something had happened to Claire — I didn't even want to think about what that might be — it was a safe bet they'd be coming back with more questions.

But I was getting ahead of myself. Teenagers took off all the time, and it didn't necessarily mean something bad had happened to them. But I knew, as well as anyone, the kind of agony parents went through when they hadn't heard from their kids, when they had no idea where they were. Like you're at the bottom of a well and can't climb out. I had an inkling of what Claire's parents had to be going through. What I didn't know was whether getting the police to handle the matter quietly was the way to go.

Like I was in any position to criticize how any other parents dealt with their kids.

I didn't want to wait to find out what progress Haines and Brindle made in their discreet search for Claire. I could find her as quickly as they could, if not quicker. I knew something they didn't. I knew what Claire's friend looked like. If I could learn who she was, and get to her, I could find Claire. This girl had to know where she'd gone. They'd cooked up this disappearing act together.

I was betting I could get her name without even leaving the house.

I went to the kitchen, past Donna, who was standing at the sink with her back to me, and grabbed the laptop sitting there. I dropped into the recliner where I'd passed time the night before, and logged on to Facebook.

But not as myself. I didn't have a Facebook profile.

After Scott died and I began looking into where he might have gotten the ecstasy, I needed to know who his friends and acquaintances were. Ten or fifteen years ago, that would have involved a lot of legwork. Once I'd found one friend, I'd have leaned on him to get the names of more. And then when I'd gone to visit those people, I'd have repeated the process.

These days, all I had to do was go to the number one social network. There wasn't, in my experience, a kid today who wasn't on it, although I suspected it wouldn't be long before the younger generation found some other way to connect. All their parents were on Facebook now, ruining it for them, crowding them out, posting videos and pictures of dogs and cats and cute babies, and tarting up clichéd aphorisms — 'This Is Your Life. Be Who You Want to Be!' — in colored boxes with fancy fonts.

When I'd started snooping around Facebook, the first thing I'd had to figure out was Scott's password.

I worked at it, off and on, for three days. I

entered everything I could think of, starting with the obvious ones many people use. Like PASSWORD. But I knew Scott was far too clever for that. So I moved on to his birthday, and tried every variation of it. Day, month, year. Year, month, day. And so on. No luck there.

Then I tried the names of pets. We hadn't had that many over the years. There was our white poodle, Mitzy, who got run over by a FedEx truck when Scott was seven. He'd accidentally let the dog out of the house when he was heading out to play with friends, and saw Mitzy chase after the truck and get caught under its rear wheels. He cried for a couple of days straight, and we swore off any more dogs at that point.

There was a gerbil named Howard that came into our lives for three months when Scott was ten. He got out of his cage, and we found him, a week later, stuck behind a bookcase. It wasn't pretty.

No joy on MITZY or HOWARD.

So then I entered everything I'd ever known him to be interested in. Movie titles and characters. Celebrity names. Favorite songs and musicians. Names of cars.

Nothing worked.

Then, one day, I thought of two words he used all the time whenever he wanted to get our attention. He might shout them from any room in the house, or blurt them out when he came into a room. Two words that he ran together as one. From the time he was little, until the day he —

You get the idea.

'Momdad!' he'd yell. 'Momdad!'

I tried MOMDAD.

I was in.

Trouble was, I was too overcome, my eyes too misted, to be able to study his list of friends for several minutes.

But once I did, I learned he had two hundred and seventeen of them. A respectable number, if not huge. While Scott was part of the network, he didn't do all that much socializing on it. He posted rarely, and when he did — a clip, say, from a favorite movie or *Family Guy* episode, or a link to an article from one of his favorite sites — few people chimed in with comments. There were only a handful of people with whom he actually exchanged messages, but those were the people I'd first checked out. Some discreetly, some not so discreetly.

As I'd thought she might be, Claire Sanders was listed as one of Scott's friends, but there was no interaction between them beyond that. No private messages back and forth.

But right now, I wasn't interested in who Scott's friends were. I wanted to know who Claire's friends were. So I clicked on her name, went to her Facebook page, and immediately saw that she had more than five hundred of them. This could take a while. But I was confident that anyone she could talk into posing as her was going to be a Facebook friend.

First, I looked at photos she'd posted, but there were only a few, including the one that Haines had shown me on his phone. I found a couple of party shots featuring a girl who looked like the one from my car, but the photos hadn't been tagged with identifying names.

I clicked on Claire's friends list and started scrolling through it, looking at all the postage stamp-sized faces, hunting for the girl who'd tried to pass herself off as Claire.

If only it were that simple.

Not only were the profile images small, but many of them were poorly shot, or featured the individual with others. Lots of Claire's friends, like millions of others on Facebook, didn't even use a picture of themselves for their profile. They used shots of famous people. For example, one boy, Bryson Davies, was passing himself off as George Clooney. Another, Desmond Flint, was Gort, the robot from *The Day the Earth Stood Still*. Several kids were animated cartoon characters, like Snoopy, or Cartman from *South Park*.

The girls also embraced this practice. Elizabeth Pink, I was sure, was not a dead ringer for Lady Gaga. If Patrice Hengle looked like her profile image, then she needed help. She'd posted a photo of a pepperoni pizza slice.

If none of Claire's female friends whose profiles featured actual pictures of themselves looked like the girl I was searching for, I would come back to these, click on their personal pages and hunt for more representative photos. At least, I would search those whose profiles I could access. If Scott and Claire did not have these friends in common, there was a strong likelihood I wouldn't be able to get into their personal pages, given that I was signed in as Scott.

All these new opportunities for digging into people's private lives presented an equal number of obstacles.

Slowly, I scrolled through the list and studied female faces. Many were easy to dismiss immediately. They were too old, or had different hair or skin color. Every time I spotted a blond girl in her teens I stopped, clicked on the pic, and went to the individual's personal page to view a larger image. When I found it was the wrong person, I went back and repeated the process.

'You're invading his privacy, you know. I still think those things matter.'

I looked up from the laptop screen to see Donna standing in the doorway to the kitchen.

'Right now, I'm invading someone else's privacy,' I said. 'It's kind of how I've made my living for some time now in case you hadn't noticed.'

'Let it go.'

'I told you, this isn't about Scott.'

'It's about this girl you picked up.'

'Gave a ride to,' I said.

'What did you say her name was?'

'Claire.'

'Claire what?'

'Claire Sanders.'

Donna's eyebrows went up. 'Bertram Sanders has a daughter named Claire. Is that who you picked up?'

'Yes.'

'And she's missing? That's who Brindle and his partner were asking you about?'

'That's right.'

She folded her arms. Concern pushed anger from her face. 'That must be so awful for him.'

'Him?'

'Well, his wife — his ex-wife — too, of course. He's divorced.'

'You seem to know a lot about him.'

'He's the mayor, and he's in the station all the time, not that he's particularly welcome there. He likes to come in and harangue Augie on a regular basis.'

Augustus Perry. The police chief. Someone whose unlisted home number was in my own phone's contact list, for reasons that were more than professional. I thought back to the item I'd read in the paper the night before, about Mayor Bert Sanders' fight with the Griffon police over allegations of brutality. Did it make sense that the mayor, who'd pissed off everyone in this town who wore a badge, could reasonably expect the cops to indulge him with a discreet search for his daughter?

Yet that seemed to be what Brindle and Haines were doing.

Maybe Augustus Perry was happy to do the mayor a favor. It could buy him leverage in the future. The chief was good at having people owe him one.

'You think the mayor would go to him directly?' I said. 'Ask for help finding his daughter, without making a big official thing of it?'

'A lot of people are willing to swallow their pride when it comes to their kids' safety,' Donna said. 'You think maybe this is something you shouldn't be sticking your nose into?'

'It's already there,' I said. I told her, briefly, about the events of the previous evening. How I might be one of the last people to see Claire before she went missing.

'What do you know about Bertram Sanders?' I asked.

'Former professor at Canisius College. Political science. Wrote a couple of books that did okay, I think. One of them was a flattering profile of Clinton. He's left of center. He could have stayed and taught there a few more years but opted to take early retirement.'

'Why?'

She shrugged. 'Maybe he'd had enough. A woman I work with, she took a course with him ten, twelve years ago. He asked her out a few times.'

'He hit on his students?'

'So they say. Didn't seem to trouble him that he had a wife, although I suspect it must have troubled her, given that she finally left him. And despite this failing, apparently he's this big idealist. Believes in something called the Constitution. Doesn't like Augie's approach to streamlining the justice system.'

A nice way to put it. Taking a felon behind a building and breaking his nose instead of laying charges was one way to keep the court system from getting too clogged.

A ten-second silence followed as Donna stood there, staring at me.

'What?' I asked.

'This is how it used to be,' she said. 'How we

used to talk. I remember how, when you'd get home, you'd tell me all about the things you were working on.'

'Donna.'

'This is the most we've spoken in weeks.' Another pause. 'You remember my friend Eileen Skyler?'

'Who?'

'She was married to Earl — he worked the border at Whirlpool Rapids before it went NEXUS only.'

'Vaguely,' I said.

'Things started to fall apart for them after their daughter, Sylvia, died in that crash at the top of the South Grand Island Bridge when she got cut off by the gas truck and there was a fire. She was thirty-two. Her husband had left her about a year earlier.'

'I remember.'

'It hit them pretty hard, which is no surprise. They were so sad, so heartbroken, that they didn't know how to talk to each other anymore. The smallest pleasures made them feel guilty. And most of the pleasure they'd found in life had been being with each other. It got to the point where they lived on different floors of their house. Earl came in the back way, right by the stairs, and lived on the top floor, where he set up a hot plate and put in a small fridge. Eileen used the front door, and lived on the first floor. Set up a bedroom down there. They lived in the same house but could go weeks without ever having to see or talk to each other.'

I said nothing.

'So what I keep wondering is, are things going to get better around here, or should I put in a call to Gill?'

Gill Strothers was a carpenter and general handyman we'd used around the house for several small projects, although he had tackled larger ones for other people. Additions, new kitchens. All cash-under-the-table jobs. He did good work.

'Do you want me to call him and ask him if he could put in a set of stairs by the back door there? Is that what you'd like me to do? I'm not saying it's what I want. I just wanted to get an idea if that's what *you* want.'

'Donna,' I said, shaking my head tiredly and looking down, my eyes scanning past the multiple square facial images, 'I don't want you — '

And I saw her. There on the screen. Her head cocked a bit to one side, blond hair cascading across her forehead, tucked behind her ear. It was her. I was sure of it.

'Son of a bitch,' I said.

I clicked on the name next to the picture. HANNA RODOMSKI.

I looked up to tell Donna I'd found her, but she'd left.

8

I got out of Facebook, called up the online phone directory, and found a C. Rodomski at 34 Arlington Street, which was on Griffon's west side.

I grabbed my keys. Heading out the front door, I called back into the house, 'Be back in a bit.' I didn't know where Donna was, or whether she'd even heard me.

The Rodomskis' house was a broad bungalow, set back from the street, with an expansive, well-manicured lawn. There was an operating fountain in the center that looked like an oversized birdbath and fit in, on this street, like a Rolls hood ornament on a Kia. The Rodomskis had what looked like the nicest house on an okay street, which I'd learned long ago, from a friend who sold real estate, is not nearly as desirable as having an okay house on a very nice street. Every other home on Arlington was pulling the value of the Rodomski place down.

A white Ford Explorer and a dark blue Lexus were parked in the double driveway. I pulled in behind the Explorer, got out, crossed the flag-stone walk to the front door, and rang the bell.

I could hear muffled shouting inside. A man's voice asking if someone was going to get it, a woman saying he was closer. I waited, figuring that sooner or later someone would get here.

The door was opened by a silver-haired man

in his late forties, early fifties, probably just home from work. The collar of his crisp white shirt was unbuttoned, his tie askew, the cuffs of his dress pants rested on black socks instead of shoes. The big toe of his right foot was peeking at me through a hole. In his hand was an oversized wineglass that was half full of red.

'Yeah?' he said.

'Mr. Rodomski?' I said.

'Whatever it is, we don't want any.'

'I'm not selling. I'm here to — '

'Who is it, Chris?' a woman shouted from someplace else in the house.

He swiveled his head around, yelled, 'I don't know!' Then, back to me, he said, 'What'd you say you're selling?'

'I said I wasn't. My name is Cal Weaver. I'm a private investigator.' I extended a hand.

Chris Rodomski shook my hand, which was clammy enough to make me sorry I'd offered it. 'Really?' he said.

I took out my wallet and displayed my license for half a second. I could have allowed him a closer look, but his eyes were glassy and I didn't see the point.

A woman I presumed was his wife appeared at the bottom of the stairs and turned toward the door. Big hair, auburn in color, and a little too much lipstick, suggesting to me that when she was little, she had a hard time coloring within the lines. Her cheeks were overly rouged, almost clownlike. She had a glass of red wine in her hand as well, but it was just about ready for a refill.

'Who's this?' she said to her husband. There

79

was a hint of slurring. She hadn't reached total inebriation, although I had a sense it was her destination.

'It's a detective, Glynis.'

'The police?' she said, and the skin beyond the red circles on her cheeks instantly paled. She set the glass down on the closest surface, a side table.

I told her my name. 'I'm not with the police. I'm private.'

'What's this about?' She'd put one hand to her chest, as though checking to see how quickly her heart was beating.

'I'm sure everything is fine,' her husband said. He looked at me apologetically. 'Glynis always assumes the worst.'

'That's because that's how things usually turn out,' she shot back.

'May I come in?' I asked, nodding toward the living room.

'Just tell me if it's about Hanna,' Glynis Rodomski said. 'I have to know if this is about Hanna.'

'It is,' I conceded. 'At least, in part. Is she here?'

'No,' her husband said quickly. 'She's not.' Which immediately made me wonder whether she was.

We sat down in the adjoining living room. I caught a glimpse of the kitchen through a doorway. Dishes piled by the sink, a leaning stack of newspapers, an uncorked bottle of wine, an open box of Cheerios. Unless they were having cereal for dinner, that box had to have been sitting there all day. By contrast, the living

80

room was pure Martha Stewart. Two matching couches, two matching chairs, with perfectly positioned throw pillows on all of them.

Chris Rodomski tossed a pillow aside before taking one of the chairs, and it hit the broadloomed floor silently. Glynis scowled at him, ever so briefly, but I was guessing my presence was more disconcerting to her than his contempt for her decorating touches. She sat on one of the couches and I took the other empty chair.

'Do you know where Hanna is now?' I asked.

They exchanged looks. 'Not right this second,' he said. 'There are a number of places she could be.' He tried to be offhand about it. 'With her friends, probably.' He adopted a look of grave concern toward me. 'We really need to know what this is about before we start answering your questions.'

'It's about that little business she has with her boyfriend, isn't it?' Glynis blurted. 'I told her that would end up biting her in the ass.'

Chris Rodomski shot her a look. 'We don't know that Mr. Weaver's visit has anything to do with that.'

'Business?' I asked.

He waved his hand dismissively at me. 'Tell us why you're here.'

I took a breath. 'Hanna has a friend named Claire Sanders, doesn't she?'

'Yes,' Glynis said.

'Claire hasn't been seen since last night, and I'm trying to find her. I figured Hanna might be able to help me.'

'What do you mean, she hasn't been seen?' she

asked. 'She's missing?'

I hesitated. There was a difference between not knowing where someone was and categorizing them as missing. 'She needs to be found,' I said, and left it that.

'I have no idea where she is,' Glynis said. 'Claire, I mean. She comes around here once in a while, but she's only going to come here if Hanna's home, and she's not home all that much.'

'But she lives here,' I said, making a statement more than asking.

'Well, sure, *technically*,' Hanna's mother said, 'but she spends pretty much every waking moment with her boyfriend.'

'Not just waking,' her husband sneered.

'Who's that?' I asked, getting out my small notebook.

'Sean,' Hanna's mother said.

'Sean what?'

'Skilling,' Chris Rodomski interjected, putting the wineglass to his lips and taking a long sip.

'That's right,' Glynis said suddenly. 'Sean Skilling. Every time I try to think of the name, I come up with 'skillet.' '

I asked, 'Does Hanna carry a cell phone?'

Glynis rolled her eyes. She seemed less tense, now that she realized I was here more about Claire than her own daughter. 'Are you kidding? It's surgically attached to her hand.' She rethought that. 'Or her head. I don't know which.'

'Could you call her, tell her to come home?'

'What will I tell her?'

'I don't know. Something's come up. A family matter. You need her to come home.'

Glynis looked skeptical. 'I can try.' She picked up the receiver on a landline phone that was sitting on a table next to the couch.

She held the phone to her ear and waited. She nodded almost imperceptibly with each ring, then said, 'Oh, hi, sweetheart. It's your *mother*. Could you please come over? There's something your father and I need to discuss with you. But' — she looked at me — 'it's not the sort of thing I can talk to you about on the phone.' A pause, then, with forced cheerfulness, 'Hope you're having fun.'

Glynis ended the call. 'She'll either call back or she won't. She probably saw it was me and didn't answer. She sees our name and generally ignores it. I could text her, but it wouldn't make any difference.'

Rodomski shook his head. 'Which is really a pain in the ass when you need to get in touch with her. You got kids?'

I hesitated. 'A son.'

Rodomski nodded enviously. 'You're better off, believe me. Girls can get into so much more trouble.'

'Have Hanna and Claire been friends a long time?' I asked.

'Since around seventh grade, I think,' Glynis said. 'They're inseparable. Sleeping over at each other's houses, trading clothes, going on school trips.'

'What do you know about Claire?' I asked.

Glynis shrugged. 'She's a nice girl.'

Her husband said, 'She's the mayor's daughter, you know.' A pause. 'That horse's ass.'

83

'You're not a fan?'

Chris shook his head. 'You watch the news? You see the kind of things going on half an hour's drive south of here? You want that kind of thing happening in Griffon? Far as I'm concerned, the cops here do what they have to do, and I'm okay with it. Bert Sanders is more worried about some troublemaker's rights than he is about our right to be able to be safe in our beds at night. I signed that petition. Signed it more than once. Every store I go into, I sign it. How about you?'

'I never seem to have a pen on me,' I said.

'You either support Chief Perry or you don't, that's how I feel.'

'The chief and I have a complicated relationship,' I said. I wasn't interested in talking politics any longer. I turned to his wife and asked, 'When's the last time you saw Hanna?'

She glanced at her husband and then back at me. 'I didn't hear her come in last night, and I guess she was off to school pretty early this — '

'Hanna didn't come home last night,' Chris said. 'For God's sake, Glynis, stop fooling yourself.'

'If she didn't come home, where was she?'

'With that boy. Sean. She's over at his house most nights.'

'He lives with his parents?'

Rodomski nodded. 'I guess they don't see anything wrong with it. A girl shacked up in their house with their son.'

'Shacked up,' Glynis said mockingly. 'What century are you from?'

84

'I need Hanna's cell phone number,' I said to both of them, 'and an address for Sean Skilling.'

'I can give you the number, but I don't know exactly where the Skillings live,' Glynis said. 'I'm sure they're in the book, though.'

She recited the number, which I scribbled into my notebook. 'They go to school together?'

Glynis nodded. 'And Sean has a car.'

'What kind?'

She looked hopelessly at her husband. 'It's a pickup,' he said. 'Probably a Ford. You know Skilling Ford, just outside of town?'

I did.

'That's them.'

'What kind of work do you do, Mr. Rodomski?'

'I'm a financial adviser,' he said.

'Here in Griffon?'

'No, we have an office down on Military Road.' He pronounced it 'milltree,' like everyone else around here did.

'I work, too,' Glynis said indignantly. 'Looking after him and our daughter. That's a full-time job.'

'One of Glynis' little jokes,' Chris Rodomski said wearily. 'She thinks if it's funny once, it's funny a hundred times.'

I handed them each a business card. 'If Hanna comes home before I run into her, give me a call. Maybe by then I'll have found Claire anyway.'

They each took a card without looking at it.

'One last question. What's this business you mentioned?'

'Hmm?' Glynis said, playing dumb.

85

'When I came in, you asked if this was about that business they've been running. You said you told Hanna it could come back and bite her in the ass.'

'It has nothing to do with Claire Sanders,' Chris Rodomski said. 'I think we've helped you out as much as we can.'

They showed me to the door.

As I walked back to my car, I took a small detour down the side of the house to get a look at the backyard. Even in the darkness, I could make out several garbage cans and an old rusted swing set. It had to have been years since Hanna had played on that. I thought of Chris Rodomski's nice suit, the hole in his sock. Perfect living room, messy kitchen. Beautiful front yard, a jungle out back.

The Rodomskis liked to make a good first impression, but didn't give a damn what you thought once you got to know them.

9

When she pops in from work to see that he is okay, and to bring him some takeout — Buffalo chicken wings and fries — he is sitting in the chair with a car magazine open on his lap.

'I don't understand these what-they-call-'em nav systems,' he says. 'All the cars have them now. Never had one of those in a car.'

'I hear they don't work that well,' the woman says. 'Heard about some idiot woman, she kept doing what the system told her and drove right into a lake.'

The man laughs softly. 'That smells like wings,' he says, taking the Styrofoam box and opening it. 'Looks delicious.'

'I brought you lots of napkins and wet wipes,' she says, handing them over. 'Try not to drop the bones all over the room.'

Like it would matter. He's always spilling his food. Once a week or so she tries to get in here and clean up the mess, but honestly, doesn't she have enough to do? The room reeks, but she stopped noticing the smells long ago.

'Did you think about what I said this morning?' he asks, biting into a wing, tearing at the chicken with his gray teeth.

'What did you say this morning?' she replies. She remembers — she always knows what it will be about — but feigning ignorance stalls things for a while.

'About going in to work? Or just going out?'

'Enough. You're wearing me out.'

She gathers some magazines on the bed — car magazines, a People and half a dozen National Geographies — and sets them neatly on the bedside table. 'You can't ask me the same thing every day and think you're going to get a different answer. You — oh for God's sake, there's toast crusts in your bed.'

The man says, 'If it's getting me out that worries you, I think I could manage the stairs myself. It'd just take a while, that's all.'

'It's not about that,' she says. 'You know that.'

Something that troubled her that morning is eating at her again. Where's the book? The one he writes in three times a day, or more? Now that she thinks about it, she hasn't seen it for days.

'Where's your stupid little notebook?' she asks.

'I told you, I write in it after you leave.'

'Since when?'

'I just do.'

'Where is it right now?'

'I think it fell under the bed. Might be stuck between the bed and the wall.'

'Move aside, I'll find it for you.'

'It's okay,' he says. 'I'll do it.'

'Better find it fast or you'll forget what to write,' she says, deciding to drop it, at least for now. She has to go.

As she turns to leave, he says, 'Wait.'

She stops. 'What?'

'The boy,' he says. 'What's up with the boy?'

She is confused for a moment, unsure which boy he's referring to. His stepson, or the one who's caused them so much trouble lately. She decides on an answer that covers all the bases.

'Everything's under control,' the woman says. 'We're doing our best to sort things out.'

'Maybe,' the man says, allowing a naive sliver of hope to creep into his voice, 'it's a good thing, what happened. I mean, it might mean things will change.' He smiles at her with those gray teeth. 'I could use a change.'

'No,' she says. 'It doesn't mean that at all.'

10

He was always on my mind. It was true all through this period, but even now, after all this time, that's still the case. Almost like a low-pitched hum, no matter what you're doing, that's always there in the background.

I thought about what he was like, the things we did together. Moments. Mental snapshots. Some of the memories were pleasant, some less so. Some of them were like signposts along a journey.

When Scott was eight, the school called because he'd been in a fight with another boy. Donna couldn't get away from work, but I was between jobs, so I headed over. I found him sitting on a bench in the office, staring down into his lap, his legs just barely long enough to touch the floor with the tips of his sneakers. He was swinging his feet back and forth.

'Hey,' I said, and he looked up. His eyes were red, but he was not crying at that moment. I sat down beside him, our thighs touching, and he leaned into me.

'I thought I was doing the right thing,' he said.

'Start from the beginning.'

'Mickey Farnsworth threw a rock at a car and I told the teacher. She told me she was busy and I guess she forgot to do anything about it and at recess Mickey said I was a tattletale and started beating me up and we got into a fight and now we're both in trouble.'

'Where's Mickey?' I asked.

'His mom came and got him. She called me a tattletale, too.'

That really pissed me off, but I had to let it go. The thing was, Scott had some history here. Of tattling. He didn't like to see others getting away with things, but seeing that justice was done often had a way of backfiring for him.

Welcome to the world.

'It's wrong to throw rocks at cars, right?' he asked.

'It is.'

'And you and Mom say it's wrong to do nothing when people break the law. Isn't it against the law to throw rocks at cars?'

'It is.'

'So why am I being suspended?'

I put my arm around him and patted his shoulder. I couldn't think of anything to say that wouldn't make me a hypocrite. I gave it my best shot.

'Sometimes doing the right thing hurts.' I paused. 'Sometimes, doing the right thing is not always worth doing. It's hard to be right all the time. It's not an easy way to live your life.'

'Don't you always do what's right?' Scott asked, turning his head to look at me.

'I'll always try to where you're concerned,' I said.

He rested his head against my chest. 'The principal wants to talk to you.'

'Okay.'

'And you have to take me home.'

'Okay.'

'Am I going to be punished?'

'You have been already,' I said. 'For the wrong things, for the wrong reasons.'

'I don't understand, Dad.'

'Me, neither,' I said. 'Me, neither.'

★ ★ ★

As I went in search of the Skilling residence, I gave more thought to what I was doing, and why I was doing it. I needed to know Claire Sanders was okay. I needed to know, having been dragged unwittingly into this mess, whether my actions had put her at risk. If they had, I'd have to see what I could do about it. I didn't like to see kids in trouble.

Yeah, but you don't mind scaring the shit out of them when it suits you.

I was confident I'd find her. I couldn't recall, offhand, how many times I'd been hired to track down missing kids — easily twenty — and only once had I failed. And that was because the kid — a twelve-year-old boy — came home on his own before I could find him.

When I finally did find Claire — at a boyfriend's place, a kids' hostel in L.A., some beach down in Florida — what would the plan be then? Drag her back to Griffon?

Hardly.

But I'd tell her that people back home were worried about her. I'd recommend that she call her folks. I'd give her shit for getting me involved.

That'd be it for me.

92

Sean Skilling would lead me to Hanna, and Hanna would lead me to Claire. One way or another.

I found the Skilling residence about half a mile away, on Dancey. It had been dusk when I'd arrived at the Rodomskis', but by the time I got to the Skillings' night had descended completely. I drove slowly down the street, looking for numbers, marveling at how many people don't make them easy to spot. If they didn't want to do it for the fire department, you'd think they'd at least do it for the pizza delivery guy.

The house was even numbered, so it had to be on the left, and I figured I was only a couple of doors away when I saw a car's headlights come on in a driveway just ahead. It had been backed in, so the lights intercepted my path. I glanced over as I passed by, blinded briefly. Brass numbers were affixed to a large decorative stone set by the curb. This was the place.

It wasn't a car after all, but a pickup. A black Ford Ranger. Once I had the headlight glare out of my eyes, I was able to spot a young man in a ball cap behind the wheel.

I pulled over to the opposite curb as the truck roared onto the street, accelerating so quickly it fishtailed, and tore off in the direction I'd come from. I executed a fast three-point turn and hit the gas. The pickup had disappeared beyond the bend, so I thought it was unlikely he'd noticed me turning around to come after him.

A left turn, then a right, and we were on Danbury. I had a hunch where he might be going.

Four minutes later, it proved right. The Ranger crossed the street and wheeled into the parking lot behind Patchett's. I pulled over to the shoulder so I could get a look at him as he got out of the truck and walked briskly into the bar. While he wasn't running, there was a sense of urgency in his stride, and he moved like an athlete. He was six feet, hundred and eighty pounds, with dirty blond hair falling out from beneath a cap branded with two broad horizontal stripes across the front. A Bills cap. He wouldn't be the only one in Patchett's wearing one of those.

Once he'd disappeared inside, I put the Honda in park, leaving it behind a couple of Harley-Davidsons with raised handlebars, crossed the street and entered the bar. Patchett's was like a thousand other bars. Dim lighting, loud music, railings and chairs and tables made of heavy oak, the smell of beer and sweat and human longing hanging in the air. There were about a hundred people in here, some standing at the bar, others at the tables working on ribs and wings and potato skins along with their pitchers of beer, about a dozen hanging out around the pool table.

I wasn't the oldest guy in the room, but the crowd was mostly made up of men and women in their twenties. And, knowing Patchett's as I did, probably several in their late teens. They were easy to spot, and not just because they looked younger. They were the ones trying the hardest to look cool while drinking. Holding the necks of their beer bottles between their index and middle fingers, like they'd been drinking this way their whole lives.

I scanned the room for Skilling, spotted him talking to a man at the bar. With the speakers blaring the 1969 hit 'Proud Mary' by Creedence Clearwater Revival — there couldn't have been a person here who was alive when that came out, and even I'd only just made it — I couldn't make out what he was saying. I'm no lip reader, so I sidled up to the bar, behind him, caught the bartender's attention and ordered a Corona, all the while trying to hear what the kid was saying.

It wasn't that hard, once I got close, considering everyone had to shout to be heard over the music. The man Sean was talking to yelled, 'Haven't seen her, man. When'd you last talk to her?'

'Saw her last night!' he shouted.

'She not answering her cell?'

He shook his head. 'Look, if you see her, tell her to call me, okay?'

'Yeah, no problem!'

Sean Skilling moved away from the bar and crossed the room to talk to someone standing in a group of three by the pool table, where a couple of overweight bearded men in black leather jackets, who didn't look like they were from around here, were thoroughly engrossed. I kept my position for about thirty seconds, then took my beer and ambled in that direction.

There was a pillar about two feet away from him. Taking the side that would put my back to him, I leaned against it, but there was too much noise to pick up anything he had to say, even though his voice was raised. So I pushed myself off and wandered close to the group, pretending to watch the two bikers play pool. I thought they were wannabes, guys who didn't make the cut for Hell's Angels but wanted to look the part.

'Sorry, man!' I heard a girl say. 'I saw her here, like, yesterday? I think it was yesterday, or it might have been the night before!'

Did Hanna know her boyfriend was so interested in finding Claire? Was Sean Skilling the guy in the pickup Claire was trying to get away from? But would Hanna have helped Claire pull a disappearing act so her own boyfriend would stop stalking her? Did that make any sense at all?

'Okay, well, if you see her, call me?' Sean asked.

Nods all around. A young man in a black T-shirt with a Batman insignia on it asked, 'Hey, can I place an order with you for Saturday night?'

'Not right now, man.'

Sean spotted someone else he knew in the far corner of the room. I didn't see much need to eavesdrop on another conversation that was going to be the same as the previous two, and besides, there was no place over there where I could lurk undetected.

I watched Sean ask some questions of a young man who was sitting at a table, wiping chicken wing sauce off his fingers with a moistened napkin. The man shook his head, and Sean nodded. Then he turned, scanned the room for anyone else he might know. Spotted a waitress, stopped her as she was crossing the room with two pitchers on a tray that she was balancing just above her shoulder. She shook her head, moved on.

Sean Skilling stood there, as if wondering what

to do. He dug into his jacket for his cell phone, probably checking for a text or message he might not have heard come in, then shoved the phone back into his pocket.

He headed for the door.

I set my beer on the closest table and went out after him.

He was about to round the corner of the building when I called out to him. 'Sean!'

He whirled around, squinted at me. 'Yeah?'

'Sean Skilling?'

'Who the hell are — Do I know you?'

'I'm Cal Weaver.'

He cocked his head at a funny angle. 'Weaver?'

'That's right.'

'Scott's dad.'

'Yeah,' I said.

'You're, like, the private dick guy.' Emphasis on the word you'd expect.

'Yeah,' I said.

He shook his head violently and raised a hand, palm out. 'I don't know anything about anything.'

'You don't even know what I want to ask you about.'

'It's about Scott, right? I got nothing to tell you.'

'I'm not here about him. I'm trying to find Claire Sanders.'

His mouth opened, but nothing came out for a second. 'What the hell have you got to do with that?'

I heard the bar door open and close behind me, a couple laughing as they walked across the street.

'Sean, listen to me. I need to talk to Hanna. I think Hanna might know where Claire is. The police are trying to find her.'

He waved a hand at me. 'Fuck you, pal.'

I took a step toward him. 'I'm not out to cause trouble for you. I just want to make sure Claire's okay. Where can I find Hanna? Is she with Claire?'

I heard the door open again behind me, the brief cacophony of voices and music spilling out into the night air.

'Come on,' I pleaded. 'We'll go someplace quieter, get a coffee, you can fill me in.'

Sean Skilling laughed. 'Yeah, like I'm going to go someplace with you, you fucking psycho.'

I thought I caught him looking past my shoulder for half a second. I glanced that way as someone yelled, 'Take off, man!' I didn't move quickly enough to stop the fist from connecting, though I did get an arm up in time to partly deflect it. But the blow still caught me in the side of the head, and I went down before I could get any kind of look at my attacker.

As I hit the ground, non-celestial stars swirling before my eyes, I heard two sets of footsteps running off in opposite directions.

'Fucking hell,' I muttered, putting a hand to the side of my head. I'd landed on my back. I rolled over and brought myself up to my knees, making sure the world wasn't rotating too speedily before I got to my feet. From the parking lot, I heard the growl of a pickup, then the squeal of tires as the truck shifted from loose gravel to pavement.

'You okay?'

Standing over me was a heavyset woman, mid-sixties, gray hair hanging straight down to her shoulders in a style she probably hadn't changed in four decades. She gave me a grin.

'Looks like you just got your ass whupped. Why don't you come in, we'll see if you're in need of medical attention. My name's Phyllis. I own this dump. And I think I got a pretty good idea who you are.'

11

Phyllis led me back through Patchett's, behind the counter, and into an office. I briefly considered protesting, telling her I was fine. But first, she had a viselike grip on my arm. And second, I thought she'd be worth talking to. As we passed the guy who'd handed me my Corona, she said, 'Get me some ice in a towel, Bill, for Sam Spade here.

'Have a seat,' she ordered, releasing her grasp on me and pointing to a leather couch across from a desk. I sat. Bill appeared with a red-and-white-checkered towel in which he'd collected half a dozen ice cubes.

'Put that on your noggin,' Phyllis said. I took the towel and held it against my temple, which, I had to admit, was throbbing. As Bill left and closed the door behind him, Phyllis parked her butt on the edge of the desk and held up a fist in front of my eyes.

'How many fingers am I holding up?'

'That's funny,' I said.

She extended the middle one. 'How about now?'

'One.'

She laughed. 'I think you'll live. But you keep that ice on there. Head injuries are no joke. Remember how Mannix got knocked out nearly every week? That guy should have been brain-damaged.'

'I'm guessing the Mannix and Sam Spade references mean you know what I do for a living,' I said.

She nodded. 'I recognized you when I saw you lying down there. You're Cal Weaver.'

'And you're Phyllis . . . '

'Phyllis Pearce.'

'If we've met before, I'm sorry, but I don't remember.'

'We haven't,' she said, shaking her head. 'But I've seen you around. I make a point of knowing who everybody in Griffon is. Lived here my whole life, so whenever a new face comes to town, I ask who it belongs to. You moved here, what, eight, ten years ago?'

'Six,' I said.

'Sorry about your boy,' she said.

I raised my head slowly to look her in the eye. 'Thanks.'

'Could have been anybody, you know.'

'I'm sorry?'

'Could have been anybody who sold him those drugs.' I must have looked surprised at what she seemed to be implying she knew, and it made her smile. 'I hear you've been asking around. That what you were doing here tonight?'

'No,' I said.

'Because,' she said, talking right over my denial, 'I can't have that. You want to go around interrogating kids about what happened to your boy — and I don't blame you one bit in that regard — you can't be doing it on my premises. Starting a fight on my front steps, I won't have that. You do what you have to do, but don't be

101

causing any trouble on my turf.'

'I didn't start a fight,' I said, feeling like some kid telling his mother he was blameless. 'And that's not why I'm here.' I took the ice away from my head for a second. 'I'm looking for Claire Sanders.'

'The mayor's kid?'

'Yeah.'

'That who slugged you out there? Some little thing of a girl?'

'No. I don't know who it was. I was cold-cocked. I wanted to talk to a kid named Sean Skilling. You seem to know everyone around here, so you probably know that name.'

'Ford dealer's kid.'

'Yeah.' I paused. The ice was so cold it was starting to hurt, but I held it in place. 'I should take you on as a partner, you know so much of what goes on. Save me a lot of legwork.'

Phyllis Pearce grinned. 'I got enough to do, running my vast empire.' She opened her arms wide. 'What'd you want with the Skilling kid?'

'His girlfriend is friends with Claire. She may know where Claire is.'

Phyllis Pearce nodded slowly. 'Got it. I think Claire was around here a night or two ago. Whatcha want to talk to her for?'

'I just want to find her,' I said.

'Who you working for?'

I looked at her and said nothing.

'Oh, I get it. Client confidentiality and all that.' She went around the desk and dropped into her oversized, overly padded office chair. There was a keyboard in front of her, but the

102

monitor was angled off to the side, so we could see one another. She brushed her long gray hair off her shoulders, raised her head so it would fall on her back. 'Although it would stand to reason it's her dad who wants her found.'

'I would imagine he does,' I said.

'Who's the Skilling kid's girlfriend?'

I told her.

'Hanna, oh yeah, Chris Rodomski's kid. We had to throw that drunken son of a bitch out of here all the time fifteen years back. Well, my husband. Not me.'

'Your husband's the bouncer?' I hadn't noticed anyone on the premises who looked like an age-appropriate match for Phyllis.

'It was among Harry's duties back then. But I lost my husband seven years ago.'

'I'm sorry,' I said.

She shrugged. 'Not easy, running this place on my own. Our son ended up pursuing a different line of work, but I've got good people working for me here.'

I stopped pressing the cold, damp towel to my temple. 'What should I do with this?'

Pearce pointed to a small sink along one wall. She had a small bar set up there. I got up, tossed the towel into the sink, the shrunken cubes clinking into the drain. I scanned the room, which had maybe twenty old black-and-white photos of Griffon from its early days. Horses and buggies in the streets in some of them.

She noticed me admiring them and said, 'No, I didn't take them myself. Even that was before my time.'

There was one shot of a much younger, slimmer Phyllis, her hair in exactly the same style but dark, arm in arm with a man I presumed was Harry, standing in the street in front of Patchett's. Maybe an inch taller, curly-haired, and thinner than his spouse.

'This your husband?' I asked.

'Yup. But not Harry. That's my first husband there. That was taken around 1985 or so, before he got cancer and passed on. Harry I met in 1993, married him a couple of years after that.' She cackled. 'I was about sixty pounds lighter then. But as I gained weight, I gained wisdom.'

I sat back down on the couch. Maybe she was expecting me to leave, now that I was done treating my injury, but I still had things to ask her.

'Obviously, you know about my son, Scott. Did you ever see him around here?'

She thought. 'It's possible, but I don't know. If they look like they're still reading the Hardy Boys, they don't get in. It's like throwing back a fish that's too small. Your boy, he was still pretty wet behind the ears.'

'Probably half the clientele here right now shouldn't be.'

Phyllis Pearce smiled warily. 'For someone who's lived here as long as you have, you don't seem to have an idea of how things work in Griffon.'

'Enlighten me.'

She leaned forward, her elbows on the desk, her heavy breasts resting on the keyboard. 'Sure, we got people having a drink here, a little

104

something to eat, who may technically be under twenty-one years of age. The State of New York, in its infinite wisdom, raised the drinking age from nineteen to twenty-one back in 1985. Based on your observations, Mr. Weaver, would you say that stopped people under the age of twenty-one from drinking?'

'No.'

'Of course not. I would imagine that in 1985 you yourself were under the age of twenty-one.' When I said nothing she continued. 'And did that law put the fear of God into you, or did you and your friends get hammered every weekend anyway?'

'We pretty much got hammered.'

'Damn right you did. We know what kids are going to do, because we know what we did when we were that age. Better it's happening in one place, where we can keep an eye on it, don't you think?'

'So we're surrendering. We've decided we can't control *what* our kids do, so we're just happy if we know *where* they're doing it.'

Pearce beamed at me like I was the smartest kid in the class. 'And not just that. I'm doing what I can to help the local economy. Because if they can't come here, they can be across the border to Canada in ten minutes, where the drinking age is nineteen. A seventeen-year-old with the right ID can pass for nineteen. But a seventeen-year-old has a lot harder time passing for twenty-one. All these kids, before and after they come to Patchett's, they buy pizza, go to Iggy's for a burger, get gas, pop into the local

105

7-Eleven. And zipping across the border ain't what it once was. How many of these kids have passports? Used to be, they whisked you through in five seconds, but now, if you haven't got a passport, you're not going across that border one way or the other, thank you very much, Osama bin Laden, may you rot in hell, you mother-fucker.'

She leaned back in her chair. 'I'm not gonna tell you I've managed to put every Griffon parent's mind at ease, thinking if their kids are drinking, they're doing it here. Kids are still having parties in their basements, having a wild time when their parents are out of town. There's quite a little business going on of getting booze to kids who aren't old enough to go into stores to buy it themselves. They even deliver.' She smiled. 'But I do my part.'

'And the police leave you alone.'

'They're very . . . supportive. Once in a while, we get some riffraff in from the south, and they look after us in that regard. Couple of fellows out there right now, monopolizing the pool table, have me a little concerned.'

'Maybe the local cops give you a pass because, as you've demonstrated, you know everybody's business. Pissing you off might not be in any-one's interest.' My eyes narrowed. 'And maybe there's a little something in their Christmas stocking, too.'

'You smooth talker,' Phyllis said, grinning. 'Thinking I wield any power around here. Nothing could be further from the truth. I'm just a simple businesswoman, trying to get by. But I will say this — that Augustus Perry, he's a good man.' She served me a sly smile. 'Not that I have to tell you.'

'One last thing,' I said. 'I'd like a peek at your security tape. See who it was who clobbered me.'

'I can't help you there,' she said.

'If you don't show me, you'll just have to show it to one of Griffon's finest.'

'Oh, don't be silly.' She gave me a look of disappointment. 'You're not going to the police about that and you know it. Is that what a real private eye does? Goes running off to the cops every time he gets a knock on the head? Please.'

She was right. I had no intention of reporting the assault.

'But that's got nothing to do with why I won't let you see the security tape,' she said, and then waved her arm around the room, like she was about to pull back the curtain to Door Number Two. 'You see any monitors in here? We have no surveillance system. No closed-circuit cameras.'

'Not even out front?' I asked.

She shook her head.

'You look surprised,' Pearce said.

'I'd heard different.'

'You were misinformed. Or you misunderstood.'

'Maybe so,' I said, getting up off the couch.

'But if there's anything else I can help you with, my door's open,' she said. 'You strike me as someone who could use a bit of guidance.'

12

As I walked out I tried to get my sore head around what Phyllis Pearce had told me. No surveillance system? That spot out in front of Patchett's was only steps from where Claire Sanders had tapped on my window asking for a ride. How was that caught on a security camera if the guy who'd sucker punched me was not?

Before I crossed the street to get in my car, I looked for cameras out front anyway. There were none. But hadn't Haines and Brindle — one of them, I couldn't remember which — told me that was how they'd been led to my door? That my license plate had been picked up on the bar's camera when Claire got in?

Had either of them actually said that? Or had they only intimated it? Allowed me to think it when I raised the suggestion that my car had been caught on closed-circuit?

I couldn't recall how the conversation had gone exactly, and the throbbing in my head wasn't helping my powers of recollection. But if they had, in fact, told me I'd been picked up on a camera, why had they lied? If there was no camera, what had led them to me? Did they already have Patchett's staked out? Were they already following Claire?

It wasn't a stretch to think the local cops might have a cruiser parked across the street from the place now and then, watching for people getting into their cars who were too drunk to drive. Or maybe they had quotas to fill, and picked up the occasional underage drinker to show they were keeping Griffon a safe and decent place to raise our children, even if they were letting Patchett's serve drinks to minors.

Maybe the cops had been called to Patchett's earlier for some kind of disturbance, and before they'd left had noticed a teenage girl hitching a ride with a strange man, and had the presence of mind to make note of a plate number. Then, later, when Claire was reported missing, some cop at the morning briefing said, 'Hang on.'

I fumbled in my pocket for my keys, hit the remote button to unlock the car, and slid in behind the wheel. I took a glance at myself in the rearview mirror before I closed the door and turned the lights out. My hair was mussed. I combed it with my fingers to the point where I looked moderately respectable.

I was about to turn the key when the two bikers came out of Patchett's and wandered across the road to the motorcycles parked directly ahead of me. As they were getting ready to swing their legs over like a couple of cowboys mounting their horses, headlights came on about a hundred yards away.

Almost instantaneously, a bank of multi-colored swirling roof lights was activated on the same vehicle. A siren whooped for five seconds before the cruiser screeched to a stop beside the bikes.

The bikers stood there and watched as two cops got out of the car. A woman from the driver's side, a man from the passenger's. I recognized the woman as Donna's friend Kate Ramsey. Late thirties, short blond hair, about a hundred and seventy pounds, no more than five six. Chin up, formidable. Her partner I didn't know, but I guessed he was in his early thirties, five ten, about the same weight as Ramsey, strong chin and cheekbones.

It looked like Kate was going to take the lead here. I put down my window so I could hear.

'Where you boys from?' she asked, She had one hand on the nightstick hanging from her belt.

Biker One said, 'What's the problem, Officer? We do something wrong?'

'I asked a question,' she said. 'Where you from?'

'Elmwood,' Biker Two said. A Buffalo neighborhood, and a pretty nice one at that.

'What brings you up to Griffon?' the other cop asked.

'We just rode up for a couple drinks, play some pool,' Biker One said.

'That'd be all you're doing up here?' Kate Ramsey asked. 'You wouldn't be up here doing a bit of business?'

Biker Two shook his head. 'Listen, we just wanted to get some air, do some riding on our bikes. That's all. We're not looking for trouble.'

Kate's partner said, 'We don't need your kind up here.'

'Our kind?' Biker One said. 'The fuck is that supposed to mean?'

'It means,' Kate said, 'we don't need greasy,

110

drug-dealing dickheads like you two fucking up our town.'

The first biker moved an inch toward Kate, but the other one held up his hand. 'Then I guess we should be on our way.'

'We don't have to take this shit,' the first one said.

Kate's partner moved forward, taking the nightstick from his belt. 'Oh, I think you do.' He walked around to the front of the second biker's bike, swinging the stick casually. 'What's a headlight like that run?'

'Come on, man, we'll go,' Biker Two said. 'We're on our way.'

'And you won't be back,' Kate said.

'Fine,' the first one said. 'Who the fuck would want to come back here anyway? Everything they say about this hick town is true.'

Kate Ramsey and her partner stood there and watched as the two got on their bikes, started them up with a roar, then navigated their way around the Griffon police cruiser. Once they were on the road, one of them stuck his hand into the air and offered up a one-finger salute.

Ramsey and her partner watched until their taillights were reduced to the size of pinheads, then got back into their car and drove away.

★   ★   ★

I was going to hunt up the Skilling house, but decided that before I did that, it made more sense to find, and talk to, Claire's father, Bertram Sanders.

111

I found his address through my smartphone. Sanders lived on Lakeland Drive. I knew Lakeland, but never understood why it was called that. The street neither overlooked nor led directly to any body of water. I was hoping that when I knocked on the door, it wouldn't be the mayor who answered, but Claire herself. After all, if she'd returned home since the cops had been to see me, there wasn't anyone who would have felt obliged to let me know.

It was a lower-income, postwar neighborhood. That'd be the Second World War, not the one in Korea, or Vietnam, or the Gulf, or Iraq, or Afghanistan. We'd had so many of them, it was hard to keep track. It was a simple two-story house with clapboard siding, painted brown, and while the place looked narrow from the front, it went back a long way. The house was better maintained than many others on the street, several of which still sported rusted television aerials that probably hadn't picked up a signal in years. Behind the house, at the end of the long, single-lane drive, stood a separate one-stall garage.

I parked on the street, went up to the door, and knocked. It was past eight and the streetlamps were on, but I didn't see lights on in the Sanders house. I shielded my eyes and peered through the rectangular window set vertically in the wooden door. No signs of life.

It seemed fruitless, but I decided to walk around and try knocking on the back door, which, once I got there, I could see entered the kitchen. Again I put my eyes to the window and

112

saw that the only light inside appeared to come from a digital display on a toaster. No one came when I knocked.

'You looking for the mayor?'

I turned and saw an elderly woman standing beneath a porch light of the house next door. She had a view of me over the fence.

'That's right,' I said slowly. 'I was hoping I'd catch Bert at home.'

'It's Thursday night,' said the woman, like I should know the significance of that.

'What's Thursday night?'

'The night the town council meets. You must not be from around here.'

All the years I'd lived in Griffon, and tonight I felt like a stranger. Everyone pointing out how little I knew.

'It slipped my mind.'

From inside her house, a man shouted, 'Who you talking to?'

She turned around and shouted back, 'Man looking for Bert!'

'Tell him to try the town hall!'

'I did that! You think I'm an idiot?' She turned back to me. 'He thinks I'm an idiot.'

'I thought Claire might be home and I could just give her a message.'

'Haven't seen her around today.' She hesitated, licked her lips, like she was weighing whether to tell me something. 'You never know where she might be. Thank God our kids are grown and gone; they hardly ever call, but frankly I couldn't be happier. But it can't be easy for Bert, raising a girl on his own.'

I recalled what Donna had told me, that the mayor and his wife had split up. 'Yeah, they can be a handful,' I said.

'What are you talking about?' the man yelled from inside the house.

'I'll tell ya in a minute!' she shouted at her husband. 'Don't mind him. He just likes to be included.' She rolled her eyes.

'Does Claire spend all her time here?' I asked. 'Or does she spend half of it with her mother?'

'That'd be tricky, spending half her time here and half across the border. Caroline's living in Toronto with her new husband, what's-his-name.'

'What *is* his name?' I asked, like I'd known it myself at one time. Maybe Claire was with her mother. It'd be worth checking.

'Ed,' the woman called back into the house. 'Ed!'

'Huh?'

'What was the name of that guy Caroline married? One that runs the jewelry store that has the ads on the Toronto station.'

'Uh . . . it'll come to me. It was Minsky.'

'No, that wasn't it,' she shot back. 'That's your sister-in-law's name.'

'Oh, right.'

She looked back at me. 'I remember. His name's Jeff Karnofsky. With a 'k.' Well, two of them. One at the beginning and one right near the end.'

'When's the last time you saw Claire around here?'

'Last night. Saw her take off in some pickup truck.'

'What time would that have been?' I asked.

She shrugged. 'I don't know. It was after the news.'

'Which news?' These days, especially with the cable networks, there was never a time when the news wasn't on.

'Brian Williams,' she said. That would be the *NBC Nightly News*, on WGRZ, the local NBC affiliate. The show ran from six thirty to seven p.m. 'He's a handsome bugger, that one.'

'So was it soon after the news ended that Claire left?' I felt my questions were starting to get too specific, but this woman seemed happy to talk, and violating confidences didn't seem to be something that troubled her.

'I don't know. Seven, eight, eight thirty, I don't know. Took off in a real hurry, tires squealing and all. Police should give them a ticket for driving like that. God knows they're here enough.'

'What do you mean?'

'Been going on for a while now. There's often a Griffon cruiser parked along the street, like they've always got their eye on the mayor's house. I was wondering whether he was getting death threats or somethin', but when I asked him about it, he said it was nothing, not to worry.' She chuckled. 'I'd sure hate to have someone come by and shoot out his windows or anything. They might hit our house by mistake.'

13

Griffon Town Hall dominated the town's center, situated at the end of the green, its spire drawing the eye skyward. It was an example, I'd been told, of Georgian architecture, with its gabled entrance and melding of red brick and white-painted wood. Like something out of Colonial Williamsburg, even though we were a long way from there. I did know that maintaining and restoring the building was a constant drain on the town's budget, and that some taxpayers were in favor of building new municipal offices just outside the downtown area, near all those big-box stores and fast-food outlets on Danbury. Sanders, to his credit, had countered that if Griffon's civic leaders were willing to abandon the downtown, what hope did the remaining merchants have? I could not recall ever meeting the man, but from what I'd read, I liked where he was coming from.

I drove the streets surrounding the town hall a couple of times, looking for a place to park. There seemed to be a lot more cars down here than usual. I was forced to leave my car a couple of blocks away, not something I wanted to do, because it meant I'd have to walk past Ravelson Furniture on my way back.

In my darker moments, I imagined conversations with my son, asking him why, if he had to end his life the way he did, he couldn't have done it someplace I didn't see every time I came downtown.

Sometimes I tried pretending it wasn't even there, which was a challenge, considering that the store was in the largest, and one of the oldest, commercial buildings in Griffon, dating back to the late eighteen hundreds. But even if I never came down here, there was no escaping the Ravelson name. They bought newspaper ads every week, delivered flyers to the door, and ran commercials on the local stations featuring the owner, Kent Ravelson, a man unfamiliar with subtlety. My personal favorite starred Kent, seated in an overstuffed leather chair, smoking a pipe and wearing a pair of professorial glasses, playing a psychiatrist dispensing advice to a blond babe stretched out on a couch.

'Now that I've got you on the couch, I'm going to *shrink* its price!' he says, trying to sound like a famous Austrian psychoanalyst but coming across more as a horny Nazi. A mental health organization in Buffalo lodged a complaint, but it only encouraged him to do more.

Even though I kept fooling myself, thinking I could sidle past Ravelson's like it wasn't there, it just wasn't possible. I'd crane my neck upward and study the corniced edge of the building's roofline. The place where Scott had stood, for how long I don't know, thinking God knows what, before deciding on a quicker way to descend four stories than taking the stairs.

He didn't jump from the front of the store, but the side, which brought him down into the parking lot. Onto a handicapped spot. It was

117

there that the police — Officer Ricky Haines — found him.

Walking past this time was no different. I stopped, and stared. The store wouldn't close for another half hour, and there were the occasional couple going in and out, cars starting up and leaving the lot.

As I always did, I surveyed the scene. Starting at the handicapped spot, rising past the four rows of windows, stopping at the roofline.

How long would it have taken? Two seconds? Three? I saw his body falling, plummeting, hitting the pavement. Three seconds seemed about right. Certainly no more than that. What was he thinking on the way down? Was he terrified? Did he realize, once he'd gone off the edge, what he'd actually done? In those two or three seconds, had he wondered whether there was anything he could do to save himself?

Or was he happy? Did he hit the ground with a blissful smile on his face? And which would have been better? To realize, in his last second, that he'd made a fatal mistake, or to spend his last moment drugged to the eyeballs, meeting his maker as happy as a lark?

It didn't do me any good to dwell on these things.

But there were so many to dwell on. Like how he'd gotten up there in the first place. I wanted to blame the good folks at Ravelson Furniture. After all, if they hadn't given Scott a job for the summer, he wouldn't have had access to the roof. But I knew that was akin to blaming Starkist for cutting your finger on the lid of the

118

tuna tin. If anything, Kent Ravelson had gone out of his way to give Scott a break. The kid didn't have much of an employment history, nor the kind of upper-body strength needed to work in a furniture store. But Kent found Scott plenty of tasks, even if they never included lifting a refrigerator. He even gave our boy a taste of sales, letting him work the mattress department one day when one of the regular salesmen was sick.

I had a sense that Kent, and his wife, Annette, who ran the store with him, had taken something of an interest in our son possibly because their own boy, Roman, didn't want any part of the family business. He was twenty-one and, from what I'd heard, aspired to greater things than running a furniture store; he spent his time hanging out at home, tapping away at zombie screenplays on his laptop, which had, so far, failed to attract any attention from Spielberg or Lucas or Scorsese.

Donna and I had hoped the responsibilities associated with a summer job would have a maturing effect on Scott. Instead, it just meant he had more money to spend on booze and drugs, which he'd consumed in considerable quantities that night on the roof.

The police investigation, such as it was, concluded that Scott, possibly with friends, had been up on that roof more than once. They found a number of discarded liquor bottles, marijuana butts, and a couple of dropped ecstasy tabs.

What fun it must have seemed, having the roof

to himself, a view of Griffon below, and in the southern distance, Niagara Falls, the Skylon Tower on the Canadian side looking like some enormous golf tee on the horizon.

I had been up there myself, twice, since Scott's death. Both times, as a father, but I couldn't help but take in the scene as an investigator. Trying to figure out how it happened, recreating the events in my head. I could picture him larking about, letting the combination of drugs and alcohol carry him away. A brick ledge, a kind of lip, ran along the roof's perimeter, but it was only about six inches high. Not a barrier that would break a person's fall if he tripped near the edge, and certainly not a barrier that would present any obstacle to someone who thought he had the ability to fly. I'm usually okay with heights, but the two times I'd been up there, standing right up next to that brick lip, I could feel the vertigo kicking in. Was I really dizzy, or was I imagining Scott's delirium at the time?

And I remembered vividly that knock on the door. Donna and I'd been in bed, but neither of us asleep, wondering where Scott was. I'd tried his cell without success, and was just about to get dressed and go looking for him when there was a hard rap on the front door.

'Oh God,' Donna'd said. 'Oh no.'

I don't put a lot of faith in premonitions or a sixth sense. But right then, when that knock came, I think we both knew we were about to get very bad news.

I'd run down to the door in my robe, Donna trailing after me. When I opened it, we saw a

Griffon police officer standing there, a name tag on his shirt that read HAINES. When he saw Donna, I could see surprise in his eyes.

'Ms. Weaver,' he'd said. 'I had a feeling, when I checked his wallet, it might be the same Weaver.'

'Ricky?' Donna'd said. 'Why are you here? What's happened?'

'It's about your boy.'

We'd both held our breath. Officer Ricky Haines took off his hat and held it over his chest, obscuring his name tag. 'I'm awful sorry, but I have some bad news.'

Donna clutched my arm. 'No,' she'd said. 'No, no, no.'

I'd pulled her into my arms as Officer Haines said —

'Hey, Cal. Cal? *Cal?*'

I was so wrapped up in my own thoughts of the past I hadn't noticed a person standing to my left in the present. It was Annette Ravelson. She was late forties, round but not quite plump, what they might have called *zaftig* in another time. She stood about five eight, but would have been five five without the heels. Gold hoop earrings the size of coasters dangled below her poufy gray-blond hair, and there was a powerful whiff of some flowery fragrance about her.

'Hi, Annette.'

We'd known the Ravelsons even before Scott went to work for them. We'd bought furniture here over the years, then got to know them better during the summer Scott worked there. But our encounters since the incident had been few.

'You okay?' she asked.

'Yeah, I'm fine.'

'I kept saying your name, but you didn't seem to hear me.'

'I'm sorry.'

'What happened to you?' She pointed to my temple, which had puffed out slightly.

'Took a tumble,' I said. 'No big deal.'

'You sure?'

'Positive. I'm fine.'

Annette stopped looking at my head and sized up my vantage point. She had to know what had been going through my head.

'Is this a good idea, Cal?' she asked hesitantly. 'I mean, coming by here all the time, standing here — '

'You're right,' I said quickly. 'Absolutely right. I should get going, anyway. I was just walking over to town hall.'

'Oh,' she said. Worry crossed her face. 'Council meeting tonight?'

'So I gather.'

'Cal, please, tell me you're not going to ask them for a new law mandating higher railings on the edges of buildings or something like that. That's what people do these days. They think some new ordinance will prevent another tragedy like — '

'No, I'm not doing that.'

Now Annette Ravelson looked mortified. 'I'm sorry. I should never have said that. That was awful of me. Forgive me.'

I waved it away. 'Nice to see you, Annette.'

She touched my arm as I began to leave. 'Cal, there's also something — this is very awkward,

122

especially after I've just been so horrible.'

'What is it?'

'Believe me, this isn't me talking. But Kent, well, he's seen you standing out here quite a few times before, and I wouldn't want you to think he doesn't understand what you've been through. Believe me, his heart goes out to you, as does mine. You know that. But when he sees you here, sometimes sitting in your car in the parking lot there, well, it kind of creeps him out, if you know what I mean.'

'Creeps him out.'

'That came out wrong. But it makes him uncomfortable. I mean, other customers, they see you there, and they ask why you're there, and — '

'I certainly wouldn't want to make Kent uncomfortable,' I said. I looked at the building. 'Is he in? Maybe he'd like to tell me himself.'

Annette Ravelson put a hand up to my chest, nearly touching it. 'He's not there. I'm sorry. I shouldn't have mentioned it.'

Now I felt sorry, too. That I had overreacted. 'No, it's okay. I understand. Give Kent my regards. I haven't seen him around in a while.'

'Everyone's busy, you know,' she said.

'Anyway, I need to go,' I said. I forced a grin. 'I'll say hi to the mayor for you.'

A startled expression overtook her face. 'Why would you do that?' she asked.

'It's a joke, Annette,' I said. 'Take care.'

14

Getting into Griffon Town Hall wasn't like entering the Capitol, or the White House, or even the Empire State Building. For a while there, after 9/11, the mayor at the time implemented harsh security measures, and he had the support of Augustus Perry, who was deputy police chief then. You couldn't get into the building without passing through a metal detector and having your bag inspected. But being that Griffon was a small town, it wasn't long before the security people, who were also locals, started getting walked all over.

'For Christ's sake, you gonna strip-search me before I can go in there and buy a fucking tag for my dog, Mittens?' Rose Tyler, a fixture around town, allegedly snapped one day. They let her keep her bag and bypass the metal detector. It got to be that way with most everyone within two or three months. It was decided that if al-Qaeda decided to attack America again, Griffon Town Hall was not likely among their top ten targets, so reason prevailed and the security measures were dropped.

I ran up the half dozen steps, past the corner-stone that reminded everyone that the building had been here since 1873. As I made my way down the hall toward the council chamber, which was actually an old-fashioned courtroom by day — think *To Kill a Mockingbird* — I could hear a murmuring of voices, the subtle movements of people shifting in their seats.

I hadn't expected to find so many people in the gallery. Four or five dozen, I guessed. Town hall meetings around here rarely got into anything more controversial than somebody putting money into a meter and not getting any time, but there was clearly something bigger than that going on tonight. A man in the audience was on his feet, pointing to the front of the room, where the mayor, flanked by a couple of town councilors, was seated at a long table.

The man, who looked to be in his seventies and was wearing a plaid shirt and a ball cap, said, 'I don't know what gives you the right to think you can tell the police how to do their job.' There were murmurs of agreement from the people seated around him as I slipped into one of the seats at the back.

Bert Sanders, who had the kind of good looks — a full head of dark hair, a strong chin, a nice set of teeth — that could have given him a shot at being mayor of someplace a lot more important than Griffon, replied calmly, 'I'm not telling the police how to do their job, but I'm not afraid to tell them who they're accountable to. And they're accountable to everyone in this room. Not just me, or the people sitting up here with me. They're accountable to you, sir.'

'Well, I think they're doing just fine,' the man shot back, still standing. 'I go to bed at night and I feel safe and that's bloody well good enough for me.'

'I'm not so sure everyone shares your

assessment,' Mayor Sanders said. A hesitant hand went up tentatively on the other side of the gallery. 'Yes?'

A redheaded woman in her forties stood up, slowly, like she wasn't sure, now that she'd been called upon, that she wanted to say anything. But she cleared her throat, and spoke.

'Some of you may know me. I'm Doreen Cousens, and I manage Griffon Dry Cleaners. I recognize a lot of you folks. I've got one of them petitions by the cash register, about the cops are tops, and sometimes I get customers, they don't want to sign their name, and what I'm wondering is, if I know who those people are, am I supposed to make a note of it?' She waved a sheet of paper in the air. 'Because I've got a list of names here of people who wouldn't sign. Should I give that to the police, or to you?'

'Oh for God's sake,' Sanders said. 'Yeah, give it to me.'

The woman moved to the aisle, walked to the front of the courtroom, and handed the sheet to the mayor. From where I sat, it looked like there were twenty or thirty names on it.

Mayor Sanders took the sheet, ripped it in half, then ripped it again. The woman who'd handed it over put her hand to her mouth as a collective gasp swept the room.

Another woman bolted to her feet and shouted, 'If there's people here don't support the police, we need to know who they are!'

'Damn straight!' someone said.

'Who's on that list?' shouted another. 'Are you on it, Mayor? Are you?'

126

Sanders held up both hands, hoping for quiet, and finally pushed back his chair and stood. 'I don't know if I'm on Doreen's or not. But if I'm not on hers, I may be on somebody else's, if they're taking down names like Doreen is. Because you're right — I haven't signed. I don't have any intention of signing. I don't have to swear allegiance to the police. My allegiance is to the Constitution, and the citizens of Griffon. I won't be intimidated into signing that petition, and no one here should feel compelled to do it, either. I support any police force that operates within the law, that does not exceed its authority, that does not take it upon itself to mete out sentences.'

Some rumblings among the crowd, but also a smattering of applause.

'When an officer wearing a badge of the town of Griffon,' Sanders said, his voice rising, encouraged perhaps that he had a handful of people on his side, 'takes a suspect down by the water tower and knocks out one of his teeth, then something is very wrong with — '

'Bullshit!'

The whole room, including me, jumped. It's hard not to flinch when a cannon goes off. I might even have jumped more than most, since the explosion came from right behind me. Like everyone else, I whirled around, and standing there, at the entrance to the courtroom, was Griffon's chief of police, Augustus Perry.

All six foot three of him. Broad-chested, thick-necked, and totally bald, he carried himself well even with that bit of a paunch he had going on. He was in uniform, although his position allowed him to be more casual about it. Black dress boots, new jeans with a visible crease, a white collared shirt and a tweed jacket with a small badge pinned to it. You half expected him to wear a Stetson, even though we were a long way from Texas, but our chief thought his shiny dome afforded him more distinction.

I was sitting no more than three feet from him, and was the first person in the room — aside from the mayor — he locked eyes with. They popped for a second — clearly he hadn't expected to see me here — and then he gave an almost imperceptible nod.

I returned it. 'Augie,' I said quietly. 'Evenin'.'

Perry took his eyes off me and turned them back on Sanders, who said, 'You're out of order, Chief.'

The way the two faced one another across the room, the only ones standing, it was like we were at the OK Corral. But I guessed that only the chief was armed — I knew he kept a weapon attached to his belt, just under the jacket — and it struck me as unlikely that shooting the mayor would be the best way to confront accusations of police brutality.

'I'd say you're the one out of order,' Perry said. 'You preach about the Constitution, yet here you are making unsubstantiated charges based on rumor and hearsay and innuendo. This individual you say was assaulted by a member of my force — is he here? Am I able to confront the accuser on behalf of my officers?'

Perry paused, his last word echoing in the hall.

128

The mayor took a moment to respond. 'No, he is not.'

'Have you a sworn statement from this person? Has he filed a complaint? Launched any kind of action against the town?'

Another moment of silence. 'No,' Sanders said again. He looked, briefly, as though he'd been slapped, but he raised his chin defiantly. 'In a town where simply failing to sign a pro-cop petition gets your name on a list' — he gestured to the torn pages before him — 'who'd dare take the police on with an assault charge?'

'Doreen might have been taking down names,' Perry said, 'but she was not asked to by anyone under my command, and I'd have torn that list up same as you.' He pointed a finger. 'You're a showboater, Sanders. A bleeding heart, an opportunist, and a slanderer. If you've got evidence that my people are breaking the law, bring it to me, and I'll weed out the bastards. But in the meantime, you'd be well advised to keep your powder dry.'

Before Sanders could respond to that, Perry turned to walk out, and caught my eye a second time.

I smiled and said, in a voice loud enough just for Perry, 'Leaving when you're on a roll, Augie? Your horse double-parked?'

He gave me a sly grin. 'Bet you're relieved the mayor tore up Doreen's list.'

I shook my head. 'You know I'm always in your corner.'

Augustus Perry snorted and left the building.

129

15

When Perry departed, the room erupted. People in the audience were yelling at the mayor and each other, while Sanders banged a gavel on the table to try to bring things to order.

When he saw he wasn't getting anywhere, he said, 'I move that we bring this meeting to a close. Do I have a seconder?'

A woman seated to his left raised a weary hand. 'All in favor?' Sanders asked, and every hand shot up. 'Fine!' he said, attempting to be heard above the ruckus.

I made my way down the center aisle to the front of the room. 'Mayor Sanders!' I shouted, fighting my way upstream as others, grumbling among themselves, began filing out.

He barely glanced up, then went back to stuffing some papers into a briefcase, eager to get the hell out of here. I got up close and said, 'Mr. Sanders, I need to talk to you.' He didn't even look up. 'My name's Cal Weaver and — '

Sanders instantly stopped shuffling papers and looked at me, like I'd startled him. 'Who did you say you are?'

'Cal Weaver.'

'What — I'm sorry, but I have to run.' His voice was agitated. 'I — I've nothing else to say about this whole business.'

'I'm not here about your dispute with Chief Perry. I'm here about another matter.'

He eyed me warily. 'What would that be?'

'I'm a private investigator, Mr. Sanders. I need to ask you some questions about your daughter.'

The eyebrows — sitting on his forehead like a couple of furry black caterpillars — went up. Almost, I thought, in relief. 'Claire? What about her?'

'I'm trying to locate her,' I said.

'Why on earth would you be trying to do that?'

'Because — isn't she missing?'

'Missing? Claire's not missing. I don't know what you're talking about.'

I was probably the one who looked startled now. 'Is there someplace we could go to talk?'

Sanders stuffed the last of his papers into his briefcase, snapped it shut, and cast his gaze tiredly across the room as the last of the people straggled out. 'My office,' he said.

I followed him out of the courtroom and up a flight of broad wooden steps that creaked underfoot. We entered a room with a twelve-foot tin ceiling and tall windows that looked as though they'd been painted shut since the Eisenhower administration. Behind his expansive desk hung a picture of him with the current president, overlooking Niagara Falls, taken when the commander in chief took a swing through this part of the state about a year back. Sanders managed to look not like some small-town mayor, but like the head of a multibillion-dollar corporation, with his perfect hair and suit that looked like it was worth more than that modest house of his I'd been to earlier.

Sanders closed the door behind us and said, 'What's this about, Mr. Weaver?'

'Is Claire home? Has she already turned up?'

'You really have me at a loss here.'

'The police came to see me,' I said. 'Earlier this evening. They're trying to find Claire. She hasn't been seen since last night. Are you telling me you didn't report her missing?'

'Of course I didn't.' But he did look concerned.

'Then where is she?'

'She's gone away. I don't see any reason to disclose her whereabouts to you. And what's your connection to this, anyway?'

'I saw your daughter last night,' I told him. 'She used me to give someone the slip, to get away from someone she must have believed was following her.'

'Used you? How?'

'I gave her a ride. She — '

'Whoa, stop right there,' he said. 'Claire was in your car?'

'She asked for a lift, out in front of Patchett's. She recognized me. She knew my son. If she hadn't mentioned that, I probably wouldn't have given her a ride. She said she was worried about someone watching her. I didn't see how I could say no.'

Sanders seemed to be sizing me up as a possible predator. 'Go on.'

'She asked me to stop at Iggy's. Said she wasn't feeling well. She went in, but it was a different girl that got back into my car. Dressed to look like Claire, with a wig. Hanna Rodomski.

132

The two of them pulled a fast one on someone who may have been watching them.'

He did a slow walk to the other side of the desk, rested his hands on the back of the cushioned high-back chair. 'Really.'

'Really,' I said.

'That's quite a little stunt they pulled.' He forced a smile. 'You sure they weren't just having a little fun? Playing a trick on you?'

'Whoever they were trying to fool, it wasn't me,' I said. 'There's no way Claire could have known I was going to be coming along at that time.'

Sanders shrugged. 'Maybe it didn't have to be you. It could have been whoever they got to pick Claire up. A practical joke.'

'I don't think so. If it's all a joke, then why are the police involved?'

Sanders' tongue moved around the inside of his cheek like a lollipop. 'It must just be some kind of misunderstanding.'

I placed my hands on the desk and leaned forward. 'Here's what I'm having a hard time getting my head around. The police seem to think your daughter is missing. They want to find her. They're either worried about her or think she's mixed up in something they want to ask her about. But you, you don't seem to be that worried at all. About your own daughter. Maybe you could clarify that for me.'

Sanders hesitated. People usually did that for two reasons. They didn't want to tell you the real story, or they were buying time while they thought up a good story.

'You saw what went on tonight,' he said.

'That meeting?'

'That's right.'

'You're telling me there's a connection between your daughter and the fight you've got going with the Griffon cops?'

He gave me a sly grin that showed off his perfect teeth. 'Like you don't know.'

'You're losing me,' I said.

'I know your connection. I know what kind of game you're working here.'

'Connection? You talking about me and Chief Perry?'

Sanders nodded smugly, like he was no fool. 'I know he's your brother-in-law.'

'What of it?'

'Didn't think I knew, did you? Figured you might get that one past me.'

'I don't give a damn whether you know or not,' I said. 'He's my wife's brother. What's that got to do with anything?'

'You think I'm stupid?' he asked. 'You think I can't figure out what's going on here? Perry doesn't like losing leverage, does he? Doesn't like it that he's got one less person to intimidate. You can tell him I know what he's doing. You can tell him it's not working. I don't care how many cruisers he has watching me, or how many people he thinks he can turn against me. Because that's what he's doing, you know. He's making this an 'us against them' kind of town, using fear to turn people to his side. If you're not with the great Augustus Perry, you're on the side of the criminals. Well, it's not gonna work. I'm

134

not backing down. He doesn't run this town. He may think he does, but he doesn't.'

'Is the chief trying to scare you? Is he harassing you?'

'Oh, please,' Sanders said. 'What'd he think? That he could send you here, trick me into telling you where Claire is?'

'So she is missing. Or hiding.'

Sanders smiled. 'She's fine. There's the door, Mr. Weaver.'

'Has Claire been threatened? Because of what's going on between you and Perry?'

He just shook his head dismissively.

'You've got it wrong,' I said. 'My concern for Claire is genuine. I gave her a lift, and she disappeared on my watch. I have to know. I have to know that she's okay.'

'Get out.'

'Call her. Just let me speak to her.'

'Get out.'

'All I'm asking is — '

Sanders held his palm up in my face. A strong gesture, betrayed by a tremble.

'Now,' he said.

16

When she gets home, she sees a sliver of light beneath his door, so she decides to check on him. He could have fallen asleep with the light on, and if that's the case, she'll turn it off. But maybe he's sitting in his chair, reading. He does that sometimes when he can't sleep.

Once she has the door open, she finds he is, indeed, awake, but not in his chair. No book or magazine in his hands. Just looking at the ceiling, as though some movie is being projected there.

'Are you okay?' she asks.

'Just thinking,' he says.

'About what?' she asks, although she has a good idea.

'I thought about what we could say.'

'Say about what?'

'About why I've been away.'

It's never been this bad before, she thinks. Him harping on things like this. The events of the last few weeks — that boy's unexpected visit — have agitated him. He's not the only one.

'Okay,' she says, since part of her is curious about what he's come up with. 'Why have you been away?'

'I was in Africa.'

'Africa,' she says.

'On a safari. I got lost. In the jungle. In the rain forest.'

'I think that's in South America,' she says. 'I think you'd have a hard time keeping your story straight.'

'We could work on it together so I'd be sure to get it right.'

'You should turn off the light and go to sleep,' she says.

'No!' the man shouts, and the woman recoils. He is usually passive, manageable.

'Don't you raise your voice to me,' she says.

'I went to the Arctic! I was on an Arctic expedition! And now I'm back!'

'Stop it. You're getting yourself all worked up. You're talking nonsense.'

'Or maybe I was in the desert. I was wandering the desert.'

The woman sits on the edge of the bed and places her hand on his clammy forehead. She pats him gently.

'You'll never get to sleep if you get yourself all wound up,' she says soothingly. 'You're overtired.'

He wraps his hands around her arm and pulls her to him so her face is inches from his. His breath smells like the inside of an old leather bag.

'I don't blame you,' he says. 'I understand. But it has to end. It can't go on forever like this.'

She's been thinking that herself for a while now.

17

As I walked back to my car, I got out my phone, called up the number for my brother-in-law, Augustus Perry, and entered it.

Something didn't add up. The police were looking for Claire Sanders, but her father claimed she wasn't missing. It didn't take Sherlock Holmes to figure out he was hiding something, lying to me. Claire had to be in some kind of trouble. She'd gone to a lot of effort to outwit someone who'd been following her.

Was it the police? An ex-boyfriend?

Her father?

If I couldn't get any satisfactory answers from him, best to go back to the police and learn what prompted them to start looking for her. But I didn't want to talk to Haines or Brindle. It made more sense to go to the top. Not that Augie was naturally disposed to help his sister's husband. He more or less considered me a horse's ass.

The feeling was mutual.

We managed to be civil to one another through most family get-togethers, so long as discussions did not turn to politics, religion, or some of the really contentious topics, like the quickest route to Philadelphia, how much it rained last week, or who was getting better gas mileage.

We'd really gotten into it summer before last, at a barbecue in our backyard, when Augie said that if we accepted that certain racial groups were more intellectually superior, from a genetic standpoint, than others, and that if we further accepted that intellectually inferior racial groups were more likely to break the law, then racial profiling wasn't racism at all because it could be supported by scientific data.

'I'd love to see that data,' I said.

'Look it up,' he said. 'It's on the Internet.'

'So if it's on the Internet, it must be true.'

'Well, if it's scientific data, it is.'

'If I saw something on the Internet that said a new study had determined that you've got the IQ of a bucket of bolts, would it be true? Because it's going to be on there in about five minutes.'

His wife, the long-suffering Beryl, had to hold him back.

I had to concede that, attitude aside, Augie wasn't all bad as a cop. He had good instincts. He was tireless. Before he was a chief, and not spending a large chunk of the day sitting on his butt behind a desk, he'd knock on doors all day and all night if that's what it took to find someone who might be a potential witness to a neighborhood crime. When we had an eight-year-old boy go missing five years ago, Augie came out from behind his desk and participated in foot searches for six days, getting less than four hours of sleep a night, until he found that kid in the basement of an abandoned mattress factory. The kid had fallen through a hole in the floor and couldn't get out. Augustus Perry was also skilled as an interrogator. He knew how to get information out of people.

But I also knew Bert Sanders had his number. My brother-in-law was a great believer in expediting the justice system. Why go to all the trouble of a trial to encourage a troublesome out-of-towner to stay out of Griffon when a good swift kick in the nuts could accomplish the same thing in a lot less time?

But the men and women under Augustus Perry's command were careful. They covered each other's asses. They didn't teach someone a lesson in front of witnesses. And the corners they cut, they cut with their heads held high because they believed, in their hearts, that they were making Griffon a better place.

I'd entered the number for Augie's cell, not his home phone. He always carried his cell. It rang several times before it went to message.

'Augie, it's Cal. I need to talk. Call me when you get this.'

I wasn't going to spin my wheels waiting for him to call back. I was going to take another run at Sean Skilling. I wasn't through with that kid.

★　★　★

I drove back to the Skilling place, an expansive two-story house with a triple garage and three different models of Fords out front, although none of them was the Ranger Sean had been driving. I parked around the corner, walked back, and pressed my thumb hard on the doorbell.

It didn't take ten seconds for someone to

answer. A small woman with porcelain skin and light blond hair to match. Without makeup, she gave the appearance of having had all the blood drained out of her.

'Hello?'

'Ms. Skilling?'

'Yes? I'm Sheila Skilling.'

'I'm Calvin Weaver.' I flashed my license. 'I'm a private investigator.'

'What do you want?'

'It's about Sean.'

Alarm consumed her face. 'Sean? Is he okay?' She turned her head. 'Adam! The police are here about Sean!'

I didn't see the need to correct her yet.

'What's happened?' a man shouted, his voice muffled. A moment later, a door swung open and Adam Skilling emerged from the basement. Running up the stairs had winded him, which wasn't too surprising, given that he looked to be at least two hundred and fifty pounds. He had a round face, his cheeks currently crimson, a moustache, and a full head of brown hair.

'What's going on?' he asked between breaths.

'Something about Sean,' Sheila said. Both sets of eyes were on me. 'Has there been an accident or something?'

I shook my head. 'More like an incident.'

'Good heavens, what?'

I went authoritarian. 'In the execution of my duties, I was attempting to elicit some information from your son, when one of his friends assaulted me. Then the two of them fled.'

'Jesus,' said Adam. 'Where the hell was this?'

141

'At Patchett's.'

'You're a cop? You don't look like a cop.'

'I'm an investigator. Private. My name's Cal Weaver.' I did him the courtesy of showing my license again. 'It'd be my preference not to involve the police in this, but that will depend largely on your cooperation. And Sean's.' I was hoping they wouldn't see through me as easily as Phyllis Pearce had. I peered beyond them into the house. 'Is he home? I don't see his truck in the drive.'

'He's — he's out,' Sheila said. 'I don't know where he is.'

Adam Skilling, no longer winded, dug into his pocket and withdrew a cell phone. 'I'll get him. I'll get him over here right — '

'No, not yet,' I said. 'I have some questions for you first. Maybe we can iron a lot of this out before we bring your son into it.'

'Who assaulted you?'

'I don't know. I was struck from behind.'

'But Sean, *he* didn't hit you,' Sheila said.

'I think that fact may help mitigate things,' I said. 'May I come in?'

They led me into the living room and motioned for me to take a seat on the couch. Sheila and her husband took chairs across from me.

'Is Hanna here?' I asked.

That one caught them both off guard. 'Hanna Rodomski?' Sheila Skilling asked.

'Is there another Hanna?' I asked.

'No, of course not. And no, she's not here. I mean, she's probably with Sean. Is Hanna in

142

some kind of trouble, too?'

'I told you that girl was no good,' Adam Skilling said. 'Didn't I?'

'Does she stay here?' I asked.

Sean's mother flushed. 'Well, I know maybe it's not proper, but yes, the odd night, she does stay here with — '

'That girl sleeps here more than she does at her own house,' Adam said. 'It's not right. She's a bad influence on the boy. Some days she parades around here in her underwear like she owns the joint.'

His wife shot him a look. 'She was just going into the bathroom. And you don't have to look.'

The man's cheeks, which had settled down some since his run up the stairs from the basement, flushed again.

'And anyway,' his wife continued, 'she wasn't here last night. I know that for sure. I think both of them might have . . . slept someplace else, because I don't even think Sean was here last night.'

'You never know where the hell they are,' Adam said, puffed up like a blowfish. 'You can't afford to take your eyes off them for a minute.'

Sheila shot him another look, which this time he seemed to take to heart. Some of the air was let out of his chest, and he shrank a size. 'All I'm saying is, they take years off your life.'

I was troubled by Sheila's comment that Hanna hadn't stayed here last night, because I had the impression from her parents that she hadn't slept in her own house in the last twenty-four hours.

'When's the last time you saw Hanna?' I asked.

'Yesterday,' Sheila said. 'Around dinnertime?' She looked at her husband, but he shrugged. 'But I don't understand. Are you here about Sean, or Hanna? Was Hanna the one who hit you?'

'I'm pretty sure she wasn't,' I said. 'But I am here about Sean, and Hanna. And Claire Sanders, too.'

'Oh, Claire, we know her,' Sheila said. 'Don't we?' she said to Adam.

'And her father,' he said wearily.

'I was trying to ask your son about her when I was struck,' I said. 'I'm trying to find Claire, and I think Sean and Hanna know where she is.'

'Why are you looking for Claire?' Adam asked.

I ignored the question. 'I think Hanna will know where she is, and I'm hoping Sean can put me in touch with her. Sean's looking for Claire, too. He was asking around at Patchett's. Sean may think he has something to fear from me, but he doesn't. My interest is in finding Claire. If he helps me with that, I can let everything else slide.'

'Have you talked to Bert?' Adam asked. So he and the mayor were on a first-name basis.

'Yes,' I said. I looked at the cell phone in the man's hand. 'This'd be a good time to invite Sean to come home. Don't mention I'm here.'

Adam hesitated, then placed the call. Sean's phone probably rang three or four times, and then his father spoke. 'Hey, where are you? . . . What do you mean, driving around? Driving

144

around where? ... Okay, listen, I don't care where you are. Just get your ass home pronto ... You'll find out when you get here ... If you're not here in five minutes you can forget driving around in that Ranger. I've got a fifteen-year-old Civic on the lot that'll suit you just fine ... Yeah? Fine, five minutes.'

He ended the call and looked at me. 'I must have done something bad in a past life to deserve all this misery.'

18

The kid showed up in four minutes. Headlights splayed across the living room window. A second later, a truck door slammed, and two seconds after that, Sean Skilling came barreling into the house like a runaway train. But he put the brakes on the moment he saw me sitting with his parents in the living room. He looked like he was going to turn and run, but his father jumped to his feet and shouted, 'Hold it right there, mister!'

Sean froze. But you could see it in his eyes, that he was still thinking of making a break for it.

'Get the hell in here,' Adam said, pointing to the living room. 'Get the hell in here and sit the hell down.' He pointed to the chair he'd just vacated.

The kid moved cautiously, like he was expecting his father to attack him before he could sit, but he got to the chair without incident. Adam stayed on his feet, moving back and forth in front of his son in short steps, like a boxer warming up before the bell rings.

'What in the hell's going on?' he asked.

Sean shot him a look. 'I don't know what you're talking about.'

That was probably true, to a point. He must have wondered whether I was here about Hanna, or Claire, or his friend punching me in the head. No doubt we'd get to all of it before the night was over, but clearly Adam Skilling wanted to address the third issue immediately.

His father said, 'Who hit him? Who hit this man? I want a name!'

'I didn't hit him. I didn't lay a hand on him,' he said.

'But you saw him get hit, didn't you?'

'I don't know, maybe — '

'That's a yes-or-no question. You saw him get hit, or you didn't see him get hit. Which is it?'

'Adam — ' his wife said tentatively.

'I'm talking here, Sheila. Yes or no?'

'Yeah, I saw him get hit. But it was dark.'

'Oh please,' Adam Skilling said. 'Was it light enough for you to see him when the two of you ran off together? What if he'd been knocked unconscious? What if he'd had some kind of brain injury or something? You want to end up with a record? Is that what you want? So I'm gonna ask again, who hit — '

'Mr. Skilling,' I said firmly.

He whirled around, looked at me as though he'd forgotten I was there, even though his questions concerned me. 'What?'

'We can get to who it was later,' I said.

'I'm trying to help, for Christ's sake.'

'I know, and I appreciate it.' I turned to Sean, who looked slightly relieved. 'In case you don't remember, I'm Cal Weaver, and I'm a private investigator.'

'I know who you are.'

'I don't think you understood what I was after when I saw you at Patchett's. I'm looking for Claire, and I think Hanna can help me.'

'I don't know where she is.' He looked at both

147

his parents quickly. 'Swear to God.'

'Why are you looking for Claire?' Sheila asked. 'I don't understand what's happened with her. Is she missing?'

Sean looked down at the broadloom and shook his head. 'Sort of.'

'What's that mean? 'Sort of'?' I asked.

'I mean, yeah, she's gone away, but that doesn't mean she's *missing*. It just means she's not around.'

'You know where she is?' I asked.

'I swear, I've got no fucking idea.'

Adam's hand came out of nowhere and slapped the kid across the side of the head. 'You watch your goddamn mouth.'

Sean winced but made an effort not to cry out. Maybe he was used to it.

'Does Hanna know where Claire is?' I asked.

Sean hesitated, bit his lower lip. 'I don't know. She might. She and Claire kind of cooked this thing up together.'

'Then we need to talk to Hanna.'

Sean said nothing.

'Where's Hanna, Sean?' I asked.

'I don't know.'

'What do you mean?' Sheila asked. 'She's practically attached to you. Did she go back to her parents' house?'

'Maybe. But I don't think so.'

Sadness washed over Sheila's face. 'Oh no, did you two break up?'

'That'd be the first bit of good news we've had around here in some time,' Adam said.

'No,' Sean said forcefully. 'We didn't break up.'

148

I was sensing something more urgent here than a teen romance in trouble. 'Sean, did Hanna and Claire go off someplace together?'

'I don't know. I'm starting to wonder. The thing is, I wasn't at Patchett's looking for Claire.'

'Don't lie to us,' Adam said. 'The man says he saw you there, and that when he tried to talk to you, somebody hit him in the head.'

'I *was* there, okay? I admit I was at Patchett's. But I wasn't looking for Claire.'

I nodded, suddenly getting it. 'You were asking if anyone's seen Hanna.'

He looked at me, his eyes starting to fill with tears. 'I don't know where she is. She's not answering her phone. She's ignoring all my texts.'

'Try her now,' I said.

'I tried her just a few — '

'Just try her and hand me the phone.'

He complied. After tapping Hanna's name in his contact list he handed the phone over and I put it to my ear.

It rang eight times before it went to voice mail. 'This is Hanna!' she said cheerfully. 'Leave! A! Message!' I ended the call. So her phone was on.

'Does Hanna have one of those tracking apps on her phone?'

Sean shook his head. 'No.'

'Still, the fact that the phone is on means we might be able to get in touch with the provider and figure out where it is.'

'Where *she* is,' he said.

'She could have lost her phone, forgotten it, even had it stolen,' I said. 'Maybe that's why she's not answering.'

I returned his phone to him and said, 'Do you know why I'm here, Sean?'

He gave me a 'duh' look. 'You told me, at Patchett's, that you're trying to find Claire.'

'That's right. But do you know why it's *me*, and not someone else?'

Sean puzzled over that one for a second. 'I'm . . . not sure.'

'You know what Claire and Hanna were up to last night.'

Slowly he said, 'Kind of.'

'Were you supposed to be Claire's ride? Were you the one who was supposed to pick her up out in front of Patchett's?'

It made sense to me. Clearly, Claire and Hanna had needed a third person for their stunt. Claire had been waiting for a ride that hadn't showed. And since Hanna was in on it, it stood to reason her boyfriend might be as well. And Bert Sanders' neighbor had said she'd seen Claire get picked up the night before in a vehicle that could have been Sean's.

When the boy didn't answer, I said, 'When, exactly, did you last see Hanna?'

'Last night,' he said. 'Around nine thirty or ten or something like that.'

'Where was that?'

'I . . . I dropped her off at Iggy's.'

'Okay. Then what?'

'I was driving around, just, you know, driving.'

'You had some time to kill.'

'Kind of. But then I got stopped by the cops.'

'What?' his father said, taking on a will-this-never-end expression. 'What for?'

150

'I went through a stop sign. Okay, not really. I mean, I didn't run it, you know? I did one of those rolling stops. I *almost* stopped. But there was this Griffon cop sitting there, and he hits the siren and pulls me over.' He shook his head in disgust. 'You know what they're like in this town. Any little thing, especially if you're my age, or you're from out of town, or if you're like Dennis and your skin's not exactly as white as everyone else's.'

Adam had briefly closed his eyes. Maybe he thought if he closed them hard enough, when he opened them once again we'd all be gone.

'And they had me sitting there forever while they ran the plates and checked my license, but it's totally clean, right? So when the cop finally came back he just gave me a warning to always come to a dead stop.'

'No ticket?' his mother said.

'That's right,' her boy said, and smiled, grateful that there was at least one thing that had turned out right.

It also helped me fit one piece into the puzzle. That was why he wasn't able to get to Patchett's to pick up Claire and drive her to Iggy's, where Hanna was waiting.

'Did you make a phone call while you were waiting for the police to run your license?' I asked.

He looked surprised. 'Yeah.'

'To tell someone you were going to be late, or weren't going to make it at all?'

I could see it in his eyes, that he was figuring it out now, too. That I was the fill-in. He'd called

151

Claire to say he was held up, and she'd told him she'd try to hitch a ride.

'I don't understand what's going on at all,' Sheila said. 'What are you two talking about?'

'What'd you do then, Sean?' I asked.

'I didn't — I didn't really know what to do. But wait.'

'Wait for what?'

'A phone call, I guess. To let me know things went . . . okay.'

Sheila interrupted again. 'I still don't — '

I held my hand up to silence her. We were finally getting somewhere.

'Did you get a call?' I asked.

Now a tear ran down his cheek. 'Yeah,' he nodded.

'Who called you?'

'Hanna.'

'What did she say?'

'She was talking real fast. She said things kind of got fu — ' He glanced at his father. 'Things got kind of messed up, but it sort of went okay, that they did the switch, but she was all kind of freaked out.'

'Switch?' Adam said. I held up my hand again.

'What do you mean, freaked out?' I asked.

'She said she just jumped out of some guy's car, and it was raining, and she was soaked, and she needed a ride, and she was really upset.'

'You said the last time you'd seen her was earlier. But didn't you go and pick her up then? The police were done with you by then, right?'

'Yeah, and I was going to pick her up. She was about to tell me where she was, and then she says — and don't be angry, Dad, because this is exactly what she said to me — she says, 'Shit, they're here.''

'Who's 'they'? The same ones Claire was trying to lose?'

'I don't know.'

'What'd Hanna say then?'

'She didn't say anything. The call just ended. And I never got to know where she'd been dropped off.'

I knew.

19

'Sean and I have to go out,' I told the Skillings.

'What for?' his mother said as we all got to our feet.

'We're going to see if we can find Hanna, aren't we, Sean?' I said to him.

He nodded. 'Yeah.'

'I don't know about this,' his father said.

'I very much appreciate your son's cooperation, and yours,' I said. 'In consideration of that, I'm inclined to let that other matter slide.'

The parents contemplated my words. Sheila spoke first. 'You help this man any way you can, Sean.'

'Yeah,' Adam said. 'You do that.'

As their son and I moved toward the door, Sheila said, 'Don't be too late, now.' Like we were heading out to catch a movie.

Once outside, I said, 'I'm parked around the corner.' We walked the short distance in silence. I hit the remote to unlock the doors and the two of us got into the Honda.

'Where are we going?' he asked as he reached over his shoulder for the seat belt.

'I was the one who gave Claire a ride last night,' I said. 'When you didn't show up at Patchett's.'

'I figured that, but why would she have called *you?*'

'She didn't. I was in the right place at the right time.' Or the wrong place at the wrong time, depending on how you looked at it. 'I was driving by, stopped at the light. Claire'd been standing there, waiting for you, and when you called and said you couldn't make it, she tapped on my window to ask for a ride. I was going to say no, but she recognized me, said she knew Scott. So I said okay.'

'If I hadn't got pulled over,' Sean said, 'I'd have been there. Stupid cop was jerking me around for no reason.'

I keyed the ignition, turned around, gave it some gas. 'Yeah. So let me guess how it went. You gave Claire a lift to Patchett's. Then you picked Hanna up and took her to Iggy's so she could wait for Claire.'

'Yeah. We figured no one would follow me after I dropped Claire off. They'd hang back at Patchett's.'

'Okay. Then, after you dropped Hanna off, you were to go back and get Claire, drive her to Iggy's. They do the switch, and Hanna, wearing that wig, gets in your car looking like Claire. How'm I doing?'

'Good,' he said, looking straight ahead.

'Hanna had me fooled for about one minute, but I guess that was okay, because I wasn't the one she had to trick. So here's what I'm wondering, Sean.'

He glanced over.

'Who's following Claire that she'd go to that much trouble to get away from him? And who picked her up after Hanna took her place?'

He shook his head. 'I don't know.'

'You're lying.'

155

'Really, man, I don't know what the fuck it's all about.' His dad wasn't here now to slap him upside the head, and I wasn't going to do it. I was tempted, but not over his foul language.

'You just agreed to help out without knowing a thing?'

'Claire didn't talk to me about it. She and I, we haven't been getting along as well as we used to since she dumped my friend — '

He cut himself off.

'Your friend?' I said.

'Yeah,' he said. 'I've got a friend she used to go out with, but then she started seeing this other guy.'

'What's your friend's name?'

'Doesn't matter.'

'This friend the same one who clunked me in the head?'

Sean shot me a cautious look. 'He didn't mean to hurt you or anything. He thought you were coming after me. He was just trying to protect me.'

'Okay,' I said. 'You want me to go back, ask your parents who, out of your friends, recently got dumped by Claire Sanders? How long do you think it'll take me to get a name?'

Sean looked ready to surrender. 'You gonna have him charged?'

'No,' I said.

'You gonna throw him in a trunk or anything?'

I glanced over at Sean, then back to the road. 'No. I won't do that.'

'His name's Roman.'

'Roman?' I said. 'Roman Ravelson? Whose

156

parents own the furniture place?'

'Yeah.'

'Isn't he a bit old for Claire?' I knew he was twenty-one.

'Whatever,' he said. 'She broke it off, anyway. But now she knows how it feels, so maybe she'll get back with him, although I kind of doubt it.'

'What, did someone dump her?' I asked.

'She started going out with this other guy, Dennis — I don't know where he's from exactly, but not from here; he was just here for a summer job — and she was all super in love with him, but then I guess he just wanted out, and went back to wherever he came from. Claire was, like, all devastated, and you ask me, it kind of looked good on her.'

I'd heard the name earlier tonight. 'Is Dennis the black guy you mentioned?'

'Huh?'

'When you told your parents about being pulled over, you said the cops pull over people your age, out-of-towners, or people like Dennis who's not as white as everyone else around here.'

'Oh yeah. He's black.' He shrugged. 'This is still kind of a white-bread town, you know. I'm not sayin' that's a bad thing — it's just some people around here kind of freak out when they see a black guy.'

Sean wasn't wrong about that.

'So even though you're pissed with Claire, you agreed to help her with this thing last night.'

'Hanna asked me, so I did it. She said Claire was being stalked or something and she needed to get away.'

157

'Who'd she need to get away from? Roman?'

'I don't know. I mean, okay, Roman has wanted to talk to Claire about why she dumped him. A guy deserves some kind of explanation, right? She wouldn't answer the phone if it was him, and she stopped texting with him because he kind of crossed a line there.'

'How'd he cross a line by texting with her?'

'Oh man, I can't talk about this. Forget I said that.'

'Sean.'

'Okay, you know you can send more than words in a text, right? You can send pictures?'

'I know.'

'So, after Claire broke up with Roman, he texted her a picture of what she was going to be missing.'

I was pretty sure I was getting his drift. 'You telling me he texted a photo of his dick to her?'

Sean shrugged. 'Pretty much.'

'And not at half-mast, I'm guessing,' I said.

'Look, it's no big deal. Everybody does it. Sends hot pictures of themselves to each other. But Claire kinda didn't like that after they'd broke up.'

'Did Dennis know Roman sent her those kinds of pics?'

'I don't think so. He'd have probably tried to kill him if he had.' He waved his hands like he was trying to clear the air. 'But, look, I don't think it was Roman that Claire was trying to ditch. I mean, Hanna wouldn't have asked me to help out if it was my own friend that was involved. That wouldn't be right.'

158

'So you have no idea who might have been following her.'

He licked his lips. 'I swear, I don't know the details. Hanna said Claire wouldn't even tell her what exactly was going on.'

'Could it have been the police?'

'Like I said, I don't know. These are all things you should ask Hanna. I was just supposed to drive, okay?'

'What about Claire's father?'

'What about him?'

'Could he be the one she was trying to give the slip to?'

Sean didn't answer right away. 'Where are we going, anyway?'

'To where I dropped Hanna off. You didn't answer my question. Could Claire have been trying to get away from her father?'

'What, you think *he's* been following her around?'

'I'm asking you. What's the story on Claire and her dad? They get along?'

'I guess they're okay. She's living with him and not her mom, so I guess that says something about how they got along. And she didn't want to have to go live in Canada and get split up from all her friends. Her mom's new husband is even weirder than her real dad, so she probably figured she was better off with him.'

'What's weird about Bert Sanders?'

'You hear stories.'

'What kind of stories?' I asked.

'I don't know. Just, he's, you know, even though he's an old guy, he really gets a lot of

159

action. I don't know where he'd find time to follow Claire around.'

'Are you talking about women? He has a lot of lady friends?'

'Yeah. I mean, Claire says he's all high and mighty about a lot of things, like what's right and wrong and all that kind of stuff and raising shit with the cops — which, by the way, I happen to think is a pretty good idea — but when it comes to gettin' some, he's right in there. It kind of embarrasses Claire. Hanna told me she said, one time — Maybe I shouldn't tell this.'

I waited.

'One time, Claire comes home from school in the middle of the day — she was sick, right? And her dad's home, and there's this woman, she's got her head in his lap, right in the living room.' He gave me a look. 'You know what I'm talking about?'

'I know what you're talking about. Who was the woman?'

'Shit, I don't know. I don't even know if Claire knew. She caught a glimpse of what was going down — ' He stopped himself. 'I wasn't trying to be funny. But when she saw what was happening, she, like, ran off.'

'Is Claire afraid of her father?'

He gave me another glance. 'Everybody's afraid of their fathers. Mothers, too, mostly.'

My mind drifted for a moment. Had Scott been afraid of me? Had he been afraid of Donna? I couldn't believe that. We were good parents.

Except for when we weren't.

'Yeah, but there's afraid, and then there's *afraid*,' I said. 'You're afraid your parents are going to find out about stuff you've done they wouldn't approve of, and if they do, there'll be consequences. You get grounded, lose driving privileges. End up with a Civic instead of that nice pickup you're driving. It's like that for all kids. But then there are parents who go too far. Who cross the line. You get what I'm saying.'

'Yeah.'

'Does Claire's father cross some kind of line?'

'I don't know what you mean,' Sean said. 'You mean, like, what, slapping her around or something?'

'You tell me.'

'I don't think so. I never seen her with bruises or anything like that.'

'What about other kinds of abuse?'

Sean made a face like he'd eaten something bad. He shook his head definitively. 'No way. I mean, I don't think so.' He paused. 'If anything, Claire's dad cares too much. That can be kind of hard to live with, too.'

'Do your parents care too much?' I said.

'Sometimes I wish they cared a little less. My dad's on my ass all the time, and he's pissed about Hanna being over and all, but her parents, they don't care that much about what she does. She's lucky that way.'

Was that what defined luck for these kids? Parents who didn't give a shit? I seemed to recall Hanna's parents being worried about something. A business Hanna was involved in with her boyfriend that could end up biting her in the ass.

161

'You and Hanna got something going on the side,' I said, not asking a question. 'To make some money.'

His head jerked. I'd hit a nerve. 'What?'

'What is it?' I thought immediately of Scott. 'You guys selling something? You selling drugs?'

'Jesus, no.'

'You're doing something. Her parents mentioned you had something going.'

'It's nothing. It's not a big deal. It's just — look, everybody does it.'

'Everybody does what?'

'Drinks,' Sean said. 'It's no big deal around here. I mean, everybody knows you can get a drink at Patchett's as long as you don't look like you're twelve. But not everybody wants to drink there. Sometimes, you know, you want to do stuff at home or someplace else.'

'Like when parents are away.'

He gave me a look. 'Sometimes.'

'So where do you and Hanna fit in?'

Sean sighed. 'Man, you just don't quit, do you?'

'Something's going on, Sean. Something with Claire. I don't know what it is yet, but you answering my questions, it helps. I'm not looking to make trouble for you. I just want to find Claire.'

'What me and Hanna are doing, it's got nothing to do with Claire.'

'Why don't you let me decide that?'

Another sigh, then, 'Okay, so, we get stuff people want, you know, to drink, and we deliver it.'

'You and Hanna. Using your Ranger?'

162

'Yeah.'

'Just to friends?'

'Like, anybody. Word gets around, people have a couple numbers they can call, they say they need some rye or vodka or beer or whatever, and we deliver.'

'With a markup.'

'Well, yeah. We're not doing it for nothing.'

'How do you get it? You and Hanna aren't old enough to be buying booze in bulk.'

Sean's lips stayed pressed together.

'Let me guess,' I said. 'You need someone who's twenty-one, who can pick up everything you need. Roman.'

He looked at me. He didn't have to admit it. I could tell from his expression.

'Roman gets a cut of what you and Hanna make?'

Sean nodded.

'You just work Griffon?' I asked.

He shook his head. 'We kinda go all over. Lewiston, Niagara Falls, Lockport. If the order's big enough. Thing is, it used to be easy to go over the border for a drink. But now, you gotta have a passport to get into Canada and back, so more kids, we gotta do it on this side. There's a market, you know?'

'How much you make?'

'We usually only do it on Saturdays, maybe on a Friday night, too. We can make a couple hundred.'

I smiled. It was entrepreneurial, to be sure. But risky, too. Driving into neighborhoods they didn't know, a truck full of liquor, large sums of

163

cash. Pretty dumb, all things considered.

We rode for a minute in silence. Then I said, 'I've got one last question for you. Not about Hanna, or Claire, or any of this.'

Sean waited.

'At Patchett's, when I told you my name, and you asked if I was Scott's father, the first thing you said was that you didn't know anything about what happened to him.'

'I don't.'

'I hadn't even asked you anything. You came out with that pretty fast.'

He didn't say anything for a few seconds. Then, 'I got another friend, Len Eggleton. Maybe you know who I'm talking about.'

I didn't say anything.

'Len says one night, this guy came to see him, said he wanted to know who sold his kid some X. Len said this guy, he'd heard a rumor that Len dealt the stuff, even though, far as I know, Len's never been into that kind of thing. Just weed, you know.'

I still said nothing.

'So anyway, Len says no way, he never sold or gave this guy's kid any X, and the guy, then he's all, okay, if Len didn't give it to the kid, maybe he knows who did. And Len says no fucking way, he doesn't know, and the guy, he says maybe Len needs time to think about his answer, and he grabs Len and he stuffs him into the trunk of Len's car. Len's, like, he's totally claustrophobic, and just about freaks out, so the guy lets him out, and I think he actually kind of believes Len now, that he really doesn't know who gave the kid the X, but the guy, he tells Len if he tells anybody about what just happened, he'll put the word out that he *did* give up a name. Len was scared shitless, so he never told his parents or the cops or anyone else but me and a couple of other friends.'

It was very quiet in the car.

'So,' Sean concluded, 'that's why, when I saw you, I told you right out that I didn't know anything. Because I didn't want to end up in a trunk like Len. That's why Roman decked you. He was trying to save my ass.'

I shot him a startled look, but said nothing. I pulled the car over to the shoulder, eased to a stop, and put it in park.

'We're here,' I said. 'This is where I dropped Hanna off.'

20

We both got out and stood a moment in the cool night air. Unlike twenty-four hours before, there was no rain. There was the sound of distant traffic, and the occasional vehicle that went right by us, but other than that it was very quiet.

A few car lengths up, the traffic light changed. The businesses were closed, and there were few lights on in the homes that were sandwiched between them.

'You let her out here?' Sean said. 'This is, like, the middle of nowhere.'

'She tried to jump out of the car when it was moving. I had to pull over. I couldn't force her to stay.' I was trying to convince myself as much as Sean.

'Seems like a shitty thing to do,' he said.

I went around to the back of the car, used my remote to pop the trunk. Sean spun around, a nervous look on his face.

'Don't worry, I'm just getting a flashlight,' I told him, and grabbed a heavy Maglite I kept in there, along with other tools of the trade, like a bright orange safety helmet that would allow you to go almost any place you wanted when you put it on your head, as well as a laptop, a mini-printer, even a Kevlar vest I'd kept from my days as a cop but had never worn since. I closed the trunk, joined Sean, and clicked the light on.

'When she jumped out,' I said, 'she ran that way.'

'Why are we doing this?' he asked. 'This doesn't make any sense to me.'

'This is where Hanna called you from. Last thing she did was show me she had a phone, which I took to mean she was going to call someone else for a ride.'

'Yeah,' he said.

'She called you. And got interrupted. Right now, it looks like you're the last person we know who's spoken to her. It happened around here. So I want to look around. Over here, by these bushes, that's where she tossed her wig.'

I cast the flashlight beam around the shrubs. Panned it low first, then went higher, in case the wig had caught on a branch before it hit the ground.

'There,' I said.

We closed the distance. I went down to one knee and took hold of the wig, tentatively at first, like it was a piece of road-kill. 'This look like the wig?' I asked him.

'I think,' Sean said.

'Me, too. How many wigs can you expect to find along the side of the road?'

'I guess.'

I got up, heard my knee crack. I walked back to the car, unlocked it, and set the wig on the backseat.

'Let's head up this way,' I said, pointing to the corner. 'When she got to the corner, she turned right.'

I kept scanning my flashlight across the sidewalk, using it like a white cane. I didn't know what I was looking for, if anything, but it seemed like a detective-ish thing to do. When we hit the corner, I saw that the cross street went only about a hundred yards before there was a short bridge. Just this side of it, on the right, was a house that looked as though it had been knocked down in one windstorm and reassembled by the next. Boards askew, eaves hanging loose. But there was activity here. Three people sitting on the sagging porch, drinking beer, sitting in what were once, perhaps in another millennium, living room chairs that now had the stuffing exploding from them.

'Hey,' I said as we came up in front of the house.

There were two women, heavyset, and a thin, bearded man between them. All in their sixties, I guessed, enjoying a night of getting buzzed in the evening air.

'Hi,' said the man. 'How you boys doing tonight?'

'We're good,' I said. 'My name's Cal, and this is my friend Sean. We wonder if you might be able to help us.'

'You lost?' the man asked. ''Cause I can't imagine anyone would intend to be walking along here at night unless they was.'

The women cackled softly.

'We're trying to find a girl,' I said.

'You can have both of these ones,' he said, and the women cackled some more. I laughed along with them, showing I could appreciate clever repartee.

Sean was drifting away, heading toward the bridge. From what I could see, it spanned little more than a creek, and was only about forty feet long.

'A girl came running along here last night, about this time,' I said. 'It was raining, and she might have been on her cell phone.'

'What she look like?' one of the women asked.

'About seventeen, five and a half feet tall, slight, with short blond hair,' I told them. 'We think that while she was making the call, someone may have stopped, given her a ride maybe.'

'What time did we go in last night?' the woman asked the man.

'We didn't even sit out here,' he said. ''Cause it was raining. We enjoyed our evening festivities indoors.'

'That's right. We didn't come out here at all,' the second woman said.

I was trying to keep track of what they were saying while keeping an eye on Sean. He was at the bridge, which had two streetlamps at each end, and was peering over the right railing.

'You didn't hear anything at all?' I asked. 'Nothing out of the ordinary?'

'Nope. Except for Mildred here, who had some terrible gas.' He pointed to the woman to his left. There was more cackling.

'And those damn dogs,' Mildred said.

'What dogs?' I asked.

The man said, 'They've been going at it, off and on, all day, like they've been fightin' over somethin'. Settled down lately.'

'Where?'

The man pointed in Sean's direction. I turned

my head. He was on the other side of the bridge now, leaning over the railing, looking down into the dark. Sean shouted: 'Come here! Come here!'

I ran.

'Down there,' he said as I came up alongside him. 'It looks like there's something down there.'

I shone the light down. Water trickled along a gravel bed, probably no more than six inches of it at its deepest point. Along the bank, close to the abutment, there was something lighter in color up against the dirt and brush.

I played the light over it. It looked to me like a foot, and a leg, up to the knee. Badly mangled. I wouldn't be able to see any more until I got under there.

Sean was starting to move, but I grabbed his arm and said, 'Stay here.'

'I gotta see if — '

'Stay here,' I repeated, more firmly.

I ran to the end of the bridge, then cut my way through brush and tall grasses that matted the hill down to the creek. I nearly fell twice, my foot slipping on a beer bottle or can. I worked my way toward the slope of the abutment, shining the light ahead of me.

It was a body. And it was a mess.

From what I could tell, it was a young woman with short blond hair. Wearing the same clothes I'd seen Hanna in the night before. Most of them, anyway.

She was naked from the waist down.

She was on her side, her legs angled down toward the creek. I shone the light on her face, and I was as sure as I could be that this was the girl I'd found in my car when I came out of Iggy's.

'Jesus,' I said under my breath.

The phone in my jacket pocket, pressed against my chest, went off. It was like someone had placed the paddles of a heart defibrillator on me.

I reached for the phone, nearly dropped it next to the body, and put it to my ear before I'd had a chance to see who it was.

'Hello,' I said.

'You left a message,' Augustus Perry said. He sounded annoyed. 'What do you want?'

'What I called about has changed. Something else has moved to the top of the list.'

21

She looks out the window and sees that their boy is home. Well, not a boy, really. He's a man now. But isn't that how mothers always view their sons? As their boys?

'I'm just here for a couple minutes,' he says to her as he comes through the door. 'I've been running around all night putting out fires and I'm not done yet. But I wanted to see how he is.'

'Wound up,' she says.

'Did you give him something?'

'No, but I may have to. He needs his sleep.'

'I'm doing everything I can,' he says. 'This'll all get sorted out.'

His mother shakes her head doubtfully. 'We started off with one big problem and you turned it into two.' She's about to say something else, but bites her lip. But he knows what it would have been. That if it weren't for him, they wouldn't have this problem in the basement to begin with.

'I told you I'm going to deal with this. There's a couple things I can do before morning.'

'You better, because I feel like this is all ready to blow up in our face. It's like waiting for the other shoe to drop, but when it does, it's going to land on a mine.' She sighs. 'You're just one brainstorm after another.'

Wearily, he takes a seat at the kitchen table. 'God, I just want things to be normal. Things

172

have never been normal.'

'Some people's lives are never normal,' she says. 'That's just the way it is.' She surveys the room, but she's really looking beyond it. More to herself than her son, she says, 'It's like we're all prisoners. I haven't had a vacation in years.'

'And I haven't had a life,' he says. 'This overshadows everything. It's no wonder she broke up with me.'

'She wasn't right for you.' His mother never thought any of his girlfriends were right for him. 'What did she say, exactly?'

'She didn't really say anything. She just ended it. But I know why. It's because she could tell something wasn't right. I mean, I couldn't even bring her here, to meet you. It had to be at a coffee shop. She had to think it was weird that everything about this house was off limits.'

The woman puts her hand to her forehead. It's late, and she's exhausted. 'You have more important things to worry about. Finding that girl, and then the boy. Making sure he can't hurt us.'

'I know. You don't have to keep telling me.'

'Even after you find them, deal with them, we may have to make some changes around here,' she says, casting her eyes down to the floor, as though she can see right through it.

'I'm going to go down and see him.'

'There's something going on with his book,' she says.

'What do you mean?'

'It's never where I can see it. He says he writes in it after I've gone. That's not like him. I'm

173

worried what he might be writing in it. I need
you to go down and find it.'

He goes downstairs, is gone several minutes.
When he returns, he says to his mother, 'It's not
there. I couldn't find it anywhere.'

'What'd he say?'

'I asked him what he'd done with it. He said
he didn't remember.'

'Tell me he didn't . . . '

'I think he did. I think he gave it to the kid.'

The woman closes her eyes, as though she's in
physical pain.

'It doesn't matter,' he says. 'It's all gibberish.
It's meaningless.'

She shakes her head. 'Maybe. But there are
dates. And it's all in his handwriting.'

22

When Scott was twelve, he had an idea for a movie. He spelled it out for Donna and me over dinner.

'It's about this guy who comes to Earth from another galaxy, or maybe it's this one, like from Mars or something, it doesn't really matter, but he comes here wanting to see what Earth people are like, and he has to take human form so nobody can see what he really looks like, which is kind of gross. Like, he has what looks like worms all over his face or something, but they're probably blood vessels.'

'Uh-huh,' I said, glancing down at my noodles.

'At first I was thinking someone like Arnold Schwarzenegger could play him, but it's not really a Terminator kind of role, so I have to think about that a bit more. His mission is to make friends with one person, and to study him, and he picks someone totally at random and watches what this person does, and how this Earthling interacts with other Earthlings. But what the alien doesn't know is, he picked a real nerdy, geeky guy who doesn't have hardly any friends, so he doesn't interact much with other Earthlings. So the alien guy goes back to his home planet and reports that all Earthlings are lonely and unhappy and don't really fit in, because they're weird and like stuff nobody else likes.'

Donna and I said nothing for a moment. Finally, I asked, 'That's how it ends?'

Scott shook his head. 'No, no. It has a happy ending. The alien guy comes back, and takes the person he was, like, shadowing, back to his own planet, because he feels sorry for him, and the Earthling turns out to be really happy there because everyone thinks he's really cool and interesting and he doesn't think about killing himself anymore.'

Donna put her hand over her mouth, got up, and left the room.

Scott said, 'Was it the worms thing? I could take that out if it's too gross.'

*   *   *

I'm not sure why that memory popped into my head after I ended my brief conversation with Augustus Perry and made my way back up to the bridge, where Sean Skilling was waiting for me. Of course, I had Scott flashbacks about every five minutes since he'd died. He was always there, just below the surface, regardless of what I was doing.

Maybe it was the notion of happy endings, how elusive they can be, and how they aren't the same for everyone. For Scott, a geeky kid transplanted to another world, millions of miles from home, finds his happy ending among aliens who appreciate his uniqueness. But was it a happy ending for the parents he left behind?

Scott was on my mind because I was starting to worry there might be no happy ending in my search for Claire Sanders. Not if she ended up the same way her friend Hanna Rodomski had.

When I got to Sean, he was a mess.

'Is it her?' he asked, tears running down his cheeks. 'It can't be her. There's no way it's her.'

'I'm pretty sure it is,' I said. 'But it's a bad scene down there.'

I had to grab him as he attempted to get past me to go under the bridge and see what I had seen.

'You can't go down there.'

'Get the fuck out of my way,' he said, practically spitting the words into my face. He was a strong kid, and I wasn't sure I was any match for him, but there was no way I wanted him going down there and seeing Hanna. First, he just didn't need that, and second, I didn't want him messing with evidence.

Although the dogs had already done a good job of that.

'Sean, listen to me,' I said, blocking his path. 'You can't go near her. I may have already screwed things up, getting as close as I did. Are you hearing me? Whoever did this to Hanna, we want the son of a bitch caught. You go down there now and you run a chance of messing up a crime scene. You hear me?'

I could feel the muscles in his arms, taut as steel, relax ever so slightly. 'Please,' I said. 'We'll stay here on the bridge, we'll stand guard, make sure no one else goes down and disturbs her, okay? Let's preserve what dignity she has left.'

He turned and walked to the other side of the bridge, put his hand on the rusted railing. His body started to shake with sobs. I put a hand on his shoulder. 'We're going to find out who did this. I swear.'

Sean turned and pointed an accusing finger at my face. 'This is your fault. You dropped her off. You left her here for whoever killed her.'

I was aware.

I thought about that black pickup, pulled over to the side of the road, that I'd noticed seconds after Hanna had fled my car. The one that had taken off by the time I'd turned around and gone back for another look. I struggled to remember any details about it. Ford or Dodge? Foreign or domestic? I was usually good at that sort of thing, but it had been dark, and it had been raining.

'If I hadn't got pulled over by that damn cop . . . ,' Sean said. 'I was supposed to *be* there. It wouldn't have happened if I'd been there. She wouldn't have tried to run away from *me*.'

The trio from the porch were cautiously approaching. The one I knew as Mildred called out, 'What's happened?'

'There's a body under the bridge,' I said.

'Mother of God,' Mildred said.

I told her the police would be here shortly. When I'd told Augie who it was I'd found under the bridge, he didn't know the first name, but he'd recognized the last. 'Jesus. That must be Chris Rodomski's kid. Chris and Glynis.'

I'd confirmed it for him. He'd wanted to know what I was doing there, but agreed to wait for details until we could talk face-to-face.

'Ten minutes,' he'd said. 'And I'll call it in.'

178

I could hear sirens in the distance as I walked back over to Sean.

'I'm gonna hafta call my parents,' he said.

'Yeah,' I said. 'Look, Sean, before the cops get here, is there anything you haven't told me? About who Hanna was helping Claire get away from?'

He shook his head. 'I told you what I know. I swear.'

'After the cops let you off last night, after you ran the stop sign, go through it with me. What did you do then?'

'I drove by Patchett's, just in case Claire was still there. Then I went to Iggy's, in case Hanna or her were still around.'

'What time did you get to Iggy's? Did you see Hanna get into my car?'

'No. I never saw you.'

'So you didn't follow me, did you, Sean?'

'What?'

'In your Ranger. Did you follow me down this way?'

He blinked at me. 'What are you talking about?'

'I saw a black pickup around here after Hanna got out of my car. I'm gonna have to tell the police that.'

The sirens grew louder.

Sean shook his head. 'Are the cops going to think I did this?'

'They always look at the boyfriend. Luckily for you, the cops are your best alibi, since they had you pulled over around the time Hanna was killed. Plus, you may have been seen at Iggy's, or caught on their security cam, if they have one, which again places you away from the scene.'

I hoped Iggy's was more diligent than Patchett's where security was concerned. If they had cameras, Claire might have been caught on them after I'd headed off with Hanna.

The first cruiser arrived at the scene, lights flashing, siren wailing. Two officers — a male and a female — got out. Kate Ramsey and her partner. The ones who'd sent the bikers on their way. Seconds later, another car rolled up. Out got Ricky Haines and Hank Brindle.

'What about you?' Sean asked.

The arrivals had distracted me. 'Huh? What about me?'

'Aren't they just as likely to think you did it?' Sean asked. 'You dropped her off just before she got killed.'

It occurred to me at that moment that pissing off the chief of police at family get-togethers over the years might not have been such a good idea.

23

And then there he was, arriving just seconds after his uniformed officers in a white Chevy Suburban. Augustus Perry had a short huddle with them before striding over in my direction.

I stood and let him come to me.

'Cal,' he said without even a hint of a nod. He looked at the teenage boy standing next to me. 'Who are you?'

'Sean Skilling.' A pause, then, 'Sir.'

Augie squinted. 'Ford dealership?'

'My dad's, yes, sir.'

Augie nodded. 'Adam Skilling. You folks do all the servicing on our vehicles. I've seen your father at our garage.'

'That'd be him.'

Augie put his eyes back on me. 'Show me.'

Leaving Sean behind, I led my brother-in-law to the railing and pointed down to Hanna's body. 'Hard to see all of her from here,' I said.

He grunted. 'Tell me how it came to be that you found her.'

'It's a long story,' I said.

'All the more time I get to spend with you,' he said.

I gave it all to him as quickly as I could. Picking up Claire at Patchett's, and everything that followed. And then, earlier this evening, two of his men coming to see me, trying to find Claire.

'This part I'm guessing you already know about,' I said.

He stared at me blankly, although I couldn't tell whether that meant he didn't know, or did and just wasn't saying.

'Go on,' Augie said.

I told him I felt a responsibility where Claire was concerned, and started asking around myself. Looking for Claire led me to Hanna, Hanna led me to Sean Skilling, and his recollection of his short phone call with Hanna had led us back here, around the corner from where Hanna had jumped out of my car. 'She tossed her wig when she got out. It's in my car.'

'Mayor's kid's missing,' Augie said under his breath. 'Girlfriend dead.'

'Yeah.'

He looked over his shoulder at Sean Skilling, who was currently being interviewed by Officer Ramsey and her partner. 'What about the kid? Girl gets killed, the first, most logical suspect is the boyfriend.'

'I know. But I don't think it's him. And he's got an alibi courtesy of the Griffon PD. One of your people'd pulled him over to write him up for running a stop sign about the time it all went down.'

'So there'll be a record of the ticket.'

'No, there won't. Sean says the cop got another call before he could finish writing it out.'

Augie scowled. 'Convenient.'

'Look, maybe it's the kid, I don't know. But I think something different's playing out here.'

'Who were they trying to trick? With the switch?'

'No idea.'

'The Skilling kid know?'

'He claims not to.' We were both looking at him now, being questioned by Ramsey and her partner. 'Who's with Kate?' I asked.

'Hmm? That's Marv Quinn.' Augie took another look over the railing. Haines and Brindle were searching the hillside around the body, flashlights in hand. 'That girl's missing her drawers.'

'I noticed,' I said.

'You think the Skilling kid and the girl were having troubles? She wants to break it off, he gets mad, things get out of hand, he wants one last go at her?'

'I don't think so,' I said.

He took one more long look at Hanna Rodomski and said, 'These sorts of things aren't supposed to happen here.' Even in the dim glow of the streetlamps, I thought I saw genuine sadness cross his weathered face.

He rubbed his mouth thoughtfully, then said, 'You think it's turned around somehow?'

'How do you mean?'

'This crazy stunt the girls pulled, fooling someone into thinking it was Claire who got into your car, which allowed her to slip away. Could it be the other way around? Maybe it wasn't that Hanna was trying to make someone think she was Claire. Maybe Claire was trying to make someone think she was Hanna.'

That made my head hurt. 'No. It doesn't play that way.'

'Maybe you're right. But it's possible, whoever

killed the Rodomski girl, they could have been thinking she was Claire. Thoughts?'

'That'd definitely cross Sean Skilling off your suspect list,' I said.

He said, 'Hmm.'

I asked, 'Why are you looking for Claire Sanders?'

'Who said I was?' the chief said.

'The collective *you*, Augie. Your minions.'

'Who was it again came to talk to you?'

'Brindle and Haines. Haines I know. He was the one . . . He brought us the news about Scott.'

Augie's face softened. 'About that. Haines should have called me. He shouldn't have delivered that news to you himself. It should have been me. I'm Scott's uncle, for Christ's sake. I'm sorry about that.'

I nodded. It wasn't the first time Augie had mentioned it.

'I honestly don't think he made the connection,' Augie said. 'If he'd thought for a half a second, seen the name Weaver on Scott's ID, thought about Donna in payroll — you're supposed to have *some* smarts if you're a cop.' He glanced down toward the creek, where Ricky Haines and his partner were still mucking about. 'Anyway, those two came to see you. Tell me about that.'

'They were looking for Claire. They knew I'd given her a lift at Patchett's. One of them said something about getting picked up on closed-circuit there, but Patchett's doesn't actually have any. So my first question is, were they already watching Patchett's? And the second is, who put them onto looking for Claire in the first place? Her father says he didn't report her missing.'

'You talked to him?'

'Right after you had your little town hall chat. Could someone else have reported her missing? Her mother? Sanders' ex lives in Toronto, right? But even if it was her, wouldn't you have gotten a heads-up?'

Augustus Perry didn't say anything. If I didn't know better, I'd have guessed he was thinking.

I interrupted whatever process was going on in there.

'It would seem to me, even with my limited understanding of the inner workings of the Griffon police department, that when the daughter of our beloved mayor, your sworn enemy of the moment, is the subject of a police search, somehow you would be in the loop.'

Augie looked back to where his SUV and the police cruisers were parked. There was another set of lights approaching.

'Coroner,' he said, and started walking.

24

A short black woman in her fifties, wearing a shiny blue down-filled jacket zipped up to her neck, approached. It struck me that she was dressed for much colder weather than we were currently having.

'Chief,' she said, blowing her nose and stuffing a tissue into one of her jacket pockets. I could see the ends of some surgical gloves sticking out of both of them.

'You okay, Sue?' Augie asked.

'Freezin' to death. It's this goddamn cold. Been trying to shake it for two weeks.'

'Sorry you had to get dragged out when you're sick,' he said.

Sue shrugged. 'Still a hell of a lot better off than that girl down there, I gather.'

'Cal, you know Dr. Kessler. She's what passes for a coroner around here.'

Sue Kessler sniffed, looked at me. 'We've met before, I think.' She was right. We'd crossed paths once or twice since I'd moved to Griffon. 'I won't shake your hand.'

I was okay with that.

'Sue, Cal found the body.'

'You touch anything?' Kessler asked.

'No,' I said. 'But I got pretty close to her.'

'Point me,' Kessler said.

Augie raised an arm, extended a finger. 'Down by the creek. Just under the bridge.'

'Terrific,' she said, pulling the gloves on. 'Give me a couple of minutes.'

She was gone more like ten. Augie talked briefly to some of his officers, then returned to my side, the two of us hugging the railing, leaning over, catching glimpses of Kessler doing her job. We walked to the end of the bridge to meet her as she worked her way back up the hill.

'I'd say strangled,' she said. 'There's impression marks on her neck, aside from the bite marks from some animals, dogs most likely. Dead at least a day, I'd guess, but I'll know more later.'

'Sexually assaulted?' Augie asked.

Kessler shrugged. 'You could presume, given that her pants and underwear are missing. But I won't know until I've had a chance to examine her.'

'Missing?' I said.

'If they're down there,' she said, 'I didn't see them. They're certainly not close to the body. Your people find any of the vic's clothes?'

Augie said he would have to talk to his people.

Kessler sneezed and said, 'I'm gonna go home, drink a gallon of NyQuil, try to get some sleep. I'll tackle her first thing in the morning.'

As Kessler walked away, Augustus Perry said to me, 'You might as well go home, too, Cal. We'll take things from here.'

I wasn't ready to leave. 'It's bugging you, isn't it?'

'I don't know what you're talking about.'

'Someone's not keeping you informed. That has to worry you.'

187

'Cal,' Augie said, bristling, 'it may surprise you to know that the chief is not informed of every single thing that goes on within the department. If you get pulled over for speeding, I don't get a call. If someone smashes a window at Griffon High, I don't get a call. A cat gets stuck up in a tree, I don't get a call.'

'Fire department gets that one, don't they?'

'There are any number of reasons why someone in my department might be asking around about Claire Sanders that would not warrant my being brought into the loop, as you put it.'

I shook my head. I was suddenly very tired, but I knew I wasn't heading home to bed anytime soon.

'See you around, Augie,' I said.

'You going home?'

'Once I've found Claire.'

I started to walk away, and then something struck me. I stopped and turned. 'Of course, the other possibility is, you do know what's going on. You know everything. Maybe you know something about Claire that Mayor Sanders would prefer didn't come out. Maybe she's into something she shouldn't be. Maybe if you find out what it is, you'll have some leverage against Sanders, get him to get the hell off your back.'

'Good thing there are a lot of people around right now,' Augie said. 'Otherwise, I'd knock you flat on your ass.'

I looked around. 'Just about all of them are cops,' I said. 'I think they'd back up whatever story you wanted to tell. Isn't that how it works around here? You may have thought you were fooling some of the people at that meeting, Augie, but you didn't fool me.'

'You got a lot of nerve,' Augie said. 'You think if this had happened anywhere else, where your brother-in-law wasn't the fucking chief, you wouldn't be getting your ass hauled in for questioning? You're the last person who saw this girl alive, Cal. You don't see me making an issue out of that.'

'Not yet,' I said.

Augie smiled.

25

On the way to my car, I stopped to check in on Sean, interrupting an interrogation by Kate Ramsey and Marvin Quinn.

Quinn said, 'Excuse me, mister, but we're working here.'

'It's okay, Marv. This is a friend of mine, the one I was just telling you about,' Kate said. 'How you doin', Cal?'

'I've been better, Kate.'

'I was telling my partner that was you I saw earlier tonight, out front of Patchett's when we were talking to our biker friends.'

I didn't know I'd been spotted sitting in the car. Kate was good. 'Yeah, that was me.'

She grinned slyly at her partner. 'Didn't I tell you that was Donna's husband keepin' an eye on me?'

'I had a feeling it was you,' I said. 'There's only two women working uniform in Griffon, right?'

'Just me right now. Carla's been on mat leave for six months.'

I thought of the kid working that convenience store, the one who'd said he'd had his tonsils spray-painted by a woman cop. Kind of narrowed it down for this neck of the woods.

'You stake out Patchett's much?' I asked.

Quinn, who'd said little up to now, said, 'We'd been watching those two ridin' in on their hogs and were waiting for them to come out, have a word with them.'

Kate nodded. 'Plenty of places for them to hoist a few and play pool back where they come from.'

Sean was watching with glazed eyes, like he didn't even know where he was anymore.

'Were you watching Patchett's last night?' I asked them. 'Around ten?'

Kate didn't hesitate. 'Nope. We were both finishing up with a fender bender south of town around then, weren't we, Marv?'

Officer Quinn nodded.

'Why?' Kate asked.

'Doesn't matter,' I said, and turned my focus to Sean. 'You gonna be okay?' He shrugged. 'You called your parents?'

'These guys are still asking me questions.'

'Call your parents,' I said. 'And don't say another word to these nice officers until they get here and hire you a lawyer.'

Kate Ramsey got her back up. 'Cal, what the hell — '

Quinn stared at me. 'Butt out, pal.'

I gave the two cops a smile. 'Have a nice evening. And you take care, Sean.'

As I was rounding the corner to head back to where my car was parked, I glanced back and saw Haines and Brindle up on the bridge again.

Brindle was looking at me. When our eyes met, he turned away.

★ ★ ★

While Ramsey and Quinn might not have been watching Patchett's last night, it was possible some other Griffon cops had been posted outside. And not necessarily Haines and Brindle. If some cop was watching the place for potential troublemakers like those bikers, and noticed a teenage girl getting into a car with a strange man, he might have made a note of my license plate. That could have been what led Haines and Brindle to have a word with me.

It still didn't explain why they were looking for Claire if no one had reported her missing. I wondered if I'd been onto something when I accused Augie of trying to get some dirt on her to strengthen his position in his fight with Sanders.

Sanders.

I wanted to talk to him again. Much had changed since we'd spoken a couple of hours ago.

A girl was dead.

His daughter's best friend.

He might not have wanted to talk to me before, but I didn't see where he had much choice now.

So I pointed the car in the direction of his house. But en route, I noticed Iggy's up ahead. It was on my mental list of places to stop, too. I figured I might as well go on and get it out of the way, especially considering it would probably be closing soon.

As I was heading toward it, I noticed a small car in my rearview mirror that seemed to be taking every turn I did. When I slowed, it slowed.

When I sped up, it did the same.

I wondered whether it would follow me into the Iggy's lot, but it didn't. As it kept on going down Danbury, I managed to get a quick look at it. A silver Hyundai. I didn't have a hope of reading even one number on the plate as it sped off.

I locked the car and went into the restaurant. A tall, thin man in his late twenties looked at me expectantly from behind the counter as I approached.

'Is Iggy around?' I asked. Always start at the top.

'Iggy?' asked the man, who had a name tag that said SAL.

'That's right.'

'There is no Iggy. At least, not anymore. Iggy — that'd be Ignatius Powell — opened his restaurant on this site in 1961, rebuilt it a couple of times, and then sold it ten years ago to my father. Last year, he died. Iggy, I mean. Not my dad. I manage this place for him in the evenings. Is there a problem with your burger?'

'Nothing like that, Sal,' I said. I showed him my license and told him I was trying to track down a girl who'd been here about this time last night.

'I'm pretty sure she slipped out your back door, and may have met someone in the parking lot,' I said. 'I notice you've got cameras.'

'Oh yeah, you have to,' Sal said. 'Especially at the drive-through window. Go on YouTube, you'll see a bunch of videos of McDonald's customers going berserk there. We had this one lady, she said she wanted a Whopper, and Gillian — she was the one on the window — told her we don't sell Whoppers, that's Burger King, but she wouldn't take no for an answer, kept screaming that she wanted a Whopper. Finally, she gets out of her truck and tries to grab Gillian through the window. We had to call the cops.'

'I'm hoping a look at last night's recordings will show me who might have given this girl a ride,' I said.

It made sense that someone other than Sean was waiting here to drive Claire somewhere, or that she'd arranged to have a car left here for her.

'I guess I can show you, you being licensed and all,' Sal said. 'I mean, I've already showed the police, so — '

'The police have already been here?'

'Yeah, like, a few hours ago.'

I nodded, like I'd expected this, which, in fact, I had. 'Would that have been Officers Haines and Brindle? We're all working toward the same goal. We just want to find Claire.'

'So you know those guys?'

'We were discussing the case earlier in the evening,' I said.

Sal called over a pimply-faced girl working the counter alongside him who couldn't have been twenty. 'I'll be back in a bit,' he told her. 'You hold the fort.' He motioned for me to follow him to a door at the end of the counter and led me through the kitchen, where one person was working.

I followed him into an office with two

monitors, each showing four views of the property. There were live shots of the drive-through, the front counter, the kitchen, another office where the safe was kept, and four of the parking lot.

'We had another nutcase one day,' Sal said. 'Came up to the counter wearing nothing but a pair of ratty shorts and flip-flops, a .38 in his hand.'

'You're kidding.'

'Yeah. Hair all sticking out, total whack job. Waved the gun around and said he'd start shooting if we didn't hand over the recipe for the special dressing we put on our burgers, which is really just mayo with some relish and a couple other things mixed into it.'

'Not exactly the formula for rocket fuel,' I said as Sal sat down in front of the monitors, started moving a mouse around.

'Yeah, right,' he said. 'So I wrote it on a napkin for him. Mayo, relish, a pinch of cayenne, like that, you know? And I hand it to him, and he says, 'No, put down what's *really* in it,' so I said, 'Okay,' and just started making shit up. Like dimorixalin diphosphate, and positronic marzipan, even calista flockhart.'

'Good one,' I said.

'I might even have written down plutonium. Anyway, I give him that, and he looks at it and says, 'Okay, good.' And I hand him another napkin and the pen and tell him he needs to sign his name. 'Whenever we give out the special mayo recipe, the person has to sign for it,' I say.'

'He didn't.'

'He did. Didn't take long for the cops to find him. Okay, here we go,' he said, pointing to the screen. It was a shot of the door on the side of the restaurant, near the back, where the restrooms were located. The camera was mounted outside and offered a broad view of the parking lot. But it was also night, so the view wasn't terrific. The date and time were superimposed across the bottom of the screen.

'So this is 9:54 p.m. yesterday,' Sal said. 'This is about where the cops had me start it from.' He froze the image. There were two vehicles visible in the lot from this vantage point. A light-colored or white Subaru Impreza and, partially hidden behind it, what looked like a silver or gray Volvo station wagon, although I couldn't be sure.

'The Soob is mine,' he said.

'Can you fast-forward that until we see some activity?' I asked.

'Sure.' He fiddled with the mouse. At 10:07:43 a black Dodge Challenger, the new model designed to look like one from the seventies, pulled up close to the door. A heavyset man got out, went inside. Three minutes later he was seen leaving, a brown Iggy's bag in hand. He got into this car, the lights came on, and he was gone.

At 10:14:33 a man appeared from the right side of the screen, limping. He looked like he was in his twenties, but he moved like a much older person. Rail thin, about five five, wearing a jeans jacket.

'That's Timmy,' Sal said.

'Timmy?'

'I don't know his last name. He lives just up

the street a bit, in that four-story square apartment building? I think, anyway. Works a shift somewhere, gets home about this time, comes by here every night on his way home for a double-patty cheeseburger, large fries, and a chocolate shake.'

'Every night?' I said.

'Yeah,' Sal said.

'He's, like, a hundred and thirty pounds. Tops.'

Sal shrugged. 'Some people handle fast food really well.'

'Every single night?' I asked again.

Sal glanced at me. 'You got any idea how many people eat here daily? Look, you're not gonna catch me knocking our food, but I couldn't eat this stuff every day of the month.'

'Hang on there for a second,' I said. I raised a finger to the monitor. 'Isn't that exhaust?'

It was coming from the Volvo station wagon parked behind Sal's Subaru. 'That car's been running the whole time,' I said.

'Yeah, I know,' Sal said. 'I was waiting to see if you noticed. I didn't want to ruin it for you.'

'It's not a movie, Sal. I'm okay with spoilers.'

'Okay. The cops — well, one of them — noticed the exhaust, too.'

'So you've already seen all of this? You know what's coming?'

'Sure,' he said.

At 10:16:13 the door of the ladies' room opens. It's Hanna. She darts out the side door. This would have been just before she got into my car. I was probably coming into the restaurant about this time. Seconds later, there I am, holding the bathroom door open, calling inside, then going in.

'Isn't that you?' Sal asks.

'That's me.'

'You're not supposed to go into the women's restroom, you know.'

'Just keep it running.'

I watched myself come back out of the restroom and head for the front of the restaurant.

The next person to appear is Timmy with the limp, at 10:23:51. He pushes his way out the door, presumably on his way home.

Sal did some more fiddling with the mouse. 'Okay. I think this is the part you're looking for.'

It happens at 10:24:03. Claire Sanders, looking exactly as she had in my car, emerges from the bathroom — she had to have been perched on a toilet seat, since I'd had a look at the stalls and they'd appeared empty — then stands at the exterior glass door, scanning the parking lot. The driver of the Volvo sees her before she spots the car. The lights come on and the car moves forward, just beyond the Subaru.

Claire waves and runs toward the vehicle, veers around the far side and opens the passenger door. The car's interior dome light comes on for two seconds and goes off.

'Go back,' I said.

Sal backed up the video a few seconds, hit PLAY again.

'Stop it when the inside light comes on,' I said.

It took him two tries to freeze the frame at just the right spot. As best I could tell, the only other person in the car was the driver, but it was impossible to determine anything about him, or her. Nothing more than a grainy smudge.

'It's hard to see anything real clear,' Sal said apologetically. 'The cops were pissed, too.'

'I'm not pissed,' I said. 'I appreciate it. Is there any way you can blow up that image, get any kind of look at that license plate?'

'Nope,' he said. 'Hopeless.'

'Let it go ahead. I want to see where the car goes.'

Once Claire's in the car, the Volvo turns hard right, does almost a three sixty, and vanishes from the right side of the monitor.

'You have any other angles that would show it leaving?'

'Nope,' he said again.

'What about arriving? If we go back before where you started.'

He took us back to 9:45:00. There is no car behind his Subaru at that point. He kept moving ahead until 9:49:17, when the car appears from the right side of the monitor, sidles up next to Sal's car, and stops. The lights go off.

I had him keep running it right up until ten p.m., just in case whoever was in that car decided to come in for a coffee or a burger. No such luck. Whoever was behind the wheel stayed there.

'Sal,' I said, drawing his name out slowly.

'Yes?'

'Can I have a coffee?'

'Sure thing.'

When I went into my pocket for some change,

he said, 'On the house. Whaddya take?'

'Two creams,' I said.

While he was gone, I dropped into his computer chair and stared at the screen. Thinking it through.

Claire thinks she's being followed. Gets Hanna to switch places. Now someone's following Hanna, who's with me. Hanna gets out and runs. Pitches the wig. Whoever's been on our tail now knows it's a trick. Figures out the switch happened at Iggy's.

Thinks: Maybe Claire's still there.

Sal returned with a take-out cup of coffee for me. 'It's really hot,' he said. 'I wouldn't want you to spill it on yourself and then sue us for millions of dollars.'

I forced a chuckle.

'I want you to take me through the rest of the evening,' I said. 'Right up to closing time.'

'Yeah, sure, I guess,' he said. 'Same view?'

I thought about that. 'No. At least, not to start. Let's go to the front counter. Yeah, that view, that shows everyone coming in, looking up at the menu.'

'If we get held up, we can get a good look at them from here,' he said. 'Where do you want me to start from?'

'Start at ten thirty.' I took the lid off the coffee and blew on it. 'Fast-forward through.'

He did. People shuffled in and out comically. Before long, I spotted someone I recognized.

'Stop,' I said.

It was Sean Skilling. He'd said that he'd dropped by here, and Patchett's, after everything had gone wrong, after the brief, troubling call from Hanna.

In the video, he bypassed the counter, disappeared into another part of the restaurant.

'Can you find him on the other cameras?' I asked, taking a sip of coffee. Still hot, but good.

Sal tapped away. 'There he is.'

Sean had poked his head into the ladies' restroom, just as I had done, but he hadn't gone right inside. Finding no one there, he returned to the front of the restaurant. Sal found him on the other camera again, and we both watched him leave. The video continued to roll.

'Well,' I said.

'Was that what you wanted?'

'I don't really know what I want,' I said. 'Mostly I just want to go home and go to bed.'

'I should have got you a decaf,' Sal said.

'I don't think it'll matter,' I said. 'I could be injecting it straight into my veins. When my head hits the pillow tonight I'm — Hello, what's this?'

The monitor was still displaying the front counter. The time was 10:58:02 and counting.

A heavyset man with brown hair and a moustache had come in. Not in a suit, but nicely dressed in black slacks, a white collared shirt with the cuffs rolled up.

'Pause that,' I said.

Sal clicked. 'You know that guy?' he asked.

'Yeah, but I only met him recently,' I said.

Just this evening, in fact. It was Adam Skilling, Sean's father.

26

When I came out of Iggy's there was a Griffon police cruiser parked behind my Honda, blocking it in. Officer Ricky Haines, along with his partner in crime prevention, Officer Hank Brindle, were leaning against their car, presumably waiting for me to show up.

'Mr. Weaver,' Brindle said, pushing himself upright. Haines followed suit.

'Evening, Officers,' I said.

'You kind of slipped away from the scene in a hurry.'

The chief had sent me home, but I didn't see why I had to explain myself to these two, so I said nothing.

'Thing is, we still had some questions for you,' Brindle said, tipping his hat up half an inch as if to get the full measure of me. So far, Haines was letting his senior partner take the lead here.

'Ask away,' I said.

'I suppose,' Brindle said, 'you may think you enjoy some kind of special status, being married to the chief's sister and all, but Officer Haines and I have to follow our investigation where it leads us, even if that might make our boss unhappy. But ultimately, I believe Chief Perry will understand.'

'I'm waiting.'

'What exactly did you and Miss Rodomski talk about before you kicked her out of your car in the middle of nowhere?' Brindle asked.

'I didn't kick her out,' I said. 'She demanded to get out of the car.'

Brindle smiled. 'All right, then. What did you and the girl talk about before she *demanded* to get out of the car?'

'I figured out right away she wasn't Claire, and called her on it. Asked her what was going on.'

'And what'd she tell you?'

'Not much. She said it was nothing for me to worry about. I told you this before, and I've told Augie.'

'*Augie,*' Brindle said, smiling and nodding. 'We don't call him that. We call him *Chief*. Or *Sir*. And sometimes, behind his back, a few other choice words, but I'm sure I can count on you not to pass that along.' That grin. 'As you say, Mr. Weaver, you told me and Ricky this before, but that was before we knew the girl was dead. So that makes whatever you two had to say to each other more relevant.'

'But it hasn't changed what we said,' I told him.

'I guess what I'm wondering is why you really picked up the mayor's kid in the first place. I mean, a man your age, giving a ride late at night to a teenage girl, that's not the smartest thing a fella can do. And I'd think, given your line of work, you'd be smarter than that.'

I took in a long breath through my nose and let it out slowly. I'd met cops before who tried to rattle you, make you do something stupid. It's just possible I might have done it myself a time or two back when I wore a uniform. I knew the drill, and the importance of keeping my cool.

'Claire said she knew my son. I couldn't say no at that point.'

'Were you hoping maybe she wouldn't say no, too?' The grin morphed into a schoolboy sneer.

'You got something to say, say it.'

Brindle took a step closer. 'You know what my take is on this?'

'I'm sure whatever it is, it'll be brilliant.'

'Looks to me like you picked up one girl, thinking you could have a little fun, and then when a different girl got into the car, you thought 'Hey, what the hell's this? These girls trying to mess with me? Play some kind of trick on me?' Did that piss you off? You were thinking of getting it on with the first girl, that she was just your type, and then the Rodomski girl gets in the car and you're all, 'Shit, that's not what I wanted. I wanted some of that *other* stuff.''

Brindle stopped, waiting for a response. Maybe he wanted me to hit him. The satisfaction would have been too short-lived. When I had no reply, he said, 'You want to hear the rest of this?'

'Knock yourself out.'

'You got angry with this Hanna girl, and she wanted to get out of the car, like you said, but when she ran, you went after her. Ripped the wig off her head. I can see it right there in your car.'

'Yeah,' I said. 'All my training and years working as a cop, and then a detective, have taught me the best place to hide incriminating evidence is on the backseat of your own car.'

I sighed. This very long night was catching up with me, and I still had, as the wise poet once

204

said, miles to go before I slept.

'You're going to have to find another way home, Mr. Weaver,' Brindle said. 'Officer Haines has informed me that we're to seize your car and search it and I think that's a pretty good idea.'

'For Christ's sake,' I said under my breath. I said to Haines, 'You telling me Augie actually asked that my car be taken in?'

So, no more Mr. Nice Guy. My brother-in-law was through cutting me some slack.

Haines turned his hands palms up in a what-can-I-tell-you gesture. 'I didn't actually hear it from him directly.'

'Who then?'

'I got the message through Marv. Uh, Officer Quinn.'

So Augie told Quinn, and Quinn told Haines, and Haines told Brindle, who was clearly enjoying himself.

He said, 'The way it looks to me, you're the last one who saw that girl alive. You're the one who had the opportunity. The other thing I figure, given the personal tragedy you've had lately, things are probably pretty bad on the home front, and chances are you're not getting any. So — '

'Come on, man,' Haines said to Brindle.

Brindle shot him a look and kept going. 'So, a nice ripe thing like that, it'd be hard to pass up.'

It took everything I had.

'But then,' Brindle continued, 'you had to shut her up, right? She couldn't go around telling people what you'd done to her.'

I got out my phone.

'What are you doing?' he asked.

'Calling a cab,' I said. 'You said I needed to find another way home, so I take it you're not arresting me.'

Not yet, anyway.

Neither of them said anything. I could see the disappointment in Brindle's eyes, that I hadn't taken the bait, that he'd missed out on a chance to slap some cuffs on me for assaulting an officer. He would never know how close he'd come.

I put the phone to my ear. 'Yeah, hi, I'm at Iggy's out on Danbury and need a lift home. Five minutes? No problem. Name's Weaver.' I ended the call and slipped the phone back into my jacket. 'On their way,' I said, digging out my keys. 'Don't want you having to smash the windshield or anything.' I got my house key off the ring, then tossed the car keys at Brindle. He didn't react in time, fumbled them comically, and they landed at his feet.

His face turned red with fury and embarrassment. He glared at me, then at the keys on the pavement, then at me again.

He'd have to shoot me before I picked them up.

'I got it,' Haines said, leaning over, snatching them up, and dropping them in Brindle's open palm.

It would have been, I had to admit, a stupid thing to die over.

27

As promised, a cab was there in five minutes. Haines and Brindle were still standing by their cruiser, babysitting my car until a truck came to tow it away. I gave them a friendly wave as we pulled out of the parking lot.

'Wonder what the cops are up to,' the woman behind the wheel said as I got buckled into the backseat.

'Hard to say.'

'You know what I bet?'

'What?'

'Bet that car's full of drugs.'

'You never know,' I said, and suddenly had a dark thought. I knew the car had no drugs in it now. I hoped that was still the case when the tow truck arrived.

'So where we off to?'

I gave her Bert Sanders' address.

'The mayor's place?' my driver said.

'Yeah.'

'Driven him home a couple of times when he wasn't exactly fit to get behind the wheel. Not that I'm passing judgment. That happens to all of us once in a while. I'm just glad the mayor's got the sense not to drive home pissed, you know? I like that in my elected officials.'

We pulled up in front of the house five minutes later. 'I might be a while,' I said. There was already seven bucks on the meter, so I handed her a twenty to ensure that she'd hang in.

'Take your time,' she said. 'I might catch a couple winks. Just don't scare the bejesus out of me when you get back if I'm asleep.'

There was a five-year-old black Buick in the driveway this time and what looked like one light on, upstairs. Aside from Sanders' expensive suits, that car and this modest house spoke to an unassuming, middle-class lifestyle. There's a perception among some that all mayors live in mansions, that they're chauffeured about in Lincoln Town Cars. Some actually do. An old friend of mine from Promise Falls used to drive that town's former mayor around in one. But the reality is, in America small towns are more often than not run by regular people. They sit on school boards, town councils, water commissions. These are our neighbors, the folks we run into at Walmart and the DMV and the Exxon station.

As small-town mayors went, Sanders was undoubtedly more intellectual than most. A former college professor, an author. But he'd persuaded voters he was one of them, still enough of a regular guy to be viewed as one of their own, although tonight's town hall meeting suggested fewer of them thought of him that way than used to. I hadn't voted for him, but I hadn't voted for anyone, in any election, in years. After a while, you stop wanting to reward liars.

They're all liars.

Sanders hadn't won me over in our face-to-face meeting, either. I wasn't expecting our second encounter to go any better.

I jammed my thumb onto the doorbell and kept it there. The chimes just inside the door rang incessantly. *Ding-dong. Ding-dong. Ding-dong. Ding-dong.*

Peering through the window, I saw a man come down the stairs, silhouetted by the light filtering down from the second floor. He was tying the sash of a bathrobe and shouting, 'Okay! Okay!'

The front porch light came on over my head, and a second later I heard a bolt being turned and the door swung open.

'Jesus Christ,' he said, a lock of his hair sticking out sideways. He'd clearly been in bed. 'You again. You have any idea what the hell time it is?'

I placed my palm on the door as he attempted to shut it. 'We need to talk again.'

'Get off my porch.'

I pushed harder until I had the door open wide enough to step in.

'I told you, get out,' he said.

'I guess you haven't heard,' I said. 'There's been what you might call a development in this little switcheroo Claire and Hanna pulled last night.'

'I told you I have nothing to say to you about this.'

'Hanna's dead.'

It was like I'd hit him in the head with a two-by-four.

Stunned silence at first, then, 'What?'

'Hanna Rodomski's been murdered. I found her body under a bridge. Someone put their hands around her neck and choked the life out of her.'

Still dumbfounded, he reached for the banister to steady himself. 'That's not — my God, that's not possible.'

'I can take you there if you don't believe me. I doubt they'll be moving the body for a while yet.'

'This is . . . this is horrible.' To himself, more than me, he said, 'Doesn't make any sense, just doesn't . . . '

'Of course it doesn't. Why the hell would it make sense?'

'I just can't . . . There's no way they'd go this far.'

'Who?' I asked. 'Who are you talking about?'

'A drink,' he said, pushing himself away from the stairs and heading off to the kitchen. 'I need a drink.'

He opened the cupboard and took out a small glass and a bottle of scotch, poured himself three fingers and downed it in one gulp. He went to pour another, but I grabbed his hand and forced the bottle back onto the counter.

'Tell me what the hell's going on, Sanders.'

'I don't know who killed Hanna,' he said. 'I swear I don't.'

'What about Claire? Where is she?'

He placed his hand over his forehead, as though all this was giving him a nuclear-grade migraine. But then, almost instantly, he got over it, and gave me a devilish smile.

'Oh, I get it. I get what's going on here.' The grin turned into a short laugh. 'Very good. You almost had me.'

'Had you? You think this is a joke?'

'Not a joke. A trick.'

'Really? Come on, then.' I grabbed a fistful of robe at his shoulder. 'I've got a cab waiting. We can go down and have a look at her. At least what's left. The dogs had some of her for lunch.'

He shook me off, the robe sliding down his right shoulder and almost to his elbow. He pulled it back up with a theatrical flourish, trying to preserve his dignity, but he was too shaken.

'Dear God, dogs?' He put his hand to his mouth, like maybe he was going to be sick, but then pulled it away. 'Okay, even if what you say about Hanna is true, there's no good reason for me to trust you. I've got a good idea what your game is. You think by telling me about Hanna you can scare me into telling you where Claire is.'

'So she's hiding out somewhere?'

'Not hiding. Just . . . away.'

'When's the last time you heard from her? For Christ's sake, Sanders. Your daughter's best friend is dead. If Claire were my kid, I'd be getting her on the phone right now to make sure she's okay.'

'If there'd been a problem, she'd have called . . . ' He was talking more to himself than to me.

'If Claire's in trouble, she might not be able to call.'

'No, her mother. She would call. Everything's fine. Everything's okay.' Sanders nodded hurriedly, looking like a bobblehead.

'Claire went to stay with her mother? In Canada?'

He put his hand over his mouth again, mumbling, as though he didn't want me to hear him thinking out loud.

'Talk to me,' I said. 'Is that where she is?'

He took the hand away. 'I know Augustus Perry's your brother-in-law. You think I don't know he's using you to find out where she is?'

'Are you kidding?' I said. 'He just had my fucking car towed. And what's Augie got to do with Claire?'

Sanders said nothing, but kept looking at me, wide-eyed.

'Look, I told you how I became involved in this, and it has nothing to do with the chief. Claire asked me for a ride. She and Hanna pulled off their little stunt with my help, and now Hanna's dead. I'll find out what's going on with or without your help.'

'I've nothing to say to you,' Sanders said.

'Tell me she's alive. Do you know that much?'

Before he could answer, lights swept past the living room from outside, casting a glow as far as the kitchen. Sanders broke away from me and ran to the window, pulling back the lace curtain for a better view of the street.

'What is it?' I said.

'There's a car sitting out there, with the lights off. Someone's inside.'

'It's my taxi. I told her to wait.'

'But the lights — '

'Probably just another car driving by,' I said. 'The woman next door said the police have been parked on the street lately. Like they've been watching your house.'

He glared at me. 'You've been talking to my neighbors? And you're trying to tell me you're not in on it?'

'In on *what*? Why are the police watching you? Why do you think the chief's involved in this?'

When he wouldn't respond, I tried a more conciliatory tone. 'Mr. Sanders, I swear, I'm trying to help you here. I'm trying to help Claire. If she's running from something, tell me what it is so we can deal with it, so she can come back.'

He studied me in the dim glow of the light filtering down from the second floor. 'How long you lived here, Mr. Weaver?'

'A few years. Six.'

'Happy here?'

'I used to be,' I said.

He picked up something in my voice. 'Your son,' he said. 'I know about your son.' He swallowed. 'I'm sorry.'

I didn't have to ask how he knew. Everyone in Griffon knew. It was a safe bet Claire had mentioned it to her father at some point.

'But before your . . . your personal tragedy . . . were you happy in Griffon?'

It was hard to think back to what our world was like before two months ago. There had been troubled times with our son for a year or more, but even through that there had been good times as well. And before Scott found comfort in substances that clouded his judgment, I suppose we were what you'd call happy. Content, maybe.

But I didn't feel like getting into that with Bert Sanders. 'I don't see your point.'

He said, 'Have you felt safe here?'

I hesitated. 'I guess.'

'The Griffon cops — they do a helluva job, right?'

I thought of the petition. 'Our cops are tops.'

That actually made him smile. 'Have you signed?'

I shook my head.

He nodded admiringly. 'That's a surprise.'

'I don't know what this has to do — '

'Down in the park one night, there was a kid with one of those air horns — you know, the kind that look like an aerosol can? One of Griffon's finest went down there, held the horn right over that kid's ear, and let it go. Kid may not get his hearing back. His parents tried to come after us, but guess what? Your brother-in-law's got three cops who say the kid was so drunk he put the horn up to his own ear and did it himself.' Sanders gave me a withering look. 'You ask just about anyone in town here whether that kid got what was coming to him, and they'll tell you yes.'

I said nothing. He was right.

'If it's just cops getting a little carried away once in a while, we can all look the other way and pretend it's not happening. That's the prevailing view in this town. Some punk gets the shit beat out of him and finds himself dumped outside the town line, who's going to lose sleep over that? But if Augustus Perry's storm troopers are willing to bend the rules there, what else are they capable of? What do you think happens to drugs and illicit cash they seize? If there's no trial, there's no need for evidence. Why do they turn a blind eye to what goes on at Patchett's? You think Phyllis Pearce isn't spreading a little cash around?'

'You have proof of any of that?'

He laughed. 'Proof. Yeah, sure.'

I didn't have time for this. 'Mr. Sanders, just tell me where Claire is. I'll bring her home. It's what I do,' I said.

He wasn't hearing me.

He said, 'You think the cops are sitting out on that street watching out for me? Is that what you think?'

'Why don't you just tell me?'

'They're not watching *out* for me. They're just *watching* me. Intimidating me. Trying to get me to back off.'

'I still don't understand what — '

I stopped. I heard something — or someone — upstairs.

28

'What was that?' I said, looking up. It had sounded to me like someone moving around. Definitely not a squirrel running across the roof.

'I didn't hear anything,' Sanders said.

'Then you're deaf,' I said. 'It was upstairs.'

'There's nobody upstairs,' he said. 'I'm alone.'

I studied him. 'Is she here? Is Claire here now?'

He shook his head quickly again. 'No.'

I raised my head to the ceiling. 'Claire!' I shouted.

'Shut up!' Sanders said. 'Keep your voice down!'

'Why do I have to keep my voice down if there's no one here?'

I made my way to the stairs, shaking Sanders' hand off my arm as he attempted to stop me.

'Get out,' he said. 'You've got no right to search my house!'

I glanced back at him. 'Maybe you should call the cops.'

He stammered something unintelligible as I ascended the stairs. I was nearly halfway up when he charged after me. I felt arms locking around my knees, and I toppled forward. I reached out to brace my fall, but my right elbow connected with one of the hardwood steps, sending a charge up my arm.

'Shit!' I said.

'You son of a bitch!' Sanders said, grappling with my lower legs.

I managed to slip one free, then placed the bottom of my left shoe against his bare right shoulder and pushed. He flew back down the stairs and landed on his ass, the sash of his robe coming undone, exposing him. Nothing looks much more foolish, or more vulnerable, than a man with his junk hanging out for the world to see.

He scrambled to his feet, pulled the robe around himself, and retied the sash. I was half sitting, half standing on the steps, giving my elbow a gentle rub.

'We can make this easy or we can make this hard,' I told him.

'Please,' he said, in a voice that bordered on whimpering. 'Just get out. What does any of this have to do with you, really? Can't you just go?'

'Stay there,' I said, and climbed the rest of the flight. 'Claire,' I called again, but not shouting this time. I didn't want to sound threatening. 'It's Mr. Weaver, Scott's dad. We met last night.'

At the top of the stairs I took a second to orient myself as Sanders, now halfway up the steps behind me, said, 'I told you, she's not here.'

I ignored him. There was a bathroom immediately to my right, and just beyond it a door to what looked like the largest of the three other rooms up here. This, I guessed, was Sanders' room. A queen-sized bed, the covers thrown back. He'd clearly been under them when I'd arrived and had thrown on the robe to greet me at the door.

To the left, what had probably been a

bedroom but was currently an office. A desk, bookshelves, a desktop iMac.

And straight ahead of me, the door closed, was Claire's room. I didn't need to be Poirot to figure that out. Stuck to the door was a miniature plastic license plate, the kind you can buy at novelty and souvenir shops, that bore the girl's name.

'Claire?' I said hesitantly before pushing the door open and running my hand along the wall for the light switch. I flicked it on. The first, most obvious thing I noticed was that the bed was empty, and made, although it was littered with about a dozen magazines.

'I told you,' Sanders said behind me.

I stepped into the room.

There were several stuffed animals, a few dogs and two furry bunnies — a pink one and a blue one — that all looked worn with age, adorning the pillow. She'd probably had them since she was a child. The magazines were not what I might have expected. While there was one issue of *Vogue*, most were copies of the *New Yorker*, the *Economist*, *Harper's*, and the *Walrus*, a Canadian magazine of news and commentary. On the bedside table were an iPad and the Steve Jobs biography that had come out a couple of years ago.

I picked up the iPad and pressed the HOME button to see what came up. An array of icons, most of them news sites.

'You've got no right to look — '

I whipped my head around and snapped, 'Enough.'

I tapped on the stamp icon and brought up Claire's e-mails. I gave recent messages in the in-box, and those that had been sent, a ten-second scan. The thing was, my generation felt so advanced, communicating through e-mails, but most kids texted, having abandoned e-mail long ago. No message jumped out at me.

I looked up, caught a glimpse of myself in a mirror. When I was young, we tucked the edges of snapshots under mirror frames, but there were none displayed here. These days, hardly anyone had a picture that was on a piece of paper. Photos were shared online, posted, e-mailed, flicked across smart-phone screens. Technology allowed us to share our photos with more people now than ever before, but where would these captured moments in time be in twenty years? On some outdated piece of hardware at the bottom of a landfill site? What happened to memories you couldn't hold between your thumb and fore-finger?

These thoughts running through my head prompted me to tap on the iPad's photo icon. Up popped the kinds of shots teenagers most often took of each other. Laughing, vamping, sticking out their tongues, standing around at parties, drinks in hand.

'Those pictures are private,' Sanders said.

He was wearing me out. 'Like I said, call the cops.'

There were several shots of Claire and Hanna together. Hanna kissing Claire on the cheek. Claire grabbing Hanna's nose. The two of them in prom dresses, hands on hips.

But there were shots of Claire with boys, too. Some that, by their placement farther down the screen, were probably taken longer ago, and featured an older-looking, round-faced kid. Young man, actually.

I turned the iPad toward Sanders. 'Is that Roman Ravelson?'

'Honestly, would you please get — '

'Is it?'

'Yes.'

'And what about this boy?' In the more recent pictures, Claire was snuggling, kissing, and laughing with a young, clean-shaven black man with closely cropped hair. He stood a good foot taller than Claire.

'Dennis.'

'Dennis who?'

'Dennis Mullavey. Someone she used to go out with.'

'From Griffon?'

'No, I don't know where from. He had a summer job here. He went back home, wherever that is.'

'Was it serious?'

Sanders shook his head in exasperation. 'I don't know. It was a summer romance. You remember those? They're all the more intense because the time seems so limited. This is a — this is a total invasion of my daughter's privacy.'

I set the iPad down and surveyed the top of the desk. It was cluttered with what I would have expected. Some makeup, bottles of nail polish, schoolbooks. I rounded the bed to see whether anything was tucked between it and the wall — I was thinking someone could have been hiding there, but no one was — then went to the closet door and opened it.

'For God's sake,' Sanders said.

I was greeted with a kind of congealed mass of clothing. I doubted it was possible to stuff one more thing in there. I turned, looked at Sanders standing in the doorway, trying to look imposing.

'You should go,' he said.

He moved aside to let me leave the room, but instead of heading back down the stairs, I walked into his office. Nothing much to look at here. The closet was already open, jammed with cardboard filing boxes.

I crossed the hallway and returned to Sanders' bedroom. There was something in the air, a scent I recognized. I had a feeling I'd smelled something similar not all that long ago.

'I'm not going to tolerate this intrusion any longer,' he said, but he didn't have an ounce of authority left in his voice.

'How long has it been since you and your wife split up?' I was looking at the mattress as I walked around it.

'What does that have to do with — '

'Hang on.'

When I got to the far side of the bed to see whether anyone was hiding, I noticed there was an en suite bathroom off the bedroom.

Sanders caught me looking at it, and his body tensed.

I moved to the doorway. A sink, a toilet, and a tub. The shower curtain was drawn across the bathtub. The fabric was too heavy to show whether there was anyone hiding behind it, but you get a sense about these things.

'Claire?' I said.

No answer.

I said, 'I'm going to count to five and then I'm going to pull back the curtain. One. Two. Three. F — '

'Okay!' Bert Sanders said in defeat. 'Okay.' He spoke beyond me. 'You might as well come out.'

From behind the curtain, a woman said, 'I'm naked.'

For a second there, I was feeling pretty proud of myself. I'd found Claire. But the feeling drifted away pretty quickly at the thought of Sanders out here, naked under his robe, and Claire in there, without a stitch on.

What the hell was going on?

'Hang on,' Sanders said, and ran to the closet, where he grabbed a second robe. I looked discreetly away as he went into the bathroom. I heard curtain rings sliding back on the rod.

'Here you go,' Sanders said. 'Just slip that on . . .'

'I tried to be quiet,' she said.

'I know, I know.'

He preceded her out. I figured it was now safe to turn around and look at Claire for the first time since I'd seen her run into Iggy's the night before.

She didn't look like the Claire I remembered at all. That's because she wasn't Claire.

It was Annette Ravelson, wife of Kent — the couple who owned the furniture store where my son had jumped to his death.

29

'Annette,' I said as she tightened the sash on the robe.

'Cal,' she said, not able to meet my eye.

'You know each other?' Sanders asked.

'Of course I know Cal,' she said, then found the strength to look at me and asked, 'You thought I was Claire? You were shouting her name all the way up the stairs.'

'I thought she might be here,' I said.

'Well, I guess it makes more sense that she might have been here than me,' Annette said.

'I can honestly say I wasn't expecting to find you here, Annette. It's late. Won't Kent be creeped out, not finding you at home?'

'I told you, he's out of town,' Annette said. 'On a buying trip. It's like a furniture wholesalers' convention. He picks what lines he wants us to sell.' She stuck out her lower lip and managed to blow a lock of hair out of her eyes. She glanced at Bert, then back to me, and said, 'I know this kind of looks bad.'

I said nothing, but peeked into the bathroom. Thrown into the dry tub were her clothes, shoes, and a handbag. She'd evidently hurriedly collected, from the bedroom, all evidence of her presence. Her purse landing in the tub was probably the noise I'd heard, and that scent I'd picked up earlier was the perfume she'd been wearing when I'd run into her earlier, before going into the town hall.

Annette said, 'Why are you looking for Claire? Bert, is Claire in some kind of trouble?'

Sanders had sat down on the edge of the bed and was rubbing his shoulder where I'd given him a shove down the stairs with my foot. 'I don't know,' he said defeatedly. 'I'm not sure I have any idea what's going on anymore.'

'Annette, vouch for me,' I said. 'I'm trying to help Bert here, but he doesn't trust me.'

'Help him with what?'

'I think Claire *is* in trouble, but Bert either doesn't think so or doesn't want to admit it to me. But there's more reason now to be concerned.'

'Why?' Annette asked. 'What?'

Sanders lifted his head. 'The Rodomskis' kid is dead.'

Annette's eyes widened. 'What?'

'She was murdered.' He pointed a feeble finger at me. 'You tell her.'

'Hanna Rodomski,' I said.

'I know who she is,' she said, aghast. 'I know her parents. My God, this is terrible. They must be devastated.'

I imagined they were, but I hadn't seen them since discovering their daughter's body. I felt a pang of guilt, as though I should be at the Rodomskis' house and not here, but I believed every minute counted now where finding Claire was concerned.

'Does Claire know?' Annette asked. 'Bert, does she know what's happened to Hanna?'

Sanders looked at me. 'I don't know. I suppose

it's possible, the way kids are all connected these days. Do regular people know yet? Has it been on the news?'

'I don't think so. But it's only a matter of time. Like you say, if Claire has access on her phone or if she's near a computer, this kind of thing will spread like wildfire on social media before it hits the news.' I hesitated. 'She should hear it from you.'

'Yes, yes, you're right,' Sanders said, and turned to look at the phone on the bedside table.

Pick up the goddamn phone and call her, I thought. But it looked like he was heading in that direction.

'She probably has her cell phone turned off,' he said.

'Why would that be?' I asked.

'They can track you, right? If your cell phone is on.'

'What are you talking about, Bert?' Annette asked. 'Who'd be tracking — oh God, you're not serious. You really think he'd do that?'

'Who?' I asked. 'Who'd do what?'

Annette gave me a critical look. 'Your brother-in-law, that's who.'

'What are you talking about?'

'I mean, do you have any idea how much trouble I had to go to, to sneak in here tonight?' she asked. 'Had to park a block over that way.' She pointed toward the back of the house. 'Had to sneak between houses, acting like Catwoman. Could have used some night-vision goggles. Ripped my nylons on some prickly bushes. It's not like Bert can go anywhere to meet *me*.

They're watching him all the time, his comings and goings. But I can sneak in through the back way and no one spots me.'

'You're worried the chief is going to find out you two are having an affair?'

'It's not that,' Sanders said, his hand resting on the receiver. 'Perry's trying to put the fear of God into me.'

'Bert, yes, Perry's being a total asshole,' Annette said, 'but why would he be tracking your daughter's whereabouts? I mean, she's on a school trip to New York. Why would he care about that? And if she doesn't have her cell on, then get in touch with the teacher or call the hotel where she's — '

'That's not where she is,' Sanders said. 'She's not on a school trip to New York. That's just what I told you.'

Annette Ravelson blinked. I could see she was hurt. Always disappointing when the man you're cheating on your husband with isn't honest with you.

'Don't be upset,' he said to her. 'You know I'm living in a fishbowl these days. Everything's on a need-to-know basis.'

Exasperation overwhelmed him as he said to me, 'You heard what my neighbor said. You never know when there's gonna be a cop car watching this house. It's all part of Perry's intimidation campaign to get me to shut up, to let this whole thing about how he runs his department just go. He's watching me, and he's got his jackbooted thugs watching me, and up until a couple of days ago, Claire, too. If Perry can walk all over the constitutional rights of everyone else who dares venture inside the town limits, why not the mayor's? Why not my daughter's?'

'Claire was feeling the heat?' I asked.

'How could she not?' Sanders said. 'She said she couldn't stand it, the cops watching me like that. She was sick of getting caught up in my battle with them, and who the hell could blame her? She wouldn't go into specifics, but one night outside Patchett's a cop stopped her, and another time, more recently, same officer, I think, took her purse from her, supposedly to search for drugs, which there were absolutely none of, and we had to go down to the station to pick it up the next day. Can you blame her for wanting to get the hell out of this town? She figured out a way to do it without the cops knowing where she went.'

'You knew she was doing this thing with Hanna.'

'I didn't know exactly *what* she was doing, but she told me she had something all worked out.'

'She must have told you where she was going.'

Sanders' hung his head in a gesture of admission. 'To Toronto. To stay with her mother, my ex-wife. Caroline. Caroline Karnofsky now.'

'Caroline picked her up?'

Another nod. 'Claire set it all up with her mother. Claire said if there were any problems, she or her mother would call. I didn't hear any-thing, so everything must have gone off just fine.'

I pointed to the phone and mimed a dialing motion with my fingers. 'You need to let her know.'

Sanders moved to pick up the receiver, then hesitated.

'This line,' he said. 'It might not be safe.'

'Seriously?' I said. 'You think the chief has your line tapped?'

'It's crossed my mind. Sometimes I think I hear clicks. You know what they say. Just because you're paranoid doesn't mean — '

I waved my hand. 'I know. But, Jesus, he wouldn't . . . ' But I knew that over the years Perry had done surveillance work. And he'd have people in his department who'd know how to do that sort of thing.

'If you really believe that,' I said, 'for all we know, the whole house is bugged. Someone could be listening to what we're saying right now.'

Annette's look of horror was immediate. 'What? You mean someone could have heard what — someone could have been listening to us in this room, like, just a little while ago?'

She was no doubt replaying in her head the things she'd said in the throes of passion. Sanders appeared to be doing the same.

'If someone recorded that . . . ' She didn't bother to finish. I could imagine what she was thinking. If someone had all this on tape — okay, more likely a digital recording — and played it for her husband, well, that couldn't be good.

'I don't suppose you'd want Kent hearing that,' I said.

Annette didn't like it when I said her husband's name. 'Don't even joke about such a thing,' she said.

I had bigger things to worry about than

Annette Ravelson's infidelities becoming public. I entered the bathroom and called out, 'Annette, come get your clothes.'

She came in, scooped everything out of the tub, and grabbed her purse, too. 'I'll go get dressed in Claire's room.'

I pulled the curtain back across the tub, then turned the cold tap on full blast. I yanked the knob that turned the shower on. Streams of water hit the plastic curtain, creating a low-level background noise like rain on a tin roof. I waved Sanders to come in, and handed him my cell phone.

'If your phone, or this place, is bugged, this should keep anyone from hearing.'

Sanders entered a number into my cell and put it to his ear.

'It's ringing,' he said. Then, 'Caroline, it's me . . . I know, I know this isn't my number. I'm using someone else's phone.'

I leaned in, my head nearly touching Sanders', so I could hear both sides of the conversation.

'Is everything okay?' Caroline asked.

'Yeah, yeah, I just — '

'Where are you? What's that noise? Are you standing in the rain?'

'I'm in the — Don't worry about that. Caroline, I need to talk to Claire. Is she there? Can you put her on? I've got some bad news for her.'

'Claire's not here. Why would Claire be here?'

'It's okay, it's safe to talk,' Sanders said. 'There's no way they could be listening in on this phone.'

'Bert, Claire isn't here.'

'When will she be back?'

'Bert, you're not hearing me. She's not staying with me. She's not supposed to be coming to see me for another couple of weeks.'

Sanders' voice went up. 'But — but you picked her up last night. Here. In Griffon.'

'Bert, I did no such thing. Where's Claire?'

Panic was creeping into both their voices.

Sanders said, 'Claire set it up. She said you were picking her up. Last night. At Iggy's. She *has* to be with you.'

'Listen to me, Bert,' Caroline said, sounding nearly breathless. 'Claire is not here. Claire hasn't been here in weeks. I have no idea what you're talking about.'

30

'I'm going to have to call you back,' Sanders said to his ex-wife. He ended the call and handed the phone back to me. The color had drained from his face.

'She said — '

'I heard.'

I turned off the cold water still streaming down from the showerhead. 'Claire told you her mother was going to pick her up?'

'That's what she said.'

'What kind of car does your ex-wife drive?'

'Um, one of those little convertibles. A Miata.'

'Not a Volvo wagon.'

Sanders shook his head. 'No, she doesn't have one of those. Neither does her husband.' He looked imploringly at me. 'Where the hell could she be?'

'Looks like she accomplished exactly what she set out to do,' I said. 'She didn't just give whoever was following her the slip. She gave everybody the slip. You think this war between you and Perry was really enough to make her want to disappear?'

No hesitation. 'Absolutely.'

'That'd suggest Claire doesn't even trust you to keep her whereabouts secret. Does that make sense?'

He raised his hands in frustration. 'Christ, I don't know.'

Annette crossed the hall and came into the bedroom in a pair of killer heels. She was wearing a scoop-necked black dress that showed off her ample cleavage, plus a hint of a lacy push-up black bra that was assisting the process. A sexier getup than when I'd seen her outside the furniture store. 'What's going on? Did you tell Claire? Did you tell her about Hanna?'

'She's not with her mom.'

'Well, then, where is she?'

Neither Bert Sanders nor I said anything.

'You don't know?'

'We don't know,' I said.

'Oh shit,' she said.

Sanders met my eye. 'What do I do now?'

I felt like telling him to pray that Claire hadn't met the same fate as Hanna, but I'm not a particularly religious man. Plus, it would have been a pretty shitty thing to say. So I came up with something else.

'Start calling around. Her other friends, boyfriends. Teachers.'

'I'll ask Roman,' Annette said. For my benefit, she explained, 'My son went out with her for a while. Maybe he has an idea where she might have gone.' She bit her lip. 'Although I kind of doubt it. It's not like they've been talking that much.'

'They used to go out,' I said.

'Yeah. But she broke it off. Roman took it hard.'

I didn't have it in me to feel bad for Roman at the moment. My head was still throbbing from where he'd hit me.

'So, anyone you can think of,' I said to Sanders.

And then I felt like slapping my head. 'Try her cell,' I said, and handed him my phone again.

He entered a number and listened. 'It's gone straight to voice mail. Claire? It's your dad. Where the hell are you? I just got off the phone with your mother. We're both worried sick. If you get this, call me right away, okay? Just call me. Or call Mr. Weaver. I'm using his phone. Please, okay? I love you.'

Sanders handed the phone back to me.

'If it went straight to message, it means the phone is off, right?' he said.

'Or the battery's dead,' I said.

'This is terrible. I just don't know what — No, I'll do what you said. I'll start asking around.'

I felt, at that moment, some small sense of relief. I didn't have to carry all the weight of this on my shoulders. Sanders had a better handle on Claire's friends than I did. He might have her tracked down before I could do it.

What nagged at me was why Claire had lied to him. She'd told him why she wanted to go, but not who it was going to be with. The surveillance video I'd seen at Iggy's showed she'd gotten into a car with someone.

'Okay, you do that,' I said. 'We'll talk in the morning, see where we are. That sound like a plan?'

Sanders nodded.

Annette had a concern of her own. 'You're not going to tell anyone about us, are you?'

'Tell you what,' I said. 'You can buy my silence

233

with a lift home. I've had some car trouble tonight.'

★ ★ ★

I ran out to the cab, rapped lightly on the window so as not to scare the driver to death, and settled up with her. I scanned the street for cop cars and didn't see any, although there were a few regular vehicles parked along the curb. I suppose it was possible someone was slunk down behind the wheel of one of those.

Then I walked briskly to the rear of Sanders' house and mounted the steps to the kitchen door, just in time to see Annette slip out of Bert's arms. He'd left the outdoor lights off, which meant Annette needed a moment for her eyes to adjust to the darkness so she could navigate her way across the yard, around the garage, and between the houses that backed onto Sanders' property.

Luckily, no dogs barked and no motion-sensitive lights flashed on. Annette was, indeed, unsteady on her feet — her heels were three inches at least — going from grass to gravel to sidewalk and taking care to sidestep trash cans, bicycles, and lumber scraps, so I took her hand and led her through the worst of it.

'Why the hell I wore these shoes I'll never know,' she said. 'Well, of course I know. Is there a man alive whose motor doesn't get a kick start from high heels?'

It struck me as a rhetorical question, so I let it go. Once we'd come out from between the houses and were on the sidewalk of the next street over, I let go of her hand. But she latched onto my elbow and held on until we were almost to her car.

'You're a nice man, you know,' she said. 'I'm sorry for all your troubles.'

We were coming up on a black Beemer sedan. 'This one,' she said, taking a remote from her purse and hitting the button. The taillights flashed. 'Why were you taking a taxi, anyway?'

'Long story,' I said, and slid in on the passenger side.

There was no need to tell her where I lived. During Scott's stint at her store, she or Kent had dropped him off several times. Scott wasn't old enough to drive, so Donna or I usually chauffeured him back and forth. But when we were occasionally unavailable, he got a lift with friends or coworkers.

'I really appreciate you keeping quiet about me and Bert,' she said as she buckled her seat belt. 'I mean, this is probably just a passing thing with Bert anyway.'

'Why do you say that?'

'I'm a realist. I know Bert. I know what he's like.'

'And what's he like?'

'Oh, come on,' she said, putting the Beemer into drive and easing her foot down on the gas. 'Like you haven't heard.'

'He likes the ladies,' I said.

'That's putting it mildly.' She laughed. 'I know I've only got a limited amount of time with him before someone else catches his eye. It's why

Caroline left him. He was screwing some other professor at Canisius.' I thought about Donna's comment, about the woman at work Sanders hit on when she was a student and he was still teaching. 'For a while there, he was even doing it with someone else at work.'

'His work?'

'No, mine. Rhonda McIntyre?'

I didn't know the name.

'Hot little thing, I admit. And about forty pounds lighter. But what she had on me in the youth department I could more than make up for in experience. Bert thinks I never knew about her, but I could tell. The way she looked at him when he came into the store, or if they ran into each other on the street. It was back in the summer. He still believes I think he was only seeing me. Anyway, Rhonda doesn't work for us anymore.'

'Did you fire her?'

'She quit all of a sudden, couple of months back. I think she actually left town, got a job somewhere else, broke it off with another guy — a cop, as it turned out, who she was finding kind of freaky, and who didn't know she was seeing Bert on the side. Or on her back.' Annette chuckled. 'Just as well she quit. I'd have had to find a way to cut her loose, dropped some hints to Kent that she was taking an extra cut off the top with cash deals, fudging some receipts, something. But in the end, I didn't have to. It's bad enough, knowing this thing I've got going with Bert has an expiration date, but while I'm still in the 'best before' days, I want him to myself. You think there's something wrong, wanting a bit of excitement in your life?'

'I guess it depends what kind. Maybe you should try white-water rafting.'

'It's just that my life these days . . . it's just *life*, you know? Today's going to be like yesterday and tomorrow's going to be exactly like today. But with Bert, even if it's just for a while, I can have a few days that aren't like all the others. You have to admit he's a handsome man. I mean, you can say that and it doesn't mean you're gay or anything.'

'He's a handsome man,' I said.

'He's got the looks to be a lot more than a small-town mayor. He could be a governor or a senator or anything like that if he decided that's what he wanted.'

'It's not what he wants?'

'He's not ambitious that way,' Annette said. 'He just wants to make a difference wherever he happens to be at the time. He cares about being a good mayor, about doing what's right. That's why he's in this fight with Perry, who, I just want to say, is not *that* bad a guy. I think he does right by this town, and I'm not just saying that because he's Donna's brother, you know? Maybe he goes a little overboard now and then, I'll grant you that. But Jesus, you don't really think he has Bert's house bugged, do you? I mean, that would be — that'd be bad.'

I shrugged.

'How'd you get looking for Claire in the first place?'

I told her, briefly, about the night before.

'God, kids,' she said. 'You can never predict what they're going to do.' She appeared to be thinking. 'This thing with Hanna — that's just so awful. You think maybe Claire ran off because she knows who did it?'

'Claire took off before it happened, so no.' I pointed. 'We're almost to my street.'

'I know.' Half a minute later, she brought the car to a stop at the end of our driveway.

'How are you and Kent doing?' I asked.

'What do you mean?' Annette said.

'This thing you have going with Sanders — you don't have to be a genius to figure out it means you and Kent are going through a rough patch.'

'It doesn't have to mean that,' she said.

'So things between you are perfect?' I asked.

'No couple on this planet has a perfect relationship,' she said. 'Do you?'

When I hesitated, Annette jumped in. 'God, I'm sorry. With what you've been through, I don't know how I could have said that.'

'Don't worry about it,' I said. 'Listen, sometime I'd like go up on the roof again.'

'Oh, Cal.'

'I just . . . I'm still wrestling with this, Annette. I keep playing it in my head, how it happened.'

'Tell you what,' she said. 'I'll mention it to Kent. If you don't hear from him, if he doesn't call you, then you'll know he's not okay with it.'

I was betting I'd never hear from him.

'Thanks for the ride. Oh, and would you say hi to Roman for me?'

She cocked her head to one side. 'Sure. Why?'

'We kind of ran into each other earlier tonight. Tell him I'm thinking about him.'

★ ★ ★

Donna's car wasn't in the driveway, so I figured she must have put it in the garage, which she didn't do very often. I let myself into the house as quietly as I could and went to the kitchen, thinking I'd have a glass of water, then realized I'd gone through another evening without any dinner. I opened the cupboard and took out some saltines and peanut butter. Not exactly fine dining, but a few smeared crackers would keep my stomach from growling through the night.

Stealthily, I put the dirty knife and glass into the dishwasher and crept up the stairs. I tiptoed through the bedroom, but I stepped on something hard and there was a sudden cracking noise. Not all that loud, but loud enough, I feared, to wake Donna. When I didn't hear her stir, I knelt down and patted the carpet until I found what I'd stepped on. One of her pencils. I'd snapped it in two. I picked up the pieces, noticed the small can of spray fixative had hit the floor, too, and scooped that up, then slipped into the bathroom.

I waited until I had the door closed before turning on the light, put the broken pencil pieces in the trash basket, the spray can on the counter, and disrobed. Stripped to my boxers, I brushed my teeth, then killed the light before opening the door.

It hit me then that Donna usually left the

bathroom light on for me.

My eyes were taking a while to adjust to the dark, so I made my way to the bed by instinct, pulled back the covers on my side, and slipped between the sheets.

I knew the moment I was in the bed that something was off. I blinked hurriedly until my eyes were accustomed to the absence of light — as though that might somehow help — then sat up and looked at the other side of the bed.

Donna was not there.

31

The porch light helps her as she slides the key into the front door and turns the dead bolt. She's surprised, when she opens the door, to see her son standing there in the front hall, having seen him only a few hours earlier.

'You scared me half to death,' she says.

'You're not usually out this late.'

'What's going on?'

'Things are working out,' he says. 'I had to tell you. I didn't want to wait till morning.'

'You've found them?'

'No, but I may have found a way to find them.'

She throws her purse on the closest chair. 'Please don't get my hopes up.'

He tells her what he's done. He has been, she must admit, a busy boy. 'That's a lot of running around,' she says. While she remains skeptical, he does seem to have thought this through.

She likes one of his ideas in particular. 'That's a good plan, to use the detective,' she says. 'I saw him earlier.'

'We put him to work for us, except he doesn't even know it,' he says.

'It could work.'

'I feel like it's coming together.'

'Don't get carried away,' she snaps. 'We're a long way from being able to put this behind us. If the boy took the book, when you find him, you have to get it back. I should have cottoned

241

to the fact that he'd given it away sooner. Usually when he fills a notebook, he asks for a new one, and I get him one. But he didn't ask this time because it was too soon. He'd probably only filled half of it. He figured I'd get suspicious.'

'You're worried too much about that damn book.'

'No, I'm not. You need to take this seriously.'

'Are you kidding? You think I'm not taking this seriously? Really? Look at the shit I've had to deal with. I've been thinkin' on my feet. Like with the other girl, how I made it look like something it wasn't. How about a little credit for that?'

'I'm going to bed. I can't deal with this one more minute.'

'It's your fault, anyway, you know,' he says.

That stops her on her way to the stairs. 'What did you say?'

'Leaving the house while the dryer was running, not being here when the lint caught on fire. If there'd never been any smoke, none of this would have — '

Her hand moves so quickly he doesn't have a chance to stop her from slapping him across the face.

'I will not have you speak to me that way. Who do you think all this has been for? Huh? Who's it all been for?'

He puts a hand to his hot, red cheek. 'It's been for Dad,' he says.

'No,' she says. 'It's always been for you. All of it. I did it all for you, and so help me, God, it looks like I'm going to have to do more before we're done.'

32

I threw back the covers and stood up so quickly I made myself light-headed. I turned the bedside table lamp on. Donna's side of the bed did not look slept in. It didn't make sense that if she hadn't been able to get to sleep, she'd have made the bed when she got up. You don't do that when it's eleven or twelve at night. You get up, wander around, have a glass of water, figuring that in a few minutes you're going to get back under the covers and try again to get to sleep.

So Donna had not yet gone to bed.

I made my way down the hall, going to Scott's room first. It never surprised me to find her under the covers there these days. But when I opened the door, allowing light to spill in from the hall, I could see the bed was empty.

Turning on lights as I went, I descended the stairs. If she had been sitting in the living room, quietly, it was possible I could have walked in and gone right past her without noticing. But she wasn't there.

She wasn't in the basement or the laundry room.

'Donna!' I shouted.

I unlocked the sliding glass doors that led out onto the deck and hit the floods, which were powerful enough to illuminate the entire backyard. It was way too frosty for her to be sitting outside, gazing heavenward, wondering how our boy was doing up there. Like I say, if you believed in that sort of thing.

I went back in, relocked the sliding doors, and opened the one at the end of the kitchen that connected with the garage.

Donna's car was gone.

'Son of a bitch,' I said.

I went to the phone on the kitchen counter and hit the button that automatically connected me to her cell phone.

It rang once.

'Come on,' I said.

It rang a second time.

'Pick up.'

It rang a third time. Then, 'Hey.'

'Where are you?' I asked.

'Driving around.'

'I came home, couldn't find you. I was starting to get frantic.'

'I should have left a note,' she said. 'I couldn't sleep.'

'What's wrong?' The stupid question to end all stupid questions, I knew. What I was trying to ask was, what made tonight worse than all the other nights of the last few months?

'I have a lot on my mind,' Donna said.

We were both silent for a few seconds. I could hear the hum of the car in the background. Finally, I said, 'What'd you have for dinner?'

'I didn't have dinner,' she said.

'Me neither,' I said. Another pause. 'I'm kind of starving.'

'I guess I am, too.'

'The Denny's would be open,' I said. 'We

could get a midnight breakfast. I feel like some eggs and sausage.'

'I'm not far from there,' Donna said. Long pause. 'I'll meet you.'

'I need you to swing by and pick me up. I haven't got a car.'

'You haven't got a car?'

'I'll tell you about it over eggs.'

★ ★ ★

Before I could fill her in about the car, I had to explain the bruise on the side of my face. She noticed it as soon as I got into the passenger seat.

'Does it hurt?' she asked.

'Not as much as my pride.'

There were two other couples and one man sitting by himself at Denny's. Donna and I took a table by the window and ordered decafs to start from the waitress, who was there before our butts had hit the seats. We clung to the hope that once we got home, we'd actually be able to get to sleep, so regular coffee seemed an unwise choice.

'The police seized the car,' I said.

Donna spooned some sugar into her mug. 'Tell me.'

I told her. Starting with my visit to the Rodomskis', followed by my visit to the Skillings', taking Sean with me to where I'd dropped Hanna off, then finding her body under the bridge.

'And Annette Ravelson is sleeping with the mayor,' I said, 'but that seems kind of anticlimactic to everything else.'

'How awful,' she said. 'Finding that girl's body.'
I thought I saw her shiver. It wasn't possible to
think about any body without imagining Scott's
in the parking lot at Ravelson Furniture.

'Yeah,' I said. 'The Skilling kid took it bad.'

'You don't think he did it,' Donna said.

'I don't,' I said. 'But I've been wrong before.'

The waitress returned and we ordered eggs
and all the greasy, wonderful things that generally come with them. An awkward silence ensued
for several minutes until the food came.

'I can't believe my brother would have the car
seized,' Donna said.

I sipped my coffee, imagined the jolt it would
give me if it weren't decaf. 'Yeah, I was
surprised, too.'

'You two are like a dog and a cat in the same
sack, but I think, at some level, he respects you,'
she said. 'Maybe he seized the car to make a
point, that he's not showing favoritism, even
though he knows he won't find anything.'

'Unless he does,' I said.

Her forkful of egg stopped halfway to her
mouth. 'Cal, Augie's not going to frame you.
That's absolutely ridiculous. You think he's going
to plant evidence against you?'

I said nothing.

'For God's sake, why would he do that? What
possible reason could he have?'

'I don't know,' I said.

'I know you don't like him — half the time I
don't even like him — but he's not capable of
that.'

'He's feeding the mayor a line of bullshit,

246

saying his people never overstep their bounds.'

She gave me a look that suggested I should know better. 'You think there's a police force anywhere that doesn't? Like, say, the Promise Falls police? I believe you used to work there.'

'Donna.'

'Augie looks out for his people. The way your chief looked out for you.'

'I lost my job,' I said.

'You could have lost more,' she said.

My time in Promise Falls was not something I liked to talk about. 'Maybe you're right. Maybe Augie's making a point. Maybe he just wants to inconvenience me. I'll have to rent something in the morning.'

'Use my car,' Donna said. 'Drop me off. If you can't pick me up, I'll find my way home.'

'Sounds like a plan,' I said.

A couple of minutes of silence followed. I had a feeling we were done talking about my evening, at least for now. We were moving to something else.

Finally, Donna said, 'I was afraid he'd stop loving me.'

I looked at her and waited.

'I was afraid, that if I — if we — got really tough with him, grounded him, cut off his money, forced him into counseling, went to war with him about what he was doing, I was afraid he wouldn't love me anymore.'

'I know,' I said.

'I even thought about turning him in,' Donna said. 'Calling Augie. Have him arrested, put the cuffs on him, throw him in jail, the whole thing.

247

Like that *Scared Straight* movie. Remember that? But I couldn't bring myself to do it. I didn't think I'd be able to forgive myself. I thought about what might happen to him when he was in jail, even if it was only for a little while, about the other people he might meet in there, what they might do to him. But now that I didn't do it, I can't forgive myself for that, either.'

I put my fork down. I wanted to say something, but it was hard for me.

'What?' Donna said.

'I'm angry all the time,' I said. 'I do my best to hide it. But it's always there. It's like I've got snakes slithering around under my skin. Millions of bugs, crawling inside me.'

'Are you angry with me?' Donna asked.

I didn't answer right away. I was debating how honest to be, because I was angry with her. But it was nothing compared to the anger I felt toward myself. It was nothing compared to the anger I felt toward whoever sold Scott that final dose.

And it was nothing compared to the anger I felt toward Scott himself.

'I don't know if there's anyone I'm not mad at,' I said, and watched her face fall ever so slightly. 'But you're far from the top of the list.' I paused. 'That's where I am.' I made two fists, trying to work out my tension, and then relaxed my hands.

'You want to punish yourself, that's one thing,' she said. 'I get that. I want to do it to myself. But you have to stop punishing me.'

'I'm not,' I said. 'I haven't said a thing.'

248

'Exactly. You have to talk to me. I've never needed you more in my life than I do now, but you're shutting me out. Withdrawing into yourself. When we lost him, what we had, part of that died, too. Are you willing to let it die completely?' Her eyes were red and moist.

I closed my own briefly.

'No,' I said.

I struggled to find words. 'I'm afraid . . . I feel like it's wrong to be happy. That if we're ever good, if we're ever happy again, it's some kind of betrayal.'

A tear ran down Donna's cheek. 'Oh, babe, we're never going to be happy. But we could be happier. Happier than we are now.'

As hungry as I'd been, I didn't have enough appetite to finish what was on my plate. I pushed some eggs around with my fork, then set it down.

'I never should have let her out of the car,' I said.

'What else could you have done?'

'Something. At the very least, stayed with her until she got hold of someone else to give her a ride. She was calling the Skilling kid when she got interrupted.'

'You said she ran away. How would that have looked, you chasing a teenage girl down some empty street late at night?'

Donna wasn't wrong. But I didn't feel any better.

'It's not my only regret,' I said. 'I've done some things.'

Donna eyed me warily. 'Go on.'

'Things I'm not proud of.'

Her face fell and her lip trembled before she spoke. 'Are you seeing someone?'

'What?' The comment caught me off guard.

'Things like that happen. After a crisis. People end up doing any number of things they wouldn't normally do.'

'No,' I said. 'Not that.' I looked her straight in the eye. 'Never that.'

I got the check.

* * *

I think we both knew it was going to happen.

We went into the house, neither of us saying a word, perhaps worried that if we said anything, it wouldn't. We got ready for bed, the way we used to. Sharing the bathroom, taking turns to brush our teeth at the sink. Crawling under the covers at the same time, turning out the lights on the bedside tables.

''Night,' I said.

''Night,' Donna said.

Neither of us pretending the other wasn't there.

I hesitated a moment, then laid a hand on her side. She turned so that her face was resting on the edge of my pillow. I pulled her body into mine, and it happened. It was slow, and undoubtedly sad in the way lovemaking can be at times, but there was something else. There was hope.

Things seemed better. Maybe we'd turned a corner.

33

The phone on our bedside table rang at six forty-five a.m.

I was already awake, staring at the ceiling, thinking about gas stations, but Donna was sound asleep next to me. She woke with a start.

'What?' she said. 'What is it?'

'Hang on,' I said, rolling over and grabbing the receiver. I glanced at the display, but the ID name was blocked. 'Hello?'

'I've called all around and no one knows where she is.'

'Who is — Is this Bert?' I said.

'Yeah,' the mayor said. 'I called everyone I could think of, at least those I had numbers for, and sent e-mails to people whose addresses I had. No one's seen Claire, no one has any idea where she might have gone. I was on the phone with Caroline for an hour after you left, and she tried to help me make a list of names. And the police showed up and had a lot of questions, too, because, you know, they had your version of events and knew Claire and Hanna had been together last night.'

'Was it Augie?'

'No, no. It was a man and woman. I can't even remember their names.' It would have been Ramsey and Quinn. 'I'm not tracking a hundred percent. I'm rattled and haven't had any sleep. I've been calling people all night, waking them

251

up, pissing them off, but I don't care.'

'Are there some you're still waiting to hear back from?' I asked.

'A few. So far, nothing. Roman, Annette's son, called me around one in the morning. She asked him to.'

I couldn't help but ask. 'He didn't wonder why his mom was getting in so late? With his dad out of town?'

'I don't know what she told him. But he was out late, too, doing whatever he does.'

Making booze deliveries to underage drinkers, I bet. Two of his employees, Sean and Hanna, weren't available.

'What'd he say?'

'He said, and I quote, he didn't fuckin' know, and he didn't fuckin' care. Said I should put in a call to Dennis Mullavey. But I don't know where to find him.'

The young man I'd seen in pictures on Claire's iPad.

'Tell me about him,' I said as Donna threw off her covers, sat on the edge of the bed and rubbed her eyes.

'Like I said, a summer romance. They were crazy about each other. A nice kid, you know? I liked him okay.'

'Where'd they meet?'

'Where does anyone meet in this town? Probably Patchett's.'

'But Dennis isn't from Griffon?'

'No. He got a job here for the summer. Working for a lawn service. Cutting grass, that kind of thing.'

'What's the name of the company?'

'I don't think I ever knew. Whenever he came by here, he'd be driving one of their trucks. It was orange.'

I could recall seeing those trucks around town, but I couldn't think of the name painted on the side. Griffon probably had three or four landscaping companies.

'I can find that out,' I said. 'So what happened between Claire and Dennis?'

'I guess it was more than just a summer job for Dennis, because he stayed on with this company into September. Most of these firms, they look after you right into the fall, raking leaves and all that. Wherever he was from, he didn't have to go back to school. He was done with high school, I know that much.'

Donna was still sitting on the edge of the bed, listening. Sanders was talking loud enough that she was probably able to hear most of what he was saying.

'Go on,' I said.

'So one day, out of the blue, he just quits his job, breaks up with Claire, and goes back home. Broke off with her with a text or an e-mail or something. Said it wasn't working out for him, he was sorry, but he wasn't interested in having some long, drawn-out discussion about it. She was heartbroken. Cried for a couple of days. I told her, 'Look, you're young, you'll have a hundred more boyfriends before you find the right one.''

'Huh,' I said.

'In case you're wondering, I didn't try to

break them up,' Sanders said defensively.

'I didn't suggest you did.'

'You'd be surprised, this day and age, how many people took me aside, said I should talk Claire into breaking it off with him because he's black. Said I should scare him off. Unbelievable.'

Sounded like the kind of thing Augie might say, but I knew Augie wasn't exactly giving advice to the mayor, except maybe to take a long walk on a short pier.

'Even Caroline,' he said. 'You know, my ex. I swear she's not a racist, but she was uncomfortable with it.'

'Did she tell Claire how she felt?'

'No, she was putting it all on me, since Claire spends most of her time in Griffon. I told her I wasn't going to do any such thing.'

'You sure she couldn't have said something to Dennis? Did he and Claire ever go visit her mother in Toronto?'

'They might have, once, but no, I don't think so.'

I wondered why Claire lived mostly with her father. So I asked.

'When Caroline got remarried and moved to Toronto, Claire put up a huge fuss. She wasn't going to move there, she wasn't going to leave her school and her friends. And honestly, I think Caroline was happy to lose that battle. She wanted to start off this new marriage without the complications of a teenage daughter at home.'

'You were okay with that?'

'Absolutely,' he said. 'Look, Cal — may I call you Cal?'

'Of course.'

'Cal, I owe you an apology. I misjudged you, misjudged your motives. I know now that your concern for Claire is genuine, and I understand how, given the way you were dragged into this, you felt an obligation to become involved. And I appreciate your discretion where Annette is concerned.' I was waiting for a 'but.'

'But up to now, you've kind of been working for yourself. I'd like to make that right, and hire you, pay you for your time.'

It wasn't the 'but' I was expecting. I thought he was going to politely tell me to cease and desist, that he'd handle things from here on.

'I want you to find Claire. I mean, look, maybe she'll call me in the next hour. Maybe she'll be in touch before the day is out. But what if she isn't? Then I'll have lost a day trying to find out what's happened to her.'

'I guess you don't want to go to the police and report her missing,' I said.

Sanders almost chuckled. 'No, I don't think so. But I have to ask, is it going to be difficult for you to help me with this, given the animosity between you and your brother-in-law?'

'Probably,' I said. 'But that's okay. Look, I have a couple of things I was going to follow up on this morning, anyway. There are a couple of gas stations close to Iggy's. Someone who'd been waiting around to pick Claire up might have filled up before or after. And I'll make some calls to local landscapers, see if I can get a lead on this Dennis Mullavey character.'

For a moment I thought I'd been cut off.

Sanders wasn't saying anything.

'Bert?' I said.

'I'm sorry.' His voice was shaky. He'd broken down. He'd been crying. 'Tell me you don't think she's ended up like Hanna.'

'I'm gonna do my best to find her.'

'I just want to know she's okay. I have to know she's okay.'

34

I hung up.

Donna said, 'I'll get breakfast going.'

A few minutes later, in the kitchen, things felt slightly different. Not unlike the feeling after a tornado whips through. You've been through this horrendous storm, wondering whether the roof will fly off, the walls will come crashing in, the car will get flipped over onto its roof.

But then the storm's roar fades away and you think it's safe to venture outside. The sun is coming out. You've lost a few trees, the power's out, half the shingles on the roof have been blown off.

But you're still standing.

We brushed against each other as we went about our morning routine without the recent awkwardness. I placed a gentle hand on her hip in a way I hadn't in some time. She made enough coffee for two. Most mornings, lately, she had been grabbing coffee on her way to work and I'd stopped by a drive-through en route to whatever job I had at the time.

While we sat at the kitchen table eating some English muffins with jam, I opened up the laptop and looked up Griffon-area landscapers. There were four listed, but when I went to their respective Web sites, one — Hooper Gardening — had photos of orange pickup trucks. I made a note of the number. It wasn't even eight a.m., so

I'd give them a call in another hour or so.

There were other things I could get started on first.

There were two self-serve gas stations within sight of the restaurant. If I checked their security footage from two nights ago, I might be able to get a better look at that Volvo. Maybe I'd be able to pick up a license plate, or see the driver.

It wasn't much, but it was something. I was also thinking about Patchett's, and whether there might be more leads worth following from there. Owner Phyllis Pearce seemed to know everybody's business. Maybe she knew something about Claire Sanders and Dennis Mullavey. I'd gone back to Claire's Facebook page to see if he was among her friends, but his name didn't come up.

Donna was ready for work ahead of schedule so she could get a ride with me in her Corolla. She didn't lean over for a kiss as she got out the passenger side, but she reached over and squeezed my hand.

Neither of us said a word.

From there, I drove to the first of the two service stations on Danbury within walking distance of Iggy's. I pulled up to the pump, got out, and put a quarter of a tank of unleaded into the car, casting my eyes around as I did so, taking in the cameras. Most self-serve places now required you to put your credit card in first and have it approved, so you couldn't take off without paying. If you wanted to pay cash, you usually had to go in and put down a deposit before they'd activate the pump.

Those cameras had been more important back in the day when people filled their tanks before they paid. Station owners no longer had that kind of trust in their customers, but the cameras remained.

Even though I'd paid at the pump, I went inside on the pretext of buying a treat. As I was getting out a five to pay the woman standing behind the counter for a Mars bar, I brought out my detective license as well.

'What's this?' the woman asked tensely. She was in her mid-twenties, and thin enough to make one wonder whether she was anorexic. 'You a cop? Because if you are, I've got the petition right here. I don't always remember to get everyone to sign it, but most of the time I do. And I get the people to write down their addresses, too.'

'I'm private,' I said. 'I don't care if anyone signs that thing or not.'

That seemed to relax her. 'That's good, because I hate asking. Why the fuck should I have to do PR for the cops, right?'

'Right.' I explained I was looking for a vehicle that might have filled up here a couple of nights ago.

'What for?' she asked.

'Some guy who may have picked up a girl out back of Iggy's.' I implied menace.

'Oh, okay. When was this?' When I told her the time period I was interested in, she shook her head. 'Sorry. We erase everything after twenty-four hours if nothing happens so the hard drive or whatever doesn't get all filled up.'

I sighed. 'Did you happen to be on night before last? Between nine thirty and ten thirty?'

This time, a nod. 'Yeah, I did a double, because Raul had the flu, although I think he was faking it.'

'You remember a Volvo station wagon coming in around that time? Silver or gray, I think.'

'You're kidding, right? I couldn't even tell you what kind of car you're driving, and it's sitting out there right now.'

I thanked her, paid for the Mars bar, and left. I was doing up my seat belt when I thought I noticed an old silver Hyundai with tinted windows parked on the other side of Danbury. I was staring at it, wondering if it could be the car that had been following me the night before, when it started up, pulled onto the road, and drove off.

The second gas station was just behind me and across the street. I wheeled out, spent ten seconds tops on the road, then pulled up at another set of pumps. I filled the tank another quarter, which pretty much topped up Donna's car, and scanned the area for cameras at the same time. When I went inside, I didn't bother buying another candy bar.

'I am very sorry, sir, but our cameras are not even working,' said the East Indian man at the cash register when I asked him about seeing surveillance footage. 'They are still up there to scare the customers, but we do not record anything.'

I asked him if he had any memory of a silver or gray Volvo wagon from two nights ago.

'I was not on,' he said.

'Who was here that night?'

'Samuel. He was here. But I can guarantee you he did not see a thing.'

'Why's that?'

The man pointed to a stack of skin magazines on the counter behind him, next to a display of cigarettes. 'Samuel looks at porn all night and only gets his nose out of the books when there is someone standing right in front of him.'

'I thought everyone looked at porn online now,' I said.

'Samuel is seventy years old. He has never got into the computer thing,' the man said. 'I am sorry.'

So was I. It had been a long shot, at best. Time to move on to something that might be more productive.

I got out the number for Hooper Gardening and dialed. I asked the woman who answered for the owner/manager, and she said Bill Hooper was out of the office. I gave her my number and she said she would have him return my call.

'How soon will he get back to me?' I asked.

'Beats me,' she said.

I couldn't sit around doing nothing, so I drove to Patchett's. It wasn't even nine thirty, and the place was dead. They opened at eleven thirty for lunch. The front door was locked, but I found a service door open around back, and two men were in the kitchen, getting things ready for the day.

'I was looking for Ms. Pearce,' I said.

'She doesn't come in until the afternoon,' one

261

said. 'Maybe two or three.'

'Thanks,' I said.

I supposed that when you ran an establishment like Patchett's, it was the evening hours when you most needed to be around. Once I was back in the car, I looked up her home address on my phone. There was only one Pearce listed for Griffon, on Windermere Drive, which was on the road heading north out of town.

It was a house I'd driven past a hundred times, but had never known who lived there. What had always caught my eye about it was that it was an imposing structure. It sat up from the road on a gentle hill, surrounded by trees. The homes were well spaced, a good hundred feet between them. The place had something of a plantation feel to it. Two stories, a broad porch with thick, sturdy columns, white wood furniture with colorful cushions. The grass was overgrown, but other than that, the property was well tended. A tan Ford Crown Victoria sat in the drive.

I parked behind it, got out, and walked up the porch steps. From this vantage point, you could see down into Griffon, rooftops, a church steeple. Sitting out here, I could imagine myself presiding over it. This would have been a better house for Bert Sanders.

I knocked on the heavy wood door, heard footsteps approaching.

The door opened about six inches, and Phyllis Pearce's face was framed between it and the jamb.

'Yes?' she said.

'Mrs. Pearce?' I said. 'You remember me? We spoke the other — '

'Oh yes, Mr. Weaver.' She opened the door wider. 'How are you?'

'Fine, thank you. Sorry to bother you so early. Patchett's must keep you working most nights.'

'It does. I'm often there till ten or eleven, even midnight, but I still wake up at six. Harder to sleep in when you're older. What do you want, Mr. Weaver?'

'I'm betting you've heard about Hanna Rodomski.'

Her face darkened. 'I have. Horrible. A horrible, horrible thing.'

'I was the one who discovered her body under the bridge and — would you mind if I stepped in?'

'Why don't we sit outside?' she said. 'It's a nice day.' Phyllis stepped out onto the porch and we each settled into a white chair. 'That must have been awful to come upon. Her body like that.'

'I was looking for Claire Sanders when I was at Patchett's last night. It was important to me to find her then, but it's far more urgent now in light of Hanna's death. Her father's asked me to find her. Once I have, and made sure she's okay, I'll be asking if she has any idea who might have killed Hanna.'

Pearce nodded. 'Of course. But what brings you to my door?'

'Last night I got the impression not much happens in this town you don't know about. And you invited me to come back if I had any questions.'

A weary smile. 'I did, didn't I? I doubt I know anything useful, but if you have something you want to ask me, go ahead.'

'Did you ever notice Claire around Patchett's with a young man named Dennis Mullavey? He might have stood out some. He's black, and Griffon's not exactly Motown.'

Phyllis pursed her lips. 'Maybe. But I think you're being a little unfair about Griffon. There are plenty of people of color living here. There's Dr. Kessler, for example. She's the coroner around here.'

'Yes, I know her. So did you ever see Claire and Dennis Mullavey?'

'I might have.'

'I have a call in to who I think he worked for, but do you have any idea where he was from? He's not a Griffonite.' I smiled. 'Is that what we call ourselves? Griffonites? Sounds like something that grows in a cave.'

'I've always said 'Griffoner.' I'm not always crazy about being a Griffoner, but it beats being a New Yorker.'

'The traffic's better,' I said. 'Anyway, he wasn't from around here, but I'd like to know where home is for him.'

'I have no idea,' she said.

'I was thinking he might have put drinks on his credit card at Patchett's. You might have receipts. If I got a number, I could check with the credit card company, maybe track him down that way.'

'And why are you looking for him, exactly?'

'He was Claire's boyfriend. Claire'd been

264

going out with Roman Ravelson, but broke off with him to go out with Dennis. But then Dennis up and left town a few weeks ago, breaking up with Claire at the same time. She was pretty upset about it. I'm wondering if they got back together, if she might have gone looking for him.' I ran my fingers through my hair. 'I was trying to think of what would make a young girl take off. I can only come up with two things: fear or love.'

Phyllis Pearce gave that some thought. 'So if she disappeared to be with Dennis, it was love. But what would she have been fearful of?'

'This trouble between her father and the chief. It's been pretty stressful in that household.'

'Or maybe the ex-boyfriend,' Phyllis said.

'Roman?'

'We've had to throw him out of Patchett's once or twice. Of course, seems we end up throwing every young man out at some point.'

'You think Claire could have been scared of Roman?'

'Who knows? As for Mr. Mullavey, I think you may have overestimated my knowledge of what goes on around here. I don't know anything about the young man, I'm afraid.'

'Bert Sanders is calling everyone he can think of who might know where Claire has gone. You have any ideas?'

She shrugged.

'Did you know that Hanna and her boyfriend, Sean Skilling, were delivering booze for Roman Ravelson?'

That made her sit up. 'I'm impressed,' she

said. 'You really are starting to find out how Griffon operates.'

'Roman's old enough to buy the product, and Sean and Hanna were delivering, and far outside the town limits. But I'm not telling you anything you don't know, am I?'

'Yes and no,' she said. 'I didn't know Sean and Hanna were involved.'

'But you knew about Roman.'

She nodded.

'That bother you?'

'Bother me?' Phyllis said. 'Does my place look like it's suffering? You come in there any night of the week, the place is hopping. If Roman wants to help out a few home parties, I couldn't care less about it. Is there anything else I can help you with, Mr. Weaver?'

'No, you've been most generous with your time.' I surveyed the porch and the surroundings. 'This is a beautiful house, and a gorgeous location. You've lived here long?'

'My first husband and I bought this house in the early eighties. Had to do a lot of work on it over the years. When I met Harry, he moved in with me.'

'You decided to hang on to it after he passed away.' Seven years ago, I recalled her saying.

'That's right.' Phyllis Pearce smiled wryly at me. 'Everyone knows the story, but if you moved here six years ago, you probably don't.'

I nodded. 'You're right.'

She had to collect herself. 'Harry could be so stupid. He was a damn fool, is what he was. Late one night, he gets it in his head to go fishing. He hitches the boat — just a fourteen-foot aluminum thing with a ten-horsepower motor bolted to the back of it — to the car and drives down to Niagara Falls, finds a place to launch the boat just off the Robert Moses Parkway, and out he goes, less than a mile upriver from the falls.'

Pearce took another moment, steeled herself. 'He had to have been drinking. There's no question in my mind. If he'd been sober he'd have had the presence of mind to have some oars in the boat, and make sure he had a full tank of gas. He got out there, buzzing around, and the tank ran empty. Motor died on him. Couldn't get it started. And the current started taking him away, over into the Canadian channel, and then over Horseshoe Falls.'

'Dear God,' I said.

'They called it an accident, but really? It was so preventable, in so many ways,' she said. 'A stupid, stupid man, Harry was.' She sniffed, and smiled. 'Doesn't mean I didn't love the son of a bitch, but that was a man who didn't always have his head screwed on right.'

Phyllis Pearce exhaled and seemed to shiver, as if to shake off the memories. 'I like to cultivate this reputation as Griffon's tough old broad. The one everyone should fear. Pretty hard to fear an old bat when she gets emotional that way.'

'I won't tell a soul you have a heart,' I said.

She smiled. 'I would appreciate that.'

I stood. 'Thanks for your time.'

She got out of her chair, too. 'If you hear anything about Claire, will you let me know? I'm not her father's biggest fan, but I hope like the dickens that nothing's happened to her.'

'Sure,' I said, and offered her a hand to shake. 'You take care.'

* * *

I was almost back into town when the Griffon police pulled me over and took me into custody.

35

I saw the cruiser in my rearview mirror a few seconds before the lights came on and the siren started to whoop. Like a good boy, I pulled over to the curb and waited for an officer to approach. Another glance in my mirror showed I was about to be visited by Officer Hank Brindle.

I powered down the window as he came up alongside me.

'Officer,' I said.

'Out of the car, Mr. Weaver,' Brindle said.

'What's the charge, if you don't mind my asking?' It sounded like such a cliché, but it seemed a logical question. 'Busted taillight?'

'Out of the car,' he repeated, resting his hand on the gun hanging from his belt.

I turned off the engine, and as I stepped out I saw Ricky Haines getting out of the passenger side of the cruiser and moving quickly to help his partner.

'Turn around,' Brindle said. 'Hands on top of the vehicle.'

I complied. Haines patted me down. I wasn't carrying the Glock today. But he found my cell phone and confiscated it.

'He's okay,' Haines said.

'Hands behind your back,' Brindle said. 'And don't do anything stupid.'

'Don't worry,' I said. 'I'll leave that to the experts.'

He secured my wrists with a set of plastic cuffs, then grabbed me by the elbow and started walking me to their car. He opened the back door and I ducked so as not to hit my head as he shoved me in. I brought my leg in just before he slammed the door.

'Isn't anyone going to help me put my seat belt on?' I asked as the two of them got back into the front seat of the cruiser.

I have to admit, being a wiseass was just covering up the fact that I was nervous as hell. What the hell had they found in my car? Or an even better question might be, What the hell had they put there?

Ricky Haines barely had the passenger door closed before Brindle had the car in drive. He kicked up gravel before getting back on asphalt.

'Last night, I wasn't a hundred percent sure about you, but I am now,' Brindle said.

'That so?'

'They got you dead to rights on this one,' Brindle said.

'Really.'

'Oh yeah. A slam dunk.' He drummed his fingers on the top of the steering wheel. 'I have to say, I've never had much use for private dicks like yourself.'

I said nothing. I was struggling to get comfortable with my hands locked together behind me.

'I figure, if you really cared about catching bad guys, you'd be a cop. Me and Ricky, we spend all our time trying to make Griffon a better place. But guys like you, you're too busy looking for husbands cheating on their wives and vicey versey. You're not doing anything that matters. You're not doing anything for the public good, and you're always getting in the way of people like me.'

'I was a cop once,' I said. I almost said 'like you.' But I wanted to think I'd never been a cop like him.

'That a fact? And this was where?'

'Promise Falls. North of Albany.'

'Pretty country up there,' Brindle said. 'So what happened? Promise Falls' high crime rate prove to be too much for you? A lot of people fishing without a license? Moose running wild in the streets?'

'Something like that,' I said. First opportunity I had, I'd call my lawyer, Patrick Slaughter, who could get started on whatever it was the police had against me. 'I'd like to make a phone call.'

'I'll bet you would.'

'When we get to the station.'

'Oh,' Brindle said, whipping his head around for a second. 'Is that where you thought we were going?'

He looked in the mirror, caught my look of apprehension, and chuckled. 'You should see your face. I was just messing with ya.' He glanced over at Haines. 'If you can't have a little fun, what's the point, am I right?'

Haines didn't look happy. Maybe not every Griffon cop enjoyed taunting suspects. 'Come on,' he said. 'I'm betting this is all bullshit, anyway.'

Brindle shot him a look.

When we reached the Griffon police head-quarters, Brindle wheeled the car around to the back and drove into an open garage. He opened my door and led me from the car to the building, a distance of not more than ten feet. From there I was taken to a basement holding cell, where I was left to spend some time on my own.

A person could be here a long time before anyone knew something had happened to him. When I wasn't there to pick up Donna at the end of the day, she would assume work had interfered, and would find her own way home. Even if she tried calling me, my failure to answer wouldn't set off any alarms.

Brindle removed my cuffs, stepped out of the holding cell and swung the door shut. It locked automatically. 'Back in a bit. Don't go away,' he said with a smile before leaving me with only my thoughts for company.

I had several of them, and they weren't good ones. I couldn't shake the feeling that they'd found something incriminating in the car. There was the wig, but that was easily explained, as was any blood that might be on the front seat, which would be Claire's. And there was no way, in this short time, that they could have done any kind of DNA testing on it.

So if they weren't nailing me with something that was already in the car, it had to be with something that had found its way into it since it had left me.

Was Augie capable of that? Planting evidence against his brother-in-law? Even if I believed he had it in him, I couldn't think of any reason for him to do it, aside from him thinking I was a horse's ass. A good reason to punch someone in the mouth, but hardly justification to send him to prison.

I heard a door opening at the end of the hall, then steps coming my way. I'd been sitting on a metal bench bolted to the floor, but sprang to my feet and went to the bars to see who it was.

A cop, in uniform, but not Brindle or Haines. It was Officer Marv Quinn, partner of Donna's friend Kate Ramsey. He seemed to be using this hallway to get from one place to another, and looked startled when he saw me with my fingers wrapped around the bars.

'What the hell?' he said. If he was pretending to be surprised, he was doing a good job of it. Given that he was the one who'd passed Augie's order on to Brindle and Haines that my car be seized, he shouldn't have been that shocked.

'Hey,' I said.

'What are you doing in here?'

'Just hanging out,' I said.

'No, really, what are you doing here?'

I eyed him skeptically. 'I guess the search of my car turned up something. Something that wasn't there before it got towed off.'

Quinn looked wounded. 'Come on, man, we don't do stuff like that.' This from a guy whose partner, if that kid at the gas station where I'd bought Tylenol was to be believed, had shot spray paint down his throat. Quinn knew how things were done around here.

'Whatever you say,' I replied.

Quinn rubbed his forehead, like there was

273

something that had just occurred to him. 'Look, sorry if I came off a bit abrupt the other night. I didn't know your wife — Donna, is it? — and Kate are friends.'

'Yeah,' I said.

'Does she know you're down here?'

'Kate?' I asked. 'Or Donna?'

'Donna.'

'No, she doesn't. Far as I know.'

Quinn nodded. 'I could tell Kate, and Kate could give her a heads-up, if you want.'

That seemed like a good idea, especially if no one was going to give me an opportunity to call my lawyer.

'Yeah, I'd appreciate that,' I said. There was something about the way he said his partner's name that struck me. 'You been partnered long with Ramsey?'

Marvin Quinn nodded. 'A year or so.' He looked at me sideways. 'I guess Donna's told you.'

'Told me?'

'I mean, if she and Kate talk, Donna probably knows, and has told you. But we'd just as soon this didn't get around.'

My mind tried to put the pieces together at silicon speed. 'Oh yeah, sure. About you and Kate.'

'The chief doesn't like it when partners are seeing each other, and in a small department like this, with only a couple of women, it's not really an issue. But he wouldn't be happy if he knew Kate and I were, you know.'

'Sure,' I said. We heard the door open.

'Anyway, hang in there,' Quinn said, and

continued on. Seconds later, Haines was looking in at me.

'I want to call my lawyer,' I said.

'Yeah, I know,' Haines said. 'My partner's not really big on that. This is kind of, I mean, it's kind of irregular, but do you want me to call him for you?'

I hardly knew what to make of that. Haines could see that I was taken aback.

'We're not all bad,' Ricky Haines said.

I weighed his offer. 'No,' I said. 'But thanks.' First of all, I didn't want to be in any Griffon cop's debt. And second, I didn't want to think about what Brindle might do to his partner if he found out Haines had done me a favor.

'Okay,' Haines said. 'Look, I'm supposed to cuff you, but I don't figure you're going to try to make a break for it.'

'Where you taking me?'

'You'll see.'

He opened the cell door, led me down the hall, up a flight of stairs, down another hall, and finally into a room with four other men. All white, all about my weight and height, but the similarities more or less ended there. One had gray hair, one had black. One man's face was long with a pointed chin, another's round with puffy cheeks. One fellow was a bit twitchy, like he was going through some kind of withdrawal. Two of them I was pretty sure I recognized as Griffon cops, although instead of wearing uniforms they were done up like they were about to go undercover as soup kitchen regulars.

You didn't need a degree in criminology to

figure out what was up. We were the cast of an upcoming lineup. Any minute now we'd be led into an adjoining room, stood against a lined backdrop that would help any audience members gauge our height, then told to step forward and turn left and right, like we were all auditioning for, instead of *A Chorus Line*, a remake of *The Public Enemy*.

No one said a word. Then a door at the end of the room was opened, and Haines told us to walk out onto the platform. I was second in line.

The five of us stood there under bright lights, unable to see what was out in front of us, although I knew it was a wall with a piece of one-way glass installed.

A voice I didn't recognize came over a speaker and said: 'Everyone turn and face left.'

We did, although the twitchy guy got it wrong and turned right. When we were all asked to face right, he went left.

'Number three, please take a step forward.' That was the guy to my right, one of the two I believed to be cops. He stepped ahead, then turned left and right as requested, then fell back into line.

'Number four, same.'

That was me. I did as I was told. Took a step forward, turned to the left again, turned to the right, then stepped back into line.

'Did we ask you to step back, number four?'

I stepped ahead again. This was pretty outrageous, putting me in a lineup before I'd even been allowed to call for legal representation. Surprise, surprise.

'All right, step back.'

I did as I was told. We stood there another minute or two before the door opened and we were told to get our asses off the stage, although not exactly in those words.

The four other men were permitted to continue beyond the door, but Brindle was there to stop me from following them.

'Guess what,' he said. 'You got the part.'

He steered me down another hall and into an interrogation room. Four pale green walls, a table and three chairs. Two on one side, a single chair on the other. He put me in the single and pulled out one of the others across from me.

'I got a few questions for ya,' Brindle said.

'I've got nothing to say. Not until I have representation. You haven't even told me why I'm here.'

'You don't know why you're here? You really don't?'

'I really don't. But I can guess. You found something in my car. Something that wasn't there when you towed it.'

He frowned. 'Why don't you come with me. Maybe I can help bring it all back to you.'

I thought of that old James Thurber cartoon, where the prosecution produces a kangaroo and says to the witness, 'Perhaps this will refresh your memory!' I doubted Brindle was going to show me any creatures from the Australian outback.

He took me out of the room and down another hall. I knew, from the many times I'd been in this building — trips that had never included visits to a holding cell or the lineup room — that we were heading toward the main entrance.

We passed through two more doors and came out behind the reception counter. On the far side of the room were a man and a woman, with, I presumed, their son. He was eighteen years old, slightly built, about five three with a short, bristly haircut, wearing jeans and a sport jacket, white shirt and tie. Looked very respectable.

I knew his age, but that wasn't all I knew about him. I knew he used to go to my son's school last year, but over the summer had moved to Lockport. I knew his name was Russell Tapscott, and that he had his own Audi convertible. Blue, with black interior.

I knew that it hadn't been forty-eight hours since I'd last seen him.

Russell was sitting in one of the chairs, next to his mother. His father was pacing back and forth in front of them.

Russell saw me first.

'That's him!' he shouted, standing and pointing. 'That's the fucker who tried to throw me over the falls.'

Okay. Now I knew why I was here. It had nothing to do with the car at all.

36

There was a time, not that far in the past, although it felt like a lifetime ago, when I'd been standing in the Griffon police department reception area with my own son. Scott had been fourteen, and he'd been picked up for being under the influence — of what, it was not immediately clear — in a public place.

The place had been a Griffon residential neighborhood, the time shortly after midnight. Scott had been running up and down the street, flapping his arms like he was trying to achieve liftoff. When he failed to get out of the way of a Griffon cruiser, he was tossed into the back and brought downtown.

Augie, as it turned out, was at headquarters at the time, and recognized his nephew as they brought him in. He waved the cops over, asked what was going on, then sent them on their way, leaving Scott in his custody.

Not wanting to upset his sister, he placed a call to my cell. I had muted the ringer, but heard it buzz on the bedside table and managed to answer it without waking Donna.

I told him I'd be right down.

Augie turned Scott over to me without a word of lecture. The boy seemed to be floating. I waited until we were in the parking lot before I tore into him.

'What the hell's going on?'

He pointed into the night sky. 'You see that thing moving. A little light is going by. It might be a satellite, or a plane.'

'I'm taking you home.'

'Wait. I have to see where it goes. What if it's coming for me?'

'For Christ's sake.' I grabbed hold of his arm and dragged him to the car, put him into the front seat.

'It's okay,' he said. 'I don't think it's coming for me. It's going too far thataway.'

'Why did the police pick you up? What goddamn stupid stunt did you pull?'

'They were in my way.'

'In your way?'

'They were blocking the runway.'

'Jesus, you're totally out of it, aren't you? When are you going to stop this kind of crap? You're killing us, you know that? You're killing me and you're killing your mother.'

He turned slowly and looked at me, like he was seeing me for the first time. 'I don't want to kill you guys.' He smiled. 'I love you guys.'

'This is a hell of a way to show it.'

'I won't do this again,' he said, and made a definitive, karate-chop motion to emphasize his point, but he ended up hitting the side of his hand on the dash. 'Ouch. Shit.'

'You've said that before, Scott. Don't even bother telling me that.'

He gazed through the windshield at the sky again. 'I'd like to go into space. Or maybe not. It's probably freezing. Where's Mom?'

I wondered if she was awake. I had left her a

note that said I'd gone out to give our son a lift home. Nothing about the police picking him up. 'At home, probably worried sick about you.'

Scott wrinkled his brow. 'Why?'

I sighed. I wondered, at the time, how much longer this would go on, whether we would ever come out the other end of the tunnel. 'We just want you to stop hurting yourself. We want you to stop doing this.'

He nodded, and for a moment there, I thought I was getting through.

Finally, he said, 'Okeydoke.' A pause, and then, 'Home, James.'

★ ★ ★

Hank Brindle, bringing me back to the present, said, 'Things clearer now?'

'Lawyer,' I said.

'God, you're a goddamn broken record,' he said.

He hustled me back through a door and out of the reception area. 'So, that kid sure seems to know who you are.'

'He does seem to have some kind of problem with me.'

'Yeah, he does. He does have a small problem with you. He says you tried to kill him.'

I said nothing.

'What he tells us is, you arranged to meet him, and that when you did, you threatened to throw him into the Niagara River, in a park not too far up from the falls, if he didn't admit to you that he was the one who sold your boy drugs before

281

he went flying off the top of Ravelson Furniture.'

I said nothing.

'He says you wouldn't believe him when he said he wasn't the guy who did it, and that you said if he hadn't done it, he probably had a pretty good idea who did. All the time, you're getting ready to push him over the railing into the water. Is any of this sounding familiar?'

I stared at Brindle blankly. We went into an interrogation room and he pushed me into a chair. He went around to the other side of the table and sat down.

'You scared that kid to death, I gotta tell ya. He says you said something to him, like, that if he told anybody about what happened, about your little encounter, that not only would you deny everything, but you'd tell the cops everything you knew about him being a dealer, so if he had half a brain in his head, he'd keep his mouth shut.'

Brindle leaned back in his chair and smiled. 'But guess what? You couldn't intimidate the little fucker. You know why? Because his father is a *lawyer* — not the one you want to get in touch with — but he's a lawyer, and the kid knows you can't get away with shit like that, even if this Russell twerp was the head of the entire Mexican drug cartel. Which, by the way, he is not. He hasn't got so much as a charge for having a joint in his pocket.'

I looked at the door, then back at Brindle.

'You've still got nothing to say?' Brindle said. 'Maybe if I just asked you a few simple questions. Where were you night before last, around eight?'

'I'm not sure.'

'You don't recall?' he said. 'Didn't you say earlier you'd been working on a job down in Tonawanda?'

'Yes.'

'So what time did you finish up down there?'

'I'm not sure, off the top of my head.'

'You seem to have some serious memory problems,' Brindle said. 'But Russell doesn't. He's able to describe what you were wearing, your make of car, lots of pertinent details. You know what I find interesting?'

I shook my head.

'You seem, from what I can tell, to be a reasonably intelligent guy. But this, threatening to pitch that kid in the river, that comes across to me as a very, very stupid thing to do. I'm guessing that you're so bent out of shape over what happened to your kid — and who could blame you there, right? — that you're going off the deep end. Does that sound about right?'

When I failed to respond, he continued. 'I know earlier, in the car, I said you were going to be going away for a while, and I'm willing to admit I might be wrong about that. A judge, a jury, they might take some sympathy on you. Understand what motivated you, even though it was the wrong thing to do. If you come clean, admit what you did, but explain why you did it, well, I could see you doing a little time, but not all that much.'

I slouched in my chair and put my hands in my pockets. My mouth was dry, but damned if I was going to ask this guy for a glass of water.

283

'But now that this kid's come forward, I'm wondering whether others will,' Brindle said. 'Because I'm guessing this isn't the only one you've scared the shit out of. If that happens, if we get a few more complainants — in fact, this kid said he knew of at least one other person, by the name of Len Edgerton or Eggleton or something — well, that might play out very differently. I think the smartest thing you could do is — '

There was a hard rapping on the door. Two distinct knocks. Brindle's head whipped around in time to see the door open.

It was Augustus Perry.

'Chief,' Brindle said.

'Officer.' Perry came into the room and took the seat next to Brindle. He looked at me with a mixture of contempt and amusement. 'I was passing by the lineup room and couldn't help but notice a familiar face.'

'I'm in the middle of an interrogation here, sir,' Brindle said, evidently not intimidated by his boss' presence in the slightest. 'I'm not unaware of your connection to Mr. Weaver, but just the same — '

Augie held up his hand to shush him. 'I understand. You're doing your job. That's fine. I wouldn't ever want it said that anyone was getting special treatment because of me.'

There was a 'but' hanging in the air. I felt it — at least I hoped I was feeling it — and so did Brindle.

'Officer,' Augie said, 'this complaint against Mr. Weaver was just brought to my attention.

This is a very serious charge.'

'Yes, sir. It is. The complainant is very specific in his allegations.'

'What times does he say this incident took place?'

'Two nights ago. Between eight and nine. Mr. Weaver called him earlier in the day to set up a meeting on the pretext of buying some drugs.'

'You have a record of that call?'

'We do. On Russell Tapscott's cell phone. The call came in from a pay phone.'

'A pay phone,' Augie said.

'Yes, sir.'

'And what was that time again, of the alleged occurrence?'

'Between eight and nine.'

The police chief nodded thoughtfully. 'Well, Officer Brindle, I'm afraid you're going to have to cut Mr. Weaver loose.'

'Excuse me?'

'A witness has come forward who can place Mr. Weaver elsewhere at that time.'

Donna.

It made sense. Quinn must have told Kate, and she'd told Donna, who in turn had gone to her brother and told him I was with her for the evening. At least until close to ten, when I'd admitted to everyone and his dog that I'd picked up Claire Sanders outside of Patchett's.

Although it was so common that a wife might lie to protect her spouse, I wasn't sure her testimony would be enough to save my ass.

Brindle shook his head vigorously. 'I doubt that, sir. I think Mr. Weaver here would have

285

mentioned an alibi if he had one. At the moment, he seems to be suffering a severe memory lapse.' He made a small snorting sound.

'Maybe Mr. Weaver thought it would be pulling rank to mention who his alibi is?'

'Chief?'

Brindle was perplexed, and he wasn't the only one.

'Mr. Weaver was with me,' Augie said, giving me as cold a smile as I'd ever seen. 'Certainly during that time you mentioned. He was at my place, in my basement, playing pool. Isn't that right, Cal?'

37

'Slipped my mind,' I said. 'I was thinking we'd gotten together the night before.'

'Nope,' said Augie. 'Night before last.' He grinned. 'And you are, for the record, the worst goddamn pool player I have ever seen.' He turned to Officer Brindle. 'So, you're going to have to go out and explain to that boy and his parents that a mistake has been made.'

'Chief, this is bull — '

'I'm sorry. What's that?' Augie said. 'Are you saying what I've just told you is bullshit?'

Brindle opened his mouth to speak, but nothing came out. 'No, of course not, Chief.' He put a spin on that last word, the disrespect coming through loud and clear.

'Terrific. You want to attend to that while I spend a moment here with Mr. Weaver to extend our apologies over this unfortunate mistake? I believe the Tapscotts are still in reception.'

Brindle kicked back his chair and stood, his face red with anger. He wasn't buying a word of it. 'Yeah. I'll do that.'

'You might also want to mention the boy could be looking at charges of mischief if I weren't in such a forgiving mood today.'

Brindle looked like he'd just been slapped with a wet fish, but I was too dumbstruck to enjoy it. I didn't know what Augie's game was here.

'Yeah,' Brindle said. 'I'll get right on that.'

He caught his foot on the leg of his chair as he turned to leave, and gave it another kick. The chair skittered across the floor and banged into the wall. Brindle didn't look back as he left the room, letting the door close just a little too hard on the way out, enough to make us both blink.

Neither of us said anything for several seconds. We sat there and looked at one another.

'I'm going to need my phone back,' I said.

'You're welcome,' Augie said. 'You and I should have a chat.'

*　*　*

There was a time when I labored under the delusion that I was an honorable man.

I believed I had ideals, that my behavior was governed by a set of high-minded principles. But as you get older you start to realize every day is made up of compromises. Bending the rules doesn't seem worth losing sleep over.

I knew when it was I'd crossed the line, just over six years ago. But just because I'd done it then didn't mean I couldn't have stepped back over that line. I could have promised myself to do better. Maybe, for a while, I actually had, but I hadn't just stepped over the line in the last couple of months. I had pole-vaulted over it. I'd run at that line flat out and jumped. I'd threatened to throw one young man into a fast-moving river, locked another in a trunk, spilled some unleaded onto a third man's pants and threatened to throw a lit match at him. I'd convinced a fourth — I think he was only sixteen

— that I was going to add his right pinky to a finger collection.

One part mourning, one part rage. Mix them together, watch out.

That first time I'd crossed the line was before I got to Griffon. It was why I was a private detective now, and no longer a member of the Promise Falls police force.

There was one night, one hot July night, when I found myself unable to treat a suspect with the kind of kid gloves the Constitution expects. It all happened in an instant. Even now, I keep playing it in my head, thinking that if I concentrate hard enough, I can make things go a different way, rearrange the past.

I put a man in hospital for a week. I cuffed him, bent him over the hood of his car, and then, God help me, placed my hand on the back of his head like I was gripping a basketball, and drove it forward into the hood of his black Mercedes.

Hard.

He slipped into unconsciousness, and he hadn't had that far to go. He was drunk. Blitzed. Twice the legal limit. Which explained why he hadn't noticed the young mother pushing the stroller across the street with her two-year-old daughter sitting inside it. He killed the two of them instantly, hit the brakes for half a second to see what he'd done, then floored it.

I saw everything from across the street, where I'd been slipping a ticket under the wiper of a Range Rover that was parked in front of a hydrant. I got on the radio for an ambulance and took off after the driver, but not before I got a look at what he'd done. When you see a young child dead on the pavement, sometimes something snaps.

I pulled him over three miles south of town. For more than a mile he ignored my siren and flashing lights, but when he drifted over to the shoulder and his right wheels caught gravel, he lost control. The Mercedes fishtailed and he hit the brakes. The car went into a skid, nearly turned sideways, then went straight into the ditch, where it came to a sudden, jolting stop.

When I got to the car, he had the door open and was swatting away at the deployed airbag like it was a swarm of bees. His nose was bloodied. As he got out, his shoes slipped on the tall grass. He struggled to his feet. He saw me and turned to run, the stupid bastard. If it had been a stolen car, that might have been one thing, but you don't leave behind your own car, and all its registration documents, and think you're going to get away with something.

I grabbed hold of the back of his jacket and forced him down on the hood.

I had the image of that dead child in my brain. I might have held it together if, just after I had the cuffs on him, he hadn't glanced at the splatters of red on his windshield and said in a puzzled voice, 'I hope that comes off.'

Snap.

I worried, for a moment, that I'd killed him. His body went limp and slid off the hood and into the grass. I immediately called for an ambulance, and was relieved to find, before it arrived, that he was still breathing. But it was a couple of days before he regained consciousness. I'd given him one hell of a concussion.

The guy recalled nothing. He didn't remember mowing down and killing two people. He didn't remember the flashing lights in his rearview mirror. He didn't remember feeling my hand on the back of his skull, or seeing the hood of his car coming up to meet him with incredible swiftness. It would have been easy to say the man had fallen while resisting arrest, that he had tripped and hit his head on the hood. There were, after all, no witnesses. That was, in fact, the version of events I put down in my report.

But I didn't get away with it. Not entirely.

My car had a dash cam — a camera mounted in the front windshield that caught the whole thing. Just in the right side of the frame. I should have known better. I didn't think my car was at the right angle to capture the scene. My chief brought me into his office and we watched the video together. Several times. No popcorn.

'I'm going to find a way to make this disappear,' he said. 'And in return, you're going to do the same.'

My excuse for public consumption: I'd decided to go private. It was something I'd often thought about, but it's unlikely I'd actually have done it. I was lulled by a steady paycheck, a benefits plan. But now those were gone, and I didn't have much choice but to get started on another career.

I was ashamed. I'd let my department and myself down, but worse, I'd let Donna down and I'd let Scott down, eight years old at the time. It was, up till then, the worst thing we'd been through, but we found the strength to get past it. Donna was the one who deserved the credit. She had every reason to be furious, to blame me for our predicament. It's not as though she was pleased with what I'd done, but it had happened, and we had to deal with it.

At one point, she said she wished there were a way to tell the family of that dead mother and child what I'd done. 'I think they'd want to thank you,' she said. It might have provided more satisfaction than the twelve-year sentence the guy got.

We decided to leave Promise Falls. Donna's brother — at that time, he was a deputy chief — told her there was an opening in the administrative offices of the Griffon department. I was in the process of acquiring my New York State private investigator's license, and it would serve me just as well in the Buffalo area as it would north of Albany.

So I really didn't have anyone else to blame for being here, today, in Augustus Perry's office.

'What the hell were you thinking?' Augie asked as he closed the door. His office had the feel of the proverbial woodshed.

'You didn't have to do that,' I said. That was pride talking, and I knew it. If my brother-in-law hadn't stuck his nose into my business, I'd have been headed for a great deal of unpleasantness.

'Really?' he said, pointing a finger. 'You think you could have gotten out of that one? You think you could have stayed out of jail? Let alone hang on to your license?'

I mumbled something unintelligible. When I eat crow I like to chew with my mouth closed.

'Sorry. I didn't catch that. So let me ask you again, what the hell were you thinking? And don't say this was some kind of bogus accusation, that you're an innocent man. Don't insult me, okay? We've both been around long enough to know bullshit when we step in it. We understand each other?'

I nodded. 'Yeah.'

'Good. So, tell me.'

'I lost my head,' I said, pacing the room, steering clear of Augie.

'Excellent. Great defense.'

'There's some truth to it,' I said.

'To what?'

'That I lost my head.' I stopped, rested my butt on the edge of his desk.

'Get your ass off my desk,' Augie said.

I did, but I didn't jump. 'Scott's death . . . has driven me a little crazy.'

Augie's hard eyes softened. 'Go on.'

'You know I've been asking around, trying to find out who sold him that stuff.'

'I don't know whether you're aware, but that's our job.'

'And how're you coming along with it?' I asked.

'These things can take time,' Augie said. 'You can do all the active investigation you want, then you stumble onto something. Eighty percent of solving crimes is luck, and you know it.'

'I'm not interested in waiting to find things out by accident. When I got a name, a good prospect, someone who might be dealing, I paid them a visit, arranged a meeting.'

'Like you did with this Tapscott kid.'

'Yeah.'

'That was, uh, that was pretty fucking dumb, Cal.'

'Any of the other kids, they've been too scared to do anything about it. They know they're dirty and they don't want to draw attention to themselves.'

'How many others?'

'Four, total,' I admitted.

He nodded thoughtfully, went around his desk and sat down and told me to do the same because it hurt his neck to talk up to me. 'It's not that I don't admire your tactics, Cal. It's just, when you're a civilian, you run a few more risks employing them. But a couple of cops using your sophisticated interrogation techniques would have each other's back. Like what I did for you.'

I managed to get the word out, but I nearly choked on it. 'Thanks.'

He glared at me.

'I don't think you made a friend out of Hank Brindle in there,' I said.

'He's a big boy. He'll get over it.'

'Brindle's a bad cop,' I said. 'He's a bully.'

Augie shook his head. 'He's okay. Cut him some slack. He's had a rough few months. His dad's been sick. He's had to take a few days off, help his mom look after him. And don't let Haines fool you. He's quieter, but he's bent out of shape these days, too.'

'What's his problem?'

'Girl he was seeing dumped him a few weeks

back, packed up and moved back in with her family in Erie. They're a pair. But you know something, Cal? This little meeting we're having isn't about them. It's about you. It's about you, and your attitude problem.'

I slumped in my chair.

'Why'd you do it, Augie?' I asked.

'Why'd I do what?'

'Why'd you save my ass? I was facing some serious charges in there.'

He struggled for an answer. 'Jesus.'

'What?'

'You're my brother-in-law.' He said it with more than a little shame.

'Seriously.'

'Don't, for a minute, think I was doing it for you. I was doing it for Donna.'

That much I believed. But I remained puzzled. 'Tell me this, then, Augie. If you're actually looking out for me, then why the hell did you seize my car?'

'Why'd I what?'

'My Honda. You've still got it. I just hope it's not in a million pieces.'

Augie's mouth hung open for several seconds. 'I don't know what in the hell you're talking about. Who seized your car?'

'Haines and Brindle. They got the word from Marvin Quinn, who said he got the order from you.'

Augie leaned back in his chair, laced his fingers together atop his stomach.

'Well,' he said, 'isn't that a kick in the head with a frozen boot?'

38

'You didn't tell Quinn to have my car taken in?'

Augie shook his head. 'I did not. You're a lot of things, Cal. Dickhead, asshole, a conceited fuck if I ever met one. And the stupidest son of a bitch I know at the moment, trying to scare these kids the way you did. But you didn't kill that girl.'

'That's the nicest thing you've ever said to me.'

'Yeah, well, don't get used to it. Why would Quinn do that? I'd understand one of my officers bringing in a car to have it searched. They don't need my approval for that. The question is why he would have said I wanted it done.'

Neither of us spoke for a moment.

'I saw Quinn while I was cooling my heels in the cell, before the lineup,' I said. 'He might be in the building.'

Augie picked up a phone. 'Where's Quinn?' He waited a few seconds. 'When did he go off shift?' He looked at me and mouthed 'ten minutes.' He hung for another moment, then said, 'Get him at home or on his cell. I want to talk to him.'

He pressed a button, then said, 'Get me the compound.' Another moment on hold, then, 'Chief Perry here. You got an Accord, was brought in last night, belongs to Calvin Weaver? Yeah, that's the one . . . Uh-huh . . . Uh-huh . . . Okay. He's coming to pick it up. I would ask

296

that you extend him every courtesy.'

He hung up.

'No one's even touched it,' Augie said. 'They were awaiting further instructions.'

'I guess I'll be on my way, then,' I said.

'What are you going to do now?'

'I'm going to keep looking for Claire,' I said.

'You don't think maybe it's time for you to take a step back? You nearly got yourself charged. Maybe you should count your blessings and go home for a while.'

'I told the mayor I'd stay on this for — '

It was like I'd poked a bear with a sharp stick. 'Hold on,' Augie said. 'Tell me you're not actually working for that son of a bitch.'

'Sorry, Augie. You so pissed with him you don't think he's entitled to get his daughter back?'

He waved an angry hand at me. 'We're already looking for her. We've got a whole load of questions for her about this game she and Hanna Rodomski were playing.'

'I'll try not to get in your people's way,' I said. 'Although that may be difficult, given the campaign of harassment you've been conducting against Sanders.'

'What in the hell are you talking about?' Bellowing.

'I'm talking about having cruisers parked on his street, watching him, trying to intimidate him. Cops frisking his daughter. Sanders is convinced you've even got his phone tapped.'

'That's the biggest crock of horseshit I've ever heard.'

'Sanders blames you and all your surveillance for his daughter having to go to such lengths to get out of town without being noticed.'

His cheeks were getting red. I was reminded of a boiler on the brink of exploding.

'All bullshit,' Augie said.

'Here's the thing,' I said. 'When you go to a public meeting and tell the mayor your officers have never violated anyone's rights, I know that's a lie, and so does everyone in the room, but no one really cares, because everyone here is happy for you to treat the Constitution like it's toilet paper. So what if you run roughshod over a bunch of punks from Buffalo? But if I know you're lying then, how am I supposed to know whether you're telling me the truth now?'

'I need my head read, helping you out.'

I moved toward the door. 'What I'm doing has nothing to do with you or Sanders or any of the bad blood between you. I just want to find Claire. Once I do, maybe we can figure out who killed Hanna.'

Augie blinked, and a smile formed in the corner of his mouth.

'Don't you know?'

'Don't I know what?'

'We made an arrest this morning.'

'You've charged someone with Hanna's murder? Who?'

'The boyfriend.'

'Sean Skilling?'

'Yup.'

I let my arm fall away from the doorknob. 'The kid's got an alibi. One of your own people

298

pulled him over for running a stop sign.'

'I asked around,' Augie said. 'There's no record of a ticket.'

'I told you, they didn't write him a ticket. He got a warning.'

'What do you want from me, Cal?' Augie said. 'I asked around — no one remembers pulling that kid over in his Ranger.'

'My gut says he didn't do it.'

'Would your gut feel any different if it knew Hanna's jeans and panties were found under the seat of his pickup truck?'

39

Augie arranged for me to reclaim my phone at reception on my way out. There were three messages. Two from Donna, who'd evidently gotten word that I was in some kind of trouble, and one from the manager of the landscaping company. Before making callbacks, I got a cab to take me back to where I'd left Donna's car on the shoulder of the road when Brindle and Haines had picked me up. Then I trekked back to the police department and parked the car in the lot.

Then I phoned Donna.

'Your car's where you usually leave it,' I said.

'I called you twice.'

'I was indisposed.'

'Which was why I called. I'd heard you were in the building. And not in one of the rooms where they hold community meetings.'

'Yeah, but it's sorted out. How'd you hear?'

'Kate heard it from Marvin, and she told me. I called Augie, but by that time you were out.'

'He intervened.'

'They didn't find something in the car, did they?' Donna said.

'No, it was something else.'

A pause. 'Something else?'

'Yeah. I guess I've been pressing my luck. Something came back and bit me in the ass.'

'How'd Augie get you out of this?'

'I'll tell you all about it later. Really.'

'Sure.' Her voice sounded flat.

'What is it?'

'Last night doesn't mean everything's okay,' she said.

'I know.'

★ ★ ★

The lockup where they were holding my Honda was a large parking lot surrounded by high chain-link fencing with a nasty string of barbed wire running along the top. In the office I found a short woman, working away at the crossword, who was expecting me. She retrieved my keys and led me into the compound past decommissioned cruisers, cars that had been in accidents, and a few untouched vehicles like my own.

Once we'd found it, the woman shoved a clipboard at me and said, 'You have to sign here.' I did. She handed over the keys, told me to have a nice day, and said to beep the horn when I reached the gate and she'd open it.

I didn't just get behind the wheel and drive off. I popped the trunk, where I kept those tools of my trade. The laptop, an orange traffic vest, a matching hard hat. Among other things.

Nothing appeared to have been touched.

I went through the glove compartment and had the sense nothing in there had been fiddled with, either. As Augie'd said, no one had touched the car yet.

Even so, I was surprised to see Hanna's wig still in the car, on the floor in front of the backseat. Maybe it didn't constitute evidence, since Hanna wasn't wearing it at the time of her death, but it was all part and parcel of what had happened to her.

There was no shortage of other things to puzzle over. Why did Quinn tell Haines and Brindle to tow my car in? If he thought it should be searched for evidence, why lay it off on the chief?

And Sean Skilling arrested in Hanna's murder?

I got behind the wheel. I inserted the key, started the engine, gave the pedal a couple of taps and listened to the engine rev. I got out my phone and listened to the message from the lawn service guy.

'Bill Hooper here, returning your call.'

He'd called an hour and a half ago. I tapped his number with my thumb to call him right back.

'You've reached Bill Hooper. I can't take your call right now, but if you leave a message I'll get back to you as soon as I can.'

Phone tag time.

When I reached the gate I tapped the horn, prompting the woman to hit the button and open it without so much as looking up from her crossword puzzle.

Sean could have been lying about a Griffon cop pulling him over. But then, if the incident never happened, what kept Sean from getting to Patchett's in time to pick Claire up and deliver her to Iggy's? The kid, at least in the short time I'd spent with him, didn't impress me as a very good liar, or a killer.

But they'd found Hanna's missing clothing in his truck. Not good. Not good at —

I blame distraction for what happened next. I pulled out of the police station parking lot and nearly hit a black Escalade. Hard to miss, given that the thing was big enough to have orbiting moons. The truck swerved and the man behind the wheel shot me the finger.

I slammed on the brakes, hard enough to make the tires squeal.

I should have seen it. But I just didn't.

I took a second to collect myself and let the Escalade get a block ahead. Gave the brake pedal a couple of soft, reassuring taps, then continued on my way.

There was someone I'd been meaning to pay a visit to, but just hadn't had a chance to get around to it. I had a feeling this person was not going to be very happy to see me.

I figured there was a good chance he wasn't even out of bed yet.

When I got to the house I was looking for, I found a red Mustang convertible, top up, parked in the driveway. There was no BMW there, which told me Annette Ravelson was at work.

Just as well. I didn't want her around when I talked to her son, Roman. I could still feel the dull thud in my head where he'd hit me at Patchett's.

I rang the bell. After ten seconds, I rang it again. Then I banged on the door. When a minute had gone by, I tried the doorbell again, but this time I held my thumb on it. Inside the house, the chime rang relentlessly.

I could hold out as long as he could.

After about five minutes of this, I heard someone inside the house shout groggily. 'Okay, okay! Fuck! I'm coming.'

I kept my thumb on the button. I heard a dead bolt turn. The second the door swung open, I got my foot in, thinking that once Roman saw me, he'd try to slam it shut.

He did.

The door hit the side of my shoe, bouncing back and catching Roman's toes.

'Shitfuckshitfuckshitfuck!' he screamed, hopped, and stumbled backward.

I stepped into the house and closed the door behind me. Roman, dressed only in a pair of boxer shorts with little red hearts all over them, was collapsed on the broadloom, holding his left foot in both hands, whimpering.

'Hi, Roman,' I said. 'How's it hanging?'

40

The man wonders who was at the door. He's always curious when he hears a knock, or the doorbell upstairs. It's been so long since he's had a chance to talk to anyone. At least, anyone other than his wife and their son.

The man sits up in bed to listen. Maybe he'll be able to hear voices. He doesn't even have a radio or a TV down here. There haven't been any unfamiliar voices in so long.

Well, other than that one visitor, just the other week. But he'd had so few words to say. Ran off in such a hurry. Scared to death, probably.

The man barely had time to ask for help. Or toss over his notebook. He figured if his visitor needed proof, the book would do it.

But all this time's gone by, and no one's come. Still, anytime he hears someone at the door, he wonders, and hopes.

In the meantime, he spends most of his time in bed. Sometimes he gets himself into the chair, wheels himself around. But where's he going to go? What's the point?

So he just stays in bed and reads magazines.

And sleeps.

And dreams.

About going out.

41

'You fucking broke my toes, man!'

I knelt down and had a look. 'Try to wiggle them.'

Roman Ravelson wiggled his toes.

'I don't think they're broken,' I said. 'But then again, I don't hold a medical degree.'

I offered my hand to help him get up, but instead he crawled two feet over to the stairs and used them to pull himself to a standing position. His skin was milky white, like he'd spent the last few years in a cave. Maybe he only came out at night. There was a little roll of fat over the elastic of his boxers, and sheet creases in his pudgy cheeks.

'Did I get you up?' I asked.

'I was out late,' he said. 'You should leave. If you don't leave, I'm gonna call my mom.'

I got out my cell. 'Want to use my phone? You can tell her how you practically knocked me out last night.'

'That Sean — Jesus — I was trying to help him and he gives me up just like that. My mom told me you said to say hi. You wanted to fuck with my head, didn't you?'

I nodded. 'Your dad home?' I recalled Annette saying Kent Ravelson was out of town.

Roman blinked a couple of times, like he was kick-starting his eyes. 'He's — my dad's away or something.'

'When's he coming back?'

The young man shrugged. 'I don't know. I don't keep track of him.'

'You want to put on a shirt or anything? I've got a few questions.'

Roman sighed. 'Fuck. Follow me.'

He started trudging upstairs. I followed him to the second floor, down the hall, and into his bedroom. Bumping his toes with the door appeared not to have crippled him for life.

His room was decorated hurricane-style. Bed unmade, clothes all over the floor. Magazines, video games, everything arranged helter-skelter. The walls were plastered with movie posters. *28 Days Later*, *The Walking Dead*, *Shaun of the Dead*, *Night of the Living Dead*, *Dance of the Dead*, *Zombieland*, *Dawn of the Dead*.

I was definitely picking up a theme here.

On the floor next to the bed, atop a pile of clothes, was an open laptop. Roman picked it up, looking for something to wear. The motion made the screen, which had been asleep, come to life. I caught a glimpse of text, arranged in what looked like play format.

A script.

He tossed the laptop on the bed, found a black T-shirt he liked, and pulled it on. It was a couple of sizes too small and just barely covered his stomach. Across the front it read WINCHESTER TAVERN.

I pointed to it. 'I don't know that place. It's not from around here.'

He gave me a 'duh' look. 'It's the pub where they're trapped in *Shaun of the Dead*. You've

307

seen it, right? It's only one of the best zombie movies ever made. It's scary, but it's also funny as fuck.'

'Sorry,' I said. Now I pointed to the laptop. 'You writing a zombie movie?'

'Maybe,' Roman said.

'What's it about? Haven't zombies been, forgive me, kind of done to death?'

'You just have to find a new angle. I've got one.'

I waited.

Roman took a breath. 'Okay, most zombies, it happens because of a plague or an experiment or something like that. But what if people were turned into zombies by aliens? A mash up of two different genres. My hero is this guy named Tim who knows what the aliens are doing and tries to stop them.'

I nodded. It sounded dumb to me, but when had dumbness ever kept an idea from being turned into a movie?

'You might have something there,' I conceded. 'You got a regular job, Roman?'

'This is my job. I'm a screenwriter.'

'So, then, how much do you make, I don't know, on a weekly basis, writing your scripts?'

'It doesn't work like that,' he said. 'It's not like some job stocking shelves in a fucking grocery store where you get some stupid paycheck at the end of the week. You write a script, and then you shop it around and sell it. So you don't make money for a long time, but then you could get, you know, a few hundred thousand or a million or something.'

I nodded. 'Oh, okay. I don't understand how Hollywood works. So how many scripts have you sold?'

'I've had some nibbles,' Roman said. 'I had an e-mail the other day from Steven Spielberg's office.'

'No shit?' I said. 'When's your meeting?'

'Okay, the e-mail wasn't exactly — it was more like thanks for your inquiry, but — Did you just come here to bust my balls?' he asked. Wouldn't have been hard, given what he was wearing. ''Cause if you're here about who gave shit to Scott, I swear to you, it wasn't me.'

'I'm not here about that,' I said. 'You're more into beverages. That's what supports you while you write your scripts.'

He raised his hands in mock surrender. 'Okay, busted. I buy beer and drive around and sell it. Big deal. I'm a fuckin' terrorist.'

'You had Sean and Hanna doing the deliveries for you, didn't you? Is that why you were out last night, because they weren't exactly available?'

'I didn't know anything about that. I called Hanna earlier and got no answer, and when I called Sean he didn't pick up, either. Fuck, I didn't know she was dead or anything.'

'Did you know they've arrested Sean for it?'

His mouth dropped open. He plopped down on the side of the bed. Quietly, he said, 'No way. Sean's my friend. There's no way he'd do that.' Roman shook his head in disbelief. 'Sean was really into Hanna. Really loved her. Son of a bitch.'

'If Sean didn't do it, who do you think did?'

He shrugged. 'I can't think of *anybody* who'd

309

do something like that. That's just — that's fucked-up, man.'

I moved some rumpled jeans off a computer chair over by the desk and sat down. I noticed a phone sitting on the desk.

'Did you like Hanna?'

'Oh yeah, sure, she was nice. I mean, she kind of pissed me off sometimes. She was late with money she owed me. But, you know, it was no big deal.'

'What do you mean?'

'Well, I'd buy, like, two dozen cases of beer, load it into Sean's Ranger, right? And they'd go around delivering. Sean drives, Hanna looks after the money. And there's a markup, right? So at the end of an evening, or a weekend, Hanna's got enough to pay me back everything they owe me, and still have money left over. We'd usually meet up the next day.'

'But sometimes she didn't have it?'

Roman rolled his eyes. 'If she passed the mall on the way to see me, sometimes she'd get distracted. Buy herself something. And a couple times, people tried to pay her in something other than cash. I am strictly a cash operation, you know?'

'What do you mean? You're not telling me some kids want to write you a check.'

Another eye roll. If he did it again they might get stuck looking at his brain.

'No, no, like, if someone didn't have enough cash, they'd hand over some weed or something to Hanna. I had to lay down the law on that one. I don't want that stuff.'

'Hanna ever owe other people money besides you?'

'Beats me. Not that I know of. I don't know why you're asking me so many questions about how I make a few bucks. Nobody cares about that, and it's got nothin' to do with what happened to Hanna.' He pinched the bridge of his nose, like maybe he was trying to stop himself from crying. 'I'm tellin' ya, there's no way Sean woulda done that to her.'

'That's why I have to find Claire,' I said. 'She may know what really happened. But you weren't exactly helpful to her father on the phone last night.'

He blinked. 'What — how do you — '

'We talked this morning. You said, quote, you didn't fuckin' know and didn't fuckin' care, unquote, where she was.'

'Okay, you have to know a coupla things. One, my mom did not tell me Hanna was dead before she made me call him. And two, that guy Sanders never liked me. He never thought I was good enough for Claire.'

Point, Sanders.

'How long did you and Claire go out?' I ran my finger along the edge of the cell phone sitting on the desk.

'Like, four months or so, till, like, July.' His lips compressed. 'Till she met Dennis.'

Now we'd reached the main reason for my visit. 'Tell me about Dennis.'

'Well, his last name is Mullavey, and he's a black guy, and he's from someplace like Syracuse or Schenectady.'

311

'Those are very different places.'

He shrugged. 'Well, I don't know. He was supersmooth, you know. Thought he was real cool.'

I picked up the phone.

'Leave that alone,' Roman said.

'You take pictures with this?' I asked.

'Every phone takes pictures. How old are you?'

'This the one you used to take the picture of your cock you sent to Claire?'

'What did you say?'

'Is this the photo app here?'

He shot forward and grabbed the phone from my hand. I didn't make any effort to hang on to it.

'Is that what makes you cool, Roman? Texting hard-on pics?'

Roman stood before me, almost shaking.

'Claire and I would goof around sometimes, that's all. Just having some fun.'

'She send you naked pictures of herself?'

'Claire's a little more uptight about that kind of thing. But she thought it was funny.'

'Even after she'd broken things off with you?' I asked. 'Did she think it was funny to get a reminder of what she was missing? Did Dennis find out about that picture? Did he come after you for it? Did something happen between you two that made him leave town in a hurry?'

'No!' Roman said. 'Nothing like that happened. This is bullshit, bringing up this stuff. It doesn't mean anything.'

'Okay,' I said understandingly. 'Just tell me

what *did* happen. Tell me about Dennis.'

'I hardly ever even met the guy. I know he had a stupid job cutting grass for the summer.'

'With Hooper's?'

'Yeah, that's right. Driving around in one of those orange trucks.'

'So what happened?'

'She started seeing him, while she was still seeing me, right? But I could tell something was wrong, because she was getting all cool, you know? And then she gives me the whole it's-not-you-it's-me thing, and next thing I know she's seeing Mullavey. I wanted to fucking bash his brains in, you know, but Sean, he talked me out of doing anything stupid like that, and I never would have anyway. You think these kinds of things, but you never actually do them.'

'But then Claire and Dennis broke up all of a sudden.'

'Yeah,' Roman said. 'Like, from what Sean told me, one day he just quits his job and goes back home. Like, maybe one day he realized cutting grass was boring. He breaks it off with Claire. At the time, I thought it kind of looked good on her. Like now she'd know how it feels.'

'You try to get back with her? With anything more tempting than your dick shot?'

Roman hesitated. 'I, you know, I called her a few times. I admit that.'

'You do anything more?'

'Like, what do you mean?'

'Did you start following her around? Stalking her?'

Another shrug. 'I wouldn't call it that.'

313

'But you followed her?'

'I just wanted to talk to her, that's all. Because I think we had a good thing going on. She wouldn't answer my calls, so what was I supposed to do?'

'That your Mustang out front?' I asked.

'Yeah.'

'Your parents bought that for you?'

'Yeah, so?'

'What's your dad drive?'

'What the hell? Why are you asking?'

'Just tell me.'

'He's got a BMW. Him and my mom both got 'em.'

BMW didn't make a pickup truck. But I was betting Ravelson Furniture had one or two for deliveries. Roman could have borrowed one.

'Do you know why Dennis broke things off with Claire?'

'Man, I don't even think Claire knew the reason, from what I hear. My guess is, he was just a total douche.'

I nodded. 'Yeah, that would explain it. Roman, you know Claire, you went out with her. Where would she go? If she was scared, or just wanted to get away from everybody, where would she hide out? Aside from her mom's place in Toronto.'

He thought, then said, 'I got nuthin'.'

I got out of the computer chair. 'Good luck with your meeting with Steven.'

42

If Roman Ravelson weren't so unlikable, I might have felt bad mocking his ambitions. If I'd had a daughter and he'd sent her a photo of his erection, I'd have made him eat his phone. And I didn't think much of him sending Sean and Hanna all over Niagara and Erie counties selling booze out of the back of a truck. It exposed them to countless risks, legal and physical. If Roman wanted to make a buck selling booze to minors, fine. But he didn't need to be getting others on board.

I got into my Honda, thinking about Roman's zombie movie, about his character named Tim, out to save the world from an alien plot to —

Tim. Timmy.

The name hit me like cold, wet spray coming over the bow of the *Maid of the Mist*. The young man with the limp who came into Iggy's every night for a late dinner. The man who left the restaurant only seconds before Claire did.

Where was it Sal had said Timmy lived? It was the four-story apartment building just a stone's throw down the road.

Maybe Timmy had noticed something.

It was a long shot, to be sure. But not only had they left at almost exactly the same time — Timmy had struck off in the same direction the driver of the Volvo had taken.

I pulled away from the Ravelson house and headed back to Iggy's.

315

★ ★ ★

There was no mistaking the building. There was only one like it within spitting distance of Iggy's. Most everything along this stretch of Danbury was commercial. Fast-food joints, gas stations, strip malls, a Target on the other side of the street. The low-rise apartment complex stood alone as a place where anyone near here might actually live.

I tried to remember what Sal had told me. Timmy came in at the end of his working day, after his shift, wherever that shift happened to be. My guess was Timmy didn't have a car. If he did, he'd probably drive to Iggy's on his way home, not walk over. Which meant he worked very close to where he lived, or took a bus from work every night. Either way, it meant he probably finished work around nine, and most shifts were seven or eight hours.

It was twelve thirty p.m. My guess was if Timmy hadn't already left for work, he'd be coming out the lobby doors of that apartment building anytime now. I parked the car where I could watch. If he didn't show in the next fifteen or twenty minutes, I'd go into the lobby and see if I could find him, but I knew the directory wasn't going to be much help. Even if last names were attached to the buzzers on the intercom system, I didn't know Timmy's. If there was no super in the building, I was going to have to go knocking on doors. The building had at least forty units, and while I was wandering the halls, my man Timmy could be slipping out the front door.

I only had to wait ten minutes.

He hobbled down the building's front steps and headed straight for the sidewalk. When he reached it, he didn't turn left or right, but watched for a break in traffic. He didn't walk very quickly, so that break was going to have to be a long one. Across the street were a Target and several other stores clustered around it like pups nursing off their mother.

I got out of my car and ran over to him before he started his trek across.

'Timmy?'

The man turned and eyed me curiously. 'Huh?' he said.

'You're Timmy?'

He looked afraid to say yes, but after a second's hesitation, he said, 'Yeah, that's me.'

'My name's Weaver. I wonder if I could ask you a couple of questions?'

'What about? Who are you?'

I handed him a card. 'I'm a private investigator. I need to ask you about something that happened a couple of nights ago. What's your last name?'

Hesitantly, he said, 'Gursky. Timmy Gursky. Has this got something to do with work? Because I'm heading over there right now and I don't want to be late.'

He pointed. Not to Target, but to one of the other businesses. An electronics store, it looked like.

'The stereo place?' I asked.

'Yeah.'

'This isn't about work. And you're not in

317

trouble. But you might have been a witness to something I'm looking into. Two nights ago, when you were leaving Iggy's, there was a car pulling out of the lot, and I'm hoping you might have noticed it.'

'Noticed a car? You kidding?'

'I admit, I'm grasping at straws here.'

'How do you even know I was there? And which night you talking about?'

I told him, briefly, about reviewing the surveillance video at Iggy's, that I'd been trying to find a girl who got into a silver or gray Volvo station wagon, and that Sal said he ate there most nights, around that time.

'Sal, yeah, he's an okay guy,' Timmy said. 'Yeah, two nights ago. You know what? I actually do remember that car.'

'Seriously?'

'Son of a bitch nearly ran over my foot. Like I need any more trouble. My knee here got all fucked-up in Iraq.'

I wanted to ask about the car, but felt obliged to ask about his knee first.

He grinned. 'That's always a good line to use with the ladies, you know? I usually come up with a better story for them than what I'll tell you, which'll be the truth. I was working in what they called the Green Zone, you know? Inside the compound but not with the actual army or anything. They had, like, this whole city inside there, with everything all American. I worked for Pizza Hut. We had this trailer in there, soldiers could come up, get a slice just like they'd get back home. So I'm coming out of the trailer one day, miss the step, and come down right on my goddamn knee. Fucked it up big-time.'

'Sorry to hear that,' I said.

'Still hurts like a son of a bitch. You figure, you go over there, if you have to come back hurt, it better be because of some car bomb or missile or something, am I right? I had to hurt myself coming out of a pizza trailer. The ladies do *not* get that version.'

'You said the driver of the Volvo nearly ran over your foot.'

'Yeah,' he said indignantly. 'I noticed the car early on, because it was parked with the motor running, and the thing was really pumping out the exhaust, you know? It was an old car and the motor was noisy and really needed a tune-up. So anyway, I'm walking toward home, right here, across the lot, which is pretty empty that time of night, and I hear this noise coming from behind, to my right, and I look around, and there's the car you're talking about, zooming out of there. For a second, I thought they're trying to run me down, but I think the asshole behind the wheel, he just couldn't see me.'

'It was a man.'

'Yeah, I mean, I could tell that much. I didn't get a real good look at him, but yeah, it was a guy.'

'With a girl in the passenger seat.'

'I didn't get a look at her. I could tell someone was there, but I couldn't tell ya if was Britney Spears or Sarah Palin.'

'But you saw the driver.'

'Yep. Not much I can tell you about him, but I

think it was a black guy.'

'Okay. What about age?'

'I don't know. Not old, but other than that, I can't really say. Except he was an asshole. He came right up alongside me. I jumped back and gave him the finger. Then I went down.'

'You got hit?'

He shook his head. 'Just lost my balance. Didn't hurt myself. But I guess the driver must have been scared he'd hit me because he hit the brakes and stopped. I was getting up, so he must have seen me in his mirror, figured I wasn't dead, and then he floored it.'

'You get a look at the license plate?'

Timmy shook his head. 'You kidding? It was dark. I mean, I think it was a New York plate, but I couldn't tell you any more than that. Listen, you need anything else? I have to get to work.'

I said I didn't, and thanked him for his time.

My cell went off as I was putting on my seat belt.

'Hello?'

'Hey, finally.' It was a man, and in two words he'd managed to convey exasperation. 'Bill Hooper here.'

'Mr. Hooper,' I said. 'Thanks for getting back to me.'

'What can I do for you? I have to tell you, right up front, I'm not taking on any new jobs. I got all I can handle for now, I'm shorthanded, and it's the end of the season anyway. What I'd suggest is, try me in the spring, we might have some people move, cancel service, and we could put you on the list.'

'That's not why I was calling. I need to know about Dennis Mullavey.'

'Oh,' he said. 'Him.'

'Yeah. He worked for you?'

'I can't believe Dennis'd put me down for a reference. That takes balls. Guy walks out on me, doesn't give me any notice at all. I'd think long and hard about hiring him. I mean, he's a good worker and all, a good kid, but you gotta be ready for him to quit on ya just like that.'

'I don't exactly have his résumé in front of me. You have a number where I can reach him? An address? I gather he's not from Griffon.'

'Haven't got any of that on me,' Hopper said. 'I could get my girl to call you. I think he's from around Rochester. Came to work for me for the summer, even rented a room in my house. Look, he's a nice kid. I liked him, he did good work, was pretty reliable, right up until the end. And now that everybody is back to school, I can't get anyone else to work for me till the snow starts to fly. I only got one other guy. People say there's all this huge unemployment, but you think you can find someone willing to push a lawn mower or ride a tractor or swing a leaf blower around? I'm behind. I got some clients, I haven't been to their place in two weeks.'

'That's rough.'

I thought of the long grass at Phyllis Pearce's house. I asked, 'You do the Pearce place?'

'Yep, that's one. I'm way behind getting to her.'

'Why'd Dennis quit?'

'No idea. All he did was leave a note. 'Thanks

for the job, sorry about leaving' was all he had to say. I still owed him some money — even if a guy quits on me I'm not going to stiff him on what I owe him — but I don't think my girl's been able to get in touch with him. He just cleared out his room and he was gone.'

'This girl — is it the one I called initially?'

'Yeah, that'd be Barb. I'll give her a heads-up that you're going to call.'

'I appreciate it. One last question. Dennis have a car?'

'Yup,' Hopper said. 'But if he needs it for work, I don't know how reliable it is. He had it parked here all summer. I let him use one of my trucks off-hours, if I had one available. He always topped up the tank, I'll say that for him.'

'What kind of car?'

'Volvo. A wagon.'

'Thanks, Mr. Hopper. I'll give Barb a call shortly.'

'Okay,' he said, and hung up.

I sat there for a moment, thinking. If Dennis Mullavey had been maintaining the grounds at Phyllis Pearce's place, why didn't she have any idea who he was? Then again, she might have never known the name of the young man tending her property, or been at Patchett's when Hopper's crew came over to —

My thoughts were distracted by another phone call.

'Hello?'

'Mr. Weaver? It's Sheila Skilling.' Her voice was shaking. 'They arrested Sean, they think — '

'I know,' I told her. 'I'm sorry.'

322

'You have to help us,' she pleaded. 'You simply have to help us.'

I wasn't sure what I could do for the Skillings at the moment. Finding Claire was the priority. What Sean needed was a good lawyer. But I did have some questions for Sheila and Adam Skilling. For example, how much did they know about what Sean and Hanna were doing for Roman Ravelson? And there was one question I wanted to ask Adam Skilling privately.

Why was he on Iggy's surveillance video, standing at the counter, so soon after Claire and Hanna had switched identities?

43

The woman says to him, 'I'm going to ask you something, and I need you to be totally honest with me.'

He sits in the wheelchair, avoiding her eye. 'Of course,' he says.

'Did you write anything in the book other than the usual?'

'I . . . I told you, I can't find it. I need you to get me another empty one so I can start writing things down again.'

'I know you gave it to the boy. You admitted it the other night. What I want to know is what you wrote in it.'

'Like you said, just the usual. Nothing to worry about.'

'But you always wrote down the dates.'

The man says nothing.

She puts her fists on her hips. 'What the hell were you thinking? Can you tell me that?'

'I don't know.' He speaks so quietly she can barely hear him.

'If he gives that to someone, someone who remembers your little habits — I swear I don't know what gets into you.'

'I'm sorry. I'm really — '

She doesn't hear the rest. She steps out of the room, closes the door and slips the lock on. Her son is standing there, by the washer and dryer.

'He'll be the death of me,' his mother says.

324

'What are you doing here?'

'I think the detective might be getting close.'

His mother nods. 'I get the sense he doesn't give up easy.'

'But this is good,' the son says. 'I'm going to drop everything for a while. Indefinitely, I guess, while I see where he goes.'

'We need a contingency plan,' she says, and lowers her voice to a whisper. 'If the girl, and the kid, show up on their own, before Weaver finds them, we need to be ready. We need to be able to deny everything. We need to be able to show the kid up as a liar. We say we don't know what he's talking about.'

The son leans against the washing machine, folds his arms across his chest and shakes his head. 'You're talking about moving Dad?'

The woman hesitates. 'I guess you could say that.'

'Where would we move him? Where could he go where we could still look after him?'

His mother says nothing. Her silence speaks volumes.

'No, Mother. We can't do that.'

'I can't keep this up,' she says. 'I just can't.'

'Look, just let me see how this plays out with Weaver. If we're going to have to get rid of anybody, I'd rather it was him and the others, not Dad.'

'Of course,' she says. 'That goes without saying.'

'That Weaver guy, God, he's as big a pain in the ass as his kid was. At least everything worked out the way it should have with him.'

44

Driving over to the Skillings', imagining what they had to be going through with their son, I flashed back to when Scott was only six years old, years before our troubles began.

Around that time, he'd been having a lot of nightmares, and he was coming into our room in the middle of the night.

'I had a scary dream,' he'd say each time. Donna and I would allow him to crawl into the bed with us, but we worried we were establishing bad precedents, being too soft, that he'd be snuggling with us every night until he left for college.

But it was something we decided we would worry about later, and looking back now, I'm glad we let him slide in between us, pull the covers up to his neck, and drop his head into the chasm between our pillows.

One night, I was the one with the nightmare. It was a recurring one, one I still get every once in a while. In it, I'm slamming that drunk driver's head into the hood of the car. I've got a fistful of his hair, a good strong grip, and I'm banging his head again and again and again until it becomes apparent that it is no longer attached to his body. I realize what I've done and turn his dismembered head around so that I'm looking him right in the eye.

'I've learned my lesson,' he says, and grins.

'Have you learned yours?'

I always woke up in a cold sweat. This particular night, I did not wake Donna up tossing and turning or, as I sometimes did, screaming. I was afraid to try to go back to sleep for fear of seeing that head again, so I slipped out from under the covers and went down to the kitchen. I ran myself some water from the tap and sat there at the table, thinking about the mistakes I'd made, about how we'd ended up in Griffon.

I'd been sitting there maybe ten minutes when I realized I was being watched. Scott was standing in the doorway, and my heart did a flip. I tried not to show that he'd nearly scared me to death.

'What are you doing up?' I asked.

'I could see a light on,' he said.

'You shouldn't be wandering around the house at night.'

'What are you doing?' Scott asked.

'Just sittin' here.'

'Did you have a bad dream?'

I hesitated. 'As a matter of fact, I did.'

'What was it about?'

'I don't really want to talk about it.'

He nodded. 'Are you scared if you go back to bed it'll start again?'

'A little.'

He gave that some thought for a few seconds. Finally, he proposed a solution. 'You can come sleep with me.'

I had a sip of water, put the glass down. 'Okay,' I said.

He waited while I put my glass in the sink and turned out the light. He reached for my hand and led me to his room as though I didn't know how to get there.

His bed was a single. I lay on my side, my back up against the wall. Scott got in and tucked himself up against me.

'Don't snore,' he said. 'You snore a lot.'

'I'll try not to.'

He was back asleep in seconds. I felt his body swell and shrink with each breath. Anticipating his rhythms calmed me. Before long I was asleep, too, and at least for the rest of that one night, the bad dreams were absent.

★ ★ ★

Once again, I found myself sitting in the Skillings' living room. Adam and Sheila were settled in chairs across from me. I was on the couch. On the table between us was coffee, which Sheila must have started making the moment she'd hung up the phone with me. Steam rose as she poured some into a china cup.

'Cream? Sugar?' she asked, hovering. It was right there in front of me. As were some cookies. Sometimes, in times of extreme stress, you had to do something to keep yourself occupied. Make coffee. Bake cookies. Clean out a closet.

'For God's sake, he can spoon in his own sugar,' Adam Skilling snapped.

Sheila promptly sat down, put her hand over her mouth and pressed hard, as though trying to hold a scream inside.

328

'Mr. Weaver,' Adam said, 'our son, he can be a bit of an idiot at times, like all kids his age, but he didn't kill Hanna.'

'Tell me what's happened,' I said.

Shortly after I had left him, Sean called his parents from the bridge where we'd found Hanna's body, and they immediately drove over. Ramsey and Quinn — the Skillings had made a note of the names on their badges — were still attempting to question him, but it seems he'd taken my advice and was keeping his mouth shut.

About six hours later, as the Skillings were getting up for the day — not that anyone had gotten any sleep — Sheila noticed the police were outside, poking around Sean's Ranger. They had the doors open, and were searching inside.

'Were these the same police who'd been interviewing Sean the night before?'

Sheila had managed to tamp down that scream hiding in her throat, removed her hand from her mouth, and said, 'They were different. Two men, instead of a man and a woman.'

'Did you get their names?'

'One was . . . ' She paused. 'One was named Haines and — '

Adam interjected. 'Brindle, that was the other one.'

'How'd they get into the truck?' I asked.

'Sean must have left it unlocked,' Adam said. 'When you were here, and we ordered him home, he ran into the house so fast he probably didn't think to lock it.'

'So it had been sitting unlocked all night?' I asked.

The two of them glanced at each other, then looked at me and nodded. 'Probably,' Adam said.

'So you saw them out there. Then what happened?'

Sheila said, 'I ran into Sean's room to tell him. He was in bed, but he wasn't sleeping. He ran out — he was only in his boxers — and I ran after him, in my housecoat. Adam was already outside — he's dressed and ready for the day before the rest of us.'

He said, 'I asked them what the hell they were doing, that they needed a warrant to search a car, and the older one, Brindle, he looked at me and laughed. Then Sean ran out and started yelling at them, too, that they had no right to look in his truck. Brindle, he got in front of Sean so he couldn't stop Haines from looking in the glove box and under the seats.'

Adam swore under his breath before continuing. 'That son of a bitch Brindle actually pushed Sean away. He laid his hands on him. I think we should be able to get him charged with assault. I've talked to my lawyer about it, that we should go after this guy. I can't believe this kind of treatment. I've always had a good working relationship with the Griffon police. They get all their cars from me. We've got service people over there all the time helping them out whenever they have a problem. How dare one of their people treat Sean like that.'

I shook my head. 'You have bigger things to worry about.'

Sheila said, 'We just stood there, while they took the car apart, feeling so helpless. We didn't know what to do.'

'I called my regular lawyer first,' Adam Skilling said. 'Right then and there. Got him out of bed. But he doesn't handle criminal stuff, so he gave me the name — '

'Our son is not a *criminal*,' Sheila said.

'Christ, I know that,' he said. 'But you don't want a lawyer who normally handles real estate representing your kid on a murder charge.'

At the word 'murder,' Sheila put her hand over her mouth again.

'Tell me about what they found,' I said.

Adam said, 'The younger one, Haines, he says something like, 'What have we got here?' He's digging around under the passenger seat, and he pulls out this bundle of stuff, which turns out to be a pair of jeans and a pair of . . . you know . . . panties.'

Sheila winced.

Adam continued. 'I thought I was going to throw up. I couldn't believe what I was seeing. We'd found out, when we were waiting for the police to be finished with Sean, that the girl, Hanna, that she wasn't wearing anything from, you know, from here down.' He touched his own belt.

'What'd Sean do?'

'He was stunned. When he realized what Haines was holding up, he started screaming at him, that there was no 'effing' way he put those clothes there, that it was impossible. He accused the police of putting it there.'

331

If Sean Skilling was Hanna's killer, we had to accept that he was stupid enough to keep the girl's clothing under the front seat of his truck for an entire day. If he were a murderer, and wanted to keep a souvenir of his crime, wouldn't he have found a better place to hide it than his truck? Wouldn't he at least have locked it? And did it make sense, if Sean had already been having sex with Hanna for some time, that he'd feel the need to keep a small trophy from the event?

I asked, 'Is Sean the only one who drives the Ranger?'

Sheila said, 'I use it occasionally. So does Adam. But mostly, it's Sean's car.'

'What I'm thinking is, if your son had done this, and had hidden those clothes in the truck, he'd have been running the risk that either of you might find them. I don't think Sean's that dumb.'

Adam nodded. 'He isn't. Kids are pretty good at covering their tracks when they're up to something they don't want their parents to find out about.' He grimaced. 'And Sean's as good as any of them.'

'So what happened then?'

Adam said. 'Brindle put the clothes into some kind of evidence bag.' A long pause, like he was afraid he might break down before he continued. 'And then they arrested our boy.'

'They put *handcuffs* on him,' Sheila said. 'They didn't have to do that. What did they think he was going to do? Attack them or something?'

Adam sighed. 'Like Sheila said, they cuffed

him and put him in their car and they took him away. We got to see him later. He's a complete wreck.'

'You have to get him out of jail,' his wife said. 'Anything could happen to him in jail.'

'And that was when they left?' I asked. 'They searched the truck, arrested Sean, and left?'

They both nodded. Sheila sniffed.

'The police didn't search anything else?'

'Like what?' Adam asked.

'Did they search Sean's room? Look in his closet? Seize his computer? Did they search the garage? Anything else?'

Adam shook his head. 'No, just the truck.'

Haines and Brindle had found what they'd wanted to find, and they'd found it remarkably fast. Was the search of the truck part of their overall investigation, and they got lucky? Had they been tipped off that the evidence was there? Was Sean's accusation, that the evidence had been planted, plausible? And if so, who'd done it? The police themselves?

I was finding it hard to keep all the various aspects of this case straight.

'I want to ask you a few questions, which may or may not be related to all of this,' I said.

Sean's parents looked like they were waiting for X-ray results.

'Did you know that Sean and Hanna were making money delivering beer and liquor to underage kids?'

'What?' Sheila said. 'That's not true — that's positively ridiculous.'

'It's true. Roman Ravelson was able to buy the

stuff legally, and then he'd have Sean drive all over the place doing deliveries. There was a markup on the booze, and Sean and Hanna would keep a cut.'

Sheila shook her head violently. 'No, I don't believe that.'

Adam Skilling hadn't said a word.

'Even if this were true, why's it important?' Sean's mother asked.

'Everything's important right now,' I said. 'Driving all over the place, making cash deals with people, there's plenty of opportunities for trouble. People feel they're getting ripped off, shortchanged. Cash transactions. Maybe someone Sean and Hanna dealt with had some sort of grudge against them. I don't know. I just need to know everything I can.'

'So you can help Sean,' Adam Skilling said. 'So you can prove he's innocent.'

I hesitated. 'I want to see that Sean gets all the help he can, but I'm not working on his behalf, or yours, at this time. I'm working to find Claire Sanders. And when I do, that may end up helping Sean, because Claire may be able to fill in the gaps. What you need is a good lawyer.'

'We have one,' Adam said. 'We've hired Theodore Belton.'

I knew Teddy Belton. 'He's a good man. You're in good hands with him.' I stood. 'I'll be in touch. If you hear anything, about Claire, or anything else, please let me know. And if I hear something that could help Sean, I'll call you right away.'

Then I spoke to Adam. 'Can I see you outside?'

334

I squeezed Sheila Skilling's hand as I moved toward the door, Adam following. Once we were both out of the house, standing in the driveway, I said, 'I noticed you had nothing to say when I mentioned what Sean's been up to.'

'I admit, I had an inkling,' he said. 'I found a couple cases of beer in the bed of his pickup one day, under the cover, and confronted him about it. He said he was just holding it for that Ravelson kid, that he'd bought some beer but had no way, at the time, to get it home, so Sean said he'd take it over later.'

'You didn't believe him.'

He pressed his lips together. 'No. I don't mean to say anything bad about that poor girl — God rest her soul — but I blame Hanna. That girl was a bad influence. She liked money and didn't mind bending the rules to get it.'

'Sean could have said no.'

He gave me a withering look. 'Can you remember being that age? What would you have done to keep a cute girl like that happy?'

The garage door was halfway open, and I could make out a vehicle in there, a pickup truck. I was surprised the police hadn't seized it, just as they'd seized my car. There seemed to be plenty more reasons to have taken Sean's Ranger in, given that they'd found Hanna's clothes in it.

I said, 'They didn't take Sean's truck?'

'Huh?' Adam said, and saw where I was looking. 'That's not Sean's. That's my vehicle.'

I squinted. Upon closer examination, I could see it was dark gray, not black like Sean's. And it was a bigger truck than the Ranger. An F-150.

'It's not exactly mine,' Adam clarified. 'Just one I borrowed from the lot for a couple of days. I have a different car every week.'

'Two nights ago,' I said slowly, drawing out the words, 'what were you doing?'

'I don't recall,' he said. 'Probably home, with Sheila.'

'You weren't out driving around anywhere?'

He appeared to be thinking. 'I might have been, actually.'

'You weren't following Sean and Hanna around, were you?'

Adam blustered. 'Of course not. Why would you ask such a thing?'

'Because you were at Iggy's. You were there not long after Claire came in, and Hanna came out and got in my car.'

I caught him speechless. He needed a few seconds. 'How — who told you that?'

'You're on Iggy's closed-circuit. I've seen it. What were you doing there? Seems kind of a funny time to leave the house to go grab a burger.'

'I didn't get — I only ordered a coffee,' he protested.

'I don't give a damn what you had. I want to know why you were there.'

'Okay,' Adam Skilling said resignedly. 'I'd been driving around. I'd been hoping I might spot Sean, see his truck. I haven't had a good feeling lately about what he might be up to, so I left the house around nine thirty and started going by places where I know he hangs out sometimes. I never did find him, never saw him anywhere. So as I was heading home, I pulled into Iggy's for a take-out coffee. Simple as that.'

'Simple as that,' I repeated.

'What, you think — what *do* you think?'

'I think it's funny you never mentioned this before. That you were driving around Griffon, looking for your son, while all these other things were going on.'

'There wasn't anything to mention. The thing is, I didn't want to worry Sheila about what Sean might be doing, so I told her I was going to the dealership to do some paperwork. That's all.'

'When Hanna stayed over at your house, that bothered you,' I said. 'You mentioned that before. You didn't like her parading around in her underwear.'

His cheeks flushed. 'It wasn't — I never said 'parading.' I just didn't think it was proper, what was going on. That's all. Are you trying to make something out of this, Mr. Weaver? I thought you were trying to help us. I thought you were on our side.'

'I'm on Hanna's side,' I said. 'And Claire's. I don't think I know yet who else's to be on.'

45

Shortly after leaving the Skillings' house, I pulled into Iggy's parking lot. I wasn't here to ask any more questions. I had a call to make, and possibly some notes, and didn't want to do it sitting in the car.

And I was hungry.

As I headed in, I walked past two parked motorcycles that at a glance looked like the ones that belonged to the two bikers who'd been rousted by Quinn and Ramsey that night in front of Patchett's after Roman had bonked me on the head.

Once I was inside, I spotted them sitting next to the window, chowing down on burgers, fries, and onion rings. They each had a soda in a cup that looked bigger than the gas tanks on their bikes. They both looked to be in their forties, short hair — not the kind of long locks one might expect on some Hell's Angels wannabes — and both carried about forty pounds more than they should have.

At the counter, I ordered a chicken sandwich and a Coke, then took a table where I could see them, and their bikes outside. I got out my notebook and wrote down their license plates. I took a bite of my sandwich, got out my cell, and put in a call to Barb at Hooper's office.

'Oh yeah, hi,' she said. 'I've been waitin' for your call. You need some info on Dennis?'

'Dennis Mullavey, that's right.'

'Okay, hang on, I just had it on my desk here, and then — here it is. So are you hiring him or something? I've got his birth date here . . . September 17, 1995. I don't know if I can give you his Social Security number — '

'Mainly I'm just looking for a way to get in touch with him.'

'Okay, I've got a cell number.' I scribbled it down as she read it off. 'And his address . . . okay, it's sort of Rochester, but it's actually northeast, a dot on the map called Hilton.' She gave me a mailing address and a home number.

'This Hilton address, that's his parents' place?' I asked.

'His dad,' Barb said. 'Far as I know, anyway. I think he said his mother died years ago, and he lives with his dad, or did when he wasn't working for us. But I don't know if it's going to do you any good.'

'What do you mean?'

'I mean, if you are trying to get hold of him for a job, good luck. We've still got one last paycheck for him, and I was going to send it to his dad's address, but I called him first to make sure, and he said he doesn't know where Dennis is. And when we call his cell, it just goes to message.'

'Doesn't he have a girlfriend in Griffon? Maybe she'd know where I could find him.'

'You talkin' about Claire?' Barb asked.

'I think that was her name.'

'Claire Sanders. That's the mayor's kid, you know. I don't have a number for her, but of course he would. Just call the town hall. He's pretty approachable. Dennis, he was crazy about that girl — at least he seemed to be just before he bailed on us.'

'Thanks for all this,' I said.

'No problem. Look, if you see him, tell him Barb said hi. I still like the kid, even if the boss would like to wring his neck for taking off so quick.'

'Will do,' I said. I ended the call and put the phone down on the table.

Took a bite of my sandwich.

Watched the two bikers continue to eat their lunch.

I tried the cell phone number Barb had given me for Dennis. It went straight to message.

I decided not to leave one.

I watched the bikers some more.

When the Griffon police abused their authority by running people out of town, it didn't mean those people were total innocents. Maybe these bikers were trouble. Maybe they'd ridden up to Griffon to make a few sales.

I hadn't shown much fear when it came to questioning Scott's contemporaries. I'd always figured he'd gotten the ecstasy from one of his friends, but I supposed it was possible he'd gotten it from a couple of guys like these. Maybe Scott had been to Patchett's one night and bought something off one or the other of them, although Phyllis Pearce had suggested kids like Scott who really looked too young were given the boot. Which explained why Scott preferred house parties and rooftops for getting drunk and high.

These two bikers were certainly more formidable-looking than the young guys I'd been putting the fear of God into.

The young men I'd bullied and terrorized.

But these bikers, for all I knew, could be armed.

'Hey, Mr. Weaver?'

It was Sal, the manager who'd been here the night I looked at the surveillance video. He was standing by my table, looking down and smiling.

'Hey, Sal,' I said. 'I thought you worked nights.'

'I'm filling in for the day guy who's sick.'

'Hope it's nothing he ate,' I said.

Sal gave me a reproachful look. 'Don't even joke.'

'Sorry,' I said. 'You got a minute?' When he nodded, I waved my hand, inviting him to take the seat opposite me.

'I hope you got what you needed the other night,' he said. 'You were looking for someone?'

'Yeah. That's kind of ongoing. I don't want you to look around, but there are two biker types sitting over that way.'

Sal turned his head anyway. 'Oh, sorry. I just couldn't help it. I'm not used to your line of work.'

'Those two come in often?'

He shrugged. 'I've seen them before. Sometimes at night. Maybe once a week.'

'Whaddya know about them?'

'I don't know that much. They just like riding around on their hogs.'

'They ever do any business here? Maybe not

341

right here in the restaurant, but out in the parking lot?'

His eyes narrowed. 'What kind of business? You talking drugs?'

I nodded.

He grinned. 'Next time you're at your computer, Google 'Pilkens, Gilmore' and 'state lottery.' Oh, and add the word 'gay' in there. You'll probably find a story about them.'

'If you know what I'll find, save me the trouble. I'll buy a milk shake.'

'They're one of those same-sex couples. They won the state lottery couple of years back, quit their jobs, bought some bikes, and they just wander around all the time. First time they came in, I recognized them from seeing them on the news.'

'So they're not dealing?'

He chuckled. 'If you had, like, six million dollars in the bank, would you risk all that selling dope to kids in Griffon?'

★ ★ ★

I called up the map app on my phone and found Hilton. I figured I could drive there in about an hour and a half. Normally, going to the Rochester area, I'd head south and pick up I-90 and take it east. But Hilton was on the north side of Rochester, and it looked as though I'd make just as good time going northeast and taking Lake Road, which would turn into the Roosevelt Highway, and finally the Lake Ontario State Parkway. Slower roads, more stops, but a more scenic route, to be sure.

I called Donna.

'I'm heading Rochester way. Not sure when I'll be home.'

'Okay.'

Donna often didn't ask where I was going. She knew my work could take me almost anywhere unexpectedly.

I didn't say anything for a couple of seconds.

'Cal?' she said. 'You there?'

'We should go away,' I said.

'What?'

'We should take a trip.'

'Take a trip where?'

'I don't know. Where would you like to go?'

'I — I have no idea,' she said.

'What about Spain?'

She half laughed. 'Why would you say Spain?'

'It was the first place I thought of. We could do Australia.'

'Just because we go to the other side of the world doesn't mean everything will be okay,' Donna said.

'You said something when we had our midnight breakfast,' I said. 'You said we'll never be happy again.'

'Cal, I'm sorry. I — '

'No, wait. You said we'll never be happy again, but maybe we could be happier.' I felt a lump forming in my throat. 'I want to be happier. I would settle for that for now.'

Now the silence came from the other end of the line. I waited a few seconds before saying her name.

'I'm here,' she said. Another pause, then, 'San Francisco.'

'What?'

'I'd like to ride on a cable car. I want to stand on the side, holding on. That's what I want to do.'

'Then that's what we'll do.'

'When?'

I thought. 'I think — and I could be wrong — but I think I'm getting somewhere, trying to find Claire. When this is wrapped up, we'll do it. If you can get the time off.'

'I can get the time off,' Donna said.

'You can start looking up hotels and stuff when you get off,' I said.

'Okay.'

'Maybe one of those small boutique hotels.'

'Okay.'

Each time she said the word, she sounded more sad.

She said, 'I won't be able to not think of him.'

'I know. Neither will I.'

'I *want* to think about him. I just don't want to think about him . . . '

Falling.

I could never stop thinking about Scott falling.

46

Driving north out of Griffon, I thought I saw the car again in my rearview mirror. That silver Hyundai with the tinted windows. But once I got out of the downtown area, and the buildings began to thin, the car took a hard right and disappeared.

It took me a full two hours to find Dennis Mullavey's house in the village of Hilton. There were still some signs up, coming into the village, advertising the annual apple festival a couple of weeks back.

There was a cool breeze coming in off Lake Ontario as I mounted the steps of the one-story red-brick house. There was a rusted green Ford Explorer from the last century in the driveway. I rang the bell and waited. Seconds later, a tall, very thin black man in neatly creased white khakis and a red pullover Gap shirt opened the door. His short hair was gray, and a pair of reading glasses were perched on his nose. I put his age at late sixties, early seventies. Retired, no doubt, given that he was home in the middle of the afternoon.

'Yep?' he said.

'Mr. Mullavey?'

'That's right,' he said. 'Doug Mullavey.'

'My name is Cal Weaver.' I got out my license, held it in front of him, gave him enough time to get a good look at it.

'You're a private eye?' he said.

'I am.'

'What brings a fella like you to my door?'

'I was hoping to have a word with your son, Dennis.'

'Dennis isn't here,' he said.

'When might you be expecting him?'

The man shrugged. 'He doesn't live here.'

'Would you have an address for him?'

'Nope.'

I smiled. 'If you wanted to get in touch with him, how would you go about that?'

'I guess I'd call his cell.'

'His cell doesn't answer. That's been my experience, and it's also been the experience of his former employer.'

'Maybe he's in a place where you can't get a good signal,' Doug Mullavey said.

I leaned into the railing that ran down the side of the steps. 'Can we speak plainly, Mr. Mullavey?'

'I wouldn't have it any other way,' he said.

'I'm trying to find Claire Sanders. A girl from Griffon. Her father's the mayor there. Your son was going out with her, might still be, for all I know. Claire's disappeared, and I'm hoping your son might have information that would lead me to her. It's even possible they're together.'

'I wish I could help you.'

'The thing is, Mr. Mullavey, Claire went to some lengths to slip away without anyone following her. She had help from a girl named Hanna Rodomski, and that girl's now dead.'

That caught his attention. 'What happened to her?'

'She was murdered. Around the same time that Claire vanished. I think Claire took off with Dennis. She got into an old Volvo station wagon, driven by someone matching your son's description. Does your son have a car like that?'

'I'm not sure what kind of — '

'Mr. Mullavey, please. You and I both know no son gets a car without his father's input and guidance. So you've as much as admitted that's your son's car. I don't have any reason to believe Claire or your son had anything to do with that girl's death, but I'm willing to bet one or both of them know something that could have some bearing on it. And if Hanna Rodomksi's murder is tied in to Claire's disappearance, it may very well mean that Claire's in danger. If Claire's in danger, and your son is with her, then your son is also — '

'I really don't think — '

I talked over him. 'Is *also* at risk. So if you have any idea where your son is, you'd be well advised to tell me.'

Doug Mullavey, lips together, ran his tongue over his teeth. His lips parted and he said, 'That's horrible about that girl. Just horrible.'

'Help me,' I said quietly.

He opened his mouth and said, 'I don't know you, Mr. Weaver. I don't know who you are. I don't know anything about you. I don't know whose interests you really represent. I don't know, if I asked you who you're working for, that you'd give me an honest answer. So I'm afraid that I don't have anything to say to you.'

I bowed my head wearily, then looked the man

347

in the eye. 'I don't mean your son any harm. I'm trying to keep him, and Claire, out of trouble. What is it you're afraid of? What is it your son is hiding from?'

'I'm afraid these are questions I can't answer. Maybe, in time, you'll be someone I come to trust.'

'Others might come with the same questions,' I told him.

'You think you're the first?' he said, and came close to a smile.

'Who else has been here?'

'You think if I wouldn't talk to the police, I'm going to talk to you?'

'The police have been here?' I asked. 'Which police? State? Griffon?'

He waved his hand like he didn't give a damn. 'Someone came around looking for Dennis. Said he'd done some things I know aren't true, that he stole from people's houses when he was cutting their lawns and they were away. That's bullshit. I sent him on his way.'

'It must have been a Griffon cop,' I said. 'Did you get a name? When was this?'

Mullavey ran a hand over the crown of his head. 'You know, I used to work for Kodak. Retired ten years ago. My wife, Denny's mom, passed away two weeks after I stopped working.'

He looked off in the direction of Lake Ontario, although we couldn't see it from here. 'I'm glad I wasn't there at Kodak for the end, when it ceased to be, what with people no longer needing film. There's a phrase I used to say there — maybe it wouldn't be so applicable these days,

348

what with everything being digital and all, but whenever someone asked me what was going to happen next, I used to say, 'I guess we'll see what develops.' I guess we'll see what develops, Mr. Weaver, but in the meantime, I have nothing to say to you.'

'I'm not the enemy,' I said.

'Would the enemy say he was?' Doug Mullavey shot back.

'No,' I said. 'He wouldn't.' I handed him one of my business cards and to my surprise, he accepted it. He called out to me as I walked back to the car. 'Mr. Weaver?'

I turned. 'Yes?'

'Dennis is a good kid.'

'I hope he's more than that,' I said. 'I hope he's smart. Because it looks like he's not just responsible for his own safety. He's responsible for Claire Sanders', too. I hope I don't have to come back here and tell you something happened to her, or to your son, and that you could have told me something that would have prevented it.'

I continued on my way and didn't look back.

★ ★ ★

On the drive back to Griffon, Donna called to say she'd be home late, probably around nine. If we were really going to try to go away, there was a lot of work she had to get ahead on. She figured she'd stay late today, a Friday, and Monday so that whoever had to do her job in her absence wouldn't make a complete mess of it. I suggested that when she got home, we order a pizza.

349

No argument.

I told her I probably wouldn't make it home much before she did, and that turned out to be true. When I pulled into the driveway at six forty-five, her car wasn't there. It was dusk, and the streetlights had come on. I felt I'd done about as much as I could today. I was running on empty. I would make a few calls from home tonight, see if I could find out anything about Dennis Mullavey online. Maybe I could track down a Facebook page for him, find out who some of his friends were. If I got lucky, some of them might be right here in Griffon. If I had the energy later in the evening, I'd go looking for them.

A lot of maybes. Everything depended on my being able to stay awake once I went through the front door. I felt a face-plant on the couch coming on.

And then it occurred to me I really owed Bert Sanders a call. If I were him, I'd be waiting by the phone, hoping to hear something, anything. That would be the first thing I'd do.

No. The second. The first thing I was going to do was get a beer from the fridge.

I put the car in park, took out the key, and sat there for the better part of ten seconds.

Decompressing.

Finally, I opened the door, got out.

Behind me, someone said, 'Mr. Weaver?'

I turned around, saw the baseball bat a millisecond before it connected, catching me at the back of the neck, just below my skull.

Then things got really bad.

47

I didn't black out completely. I was pretty fuzzy
at first, no doubt about it. But I could hear
things, like when you're having an afternoon nap
on the couch but are still distantly aware of
things going on in the house around you.

I heard someone say, 'Fucker!'

A second voice said, 'Got him good.'

Male voices.

After I hit the driveway, I slapped my palms
onto the asphalt and woozily tried to push myself
up, but a sharp kick to my side hindered my
efforts, knocking the wind out of me. I dropped
and rolled over onto my side. I could hear pitiful
moaning.

That was me.

I opened my eyes, saw them looking down on
me like a couple of skyscrapers. Hard to judge
how tall they were from my vantage point. They
could have been five one and still looked like
giants. Stocky builds, thick arms. Their faces
remained a mystery. They wore ski masks, so all I
could see was their eyes and mouths. One wore a
red mask, with knitted snowflakes on it, while
the other had pulled a solid blue one down over
his face.

Red Mask said, 'How do *you* like it, huh? You
like that?'

Blue Mask said, 'You better check and see if
he's got a gun on him.'

Red Mask said, 'Shit, yeah, okay.'

He dropped to his knees, patted me down. 'Nothing,' he said.

Just as well I'd decided not to carry the Glock today. I stood a chance of surviving a beating, but a shot to the head was a lot harder to recover from. I made an unsuccessful attempt to punch Red in the face, but he deflected the blow. Then I went for his mask, trying to slip my fingers under the bottom edge. Stubble under his chin rubbed against my fingers like sandpaper.

'Fuck off!' he said, ripping my arm away and hitting me backhanded on the cheek.

'Sit on him,' said Blue. 'Hold him down.'

I was straddled. He grabbed my wrists and with his weight pinned them to the pavement. Then I heard the unmistakable sound of duct tape being torn off a roll. Next thing I felt was tape being wound around my ankles, binding my legs together.

'Hold him!'

'I've got him. Work fast before someone comes.'

Blue moved up by my head. While his partner crossed my wrists, Blue taped them together. He wound the tape around half a dozen times, did a pretty good job of it. What he hadn't thought of was, when I brought my arms down, my wrists would be in front of me. That was a lot better than having them bound behind my back. He tore off a couple more strips and slapped them over my mouth.

'Okay, asshole, stand up.'

They had to help me to my feet, then bent me

over the hood of my car so I all I could see was metal. Blue held me there while Red ran off. Seconds later, I heard a car start up, then the whining noise of a car backing up speedily. I managed to turn my head enough to see the car back in right behind me. I couldn't see what make it was. A trunk popped open.

Red jumped out of the car and with Blue's help they hauled me off the hood and turned me around. Suddenly, I raised my arms in front of me, wrists still crossed, and attempted to bat Blue across the head. Got him, too, but not hard enough to hurt him. That was when he got the roll of tape again, making several turns around me at waist height, pinning my arms down.

Shit.

They shuffled me over to the back of their car, the trunk yawning open to receive me.

'Yeah, see how you like it,' Blue said. The two of them loaded me in. I lay on my side, looking up.

'The fun's just beginning,' said Red.

And then everything went dark.

★ ★ ★

I heard some muffled chatter through the trunk lid, then both doors opening and closing. We shot out of the driveway like a sprinter coming out of the blocks. I was tossed around, hit my head.

The car accelerated, made several turns, and within five minutes we were traveling steadily at what I guessed to be sixty or more miles per hour. We were on a highway. Most likely the Robert Moses, but heading where, I could only guess at this point.

The dumb-asses had searched me for a gun, but they hadn't grabbed my phone, which told me I wasn't exactly dealing with professionals. Although I had to concede they'd been smart enough to get the drop on me.

My cell was still tucked way down in my inside jacket pocket, but it was of little use to me now. I couldn't get at it, and even if it somehow slipped out and landed on the floor of the trunk, I was going to have a hard time manipulating it.

Most cars made in the last few years are equipped with an escape latch in the trunk that can be pulled from the inside. I'm not sure the manufacturers were thinking primarily of kidnap victims. They just wanted kids who'd accidentally locked themselves in a trunk to be able to get out before they suffocated.

I didn't know how recent this car was or whether it had such a latch. And even if it did, I didn't know where it was located. If I could untie myself, I could start patting around trying to find it. I couldn't exactly roll out while the car was moving, but someone traveling behind us might see the trunk pop up, spot me in here, and call the cops. Failing that, maybe I could get myself into position, wait until the car stopped and they opened the trunk, and see if I could drive my heels into the face of one of these sons of bitches.

The tires hummed on the pavement below me, the noise much more audible than if I'd been behind the wheel. There was a rhythmic *thunk* as we drove over pavement seams. But then the sound changed, became more hollow. We were crossing a bridge.

Then we were back on solid pavement.

I didn't know where we were going, but I had an inkling. I also had an idea who my two kidnappers were.

They were my chickens coming home to roost.

The car slowed, turned, sped up, turned again. We were off the highway, and had been traveling for about twenty minutes.

My cell rang. I felt it vibrating against my chest. There wasn't a damn thing I could do about it. I wondered if the phone's ring could be heard inside the car, whether it would prompt them to pull over, pop the trunk, and take it away from me. But I could detect a lot of muffled chatting in the two front seats, and when they didn't pull over, I figured they hadn't heard it.

I was still struggling with the tape, and while I felt like I was making headway, I wasn't making it fast enough. If I could free my wrists first, I could remove the rest of the tape in seconds. If I could break the tape wrapped around me, I could get my hands to my mouth, peel off that tape, and bite my way through the tape that held my wrists.

The car slowed. We were on gravel now, rubber crunching on stone.

I continued to shift and flex my arms. My body was soaked with sweat. Some of it had run into my eyes and stung like hell.

The car stopped and the engine died. The two

doors opened and slammed shut.

'This place is good,' one said.

'I like it.'

'Put your mask back on.'

'Oh yeah.'

Although the engine was now off, I could hear something. A dull kind of roar. Not traffic on a nearby highway. Something else. Something not far away.

I made one last effort to break the tape wrapped around my body.

No joy.

The trunk popped open. A hand slipped under the edge to swing it wide. Red and Blue stood there, looking in on me.

'He's almost got loose,' Blue said.

'I'll get the roll.'

He was gone ten seconds. When he returned, the two of them swung my legs out over the bumper, then sat me up, my butt still parked on the trunk floor. Red ran more tape around my body, then added more to my wrists.

Once that was done, they hauled me out of the trunk and stood me up. We were in a wooded area, maybe a park. I blinked a couple of times, having spent the better part of half an hour in the pitch-dark trunk.

I recognized where we were. I had been here a couple of nights ago. It all made sense now. I knew what that roar in the background was.

Water.

Millions upon millions of gallons of it. Moving very, very quickly.

A river. The Niagara River. Just a short

distance upstream from the falls.

'You're going to have to hop,' Blue Mask said. 'Either that, or we're going to have to drag you to the railing.'

'Let's just drag him,' Red Mask said. 'Hopping's going to take for-fucking-ever.'

And that's exactly what they decided to do. They each grabbed me under an arm, and hauled me toward the river.

48

'I've been thinking,' the woman says, having unlocked the door and entered the man's room.

'About what?' he says groggily. He is on the bed, covers pulled back, an open magazine on his chest. He'd fallen asleep reading. He sleeps more and more these days.

'Maybe it would be a good thing for you to get some fresh air.'

He looks at her warily. 'Are you serious?'

'Of course. You've been cooped up in here so long.'

'I don't even — I don't even know how long it is anymore.'

'The time does kind of fly by,' the woman says. 'It seems like only yesterday.'

'I'd love to sit on the porch. Could I sit on the porch?'

'Oh, I was thinking of something much better than that. I was thinking that we could go for a drive. Not just you and me, but all three of us.'

He sits up, swings his legs over the side of the bed. 'Where would we go?'

'Where would you like to go?'

'I . . . I don't even know. Just getting out of the house, that'd be so wonderful. Just to go for a drive and — you know what I'd love to do?'

'What?'

'I'd love to go for an ice cream.' He frowns.

'But I guess we can't go any place where I'll be seen.'

'I don't know that we need to worry about that. If you could get some ice cream, what kind would you get?'

The man thinks. 'I guess chocolate. I'd get chocolate.'

'You could have more than one flavor, you know. You could get a big bowl of it. You could have two or three kinds.'

He looks like a child who's been promised a trip to Santa's Village. 'What other flavors are there?'

She laughs. 'Where to begin? There are so many. Jamoca Almond Fudge. Strawberry. Heavenly Hash. They have ice creams with crumbled-up candy bar in them.'

'They do?'

'Cookies, too.'

He shakes his head, like it's all too much. 'Chocolate. That's all I want. If I can have three scoops, I'd want them all to be chocolate.'

'It's settled then,' she says.

'When is this going to happen?' he asks.

'Soon. Very soon. There are just a couple of things to work out.'

The man smiles. It takes a lot out of him. The muscles that are employed to make a person smile have not been used by the man in some time.

'You've made my day. That's great news.' He puts his hands together. 'I can almost taste the ice cream on my tongue.'

'You just keep thinking about that,' the woman says as she retreats from the room and relocks the door.

359

49

I put up as much fight as I could.

I writhed and twisted and kicked and made a general pain in the ass of myself. Trouble was, even if I could break free, they still had my ankles bound. I wasn't going to be able to make a run for it. Best I could hope to do was delay the inevitable.

At one point Red lost his grip on me and I tumbled to one side. Blue couldn't hold me alone, and I hit the dirt path.

'Dickwad,' Blue said. I wasn't sure whether he was addressing me or his partner.

I looked back where the car was parked. A red Civic. I was expecting a silver Hyundai, thinking that whoever'd been following me around had to be these two.

They got their hands under my arms again and dragged. I could see where I'd been, but not where I was going. I forced my heels down into the dirt, trying to create more resistance.

The roar of the water grew louder.

Then they stopped, hoisted me up, spun me around, and pushed.

Jesus.

They scared the living shit out of me. They threw me right up against the railing, bars pressing into my knees and chest. Below, and ahead of me, the rushing waters of the Niagara River.

The sound was nearly deafening.

They both got behind me, pinning me to the railing. Red put his mouth to my ear and said, 'Pretty fucking scary, isn't it?'

I nodded.

Then it was Blue's turn. I could feel his breath on the side of my face. 'You know what someone once told me?'

I waited.

'Some asshole once told me that unless you're going over in a barrel — and even then your chances aren't good — you're pretty much fucked. You might try to grab onto a rock before you get to the edge, but you'd hit it so hard, it'd probably kill you anyway.'

He said to Red. 'Whaddya think?'

'I guess now is as good a time as any.'

Together, they knelt down, grabbed me around the knees, and lifted.

I made a hell of a noise of protest behind the tape. I forced my hands, bound together in front of me, up slightly, just enough to catch under the uppermost railing.

'Let go!' one of them shouted at me.

I hugged the railing as hard as I could. They dropped me a few inches and tried to hoist me up again, but I managed to do the same thing again.

The water sounded like a low-flying 747.

'Fuck!' Red said.

They put my feet back on the ground. 'Turn him around,' Blue said. 'We'll send him over on his back.'

But this time, as they bent down, I pitched

myself forward. I hit the ground and rolled.

'Goddamn it!'

They came at me from either side, corralled me, and hauled me back up onto my feet one more time.

'Okay,' said Blue. 'This time we just keep hanging on to his arms and lift him over.'

'Asshole.'

Seconds later, we were at the railing again, my back pressed against it. But because the railing came up to our chests, they couldn't get any leverage with their hands positioned so high on me.

'Okay, this isn't working,' Blue said. 'On three, we get him around the knees and again heave him over.'

They pulled their hands out from under my arms and quickly got them around my knees.

'One . . . '

'Two . . . '

I started bucking and writhing again.

'Three!'

My feet came off the ground. With my back to the railing, there was nothing I could even attempt to grab onto. My head and shoulders began leaning out over the railing.

I thought of Scott.

I guess I've mentioned this already, but it bears repeating now. I'm not a particularly religious guy, but in that moment, I thought, *Maybe I'll see my son again.*

Maybe not in heaven. But in some kind of ethereal place, some otherworldly dimension. I figured, wherever it was, I wouldn't be long getting there. If I wasn't dead before I went over the falls, I'd be dead soon after.

I thought of Donna. Wondered if she would ever know what happened to me. Wondered what that would be like, the not knowing.

I'd miss her. At least until she came to join Scott and me.

I was wondering what it would feel like, actually going over. Would you feel that you were falling, or would it be more of a floating sensation? Did you get your name in the history books if you went over as a murder victim, or did that honor go only to daredevils who went of their own free will?

These thoughts and others were flashing through my head at such a speed I can't tell you what, exactly, I was thinking of when the shot rang out.

Just one shot. And then someone yelling.

'Put him down!'

Augie, I figured. Somehow, he knew. Maybe he'd been coming by the house just as these two clowns grabbed me. Followed us here.

'Shit!' said Red.

'What the — ' Blue said.

They didn't just put me down. They threw me onto the ground, hard. I rolled over, craned my neck around to get a look.

I couldn't make him out at first. It was dark, and the man was silhouetted against the moonlight. But I could see the gun in his hand.

'You dumb fucks,' he said.

'We weren't gonna do it!' Blue shouted. 'We were just scaring him!'

'That's right,' Red said. 'Just wanted to scare the shit out of him!'

'Didn't look that way to me.'

He came a few steps closer. Close enough that I could now make out who it was.

It wasn't Augie.

Almost didn't recognize him with a gun in his hand. Last time I'd seen him, he was wielding a meat cleaver.

50

Tony Fisk, pointing the gun at my two abductors, said, 'Take 'em off.'

'Huh?'

'The masks. Take off the fucking ski masks.'

Slowly, and clearly with great reluctance, they did as they were told. I was not surprised to see Russell Tapscott and Len Eggleton.

I had to hand it to them. The execution of their plan — and the near execution of me — was certainly fitting.

Tapscott I'd threatened to pitch over this very same railing. Eggleton I'd tossed into my trunk, although only for a couple of minutes. Their names had come up when I'd been asking around about kids who might have sold drugs to Scott. They were both a couple of years ahead of him at school, both from well-off families, and despite Brindle's assertion that the Tapscott kid had never been in any trouble, I still believed these two had, in fact, made the occasional sale. But I'd also been satisfied that they'd not sold anything to Scott.

Tony, the former Brott's Brats employee, pointed his gun at Tapscott, waved it in my direction.

'Untie him.'

'Sure.'

He knelt next to me and started on the tape wrapped around me, picking and tearing at it.

365

That allowed me to reach up and gently pull off the strips that were plastered across my mouth. Tapscott was working on my ankles. When he was done there, I held out my wrists so he could work on them.

Once he had me free, he backed away hurriedly, no doubt wondering whether I was going to take my revenge on him right then and there. But I was more consumed with getting the blood flowing to my fingers again. I gave my hands a few shakes, picked off the pieces of tape that were stuck to my clothes, and slowly rose to my feet.

I looked at Tony and said, 'Thanks.'

'I don't know whether thanks are in order,' he said. 'I almost let them do it.'

'Listen, Mr. Weaver,' said Eggleton, 'we're really, really sorry. Swear to God, we had it all worked out, we were going to hang you over the edge, and then pull you back.'

'It's true!' Tapscott said. 'We just wanted to give you a taste of your own medicine.'

I slowly walked over and stood next to Tony.

'Whaddya want to do with them?' he asked me.

'Let 'em go,' I said.

'What? Are you fucking kidding me?' Tony looked like he'd shoot them if I asked.

'Let 'em go,' I said again.

'Hold on. I lose my job over a few steaks and these guys nearly kill you and they walk?'

I nodded wearily. 'Yeah.'

'I don't get it,' Tony said.

'I know.'

I walked up close to Tapscott and Eggleton. They each took a step back.

'It ends here,' I said.

They nodded so quickly they looked like bobbleheads.

'We're real sorry,' Tapscott said.

'Yeah,' said Eggleton. 'Like we said, we never — '

'Get the hell out of here,' I said.

Together, they ran to the car. Tapscott got behind the wheel, started the Civic, and sprayed gravel with the front tires as they took off.

I walked back to Tony, who now had the gun pointed at the ground.

'I could use a ride,' I said. 'And I'd be much obliged if you'd let me buy you a drink.'

★   ★   ★

I got in on the passenger side of his silver Hyundai. 'You've been following me for what, a day and half?'

''Bout that,' he said. 'You need to go to a hospital or anything?'

I hurt. I'd been hit in the gut and the head, and I'd cramped up pretty bad during my time in the trunk. But I didn't have time to spend the night waiting to be looked at in an emergency room. I'd just down a handful of Advils when I had the chance.

'I'm okay,' I said.

We drove out of the woods. Once we were back on a main road, I spotted a place where we could get a drink. A small bar, neon SCHLITZ and GENESEE signs fuzzily glowing in the window.

We slid into a booth, didn't say anything to each other until after we had our drinks in front of us.

'I know you weren't following me around waiting for the chance to save my life,' I said.

'No,' Tony said.

'What was the plan?'

He took a long swig of his beer. 'I'm not sure. I was mad.'

'Sure,' I said. 'You lost your job. If you're expecting me to apologize for that, I'm not going to. I was hired to find out who was stealing from Fritz and I did.' I paused. 'You took a chance and you lost.'

'Yeah,' he said, looking down at the table.

'But you blamed me.'

Tony looked up and faced me. 'Fritz is a prick. A lousy, miserable prick.'

'That may be.'

'What I did, it was to pay myself back. For when he docked me because my kid was sick. It wasn't fair, my getting fired for that. You made that happen.'

I said nothing.

'I was so pissed. My wife, she's hardly making anything at all. Without me bringing money in, we're totally fucked. All I could think about was I wanted someone to pay for what had happened to me.'

'So you decided to start with me, not Fritz.'

Tony Fisk shrugged. 'I thought maybe you were still watching Fritz's place, maybe watching his back. So it made more sense to make you the priority.'

'You brought a gun.'

'That was just . . . I don't know. You pulled one on me in his office. I needed to be ready for anything that happened.'

'You found out who I was, where I lived.'

Another swig, another nod. 'Yeah. Followed you around here and there. Kind of lost track of you this afternoon. Where'd you go?'

'Drove out almost to Rochester.'

'So I was down the street, waiting for you to come home, and I noticed there was this other car with those two kids in it, and soon as you pulled in, they got out. I wondered, what the fuck? What are they gonna do? I saw them put you in the trunk, and decided to see what was going on.'

I sipped. 'You were worried they were going to get to do what you wanted to do.'

He grimaced. 'The thing is, I'd had a lot of time to think while I was following you around. At first, yeah, I wanted to get even with you. Not kill you, exactly, but something, you know? And the whole time I was following you, I was wondering what it'd be. And then the more I followed you, I wondered what the fuck I was doing.'

I listened.

'I mean, what was the point? Suppose I beat the shit out of you? I'd still be out of work. If the cops figured out who did it, then I'd end up in jail. And that'd make things only a thousand times worse for my wife and kid. By the time I

369

was down the street from your house tonight, I was thinking maybe it was time to do something more useful with my time.'

I smiled. 'Yeah, well, I'm grateful you didn't come to that conclusion yesterday.'

'When they shoved you in the trunk I thought about what I *wanted* to do, and what I *should* do. Part of me thought, fuck it, it's not my business. But then I thought, maybe I was there for a reason, you know?'

'Go on.'

'Do you believe in that kind of stuff? That things happen for a reason?'

It was a good question. Any other time I'd been asked something like that, I'd always said no. I didn't believe in fate. I didn't believe in destiny. Things just happened in this world for no rhyme, no reason. But I was undergoing a subtle shift in attitude. If Fritz Brott hadn't hired me to find out who was ripping him off, Tony Fisk wouldn't have been parked down the street from my house tonight.

If Fritz Brott hadn't hired me, I might very well be dead.

'I'm reassessing my position on that,' I said.

'I thought, maybe I'm here because I'm supposed to save your sorry ass.'

I leaned my glass forward and clinked it against his. 'You might be right.'

''Cause you know, they might never even have found you.'

'What do you mean? Those two guys?'

'No, no,' Tony said. 'After they did it, and you went over the falls, they might never have found

370

you. I've read a lot about this, about people who've gone over. Some on purpose, some by accident. You think the body will wash up somewhere, right? But some have gone over, and they've never ever recovered them. Your wife, nobody, would ever have known what happened to you.'

I thought about Harry Pearce. Taking his boat out one night seven years ago. Did they ever find him? Would I have ended up wherever he had?

Tony wiped the moisture from the outside of his glass with his thumb. I could tell he still had something on his mind.

'What is it?' I asked.

'I was wondering, you know, if you'd talk to him.'

'Sorry?'

'Would you talk to Fritz? Would you tell him I'm sorry, and that I'll pay him back for the meat I took? Or work a week for free or something like that?' He swallowed hard. I was guessing this wasn't easy for him. 'I need the work. I need the job.'

'Yes,' I said. 'I'll do it.'

His eyebrows shot up. 'Seriously.'

'Yeah. I don't think he'll change his mind. But I'll do it.'

'Thanks, man,' Tony said. 'Let me ask you something.'

'Sure.'

'Why'd you let those kids go?'

I paused. 'If I press charges, I'm going to have to testify. And that means I'm going to have to come clean on stuff I've done.'

His eyes narrowed. 'So you ain't so lily white neither.'

'No,' I said.

Tony's head went up and down slowly, and he smiled. 'You know, another reason, and I'm not saying this was the only one, I didn't try anything with you is, you've got someone watching your back. Although I think I'd have a word with him. He shoulda been watching you tonight.'

'What are you talking about?'

'The guy in the black pickup. He was keeping an eye on you today. But he's good. He was able to stay way back where you'd never, ever see him. What'd you do? You tell him where you were going to be?'

'You get a good look at the driver?' I asked.

Tony shook his head. 'Wait, so he's not watching out for you?'

'Describe the truck.'

'Just a black pickup. Dark, anyway. Tinted windows. Might have been blue.'

'Plate number?'

'Nope, never made note of that.' He grinned. 'So, like, is there anyone who *hasn't* been following you around?'

51

On the way back to Griffon, I got out my phone. It had rung once while I was tied up in the trunk. I had one message.

'Hey, Cal. Augie. Call me when you get a minute.'

He could wait.

I tried to give Tony some cash when we got back to my house. It was a feeble gesture, I know. Kind of, 'Hey, you saved my life, here's forty bucks.' I had my wallet out, ready to give him the two twenties that were in there, but he refused.

'Think of it as gas money,' I said.

'No,' he said. 'Just do that thing for me.'

'Okay,' I said. 'But it'll have to be in person. I can't do it over the phone. So it might be a couple of days. I've got some other things to wrap up.'

Tony nodded his understanding. As he drove off, I glanced down the street and saw Donna's car turn the corner. I waited, watched her pull into the drive, moved over by her door, pulled it open for her.

'Hey,' she said. 'Did you order the pizza?'

'Not yet,' I said.

'Whaddya been doing? I'm starving.'

'This and that,' I said.

'What the hell have you done to your clothes? You been playing football or something?'

Rather than answer, I pulled her into my arms and held her tight.

'What's going on?' she said, her voice suddenly full of worry. 'Tell me everything's okay.'

'You remember what you said, the other night? I agreed with you, but now I'm not so sure.'

'What, Cal? What are you talking about?'

'Right now, at this very moment, I'm happy.'

She buried her face in my chest and wept.

★ ★ ★

Donna had questions. She saw the bruise on my face, the handful of painkillers I swallowed, the way I winced when I moved certain ways.

'I had a run-in with someone,' I told her. 'No big deal.' I grinned. 'You should see the other guy.'

'You don't want me to know,' she said.

I smiled. I couldn't tell her what had really happened. She couldn't know how close she had come to losing me. Not now. Maybe not ever.

She ordered the pizza. While we waited, she said, 'I'm going to start researching the trip tonight. If I find something, should I go ahead and book it?'

'Give me a week to wrap things up. Anytime after that.'

'Okay.'

The pizza took forty minutes to arrive. We opened a bottle of Pinot Grigio. After dinner, she worked for a while on her charcoal sketches of Scott. Took three of them out back onto the deck, held them at arm's length and gave them a shot of the fixative. She spread the drawings on the kitchen table after.

'They're good,' I said.

She was silent for a moment. 'I haven't got it yet. I have to do this. I want to get it right. Before we go away.'

I didn't say anything.

'Enough for now,' she said. 'Where's the laptop? I've got work to do.'

Even though Augie had called, it was Bert Sanders I phoned when I went to my office.

'God, what's going on?' he asked. 'I've been waiting to hear from you.'

'If I'd found Claire, I'd have called, believe me. Did you find out anything?'

The mayor said no. 'Not much, and I don't know who else to call. Nobody knows where she might have gone, but Dennis' name came up a few times.'

'Yeah. I went to see his father today. He's not talking. I'm — '

The call-waiting beeped.

'I have to go,' I told him. 'If I hear anything, I'll call.'

'But — '

'I'll call.' I hit the button, thinking I might have waited too long, that I'd lost the other caller. 'Hello?'

'Jesus, you don't return messages?'

Augustus Perry.

I said, 'You were next on my list.'

'Yeah, sure, I believe you,' Augie said. 'I talked to Quinn. Got his ass down here.'

'And?'

375

'He denies it.'

'Which part?'

'Quinn says he never told officers Brindle and Haines to take your car in.'

'Somebody's lying,' I said.

'Thank you, Cal,' Augie said. 'You're good at this.'

'Have you talked to Brindle and Haines?'

'Can't raise either of them. Haines is off sick.'

'So you've only talked to Quinn. You believe him?'

Augie hesitated. 'I don't know. I've never been high on him. Something about the guy. Don't know what it is. But someone wanted your car brought in. I want to know whose decision it was.'

'It wasn't touched,' I said. 'Everything was in its place.'

'Where've you been?'

'Looking for Claire.'

Augie grunted. 'When you're talking to Bert, tell him I said he could kiss my ass.'

'You should have called earlier. I just got off the phone with him. You'll have to call him yourself.'

Augie hung up without saying good-bye.

I sat there, thinking.

Why would someone take my car in if they didn't want to search it?

Something Tony had said to me at the bar popped into my head.

'The guy in the black pickup. He was keeping an eye on you today. But he's good. He was able to stay way back where you'd never, ever see him. What'd you do? You tell him where you were going to be?'

I got out of my chair and went back down to the kitchen. Donna looked up from the laptop. 'What about walking the Golden Gate Bridge? You up for that?'

I breezed through. 'Sure.'

I grabbed my car keys, went outside, hit the UNLOCK button. Interior lights came on as I opened the trunk and all four doors, like I was getting ready to vacuum it. Then I stepped back and stared at the car.

Looking for anything that seemed different.

My sunglasses were still in the storage compartment in front of the console shift. The cord I used to recharge my phone off the cigarette lighter was there. The wig Hanna wore was on the floor of the backseat.

I looked in the trunk. All my stuff appeared to be in order.

I got down on my knees by the right front tire and felt inside the fenders. If someone were going to attach a GPS device, this would be a good spot. It could be fitted with a magnet that would allow someone to reach under and attach it to a car in seconds. I reached into all the wheel wells, felt around.

Nothing.

It would have been easy to slap on a tracking device under a fender without hauling the car into the garage. So maybe one had been tucked away in a much better hiding spot.

Coming up to the open driver's-side door, I got on my knees and reached in under the seat.

I ran my hand over the carpet, then reached up into the springs of the upholstery.

Donna had come outside and was watching me.

'It's always the last place you look,' she said.

'Yeah.'

'What, exactly, did you lose?'

'Nothing,' I said.

I'd gone back to the open trunk. Could someone put a tracking device right *into* a spare tire? It was tucked away under the trunk floor. I cleared things out of the way enough to lift up the access hatch and get a look at the spare. Without X-ray vision, I really couldn't tell, but it struck me as unlikely. Suppose I got a flat and had to put on the spare? The tracker would be spun to death. It'd throw the wheel off balance.

I thought about that scene in *The French Connection* where they dismantled that Lincoln Mark III, searching for heroin, finally finding drugs in the rocker panels that stretched along the frame beneath the doors. (That was the one thing I never figured out in that movie — how they'd put the car back together so quickly, and so perfectly, before they returned it to the unsuspecting Frenchman. Had they replaced the car with an exact duplicate? And if so, how did they get one that fast? And did the NYPD really have the money to buy replacement Lincolns?)

I went around to the open front passenger door, looked at the rocker panel. If someone had ripped out the plastic molding and bored into the metal with a jackhammer, surely there'd be some evidence. I ran my hand along the top and felt nothing out of the ordinary.

Maybe I was being paranoid. I stepped back from the car again and stared. Donna stood and stared as well.

I looked at the wig.

Something about the wig.

When I'd been with Sean, and found it, I'd tossed it onto the backseat of the car. But now the wig was on the floor. Nothing else in the car appeared to have been touched. Of course, the wig could have just fallen off the seat. But it got me thinking that there was another spot worth searching.

I got into the car, tossed the wig to the other side of the center hump, and put my knees on the floor so I could dig my fingers into the crack between the seat and back cushions, like I was looking for lost change in a couch. I moved my fingers across the entire width of the seat and found nothing.

So I reached deeper into the crack with both hands, got hold of the seat cushion from the inside, and tugged. The entire seat tipped forward, revealing the car's frame and various wires snaking their way back toward the rear taillights.

And something else.

A GPS transmitter, held in place on the frame with a strip of duct tape. I ripped it off, freed the transmitter, and got out of the car holding it delicately in both hands. A small red light pulsed silently at one end.

'What is that?' Donna asked, standing now by the open front door on the passenger side.

'GPS,' I said. 'So someone knows where I am at all times. So they don't have to follow close.'

She blinked. 'Who put that in there?'

'That's a good question,' I said, holding the device and studying it as though it were some ancient artifact.

Donna glanced down at the rocker panel I'd just been investigating. At least that's what I thought she was looking at. She reached down between the doorsill and the passenger seat, grabbed hold of something, and held it up for me to see.

'You been looking for your phone?' she asked.

I put the GPS device on the roof of the Honda and patted my jacket for my phone. I felt it, but reached in to be sure and withdrew it.

'I have my phone,' I said.

'Well, this isn't mine,' Donna said.

'Son of a bitch,' I said.

52

Donna handed me the phone. It was the same type as mine. I tried turning it on, but the battery was dead. Assuming it belonged to the person I figured it belonged to, it had been sitting in my car for a couple of days. Even before it had run out of power, I wouldn't have heard it because the switch on the side had been set on MUTE.

'Whose is it?' Donna asked.

'I'm guessing Claire's,' I said. 'She had it on her knee before she got out of the car. Even if she realized pretty soon that she'd lost it, once Hanna had come out, she could hardly run back out to my car to get it, not with Hanna inside.'

I wouldn't have to wait for it to fully recharge to see what clues it might hold. All I had to do was plug it into my charger in the kitchen.

'What are you going to do with this?' Donna asked, pointing to the GPS on the roof.

'For now,' I said, 'I'll just leave it on and keep it in the car.'

'You're not going to turn it off? Smash it? Do something to it?'

'Not yet. I don't want whoever put it there to know I've found it,' I said. I tucked it under the passenger seat, closed up the car and locked it. 'Let's go see what's on this baby.'

We went back into the house. On the kitchen counter, by the phone, was my charger. I plugged it into the receptacle at the base of the phone. The screen lit up, showing a battery icon completely drained of power.

'It might take a minute,' I said. 'Given that it was totally dead.'

It took half that long. If the phone had any kind of password lock on it to keep others from using it, it hadn't been engaged.

Given that the phone was tethered to an outlet, I read it leaning over, my elbows on the kitchen counter. A screen full of apps and icons appeared. It immediately showed that Claire had missed countless phone calls and that she had several voice mail messages. I was betting most of those were from her parents, wondering where she was.

I might have some trouble retrieving the voice mails, since I didn't know Claire's four-digit password. But I wouldn't need a password to check her text messages.

I went straight to the green box with the cartoon word bubble on it, and MESSAGES underneath, and tapped the touch screen, which was lightly smeared with makeup from Claire's cheek.

A specific conversation popped out. Within the banner across the top of the screen, the word ROMAN. Texts in pale gray boxes on the left side of the screen were messages from him, while those in pale blue on the right were Claire's. Donna was huddled next to me, as curious as I was about what we might find.

The most recent texts were these:

ROMAN: so hows it feel huh?

ROMAN: come on talk to me

ROMAN: i forgiv u lets just get back togthr

ROMAN: i desrve better than this

CLAIRE: lve me alone

I scrolled back to some earlier conversations.

ROMAN: hes not so smart

ROMAN: whats he got

And then, a texted photo.
Donna said, 'If that's what I think it is, for his sake I hope it's not actual size.'
I scanned another screen filled with his texts to Claire. She'd responded only twice, both times telling him to leave her alone. I tapped the screen to see who else Claire might have been having chats with.
I tapped on DENNIS.
The last message from him was: *k. luv u*
The one immediately before that, from Claire: *looking for ride, b there soon i hope.*
Donna, leaning on the counter next to me, our shoulders touching, said, 'Scroll back up a ways, get it from the beginning.'
I started to do that, and realized their chatter seemed to extend back to the beginning of time. I decided on an arbitrary starting point and started reading.

DENNIS: miss you 2

CLAIRE: really pissed at u. unfriended you on FB

DENNIS: i know. will expln evrytng when i c u

CLAIRE: better

DENNIS: i will. nvr wantd to leve like tht felt like a shit

CLAIRE: u r a shit

DENNIS: told you will expln. just hv to c u

CLAIRE: things shtty here

DENNIS: y

CLAIRE: stupid cops watching me all time mad at my dad trying to scare us dad still in pissing match with cheef

DENNIS: no

CLAIRE: ?

DENNIS: maybe not b cause of dad

CLAIRE: wtf

DENNIS: looking 4 me

CLAIRE: cops looking 4 u?

DENNIS: yeah

CLAIRE: y

DENNIS: cant say now y i ran off sudden, couldnt expln

CLAIRE: what u do?

DENNIS: nothin

CLAIRE: so y?

DENNIS: cant say now. have to c u. have to figure out what to do

CLAIRE: ok. so then com see me

DENNIS: not that simple

CLAIRE: not getting this

DENNIS: think cops watching u has nothing 2 do with your dad

CLAIRE: huh?

DENNIS: cops watching you bcause they think you'll lead them to me

CLAIRE: no way

DENNIS: yeah so we can meet but you have to shake cops

CLAIRE: wtf did u do

DENNIS: nothin

CLAIRE: so cops following me to get to you bcause u did nothing

DENNIS: told u will explan 18r

CLAIRE: have to get back 2 u

There was a time gap indicated in the message stream. The following day the conversation resumed.

CLAIRE: where r u

DENNIS: not at home.

CLAIRE: figured that where are u now

DENNIS: remember jeremy's cottage canoga springs

CLAIRE: on the lake?

DENNIS: yeah, it's safe here

CLAIRE: safe from what

386

DENNIS: pls, will tell u when i c u, have you figured out way 2 get away from cops?

CLAIRE: hanna helping me have something worked out

DENNIS: what plan

CLAIRE: you still have car

DENNIS: yes

CLAIRE: will phone u when its the day

DENNIS: k

CLAIRE: park at back of iggy's where no one can see you at 10

DENNIS: k. miss you. luv u so much

CLAIRE: luv u 2

Another time gap of a few hours. Then:

CLAIRE: u there?

DENNIS: here

CLAIRE: k. b there soon. at patchetts waiting for ride. sean coming hanna in position

387

DENNIS: k

CLAIRE: hungry?

DENNIS: lol. kinda

CLAIRE: wont have time to get anytng at igg

DENNIS: once we get on road

CLAIRE: k. i just wnt to eat you up

DENNIS: oh yeah

CLAIRE: shit

DENNIS: ?

CLAIRE: sean got pulled over.

DENNIS: what happen

CLAIRE: dont know black truck watching me

DENNIS: cant pick u up there not safe

CLAIRE: shit

DENNIS: hitch it

CLAIRE: looking for ride, b there soon i hope

DENNIS: k. luv u.

I said to Donna: 'Laptop.'

She grabbed it off the kitchen table and set it in front of me. I went to Google maps and entered 'Canoga Springs.'

'It's in the Finger Lakes area,' I said. 'Yeah, here we go. On the west side of Cayuga Lake. Couple hours' drive, maybe. Not all that far from where Dennis' dad lives. Good place to hide out.'

'You think they're still there?' Donna asked.

'I'd bet yes.'

I went to Facebook, back to Claire Sanders' page, entered the name 'Jeremy' to see if she had a friend by that name. I found a Jeremy Finder, who lived in Rochester. Then I went to the online phone directory to see if there might be a Finder listed in the Cayuga Lake area, and found an M FINDER on North Parker Road. I went back to the map page and found the road.

'Ta-da,' I said, pointing to the screen.

I got out my cell and placed a call.

'Didn't we just talk?' Augie said.

'Why are you looking for Dennis Mullavey?'

'Who?'

'Dennis Mullavey.'

'I have no idea who that is,' he said gruffly.

'You sent one of your people almost all the way to Rochester to try and find him.'

'I'm drawing a blank here, Cal.'

I was about to tell him what I'd found in my car, taped to the frame beneath the rear seat, but then held my tongue. He seemed to be playing straight with me lately. He'd gotten me out of a tight fix when I'd been in that interrogation room. He'd brought me up to speed on Quinn.

But the Griffon police were looking for Dennis Mullavey. And those text messages between Claire and Dennis seemed to confirm that they were following her in hopes that she would lead them to him.

Augie knew I was looking for Claire. Why not slap a GPS on my car and let me do the work for his department? Maybe that was why he'd lied to save my ass when Haines and Brindle had brought me in for threatening Russell Tapscott. Augie needed me out in the field.

'You still there?' Augie snapped.

'Yeah.'

'Was there something else?'

'Why'd you really lie to get me out of that mess, Augie?'

'What?'

'Because I'm family? Or did you need me to do your work for you?'

'By God, you're a horse's ass.'

Augie hung up.

When he and I had talked earlier, and he'd told me Quinn denied telling Brindle and Haines that the chief wanted my car towed in, I'd brilliantly deduced that someone had to be lying. I'd meant Quinn, or Brindle or Haines.

I'd left out someone.

'You didn't tell my brother about that GPS thing,' Donna said.

'No,' I said. 'Slipped my mind.'

53

I decided against leaving right then and there for Canoga Springs, although I contemplated it. I'd be getting there after midnight, and I didn't want to scare Dennis Mullavey and Claire Sanders to death. I just wanted to find them. Also, I didn't have an exact address on North Parker Road for the cottage, so I'd need daylight to look for Dennis' old Volvo station wagon.

Even though I set my alarm for five, I was waking up every half hour through the night to look at the clock radio to see what time it was. At four thirty I decided to just get up. I tried not to disturb Donna, but she was already awake.

'It's okay,' she said. 'You can turn on a light.'

'No, no, go back to sleep. You can get in another couple of hours before you have to get up for work.'

'It's Saturday, Sherlock.'

Still, I left the bedroom lights off, and turned on the one in the bathroom only after I had closed the door. I showered and shaved. When I came back out, turning off the light first and figuring I could hunt up what I needed from the dresser in the dark, I realized Donna was not there. The smell of coffee wafted up from the kitchen.

I got dressed and went downstairs. Donna was in her blue bathrobe, sitting at the kitchen table, her index finger looped into the handle of a mug. There was a pencil in her other hand, and a sketch in front of her.

'It's cold,' I said. 'The furnace not cutting in?'

'It's something with the thermostat. If you jiggle it, it comes on. I'm gonna have to call somebody. There's two slices in the toaster. All you gotta do is push it down.'

'I was just going to go and grab — '

'Eat some toast.' She got up, poured another cup of coffee and handed it to me, then took some strawberry jam out of the fridge and a jar of peanut butter from the cupboard. 'We have a vast array of choices.'

When I shifted over to see what she had been drawing, she cut in front of me and tucked the picture into a folder.

'What?' I said.

'I don't want you to see that one,' she said. 'Not till it's finished.' Her eyes glistened. 'I think this might be the one.'

I took that comment a couple of ways. Maybe this was turning into the best drawing of Scott she'd ever done. Or, if that was the case, this was the sketch that would allow her to move forward. To the next step, whatever that step might actually be.

I backed off. 'Okay,' I said.

Once the toast had popped, I slathered jam on one slice and peanut butter on the other. I washed it down with the coffee.

'Something that's always troubled me,' Donna said, letting the half sentence just hang there.

'What?' I asked.

'We loved him,' she said. 'We loved him unreservedly.'

'Of course we did.'

'But I don't know if . . . I don't know if he was lovable,' she said softly. 'To others. He didn't have a lot of friends.'

'Donna.'

'He was always . . . you know what he was like. He had a bit of the tattletale in him.'

'I know,' I said, and forced a smile. 'Maybe he was just trying to pull people up to his standards.'

Her face fell. 'What standards were those?' She shook her head. 'He destroyed himself.'

I looked at her across the table from me, unsure what to say or what to do. Two steps forward, one step back. Sometimes you just run out of gas.

'I need to go,' I said.

* * *

I opened the garage, even though my car was already in the driveway. I fished out the still-active GPS device from under the front seat and walked it into the garage, setting it on a shelf where I kept gardening equipment. Whoever was minding this thing, from whatever location, if they could detect that small a movement, they'd figure I'd just moved the Honda into the garage.

While I left the GPS behind, I didn't set off without my Glock. For the drive, I put it in the glove box.

When I got to the other side of Buffalo, the sun was coming up, nearly blinding me as I drove due east. I flipped the visor down and slipped on my shades to keep from squinting. One of those interstate highway service centers served as a pit stop for me. Got back in the car with another coffee and a blueberry muffin.

Once I'd passed the last of the exits for Rochester, I kept my eye out for the sign for Interchange 41, Waterloo-Clyde. I got off, paid the toll, then went south on 414, taking me past the Seneca Meadows Wetlands Preserve. I stayed on 414 as it bore east into Seneca Falls, then followed it south of town, past the Finger Lakes Regional Airport. When I hit Canoga Street I took it east to 89 through farmland. Finally, I found my way down a narrow road to the shore of Cayuga Lake and North Parker Road.

Cayuga was one of the north-south Finger Lakes, a popular place for people across New York State to buy summer properties. Some of the cottages appeared to date back decades, while others weren't cottages at all, but proper homes, no doubt built to replace cabins that were no longer worth fixing up.

I traveled slowly down the lane. In a lot of the driveways, there were no cars at all. The summer season was over. Some of the cottages had been boarded up and wouldn't be opened until spring.

I drove to the end of the road without seeing the Volvo wagon. I turned around, made the trip back just as slowly, in case I'd missed something. The road was littered with leaves, but there were still quite a few clinging to the trees. I got back to where I'd turned onto North Parker, again without seeing the car.

It was possible Claire and Dennis had been here but had now moved to another location. I sat there in the car, the engine idling, wondering if I'd wasted my time coming out here. I decided to do one more drive to the end and back.

It was on the way down, passing one of the cottages where there appeared to be little life, and no car parked outside, that I noticed the smoke.

A thin gray wisp of it, drifting up from the chimney.

I stopped the car, backed up thirty yards, and turned in. The driveway amounted to two ruts with grass growing in the center. I could hear the blades brushing along the underside of the car as I drove down between the trees. The cottage was a simple rectangular box, one story, painted dark brown. Beyond it was a separate building at the edge of the water that looked like a place to store a boat, but the big doors on this side suggested a car could just as easily fit inside.

I parked, killed the engine, opened the glove box and took out my Glock. Once I was out of the car, I slipped it into the holster on my belt and pulled my jacket over it.

The cottage was still. I didn't think my car had made a lot of noise coming in, and it was possible that whoever was inside was still sleeping. I decided to walk down to the outbuilding first.

There were two windows set high on the door, and I peered inside.

The Volvo was there. Tucked in the way it was, with the door closed, they weren't going to be making any fast getaways. A few steps away from

395

the garage was a wooden dock and, tied to it, an aluminum boat — a fourteen-footer, I guessed, with a small Evinrude outboard motor bolted to the transom.

I walked over to the cottage, stepped up onto a deck that faced the lake and rapped my knuckles on one of the sliding glass doors. There were no curtains drawn across them, so I made my hand into a visor and peered inside. Looked like one big room that was a kitchen and living area with a large television, an older, non-flat screen that looked like it weighed five hundred pounds. There were three doors facing onto the room, probably two bedrooms and a bathroom. What looked like one of the bedroom doors was open. There were dirty dishes in the sink, a pizza box on the dining table.

At one end of the main room sat a small stack of firewood, about a foot away from a wood-burning stove from which a black pipe snaked its way up and out through the roof.

I rapped again, a little louder this time, then heard a rustling in the leaves behind me. I whirled around in time to see a young black man, dressed only in blue boxers and a pair of sneakers, leap up the three steps to the deck and charge me.

I'd been caught off guard the night before, but this time I was ready. He came at me with his right fist, but before he could connect I had my left arm up to block the blow and simultaneously drove forward with my right, catching him just below the ribs. I pulled the punch some before it connected. I didn't want to hurt him that bad.

He doubled over and stumbled back a couple of steps, but he wasn't done with me. He raised his head and got ready to attack again, but by this time he was looking down the barrel of my Glock.

'Whoa,' I said, my arm locked into position. The man froze.

When I heard the glass door behind me start to slide, I took a few steps to one side so I could keep my eye on the man and still see whoever was at the door.

It was Claire, dressed in a pair of panties and a T-shirt.

'It's okay, Dennis,' she said. 'It's Mr. Weaver.'

Dennis Mullavey looked from Claire to me and back to Claire. I slowly lowered the Glock.

'You got coffee?' I asked.

54

The woman is awakened from a sound sleep. She looks at the clock, sees that it is five forty-five a.m. She grabs the phone next to her bed.

'Hello?'

'He thought he could outsmart me,' her son says.

'What are you talking about?'

'He found one of them. But he didn't find the other.'

She throws back the covers and sits up. 'What?'

'He found the one I put under the backseat. But he didn't find the one I put inside the headrest.'

'Where are you now?'

'I'm on the road. I think he's figured out something. He took off half an hour ago. I've got a good feeling.'

The woman allows herself nothing more than cautious optimism. Her son's successes are often followed by catastrophic lapses in judgment. Just the other night, he tells her this is the night Claire is going to meet with the boy, but before the night is over he's been fooled. He loses his temper under the bridge, trying to get the other girl to tell him where Claire has gone. And that software he downloaded to Claire's phone was supposed to allow him to see texts, and track her position, but all it did was let him hear her phone calls.

But she is willing to concede that the second GPS tracker in Weaver's car was a shrewd move.

'Where do you think he's going?' the woman asks.

'No idea. But wherever it is, I can find him. He'll never see me in his rearview mirror.'

'You know that when and if he finds them, it'll be three who know. If we could have just found Dennis, and dealt with him . . . But he'll have told the girl, and they'll tell Weaver.'

'I know,' he says.

'You have to let me know. The minute it's done.'

'I'll let you know. I will. Don't worry, Mom. It's going to be okay.'

But she's still going ahead with her backup plan. She's going to start moving the boxes to just outside the locked door.

55

'Why don't you two put some clothes on?' I said to Claire and Dennis. 'I'll get the coffee going.'

The two of them went back into the bedroom. There wasn't a lot to do for the coffee. All they had was a jar of instant. So I plugged in the kettle, cleaned three mugs that had been sitting in some gray water in the sink, and looked in the fridge — a hulking thing that had to be from the 1950s — for cream. I found milk.

I spooned some instant into each of the cups. When they reappeared, I poured in the water and stirred. Dennis Mullavey looked presentable in jeans and a black tee, but Claire, who was similarly dressed except her tee was blue, had hair sticking out all over the place, like she'd just walked through some briar bushes to get here. She had a small black notebook clutched in her left hand, but what really caught my eye was the cut. The one that was missing from Hanna's hand when she got into my car. It was healing nicely.

'I found your phone,' I told her as the two of them sat down and I put the cups in front of them.

'Oh God, I was going crazy trying to find it,' she said, placing the notebook on the table.

'But you couldn't come back, could you? Once Hanna was in my car.'

'You've kinda figured it all out, right?'

'Pretty much.'

'You almost found me,' she said. 'I was in the last stall when you came into the bathroom looking for me. That was about when I realized I'd lost my phone, that it was still in your car. But I couldn't exactly call Hanna and tell her to get it for me. It didn't matter all that much, though, because once I took off, I wasn't going to use it anyway.'

I looked at Dennis, who'd also taken a seat. 'And you were parked out back, waiting.'

He nodded slowly, but I could tell he wasn't yet ready to trust me, even though I'd heard Claire, in the bedroom, trying to assure him I was one of the good guys.

'What's that?' I asked, nodding at the notebook.

'Damned if I know,' Dennis said, shaking his head. 'Craziest diary ever, I'd say.'

Before I could examine it, Claire said, 'Have you talked to my parents?'

'They're worried sick,' I told her.

Guilt washed over her face. 'I thought since they hardly even talk to each other, if I told my dad I was going to see my mom, I could go days without either one of them knowing what was up.'

'You shouldn't be telling him this,' Dennis told her.

'He *knows*, okay?' She looked back at me and rolled her eyes. 'I guess Hanna must have told you everything. I mean, once I was gone, it didn't really matter, since I didn't tell her where I was going. And the whole thing worked, because here we are, and other than you nobody's found us.'

A chill ran the length of my spine.

'Have you talked to *anyone* since you took off?' I asked her.

Claire shook her head. 'Nope.'

I looked at Dennis. 'You? You been in touch with your father?'

'I'm not talking to you,' he said, but added, 'He knows I'm okay. He just doesn't know what all's happened. I told him I needed some time to figure it out.'

'So he didn't have any news for you from Griffon,' I said.

'No.'

I could see concern clouding Claire's face. 'What's happened? Has something happened to my dad?'

'No,' I said. 'Your dad's okay.' I hadn't wanted to be the one to break this news to the mayor's daughter. I swallowed, and said, 'Hanna's dead, Claire.'

Her mouth opened, but no sound came out.

'She was murdered. Her body was found under a bridge. She was killed soon after you two pulled your stunt.'

Claire had her hand over her mouth, but there still wasn't a sound coming out of her.

'I figured out what the two of you had done, the switch you'd pulled off to keep someone from following you, and I called her on it. She wanted out, tried to get out while my car was moving. She ran, wouldn't let me take her home.' I paused. 'I'm sorry.'

The wailing began like a siren. Loud arid piercing. 'Oh God,' she cried, and burst into tears. 'Oh God, oh God.'

Dennis looked stunned, and tried to take Claire into his arms, but she shoved him away.

'Leave me alone!' she screamed. 'Leave me the fuck alone!'

She slid the glass door open, went outside without closing it behind her, and ran toward the lake.

Dennis kicked back his chair and started after her, but I caught up to him and put a hand on his shoulder. 'No, you've done enough,' I said.

'What's that supposed to mean?'

'We've all got baggage where Hanna's concerned, but it's starting to look like none of this would have happened if you hadn't made it so damn important for Claire to sneak away to shack up with you here.'

Even as I said it I regretted it. I knew there was more going on here than teenage lust. But I was so damned angry. Angry that I'd ever been dragged into this, angry at all the heartache and misery that stemmed from the stunt they'd pulled. Angry about Hanna.

'You think that's what this is all about?' Dennis shouted. 'Really?'

'Then maybe you should tell me. Why the hell did you leave Griffon? What the hell happened? Why are the cops looking for you?'

He turned away. 'Shit,' he said under his breath.

'If you don't want to trust me, then I don't know who else you're going to find,' I said. 'I can

403

help you. Is that why you're hiding out here? Trying to figure out what to do next? How long you gonna stay? A week? A month? A year? What's the plan, Dennis?'

I glanced back toward the lake. Claire was standing at the end of the dock, staring out into the lake. It made me nervous, seeing her there, knowing how unsettled she had to be at this moment.

'You stay here,' I said, and ran down to the lake.

When I got to the dock, I slowed my pace. I didn't want Claire to feel me stomping on the planks, charging at her like a bull. I walked out gently, but the dock still bounced slightly underfoot.

'Claire.'

Her shoulders were trembling. I stood a foot behind her, close enough that she could feel my presence, but I didn't touch her.

'It's all my fault,' she said, sniffling.

'I just told Dennis we're all feeling some blame where Hanna's concerned. I know I am.'

'Have they got who did it?' she asked, twisting her neck and wiping her nose on the shoulder of her shirt.

'They've arrested Sean.'

Claire whirled around, her eyes red. But grief had turned to shock. 'What? You're kidding. That's insane. There's no way. He was trying to help us. He was helping me and Hanna. He was supposed to pick me up, but he got pulled over and that's why I asked you for a ride and — '

'I know,' I said. 'I don't think he did it, either.

But the police, they found evidence in his truck. From Hanna.'

'The police?' she shrieked. 'The fucking Griffon police? Oh, well, I guess it's all wrapped up, then, if the Griffon police arrested him. Fucking assholes, all of them.'

I nodded. 'You and Dennis need to come back with me. We have to get all this sorted out.'

She shook her head violently. 'There is *no way* he's going to go back there. Not a chance.'

'What happened, Claire? What happened? What was Dennis running from? Why do the police want him? Do you know who killed Hanna?'

She sniffed. 'I never should have asked her to help. Never, never, never.'

Tears were still running down her cheeks and her nose was dripping over her top lip. I found some fresh tissues in my pocket and handed them to her.

'We have to go back and sort this out,' I repeated. 'For Hanna. And for Sean.'

Claire started to go into short, rapid breaths, and I was fearful she was going to pass out. She leaned my way, and I held on to her. She wrapped her arms around me and rested the side of her face on my chest.

'Everything is so awful,' she whispered. 'It's all so fucking awful.'

I patted her back lightly. Such an empty, pitiful gesture.

'We'll go back,' I said. 'Okay? We'll go back. You and Dennis can explain everything to me on the way. And if he doesn't want to come, so be it.

But I'm not going back without you.'

Her face went up and down on my chest.

'Come on,' I said.

I held on to her as we walked back to shore, but I had to watch my step, as the dock was barely wide enough for both of us. We walked slowly across the grass and up a slight hill back to the cottage. Stepped up onto the deck. The sliding glass door was still open. I was expecting Dennis to be standing there, waiting for us, but he was not.

'Dennis?' Claire called.

There was no response.

We had another three steps to reach the door when I gripped Claire's shoulders, made her stop in her tracks.

There was something on the floor of the cottage.

Something wet and dark and sinuous snaking across it.

Blood.

56

'You know,' I said, suddenly steering Claire hard left, away from the door, 'I need to check one thing before we go anywhere.'

'What are you — '

I was pretty sure she hadn't seen the blood. If she had, she'd have reacted. Rushed inside, screamed, something. But I could tell, judging by how her body had tensed, that she knew something was wrong.

'Shh,' I said. Then, in a more normal voice that was just slightly louder than necessary, 'I don't know whether we should take both cars back or whether we should all go back in mine.'

We were up against the cottage wall, between the glass doors and a set of windows. There was a second set of three steps here that led down from the deck. I had the Glock in my hand as I whispered to Claire, 'Get under the deck.'

She started to ask why, but I put my finger to my lips and gave her a stern, urgent look, then pointed. She slipped down the steps, got on her knees, and crawled into the roughly two feet of space below the deck.

I went down the steps, too, but kept on walking along the edge of the cottage, maintaining a conversation. 'We're going to need you and Dennis to make a full statement, explain this whole thing from the beginning. I know it's not going to be easy, having to talk about this, but there really isn't any choice.'

Whoever it was had a silencer on his gun. I hadn't heard a shot when I was out on the dock with Claire. Not that so-called silenced guns don't make a sound. But down by the water, it might not have made much more noise than a snapped twig. I hadn't heard a car pull up, either. Our shooter had probably parked a ways down the road, then hiked in.

I'd had my eyes on the rearview mirror the whole way here. There were long stretches on the interstate, and coming down from it to the Cayuga Lake area, when there had not been another car on the road at all.

But someone knew I was here. Someone had followed me. There had to be a second GPS device in my car. Not just the one under the backseat. I should have checked the rocker panels, or looked inside that damn spare tire.

As I crept along the edge of the cottage, I strained to hear anyone moving inside. A floorboard creak, a door opening or closing. Anything that would give me a sense of where he was. I looked forward, then back at the open sliding glass door, then forward again. The ground was layered with fallen leaves. If someone came out the back of the cottage and started walking around, there was a good chance I'd hear something.

The cottage sat on a high foundation, so when I reached a regular window, as opposed to those floor-to-ceiling glass doors, I had to duck only a few inches not to be seen. I wasn't keen on getting shot in the head.

I glanced quickly at Claire Sanders, huddled under the deck, eyes wide with fear.

I continued with my monologue. 'I know you may not think much of Chief Perry, but he's a good man, and we can trust him.' Just because I was saying these things didn't mean I had to believe them. 'And the first thing we're going to want to do is let your father know you're okay. And your mother. This has been a very difficult time for both of them.'

I'd reached the corner of the cottage, my back glued to the wall. I peered around the edge, saw no one, slithered around to the other wall. From that vantage point, I could just barely see up to the road. Through the trees I could see a dark-colored pickup with tinted windows parked there.

'And I'm not saying that about the chief because he's my brother-in-law. If anything, that kind of leads me to think of him as a total asshole. Sometimes he is, and I know he and your dad have been having a running battle, but the fact is, when it comes to being a lawman, I think he more or less knows what he's doing.'

Sooner or later, someone was going to think it odd that Claire wasn't contributing to this conversation.

'My wife, Donna, she'll defend him till the cows come home, but she grew up with him and she knows what he's — '

Leaves rustling. Around the next corner. Someone was creeping along the back wall of the cottage.

' — like, so she'll only defend him for so long, you know, and — '

It happened fast.

The barrel of the gun appeared first, and as I'd figured, there was a silencer screwed onto the end of it. A millisecond later, the whole gun, and the hand that was holding it. A glimpse of a jacket cuff.

I fired.

The shot rang out in the cool morning air. Birds in nearby trees broke into frightened flight.

It was more reflex than anything. I should have waited another half second, for a body to appear. Would have given me a better chance of actually hitting something. But the truth was, I'd never fired my weapon in the line of duty before. Not as a cop, and not since I'd gone private.

So it was no surprise I failed to hit that hand. It withdrew instantly at the sound of the shot. There was the sound of more leaves rustling. Faster this time. Running.

And another noise, one I wished hadn't been made. Claire shouting, 'Mr. Weaver? What was that?'

The man — I'd figured it was a man, and a glimpse of that hand proved it to me — was on the move, running around the cottage. I went the other way. I didn't want the shooter coming upon where Claire was hiding before I got there. He'd have heard her and would have a good idea where to look.

I moved back to the first corner I'd rounded, took a peek around it, then hugged the wall that faced the lake, which gave me a view of the deck. Claire was crawling out from under it.

'Stay under there!' I screamed.

'Dennis!' she shouted, ignoring me. 'Dennis, someone's shooting!'

She grabbed the railing, started mounting the steps to the deck, heading for the sliding glass doors.

'Goddamn it!' I yelled at her.

The barrel of a gun appeared around the far corner of the cottage, then two outstretched arms.

'Claire!'

She glanced back at me.

I heard a sound like someone lightly hammering a nail, once. He'd taken a shot. The wood railing by Claire's hand splintered.

Claire went down.

The top half of her body landed on the deck, her legs splayed across the steps.

'No!'

The word came out of me as a primal scream of anguish.

But then Claire stirred, pushed herself up. She hadn't been hit. She'd tripped on the stairs.

I raised my Glock and fired over her, putting a bullet into the corner of the cottage. Fired again. And again. Thinking maybe I could shoot the bastard through the building.

I moved to the corner, hugging the wall, crouched down, so that when I peered around it, my head would be lower than he'd be expecting. I kept the Glock gripped in both hands, held my breath, hoping to hear something besides the pounding of my heart in my ears.

More rustling.

Distant running.

411

I peeked around the corner.

He was on the move.

Almost to the end of the road that led in here. Running flat out. Dark pants, black Windbreaker with a hood up. I sprinted after him. I could see he was headed for the pickup.

He stopped suddenly, turned, pointed his weapon my way. I threw myself to the ground like I was tackling an imaginary football player, heard a bullet slice the air over me.

More running.

By the time I was on my feet, he'd reached the truck and was getting in. It sped off, tires kicking up gravel. I wasn't close enough to see a plate before the vehicle disappeared beyond a curve in the road.

Back at the cottage, another scream.

I ran back, coming around the front side. Claire stood at the sliding doors, looking inside, a hand floating over her mouth.

She didn't have to step inside to see what had happened to Dennis. He was sprawled on his side by the kitchen table, his back to us. The chair had tipped over with him when he'd gone down. The blood puddling its way toward the middle of the room was coming from a hole in the back of his head.

'No no no no,' she whispered.

'Stay here,' I said, sliding the door open and delicately entering the room, careful to avoid stepping in the blood. I knelt next to him, put two fingers to the side of his neck. A futile gesture, I knew, but I had to be sure. I looked through the door into the bedroom, at a tiny hole in the screen in the window on the far wall. The killer'd never stepped inside; he'd just aimed from outside and taken his shot. Didn't have to shoot through glass, so we didn't hear anything down by the water.

I stood, saw that black notebook on the kitchen table, picked it up and slipped it into the pocket of my jacket.

'Dennis,' Claire said, standing just inside the door. 'Dennis?'

'We have to get out of here,' I said. 'That man may come back, or he may be waiting for us down the road.'

Claire was trembling, both hands over her mouth. I was worried she might be going into shock.

'Claire, listen to me. We have to get out of here.'

I'd already decided I didn't want to take my car. It still had a GPS device hidden in it somewhere. I could get the keys to the Volvo, but there was only one way out, down North Parker Road, and we could be driving into an ambush.

I looked out at the lake.

'What's over there?' I asked.

'We have to get him to the hospital,' Claire said quietly. 'We have to get a doctor.'

'Claire, Dennis is dead. I have to get you out of here. The other side of the lake, it looks like it's only a mile away. What's over there?'

'Union Springs,' she whispered.

'A town?'

'A little town.'

I grabbed her by the wrist with my left hand,

413

the gun still in my right. 'We're going to take the boat. We're going to run like hell to the dock and get in the boat. Do you know if there's gas in the tank?'

'How do you know he's dead?' she said. 'How can you be sure?'

'Claire!' I said sharply. 'Is there gas in the boat?'

'I . . . I think so. Dennis and I went out in it yesterday. Just wandering around.'

'Come on.'

We ran down the hill to the dock. I got her into the boat first, put her in the middle of the three seats. I stepped in, lowered the motor so the prop was in the water, gave the rubber bulb on the fuel line several squeezes, put the motor in neutral, pulled the choke, and yanked on the cord.

It started on the first pull. I shoved the choke back in, powered the throttle back, then untied the stern and bow lines from the dock. I pushed off, put the gear lever into forward, and cranked it. It was cold out on the lake. Claire had no jacket. I slipped mine off and gave it to her. She put her arms into it robotically, her eyes glazed.

It only took about five minutes to cross Cayuga. There was a marina up ahead. Lots of docks, but only a few boats still in the water. A huge building just up from the shore where people stored boats for the winter. I found a spot to tie the boat up, jumped onto the dock and helped Claire out.

'Is there a business area?' I asked her.

She raised a weak finger. 'That way, I think.'

We walked briskly up Basin Street to North Cayuga, which seemed to pass for the main drag around here. I saw a used-car dealer across the street. I didn't have to hold on to Claire's wrist all the time; she was keeping up with me. But she was so dazed I held her hand as we crossed the road. She wasn't in a state of mind where I could trust her to look both ways.

We went straight into the sales office. A heavyset man in an ill-fitting blue suit got up from behind his desk, turned on a smile like he'd just flipped a switch, and approached us. But his smile didn't last long. We didn't look like typical customers, Claire's eyes red from crying, and me sweating profusely.

There was also the small matter of the Glock strapped to my waist.

'We need a car,' I said.

His eyes on the gun, he said. 'Take whatever you want.'

'I'm not stealing one,' I said. 'I'll rent one.' I got out my wallet, showed him my private investigator's license, and handed him my Visa card. 'How's five hundred?'

He took the card. 'Sure. And I'm going to need to see your driver's license.'

'You're going to do this fast,' I said.

'Of course.'

He did, too. Within two minutes he was handing me a set of keys to a white Subaru sedan.

I said to him, 'Call the police. There's been a murder directly across the lake. Brown cottage, front doors on the lake side open. Tell them the shooter may still be in the area. Male, five ten to

415

six feet. He's driving a dark-colored pickup truck. Black, dark blue, tinted windows. You got that?'

'Yeah,' he said.

I hustled Claire into the front seat of the Subaru and got myself behind the wheel.

'We're going home,' I told her.

★ ★ ★

We went north through the village of Cayuga, then headed east through the Montezuma National Wildlife Refuge. Once we'd driven out the other side of it, I found my way back to the thruway. It was the same interchange where I'd gotten off. Before I rolled through the tollgate and picked up my ticket, I asked Claire if she needed anything.

'I don't know,' she said.

I pulled into a gas station — as it turned out, I'd rented a car that had less than a quarter of a tank in it — and filled up. Then I ran into the convenience store and loaded up on bottled water, candy bars, potato chips. Anything to keep us going.

'Help yourself,' I said when I got back into the car.

As I was grabbing my ticket and speeding up the ramp to get back on the thruway, Claire looked into the bag and pulled out a Mars bar. It pleased me when she peeled back the wrapper and took a bite.

'I've got questions, Claire. Can you handle some questions?'

She chewed some candy, swallowed, and looked blankly at me. 'I guess.' She sounded like she was in a trance.

'Do you know who it was? Do you know who killed Dennis?'

'I didn't see him,' she said.

'But do you have an idea?'

She nodded.

'Who?'

'Phyllis Pearce's son,' Claire said.

'What? She has a son? Who's that?'

'You don't know?' she asked.

I waited.

'Ricky Haines,' Claire said. 'The cop. Maybe the creepiest guy on the Griffon force, because he's all nice, but when he starts feeling you up, you start thinking maybe he's not what he pretends to be.'

57

He's driving so quickly, when he has to make a turn from a gravel road to pavement, the truck skitters on its back wheels, nearly flips over. But he wrenches the wheel, manages to right the vehicle, and once he hits blacktop he floors it.

Now, driving in a straight line, he can manage the phone. He grabs it with his right, places a call, puts the phone to his ear.

'Hello?' his mother says urgently.

'It's me,' he says.

'What's happened, Richard? Did you find them?'

'I found them,' Ricky Haines says.

'And?'

'I got them.'

'You did?'

'I got Mullavey. And I'm pretty sure I got the girl, too.'

'Pretty sure?' Phyllis Pearce likes to deal in absolutes. 'What do you mean, pretty sure?'

'I saw her go down. I couldn't exactly check her pulse, with Weaver shooting at me.'

'What about him? What did you do with him?'

'I told you. He was shooting at me. I had to get out of there. I couldn't get a good shot at him.'

'What about the notebook?'

'I don't have it.'

'God, you're hopeless! Where are you now?'

'On the road. I'm coming home.'

'No!' she says. 'You have to go back! You have to finish this!'

'No, listen. I waited, a little while, at the end of the road, the only way out, figuring Weaver'd drive out eventually. I hid the truck and I was in the woods. When they didn't show up, I drove back past the place, saw that the boat was gone. Decided then I better get out of there.'

'Boat? What are you talking about, a boat?'

'I followed them to a cottage on Cayuga Lake. Weaver must have took off in a boat.'

'Did he see you?'

'I don't know. Maybe. And I don't know what Mullavey and the girl told him before I got there.'

'My God, what a mess,' Phyllis says.

'It's not that bad, Mom. The only one left who might know anything is Weaver.'

'And he's probably got the book, too.' She can't hold back any longer: 'You should have gotten Mullavey that first day! That's what you should have done!'

Ricky thinks she's losing it. But he knows his mom. He knows she freaks out at first, but then she calms down, thinks things through. Mom usually has a plan. When he hears nothing from her for several seconds, he's pretty sure that's what is going on.

'I know all that,' he says. 'I know I've made some mistakes. But some things I got right, you know that.'

'Shut up,' Phyllis says. 'Just shut up and let me think.'

419

He waits. He feels tears coming on, blinks a few times to clear his vision. He thinks of all the things that could have been done better, the different decisions that could have been made. And not just by him. She deserves plenty of the blame, too, but she gets so angry when he reminds her of that.

Finally she says, 'You come home. I'll see what I can do.'

Ricky tosses the phone onto the seat next to him. He's not relieved, but he feels slightly better.

Mom will figure something out.

58

Ricky Haines.

Tumblers fell into place.

If it was Ricky who'd followed us to Cayuga Lake, it was most likely Ricky who'd planted the tracking device in my car. It had to have been Ricky's idea to seize my car. To avoid suspicion, he'd said that he'd been told to do it by Quinn, who in turn had been told to do it by Augie.

Once the car'd been brought in, Ricky could have had access to it and planted the trackers. And since no one had actually given an order to have the car searched, no one was going to find them before the car was returned to me.

Brindle, I was guessing, wasn't in on it with his partner. If he had been, he wouldn't have been so pissed when I got sprung by the chief on the Tapscott business. It also explained why Haines had offered to call my lawyer for me. It wasn't in his interest that I be held in custody. He needed me on the outside, leading him to Claire and Dennis.

What else had Ricky probably done?

I felt I should be calling Augie, but I still had what you might call trust issues. I wanted to hear what Claire had to say before I called anyone with the Griffon police.

She started her story, more or less, from the beginning.

'I had a job for the summer working at

421

Smith's. The ice cream place? Down by the water?'

I nodded. We used to go down there, Donna and Scott and I, after dinner on a warm summer's evening.

'That's kind of close to Hooper's office, and Dennis would drop by every day after work and get an ice cream. He kept coming so often, I could tell he was kind of into me, and things weren't going so well between me and Roman anyway. You know Roman?'

'Yes,' I said.

'I don't know what I was thinking there. He's kind of a douche, to be honest, but I guess I kind of thought it was cool that he wants to be a movie writer, you know? But he was into some sketchy stuff, like — okay, I probably shouldn't tell you this, but Roman's twenty-one and he makes money by buying beer and — '

'I know all about it,' I said. 'And that he had Sean and Hanna delivering for him, and they got to keep a share of the profits.'

'Wow, okay. Anyway, I didn't like the way he'd send Hanna out there to deal with stuff. And there was other stuff with Roman. I mean, he creeped me out sometimes.'

'The texts.'

'God, did you see that on my phone? It wasn't just the picture. He was always asking me to send pictures of myself and I didn't want to do it. So, I started going out with Dennis, and Roman was pretty pissed.'

We were booting it down the interstate, cruising at eighty, Buffalo nearly an hour away,

Griffon half an hour after that.

'Things between me and Dennis were pretty serious. I mean, we really liked each other, even talking about whether he'd go back home after the end of the summer or what, and then one day he's just gone.'

'What do you mean?'

'One day he just disappears. Sends me a message that it's not working out between us, that whole thing about it not being me but him, right?' She sniffs, looks in the glove box for tissues, but the Subaru is clean. The glove box, the ashtrays, the console, everything is empty.

'I grabbed some napkins. Look in the bag.'

Claire finds them, blows her nose and wipes away tears.

'That must have hurt, him breaking it off with you all of a sudden, no apparent reason,' I said.

'Yeah. I thought, what'd I do? I thought everything was great. I was kinda destroyed by it, bummed out, everything. And then, a couple of weeks go by, and I hear from him.'

'He texted you,' I said.

'Yeah. He said he had to explain, that he had to leave Griffon because of the cops, that something happened. I had no idea what he was talking about, but I really wanted to see him, at least to find out why he dumped me all of a sudden. This was during all that stuff between my dad and your brother-in-law. We had cop cars watching our house a lot, and Dad figured it was Chief Perry trying to screw with us, you know? Scare us, let us know he and his people were watching us all the time. I figured that's what it was about, too, until Dennis said in his texts that the cops were probably just watching me.'

'Because they thought, since you two had been an item, you might lead them to him.'

'Item?' she said.

'A thing. A couple.'

'Oh yeah, exactly.' She paused a moment. 'So he said if we were going to get together, I had to be sure the cops weren't watching me. That was when I got the idea to do the switch with Hanna.'

'Sean was supposed to pick you up, and when he couldn't come, you hitched a ride with me.'

Claire nodded. 'I didn't mean to pick on you, honestly. I'd have gotten a lift with anyone. But when I saw it was you, that you were Scott's dad, that you'd be a safe person to go with . . . ' She paused. 'Even if you have been going around scaring the shit out of everybody.'

'That's over,' I said.

'So, you found out who gave Scott drugs?' she asked.

'No. Go on with your story.'

'There's not much more about that night. I mean, the switch worked, at least from my point of view.' She looked out the window, not wanting me to see her face. 'Hanna . . . went out and got in your car, I slipped out the back and went off with Dennis. We drove straight to the cottage.'

'So who was following you in the pickup that night? Ricky?'

Claire nodded. 'I got a look at him a couple of times. Once, when he was in a Griffon cruiser, watching our house, I went right up to the car and looked in the window and said, like, 'Fuck off and leave my father alone.' Because then, I figured that was why we were being watched, that it was about my dad, and the chief had probably told everyone on the force to give us a hard time. And then, another time, instead of being in a cruiser, he was in a pickup, and it was Ricky again. But even that time, I just figured he was doing off-duty stuff for the chief. It was him that night you gave me a ride. For a cop, he's not the greatest at not being seen.'

He got smarter with me. But Claire didn't have a car.

So it's Ricky who gets played when Hanna gets into my car. Ricky who stays on my tail.

Ricky who sees Hanna jump out of my car.

Ricky who sees Hanna tear the wig off her head and toss it.

Ricky realizes he's been tricked, that Claire has gotten away, most likely with Dennis.

Ricky goes after Hanna to find out where Claire has gone.

More tumblers falling into position.

I had an immediate question for Claire. 'Did Hanna have any idea where you were going with Dennis?'

'No,' Claire said. 'He said it was better that nobody knew.'

Ricky grabs Hanna, tries to get her to tell, but Hanna hasn't a clue. Ricky gets angry, frustrated. Ends up choking the life out of her. But he has the presence of mind to strip her from the waist down, plant the notion of sexual assault, put the clothes in Sean Skilling's car.

Claire continued. 'It wasn't till Dennis filled me in that I realized that Haines was just watching me, not me and my dad. In fact, I never noticed any other Griffon cop watching me.'

'Tell me about Dennis.'

She nodded. 'Okay, Dennis, he just didn't know what to do. He'd been hiding out ever since he'd left Griffon, at the cottage. He saw his dad once, just popped in. He lives up around Rochester.'

'We've met,' I said. 'He seems like a good man.'

Claire's eyes widened. 'Wow, like, you've really talked to everybody. But, yeah, Mr. Mullavey is really nice.' Again she looked away. 'It's going to kill him when he finds out about Dennis.'

I didn't have anything to say to that.

'He told his dad he was in trouble, but that he hadn't done anything wrong, and that when the police came around looking for him, he had to remember that. He said he needed time to figure out what to do, and he wanted to talk to me about it.'

'What happened, Claire?'

'So, one day, Dennis is cutting grass at the Pearce place.'

'Phyllis Pearce.'

'That's right. The lady that owns and runs Patchett's.'

'Right.'

'So Hooper usually sends out a crew, right? Like, there'll be two of them, but this day, the guy who usually went out with Dennis was sick, so Dennis said he could handle it on his own. And he gets to the Pearce house, and he can tell no one is home because there are no cars there. He's cutting the grass when he notices what looks like smoke coming out around one of the basement windows.'

She opened one of the water bottles and took a long drink, kept the bottle in her hand.

'So Dennis runs up and goes banging on the door, even though he knows no one is there, right? But just in case, because he doesn't want to barge in, you know? But when no one comes, he figures he better do something, so he kicks in the door, and he can see that the smoke is coming up from the basement. He runs down, and there's this fire coming from around the dryer.'

'Go on.'

'There's actually a fire extinguisher on the wall, so Dennis, he grabs it, and pulls that little pin or whatever they have on them.'

'Okay.'

'And he squirts out all this foamy stuff and he puts out the fire pretty fast.'

'Smart thinking,' I said. 'Although it might have been smarter for him to stay out and just call the fire department.'

'Yeah, well, he sure wishes he'd done that.' Claire realized she'd spoken of him in the present tense, and bit her lip. Tears welled up in her eyes almost instantly. I wanted to keep her focused on the story, so I asked her what happened next.

'That was when Dennis heard someone coughing.'

I turned and looked at her. 'So someone *was* home?'

'Yeah.'

'Phyllis Pearce?'

'No,' Claire said. 'It was a guy. An old man. I mean, Dennis didn't know he was an old man at first. All Dennis heard was the coughing. It was coming from the basement, just down this hall from the laundry room.'

She took another sip of her water.

'So Dennis goes to this door, but it's got a lock on it. Like, with a key? Kind of like what you have on your locker at school, but not a combination. There's someone behind the door, locked in. He's coughing and shouting, 'Fire,' but he can't shout very loud because it's all smoky and the man is really old and sick.'

'What'd Dennis do?'

'He figures he should get the guy out right away, get him some fresh air, and he looks around for a key, and it's right there, sitting on a windowsill, so it's really easy to find, and he takes off the lock and opens the door and he's, like, totally freaked out by what he finds.'

Claire stops her story. She seems almost afraid to continue it.

'What did Dennis find, Claire?'

She swallowed. 'First of all, Dennis said, forget the smoke. It was the other smells that just took his breath away. Like, shit and piss and stuff like that. So there's this guy in there, he's, like, seventy or eighty years old or something, and there's a wheelchair in the room, and this guy's sitting up in bed, he can't walk or anything and

428

he wants Dennis to get him out of there if the place is on fire. And Dennis calms him down, says the fire is out, but he's, like, what the fuck, right? Who is this guy and what's he doing down there?'

I got out my phone and handed it to Claire. 'Open up Safari,' I said. 'Google 'Harry Pearce, Griffon, Niagara Falls' and see what you get. While we're waiting, keep talking.'

She tapped the app, typed the words into the search field. 'It's taking a while.'

'That's okay.'

'So anyway, when the old man realizes he's not going to burn up, he tells Dennis he has to get him out of there. That he has to do it fast before his wife gets back because she'll get really mad. But then Dennis hears this noise from upstairs. Someone racing into the house. See, what Dennis figured was, the house had, like, an alarm system, but instead of going to a security company, it just sent a message to a couple of people.'

'Phyllis Pearce, and Ricky Haines,' I said.

'Yeah. The old man knows someone's coming, so he throws this thing to Dennis. That notebook I was going to show you.'

I tapped my chest. 'I got it.'

'Okay. So Dennis picks up the book and stuffs it in his pocket just before Ricky shows up, yelling 'Dad, Dad, Dad!' And he comes into the room, and he finds Dennis standing there. Ricky's all, like, who the hell are you, and Dennis says there was a fire, and by the way, what the fuck is this? You got an old guy prisoner in your basement?'

She looked down at her phone. 'Okay, some stuff's coming in. There's a story here about Niagara Falls tragedies.'

'See what it says about Harry Pearce.'

Claire moved the story up the screen with her thumb. 'Okay, so it says here he went out in a boat one night, didn't have oars with him and the motor didn't work, and he went over.'

'What else?'

'Okay, it was, like, seven years ago and — '

'What's it say about a body?'

'A body?'

'Did they find him?'

'Hang on.' She continued reading. 'Okay, they found the boat, but his body was never found.' Claire looked up from the screen. 'So, that's him? In the basement?'

'Evidently,' I said.

'That's messed up,' she said.

'So Ricky finds Dennis with Harry Pearce. Then what?'

'Ricky says something like, 'You're a dead man,' to Dennis, and starts to go for him, except Dennis is still holding the little fire extinguisher, right? And he aims it up and shoots shit right into Ricky's face. It buys Dennis enough time to get past him and get the hell out of there.'

'Why doesn't Dennis go straight to the cops?' I asked.

Claire looked at me like I was an idiot. 'How many reasons do you want? First, Dennis tells me, when you're black, you don't *ever* go to the cops. Not for anything, not ever. Second, Ricky *is* the cops. Then Ricky shouts out to Dennis as

430

he's leaving, 'You go to the police and you're dead. Totally dead.' That if he goes to the cops, Ricky'll know.'

I wasn't convinced. If Dennis didn't feel it was safe to go to the Griffon cops, he could have gone to the state police.

'And there was one more thing,' Claire said. 'Ricky says to Dennis, he says, 'You tell anyone, and I'll find your girlfriend, that fucking mayor's kid' — that's what Dennis says he said — 'and slice her goddamn tits off.''

I shot Claire a look.

'Yeah,' Claire said. 'Harsh, huh?'

59

'So that's why Dennis had to see me. He was scared for me, and he didn't know what he should do,' Claire said.

'After a couple of days, you must have come to some decision.'

Claire nodded. She found another napkin, blew her nose. 'I said to him that we should talk to my dad, that he'd know what to do. Dad doesn't trust the Griffon cops, but he would probably know someone, like, in the FBI or something like that.'

'That was a good plan,' I said.

'He was still scared to do it, but we talked about it for hours and hours, looking at the pluses and minuses. But we both realized we couldn't go on like this forever, hiding out.'

'No.'

Claire nodded. 'I can't believe they're both dead. Hanna and Dennis. My best friend, my boyfriend.' She started to sob quietly.

I let her cry for the next few miles, figured she might as well get it out. Not that she was likely to be finished before we got to Griffon. She'd be doing this for weeks. When her crying subsided somewhat, I got out my phone and placed a call.

I thought it was time.

Augustus Perry answered. 'What?'

'I didn't know one of your guys — Ricky Haines — was Phyllis Pearce's son.'

'If you're going to start telling me things you don't know, I'm gonna be on the phone with you all day,' he said.

'Why's his name not Pearce?'

Augie let out a long sigh. 'What the fuck does this have to do with anything?'

'Bear with me, okay?'

'Okay, from what I know, Phyllis was married once before to some guy with the last name Haines. They had Ricky, but when Ricky was a kid his dad had lung cancer or a heart attack or something. Few years after that, Phyllis started living with Harry Pearce and eventually married him, but she wanted the kid to keep the real dad's name. And Harry Pearce is dead, too.'

'Which leads me to my next question. He went over the falls seven years ago.'

'Why are you wasting my time if you already know this stuff?'

'They never found his body, right?'

I could almost hear Augie thinking through the connection. 'That's right. Just bits and pieces of the boat.'

'There's a reason,' I said. 'Harry Pearce is alive. He's living in Phyllis' basement.'

'What the hell are you talking about?'

'He's been there for years. He's some kind of invalid. Can't walk. They've been keeping him in a locked room.'

'Where are you getting this shit?'

'You think I just make this stuff up, Augie? If I had time to explain all this now, I would.'

'Where are you?'

'About an hour from Griffon. I found Claire

Sanders. Her boyfriend, Dennis Mullavey, cut the lawn for Pearce. There was smoke coming from the house one day. He broke in, put it out, found Harry Pearce locked up downstairs.'

'Jesus. You got Mullavey with you, too?'

'No,' I said. 'He's dead. Haines killed him.'

'What?'

'Hanna Rodomski, too, by the look of it.'

'What?' Augie asked. 'You know we've got the Skilling kid for that. They found — '

'I know what they found. I think Haines planted it. He could have done it anytime during the night.'

Another long pause from Augie. I filled it. 'Soon as I drop Claire off, I'm going to that house. I'm getting Harry Pearce out of there.'

'Not without me,' my brother-in-law said quietly.

'Fine,' I said. 'I'll meet you down the corner from the Pearce house. I'm still the better part of an hour away.'

'I'll be there,' Augie said, and hung up.

Claire looked over at me as I put the phone away. Her hand was full of damp tissues. 'You really trust him?'

'Not entirely,' I said. 'But I have to right now.'

I reached back into my jacket and handed her my phone. 'Call your dad.'

She entered the number, put the phone to her ear. 'No, Daddy, it's me,' she said. Bert Sanders must have seen the caller ID and been expecting to hear my voice.

'I'm okay, I'm okay,' she said. 'But Dennis, oh Daddy, Dennis is dead.' And she began to weep again.

I reached back into my jacket for the black notebook. With one hand on the wheel, I opened the book on my lap, got my thumb jammed in the middle to prop it open, then raised it to dashboard height so I could glance back and forth between the pages and the road.

I read a few parts at random.

'What the hell?' I said.

A different date was written at the top of every page in a small, precise handwriting. Then, *Breakfast: Rice Krispies with milk, orange juice, banana, coffee with cream, Lunch: Peanut butter sandwich on white bread, two chocolate chip cookies, milk, apple. Dinner: Lasagna, Caesar salad, chocolate cake, tea.*

I flipped to another day. *Breakfast: Oatmeal with raisins and brown sugar, orange juice, coffee with cream. Lunch: Big Mac, french fries, Coke, apple pie. Dinner: Shake and bake chicken, rice with butter, peas, glass of water, no dessert.*

Every page was the same.

Harry kept a record of every single thing he ate.

★　★　★

Claire had been talking to her father for about five minutes, filling him in on what she'd done, where she'd been, when she handed the phone to me. 'He wants to talk to you.'

'Hey,' I said.

'Mr. Weaver, I can't thank you enough. You saved her life.'

I wasn't so sure it would have needed saving if

I hadn't led Haines to the cottage. 'We'll be back soon.'

'I'll meet you on the way in,' he said. 'I want to see her as soon as possible.'

'Okay,' I said. 'The police are going to want to talk to her. First thing I think you should do is take her to a doctor. She may be suffering mild shock. She's been through a hell of a lot.'

'Of course,' Sanders said. 'I can't tell you how grateful I am.'

It occurred to me I'd be passing the hospital just south of Griffon on the way. I told Sanders to meet me at the emergency room entrance. I was guessing no more than forty minutes.

'I'll be there,' he said.

When I was done with the call I said to Claire, 'Almost home.'

She nodded tiredly.

I handed her the book. 'Have you looked at this?'

'Yeah. Dennis and I looked all through it. It's kind of nuts.'

'Did you read through the whole thing?'

'Yup.'

'Is there anything else in it? Did he write about what was being done to him, about being kept locked up?'

'Nope. It's just all about food. What he ate every day. Why would someone do that?'

'It might be a kind of obsessive-compulsive disorder,' I ventured.

'Dennis and I couldn't figure out why he'd have wanted Dennis to have it.'

I thought about that. 'It's dated. And someone

might recognize the writing. And Harry Pearce's obsession with his diet probably predates his so-called death. It's proof that he's alive, that he has been for the last seven years.'

I wanted to take the conversation in another direction. 'You said something, a while ago, that you haven't explained. About Officer Haines. You said — your words — about him feeling you up. What was that about?'

'Oh yeah,' she said. 'That's actually a story about Scott.'

'Scott? What do you mean?'

'Okay, so, I told you the other night I didn't really know Scott all that well.'

I glanced over. 'Uh-huh.'

'And I didn't, but sometimes he'd hang out with me and Hanna and Sean. Like, not a lot, but sometimes.' She paused. 'He was okay. Kind of different, and a bit weird, but okay.'

'Thanks.'

'The thing is, he really stood up for me once. And it had to do with Ricky Haines.'

'What do you mean, he stood up for you?'

'Like, sort of protected me, that kind of thing.'

I gave her a look that said I wanted to know more. 'When was this?'

'I don't know. Not long before he, you know, before he died.'

'What happened?'

'A bunch of us were at Patchett's, and okay, we're all underage, I get that, but everyone does it. But we were coming out one night, and Scott happened to be there, kind of hanging around, and I was going down the side of the building, to

437

the parking lot, you know?'

'Yeah, I know.'

'And Haines, he stops me and says, 'We have to check you for drugs.''

'Did you have any on you?'

'Jeez, no,' she said.

'So Haines, he says he has to search me, and I tell him he's got no right to do that, but you know our cops, like they've ever worried about that kind of shit.'

'Go on.'

'So he puts me up against the wall, with my arms spread and everything, and he starts patting me down. And he starts coming up my body, and when he gets here' — and she pointed to her breasts — 'he starts really checking them out.' She made her hands into cups. 'Like that.'

I felt my cheeks flush with anger.

'So anyway, Scott, he's been watching the whole thing, and when he sees the cop, you know, getting his rocks off, Scott kind of goes nuts.'

'What . . . did he do?' I asked. I remembered Scott telling us this story.

'He starts yelling, 'Hey, pervert, why don't you grab onto yourself!' and other stuff, like 'Rapist!' and just general stuff like leave me alone,' she said.

I felt a small lump in my throat.

'What happened then?' I asked.

'The cop looked at him and told him to get lost or, you know, worse, and then Scott says something like 'I'm gonna tell my uncle' and 'I'll remember you.' That kind of thing.'

'Scott threatened him?'

Claire nodded. 'Yeah, kinda. Later, Scott says I

438

should charge the guy with sexual assault, but I just didn't want to get into it. I mean, it was all so complicated, with my dad having this political kind of fight with the chief, and I thought, right, if I say some cop assaulted me, the chief'll just say my dad put me up to it to make the cops look bad. It'd be, like, this huge can of worms, you know? So I never even told my dad about it, because I knew he'd just go insane. But Scott, man, he was something, telling that cop he'd get him fired. He wasn't even high when he said it.'

She winced. 'I'm sorry. I didn't mean it like that or anything. But I wanted you to know. Scott, he really hated that cop. He even had a run-in with him another time, saw him in his cruiser, pointed to him and called him a perv again. Took off running when the cop started to get out of his car and come after him. Haines really hated Scott, you could tell. That might even be why he rousted me a second time, not that long ago, just to get even for what Scott did. Took my purse and we had to go in and get it the next day.'

I felt numb.

'Oh yeah, and here's another thing,' Claire said. 'Scott told me, that time he saw Haines in his cruiser, Haines did that thing where you shoot somebody with your finger.'

Ricky Haines, the cop who found Scott's dead body in the parking lot of Ravelson Furniture, the cop who'd come to our door to deliver the bad news, the cop I now knew wasn't afraid to kill anyone who presented a threat to him.

He knew our son, and had it in for him.

60

I was rattled when those kids nearly pitched me into the Niagara River. I was more than a little shook up a couple of hours earlier when we were being stalked at the cottage.

But that was nothing compared to this.

All this time we'd believed Scott had killed himself. Maybe not intentionally, but he'd been the author of his own misfortune, as they say. He was under the influence of ecstasy and either jumped off that roof thinking he could fly or stumbled over the edge while he was high.

Not an easy thing to live with.

But this changed everything. What Claire had just told me suggested Scott didn't die by misadventure. What Claire had just told me suggested Scott had been deliberately killed.

'Mr. Weaver, you okay?' Claire asked.

We were rounding Buffalo to the north on the 290 bypass, almost to the bridge to Grand Island. A mixture of rage and anxiety was clouding my vision, like someone had misted the inside of the Subaru's windows with blood red spray paint. I had to shake my head to clear things. My hands were wrapped so tightly around the steering wheel, my arms were starting to ache.

That son of a bitch. That goddamn motherfucking son of a bitch.

He threw my kid off the roof.

No, I told myself. *I didn't know that. I didn't*

440

know that at all. I didn't have any evidence of that.

But a feeling in my gut that felt like a cancer was telling me otherwise.

Haines could have seen Scott as a serious threat. Sure, the Griffon cops took a lot of liberties and the locals didn't mind turning a blind eye to them. But this was different. A cop who took a vandal out by the water tower and busted a few of his teeth was one thing, but a cop who went around touching young girls? Feeling them up? That was something else altogether.

And Haines had to know that Scott's uncle was the chief. What if he told Augie? How many other times, that Claire didn't know about, had Scott crossed paths with Haines? How many times had he taunted him?

A tattletale.

That's how Haines must have seen him. A tattletale who could derail his career, have him brought up on charges.

I imagined various scenarios.

Did Haines see Scott walking down the street, maybe get out of his car and chase after him? Did Scott, using the key he had, let himself into Ravelson Furniture and run up to the roof, thinking he could get away? Did Haines chase him all the way up there, then pitch him off the side?

Or was Scott already up there, making noise, causing a disturbance? Did Haines drive by and see something suspicious on the roof? And when he got up there, and discovered it was Scott, did he see an opportunity?

'Really, Mr. Weaver, talk to me.'

I looked over at Claire suddenly, as though she was a hypnotist who'd snapped her fingers to bring me out of a trance.

'What?'

'Are you okay?'

'Yeah.'

'After I mentioned Scott, you went all kind of weird.'

'It was nothing,' I said. 'Just . . . when you mentioned him, it brought back some memories.'

'God, I'm sorry. I only wanted to say something nice.'

'No, it's okay. I'm glad you said it. I really am.' I tried to focus. 'Did Scott ever say anything to the effect that he was scared of Haines? That he thought Haines might do something to him?'

Claire shook her head. 'No. I mean, everybody my age in Griffon figures the cops are going to do something to us eventually. We're teenagers, so we must be guilty of something, right?'

I didn't say anything. I was still fighting the red mist, determined to deliver Claire to her father without running off the road before I could get to the hospital.

As if reading my mind, Claire said, 'I feel okay, you know. I mean, I feel horrible, but I don't think I have anything wrong with me.'

'You and your father can decide what to do.'

I was worried I'd sounded as though I didn't care anymore. That now that I'd found Claire, that I'd dealt with the burden of responsibility

I'd felt since she'd hopped into my car, she was no longer my concern. That once I handed her off to her father, I could walk away from this.

That wasn't how I felt. Not really. But a big arm had just swept everything off my very cluttered desk and thrown it to the floor.

There was nothing on it now but Scott.

We crossed Grand Island saying nothing to each other. As we were passing the discount outlet malls in Niagara Falls on our right, Claire asked, 'Who's going to tell Dennis' dad?'

Another father about to experience unimaginable grief. I felt as though we were all being sucked into a black hole of never-ending emptiness.

'I don't know,' I said. 'Probably the state police. Once they figure out what's happened at the cottage.'

'Shouldn't you be helping them with that?' she asked. 'Shouldn't you be the one to go see Dennis' dad?'

As long as I live, I'll be sorry for what I said next.

I turned and snapped, 'Haven't I done enough? If it hadn't been for you knocking on my goddamn window I wouldn't have been dragged into any of this.'

Her face fell like a stone and her eyes welled with tears.

'I'm sorry,' I said. 'I'm sorry.'

'Nobody asked you to come looking for me!' she said. 'We'd have figured out what to do! We didn't need you! Dennis wouldn't even be dead if it wasn't for you!'

'Claire — '

'Leave me alone,' she said. 'Just get me to my dad. I want to see my dad.'

I saw the blue 'H' on the horizon. Four minutes later, I was wheeling into the Emergency entrance. Bert Sanders was standing there, not knowing what car to look for, but when he saw Claire in the passenger seat he started waving and ran up to meet us.

He had Claire's door open before she could get to the handle, and he scooped her into his arms, the two of them crying.

Sanders, looking over his daughter's shoulder at me, smiled and said, 'Thank you so much, Mr. Wea — '

I reached over to pull the passenger door shut. 'Later,' I said, and stomped on the accelerator.

61

Augie was waiting for me on the corner, a few hundred yards down the street from the Pearce house, sitting high in his white Suburban. I pulled up alongside him and powered down the passenger window. Augie, who probably remembers what everyone in Griffon drives, looked at the Subaru and said, 'With all the shit that's going on, you had time to get a new car?'

'Noticed whether anyone's home?' I asked, pointing down the street.

'No one's come or gone, but there's no car there, so I'd say nobody's at the house.' He paused. 'Except, of course, Harry in the basement.' Augie looked at me skeptically, and who could blame him, really?

'There's something else I need to talk to you about,' I said. 'About Scott.'

'This got anything to do with what you think is going on in that house?'

'Not exactly,' I said.

Augie's expression turned slightly sympathetic. 'Nobody cares more about Scott than me, Cal, but could we tackle one thing at a time?'

I was churning inside about Ricky Haines, but I took his point. We were here to find Harry Pearce.

Instead of answering him, I drove the hundred yards up the street and parked in front of Phyllis Pearce's house. Augie followed and pulled into the driveway, coming to a stop close to the front porch. Walking up to join him, I noticed again how long the grass was. After Dennis quit, Hooper's hadn't had enough staff to meet all their customers' needs.

We mounted the porch steps together. Given that Augie was the chief of police, I let him go first and be the one to ring the bell.

'You said no one was here,' I said.

'Just in case,' he replied.

Twenty seconds passed with no one opening the door. Augie tried it, but it was locked. I wasn't naive enough to ask Augie whether he needed a warrant. I wouldn't have wanted to wait around for one, anyway.

'Let's take a walk around,' he said. 'Before I go busting down a door I might as well see if one's been left open.'

We went around to the back and tried that door, but it was locked, too. Nor did we find any reachable windows that could be forced open. There were several basement windows at ground level, but Augie had no interest in smashing any of them. 'I'm too old to get into a house that way.'

So we went back to the front door.

'Here goes,' Augie said, reared back, and drove the heel of his boot into the door just below the knob. The door didn't open.

'Shit,' he said. 'Nearly broke my knee.'

'Let me give it a shot.' I hit the door hard enough for the jamb to start splitting. Then Augie took another turn, and the door swung open.

'Probably going to get a bill from Phyllis for that,' he said.

We entered the house. Augie called out, 'Hello? Police! Anyone home?' We heard nothing back.

We opened several doors. A couple opened onto closets, another onto a bathroom. The fourth door, just as you stepped inside the kitchen, opened onto a set of stairs that led down.

'After you,' Augie said.

I flicked on a light. The basement was low-ceilinged and unfinished. Bare bulbs instead of light fixtures. Cement-block walls instead of paneling. There were half a dozen rooms. One was a workshop, with tools hanging on the wall. A couple of them held old furniture. Another was jammed with metal filing cabinets. Augie opened the top drawer of one of them, glanced in.

'Business stuff for Patchett's,' he said.

Another room contained a washer and dryer and rack. A shelf, grungy with spilled fabric softener and liquid detergent, was heavy with cleaners and chemicals.

'This is where the fire started,' I said.

'Huh?'

'It's what got Dennis down here. Smoke from the dryer. Lint catching on fire, probably. Look, there's the fire extinguisher on the wall.' Off the other end of the laundry room was a short hallway, and a door at the end.

'Augie,' I said.

He looked at the door, then at me.

'Guess we should have a look.'

I got ahead of him. There was a lock hanging from the door. I banged on it.

'Mr. Pearce? Are you in there? Mr. Pearce?'

Augie joined in. 'It's Augustus Perry, Mr. Pearce. Chief of police. We're going to get you out of there.'

There was a shallow basement window by the door that came down a foot from the ceiling, and just as Claire had said, there was a key sitting on the sill. I grabbed it, fitted the key into the lock, twisted it, and the lock opened. I set it on the sill with the key.

I made an effort to keep my hand from shaking.

Augie placed his hand on the door and started to push.

'Whew,' he said, as we both caught a whiff of something unpleasant that someone had tried to mask with Lysol. A mix of mustiness, dead mice, urine, and God knows what else.

The door was wide open. I wasn't prepared for what I was about to see. It wasn't what I was expecting at all.

The room was littered with odd bits of furniture, stacks of old magazines, a busted record player with no arm, a box of eight-track tapes. An old metal rollaway bed that was folded up at the middle, a soiled-looking mattress trapped within it, was tucked into a corner behind more cardboard boxes. A junk room, illuminated by a bare bulb in an exposed ceiling receptacle.

That was it.

No Harry Pearce.

Augie turned and looked at me. 'When Phyllis sends me the bill for her front door, I'm giving it to you.'

62

Phyllis unlocks the door and says to him, a broad smile on her face, 'This is your lucky day.'

Harry Pearce sits up in bed. 'What are you talking about?'

'Ice cream,' she says. 'We're going out for ice cream.'

Harry looks skeptical. 'Don't tease me.'

'It's true. We're going to do it.'

He's a kid getting a new puppy. 'This is the best day ever.'

It amazes her sometimes how childlike he has become over time. Once so argumentative and abusive, now so compliant and captivated by the thought of the simplest pleasures.

Phyllis nods. 'It's time,' she says. 'It's really time. But it's going to take a bit of work to get you out. It's not like we've installed ramps over the years.'

'That's okay,' he says, swinging his legs out of the bed and leaning forward to grab onto the arm of his wheelchair. 'We'll figure something out.'

He pulls himself out of bed, twists, and drops into the chair. While his legs have withered away to sticks over the years, his arms are roped with muscle from lifting himself into and out of the wheelchair. Not that he's had a lot of places to wheel himself around. The room he's lived in for seven years is only ten by ten feet, and not the most hospitable environment. Cold cement floor, cinder-block walls. Every once in a while, she has let him wheel himself around the basement for exercise, past the washer and dryer, into the sewing room, or the workshop he once enjoyed, with his wrenches and other tools all arranged so perfectly.

But even those short times outside the walls of his cell have made her nervous. If someone were to show up unexpectedly, she'd have to return him quickly, close the door, get the lock on in a hurry.

She tried to tell herself the room was not a cell. For the longest time, it was Harry's recovery room, where she and Richard treated him, looked after him, nursed him back to health. Sure, he was never the way he was before. Not even close. But what was done was done. One had to make the best of a bad situation, and hadn't they done their best to do that for him? All this time?

In retrospect, sure, there were things they could have done differently. Maybe, if they'd called for an ambulance right away, the moment he tumbled down those stairs, they might have been able to do something for him. But who knew he was paralyzed from the waist down and that his spine was in all likelihood broken? How were they supposed to know that? And there was more at stake, too. After all, Richard had just joined the Griffon police. He had his whole future ahead of him. Was it right for him to give up all that for a momentary lapse in judgment? Was that fair?

In many ways, really, Harry only had himself

to blame. He'd been a good man, most of the time. He'd been there for Phyllis when her husband died years earlier, had comforted her, helped her settle the estate, taken her to dinner, invited her, and her son, to join him on trips to California and Mexico. He'd treated Richard like he was his own son. Harry loved the boy, there was nothing fake about it, and Richard, who so desperately needed a father figure, loved him right back. If anything, it was the bond between them that persuaded Phyllis to let Harry move in with her, and eventually accept his proposal to let him be her second husband.

She should have paid more attention to the signs. There was something not quite right about Harry. Before their marriage, his obsession with record-keeping, with saving every receipt — he had six-year-old receipts from donut shops, for crying out loud — seemed like nothing more than charming eccentricities. In fact, he'd be a real asset at the bar, making sure the books balanced. But there were other things. Those books where he recorded everything he ate, in that small, precise handwriting of his, always making note of the date. Didn't matter how often folks at Patchett's teased him about it. It hadn't occurred to Phyllis back then that maybe Harry was obsessive-compulsive.

Maybe, if that had been it, things would have been manageable. But there were the mood swings. One day he'd want to take her and Richard to the movies or the outlet mall to spend some cash, and then the next he'd be plunged into the depths of depression. And with the depression, there was often anger. And drinking. He refused to see a doctor — let alone a psychiatrist or psychologist — but Phyllis figured that in addition to his OCD tendencies, he might be bipolar, or manic-depressive. As time went on, he became a compendium of psychiatric tics.

At his low points, nothing was too trivial to find fault with. Lights needlessly left on, getting in the car after Phyllis or Richard had used it and finding less than a quarter tank of gas. Phyllis had to make sure the spoons stood up in the drying rack so water wasn't trapped in them. Made Harry crazy when that happened. He believed Phyllis and her son discussed him behind his back, which, of course, was true.

On rare occasions, there was violence.

Like the time Phyllis lost the phone bill. Harry, who paid the bills every two weeks, couldn't understand why it wasn't with all the others. He searched the trash and determined that Phyllis had inadvertently pitched it with the junk mail. Harry was apoplectic. In a fit of rage, he grabbed her by the wrist, held her hand flat on the kitchen table, and slammed a mug down on it.

No broken bones, but she couldn't move her hand for a week. Harry was instantly remorseful. Became the world's most attentive husband. Made all the meals for days. Bought Phyllis flowers. Took Richard to a Bills game to prove he was a solid stepfather.

But he couldn't hold it together indefinitely, especially if he'd had too much to drink.

Sometimes it'd just be a slap. And there was that time, while behind the wheel, he punched her thigh when she thought she'd left an iron plugged in. (She hadn't, which only further exasperated him.)

And yet, in spite of everything, Phyllis and Richard did not hate the man. Phyllis made apologies for him, said they had to cut him some slack. He was a tormented person. He'd served in Vietnam, seen things no one should have to see, done things no one should have to do. Often, in the middle of the night, he'd wake up screaming, the mattress soaked with perspiration, as he relived some horror from over there in the late sixties.

'Harry served his country,' Phyllis often said, 'and it left him scarred.'

Phyllis had her hands full with Richard, too. Maybe, when your real father dies and you're just a boy, it messes up your head. Or when you get a new dad who's got a slew of problems, you find a way to inherit them, even though there's no genetic link. Who knew? But as Richard moved through his teens, he showed signs of not being able to control certain impulses. There were those two incidents — at least two that Phyllis knew about — where he inappropriately touched some girls at school. Okay, call it what it was: fondled. There were meetings with the principal, apologies, a suspension. Luckily, nothing more than that. And then there was his propensity to erupt in anger. Calm and serene on the surface, but simmering underneath, like lava bubbling in a dormant volcano. Then,

boom. *Phyllis wanted to take him to see someone, too, but Harry wouldn't hear of it. 'He's
just a boy,' he said. 'He's burning off steam.'*

That's certainly what happened that night,
seven years ago.

Harry was in the grips of the black dog, as
Winston Churchill had famously said, and had
been that way for the better part of a week.
Phyllis and Richard had tried their best to steer
clear of him. Phyllis was looking after Patchett's
on her own, insisting that her husband stay
home until he was feeling more up to it.

One Monday night, when the staff were
trusted to run Patchett's so that the Pearces
could have a night off, after Harry had recorded
in his notebook what Phyllis had served for
dinner — pork chops, macaroni and cheese, and
canned peas, as it turned out — he announced
he wanted ice cream.

Phyllis said they had no ice cream. Harry
wanted to know how this was possible, since he
had prepared a shopping list for Phyllis and he
knew he had written ice cream on it.

'I missed it,' she said. 'I'll get some next time.'

'What is the point,' he wanted to know, 'of my
writing things on your shopping list, if you're not
going to look at it and read what's on it? Maybe
you got it and forgot.' He rooted around in the
freezer atop the refrigerator, knocking frozen
steaks and containers of Minute Maid orange
juice onto the floor. 'Goddamn it.'

'Harry,' Phyllis said.

Richard watched this play out, standing in the
doorway between the kitchen and the dining

454

room, arms folded across his chest. A member of the Griffon police department for only a few months but still living at home, he hadn't yet changed out of his uniform after a day of writing tickets and directing traffic at an accident scene.

'Is it too fucking much to ask that we always have some ice cream in here?' Harry asked, tossing out more items. An ice cube tray hit the floor, scattering tiny blocks of ice across the linoleum. 'What about the downstairs freezer?' he asked. 'We have any down there?'

'No,' Phyllis said.

He flung open the door to the basement anyway.

Richard, up till now, hadn't moved an inch.

Harry spun around, took a step in her direction, pointed a finger, holding it three inches from her nose. 'After all I've done, helping you and your boy all these bloody years, do I ask for that much? Do I? I swear to God, if I — '

It all happened in less than ten seconds.

'Shut up!' Richard said, storming into the room, grabbing one of the wooden kitchen table chairs, holding it by the back with both hands, swinging it like a bat toward his stepfather.

He instinctively turned away, and the chair hit him across the back. Hard. Harry Pearce stumbled forward, his foot landing on one of the cubes of ice.

In a Three Stooges episode it might have been comical.

Harry's foot went out from under him and he pitched forward, right through the open doorway to the basement. Made a hell of a noise going down. But when he reached the bottom, there was total silence.

Phyllis screamed.

'Dad!' Richard cried, throwing aside the chair.

The two of them ran down the steps, finding Harry in a twisted heap, eyes closed, not moving.

'Oh my God, he's dead,' Phyllis said.

Richard knelt, laid his head sideways on his father's chest. 'No, he's not. He's breathing. His heart's going.'

Phyllis dropped to her knees, put her head to his chest as well, needing to confirm it for herself. 'Yes, I hear it. I hear it. Harry? Harry, can you hear me?'

Harry, who had adopted the shape of a pretzel, did not respond.

'I'll call an ambulance,' Richard said, getting up. He went up the stairs two at a time and as he was disappearing into the kitchen his mother called up to him.

'Wait,' she said.

His head reappeared, framed in the doorway, silhouetted against the kitchen lights. 'What?'

'Don't . . . I mean, just . . . wait.'

'Mom, every second counts.'

'He'll be okay,' Phyllis said. 'He just needs a minute. Help me straighten him out.'

'We shouldn't move him,' her son said.

'We'll be really careful. I've got that old rollaway bed in the back room. I'll bring it out and we can put him down on that.'

'Mom . . . ' Richard came back down the stairs halfway.

456

'Richard, listen to me,' she said. 'If you call the ambulance, they're going to call the police, too.'

'I'm the police,' Richard said.

'I know. But others will come. And when Harry wakes up, and tells them what you did . . . '

'I . . . I didn't mean to do it. He just made me so angry. I thought he was going to hit you.'

'I know, love, I know. I totally understand. But the police, they won't. They won't understand. You're just starting out. It wouldn't be right, it wouldn't be fair for them to hold this against you.'

'I . . . I don't know . . . '

'Get the bed set up. Set it up right here. I'll straighten him out.'

Richard brought in the rollaway, the rusty wheels squeaking in protest. He opened it and flattened it, patted the mattress to smooth it out.

'Help me lift him,' Phyllis said.

Together, they got him onto the bed. 'He's still breathing,' she said. 'He seems to be breathing just fine.'

'I couldn't stand what he was doing,' Richard said. 'He just wouldn't stop. He couldn't let it go, he — '

'It's okay. Everything's going to be okay. We'll look after him. He'll probably be fine in a few hours. He'll have a bad headache is all. You wait and see. It doesn't make any sense to make a bigger deal out of this than it really is.'

'If that's what you think, Mom,' Richard said. She always seemed to know the right thing to do.

But was this right? It had seemed so at the

time. But Harry was not fine in a few hours. He didn't regain consciousness for two days. When he did, he wasn't the same. He was simpler, somehow.

When Richard and Phyllis tried to coax him out of bed, they discovered he could not move his legs.

'We should call a doctor,' Richard said. 'He probably needs an X-ray or something.'

'We'll give it a few more days,' Phyllis insisted. 'Maybe — maybe whatever broke that keeps his legs from working will fix itself.'

Neither one of them really believed that, but they were willing to give it a go.

At Patchett's, people asked where Harry was.

'He's got that nasty flu bug that's been going around,' Phyllis told them. 'Last thing I want is him coming in here and sneezing on the chicken wings.'

After a week had gone by, Phyllis and Richard knew they had a real problem on their hands.

They'd waited too long to call for help. How were they going to explain their actions? Letting a man fall down a full flight of stairs and not calling for help? It was a bit late to start claiming self-defense. If what Richard had done had been to save his mother's life, they could have called the police that night. After all, as a spanking-new police officer, Richard would have a pretty good idea what constituted self-defense.

But they didn't.

And while Harry Pearce was a little groggier than he used to be, every time Richard descended those stairs to see how his father was coming along, the man would raise one arm weakly, point at him, and say, 'You. You son of a bitch.'

Meaning that pretty damn literally.

Getting him medical attention now posed a considerable risk to Phyllis and her son, but particularly to him.

And at work, people continued to ask, 'How's Harry? Where the hell is he? When's he coming back?'

'What are we going to do?' Richard asked one night as the two of them sat at the kitchen table, listening to Harry snoring downstairs.

'I don't know,' his mother said.

'People are going to keep asking and asking where Dad is,' he said.

'We have to stop them from asking,' she said. 'This needs to end, somehow.'

Richard leaned back in his chair. 'What are you saying? You're not thinking we should — '

'No, no, of course not. But everyone needs to think something has happened, something permanent, so they won't be asking where he is anymore.'

'Like, maybe he went to see his cousin,' Richard said. 'In Calgary.'

Phyllis shook her head. 'People would keep asking when he was coming back. No, we need to tell a story that will stop people from asking questions once and for all.' Her mouth tightened. 'I went to the library today. I found out something interesting. I found that over the years, quite a few people who've fallen into the river accidentally and gone over the falls — some of them were never found.'

459

'Wait,' Richard said. 'I thought you just said you weren't saying we'd do anything like that. We're not going to send him over the falls. We can't . . . I mean, he's my father. Okay, not my real father, but that's what he's been to me for a hell of a long time.'

She reached out and held his hand. 'I know that. But I was thinking, if we could make people think he went over the falls, then we can just keep looking after him. Right here.'

'For how long?'

'As long as we have to.'

'But he might . . . what if he actually gets better? Well enough to, you know, walk up those stairs and out the door?'

'Richard, he's not going to get better. His spine is broken. Something's happened to his head, too. He's gone a bit simple. He's not even obsessed with things the way he used to be, other than still writing down what he eats in that stupid book. I'm telling you, he's not going to get up and walk out of the house one day and tell everybody what happened to him.'

They came up with the boat idea. That Harry got drunk one night, decided to take his boat out into the river. They'd leave his car and trailer at the river's edge. Leave the oars in the car so later, when the boat, and its empty tank of gas, was found downstream from the falls, the authorities would be able to put it together. They'd search for his body, maybe for a few days, before they gave up.

And that's what they did.

There was an article in the paper, an item on

460

each of the local stations. CNN even picked up the story. There was a funeral, even though there was no corpse to bury. Phyllis wept. Richard held her and consoled her.

A lot of attention for ten days or so.

And then everyone moved on. No more questions about what was up with Harry.

Richard got his own apartment soon after. He couldn't bear to be in the house twenty-four/ seven. But he returned nearly every day at some point — usually before or after his shift — to check on his stepfather. Brought him meals, helped with his toileting needs, cleaned up after him, found books and magazines for him to read, but mostly magazines, since Harry found it hard to concentrate on books.

Everything seemed to be going along okay.

Until one day Phyllis came home late one night after closing down Patchett's, and there, ten feet from the door, dragging himself across the living room carpet, was Harry.

Nearly gave her a heart attack.

Another twenty minutes and he'd have been on the front porch. Another ten after that, and he'd have crawled down to the sidewalk, where anyone might have seen him.

From that day forward, a lock went on the door of his room in the basement.

You had to do what you had to do.

'What happens,' Richard asked once, 'when he really does . . . you know, pass away?'

It was something Phyllis had definitely thought about.

'We'll take him out into the woods,' she said,

'and dig a nice hole for him and cover him up, and we'll have our own little private funeral for him. That's what we'll do.'

But today, after seven years, Phyllis has determined that process may have to be sped up a bit.

Because it's only a matter of time before someone starts putting things together, comes to the house armed with a search warrant, finds Harry down in that room.

Now, it's all about getting rid of the evidence.

Harry is the evidence.

If the police show up, claiming to have been told some cockamamie story about keeping Harry in the basement, she can say, 'What are you talking about? Go down there, have a look. That's just crazy talk.'

The only one who's seen him down there is Dennis. And Dennis will have told Claire. The good news is, Richard has taken care of both of them. The only things left to worry about now are that detective, and the book.

Phyllis is betting he has the book. If she can take care of both those matters at once, she might find a way to get out from under all this. For herself, and for her son.

Soon, she'll put in a call to Cal Weaver. But not just yet. There are more immediate concerns.

'What are all these boxes?' Harry asks when she wheels him out of his room and past the washer and dryer.

'I'm moving you upstairs,' she says. 'With you out of the basement, I can store some more stuff in there.'

462

'Where? What are you talking about?'

'I thought I'd give you Richard's room. It's been empty a long time. You'll have a window and a view and a fresh breeze when you want it.'

'I don't know what to say — Really?'

'You wait here for a few minutes while I deal with your old room.'

'I won't be going back in there?'

'I can promise you, Harry, you won't be sleeping another night in there.'

She feels something catch in her throat. She goes into the room with a garbage bag, stuffs it with anything that says 'Harry.' Clothes, adult diapers, scraps of food, a bag of cookies, used tissues, bedding.

She forces the rollaway back together, pushes it into a corner of the room, piles some boxes in front of it. Brings in a few more boxes that she's been storing in other rooms. Sprays some air freshener, takes a sniff, concludes that it's not that bad. Working feverishly it takes her the better part of twenty minutes to do it all, but she is a strong woman. Attributes it to years of lugging cases of beer.

'Okay, we're good to go,' she says, closing the door and locking it, more out of habit than anything else.

'I'm going to need help on the stairs,' he says.

He wheels the chair up to the bottom step. Phyllis gets her hands under his arms, lifts. He grabs onto the railing with his right hand, and with Phyllis on his left, he manages to get to the kitchen. He crawls onto the floor and stays there while Phyllis runs back down, folds up the

463

wheelchair, and brings it up one flight.

'That's a new fridge,' Harry says, scanning the kitchen.

Had to grind up sleeping pills and put them in his food the day they replaced the old refrigerator when it conked out. At least that was upstairs. That time the furnace went out in the basement, she not only drugged Harry, she tied him down to the bed and taped his mouth, just in case he woke up, which, thank the Lord, he didn't. When the washing machine broke down, she got Richard to research it on the Internet and fix it himself. Still leaked a bit, but it did the job.

Phyllis gets him back into his chair, steers him toward the back door. 'Aren't we going out the front?' he asks.

'It's easier to get you into the car this way,' she says.

She realizes, as she grips the handles of the wheelchair, that her hands are shaking. She gets ahead of the wheelchair, opens the door, then gets around behind him again and pushes the chair outside. Phyllis tips the chair back slightly to ease it down the two steps.

The car is there, backed right up to the bottom step. The trunk is open.

Harry says, 'Why you got all that plastic lining the trunk, Phyllis?'

It has a low lip, this trunk. Phyllis tips Harry forward, like she's emptying a wheelbarrow. The top half of his body falls in. He throws his hands forward, trying to brace himself.

'The hell are you doing, Phyllis? Damn, I hit my head.'

'Sorry, honey,' she says. 'Can't have anyone seeing you on the way to Baskin-Robbins.'

'For Christ's sake, I can scrunch down in the seat!'

She tips the lower half of his body into the car, pulls the chair away, folds it, and puts it into the backseat of the sedan.

'Phyllis! Get me the hell out of here!'

'One second,' she says, and runs back into the house, opens the kitchen drawer where she keeps her knives.

'I've been good to him,' she tells herself, her eyes starting to fill with tears. 'I've done the best I can.'

Phyllis grabs the knife she always uses to carve the Christmas turkey and runs back outside.

63

'Phyllis must have moved him,' I said to Augie. 'She had to know we were coming, so she got him out of here.'

'This is insane,' Augie said.

I shifted some boxes around. 'I think this stuff was just moved in here. There's no dust on the floor around the boxes. And — hang on. There's half a sandwich down there, and the bread's not moldy. Would you come eat a sandwich in this room if you didn't have to?'

'I can barely breathe,' my brother-in-law said. 'Wait a second.' He left the room.

'What?' I said.

'Marks on the floor,' he said. 'Like something was wheeled through here. Went through some water on the floor, leaking out from under the washing machine . . . '

'A wheelchair,' I said.

'Maybe.'

'I'm not making this shit up,' I said.

'Let's go back up,' he said. We rendezvoused in the kitchen. 'Think Phyllis drives a Crown Vic. Tan-colored one. Looks sort of like a cop car without the bells and whistles.'

He got out his phone, told the Griffon police dispatcher to have everyone looking for Phyllis Pearce's car. 'Try Patchett's first. If you see it, don't do anything. Just let me know.'

He put the phone away and said, 'We might as

well head over there anyway.'

'I need to talk to you about this other thing.'

Augie pulled back a kitchen chair and plopped himself down. He gestured for me to do the same, and I did.

'Go ahead,' he said wearily.

'I think Ricky Haines killed Scott.'

I'd found, over the years, it was nearly impossible to shock Augustus Perry. Provoke, yes, but not shock. Even if you managed to say something that surprised him, he'd do his best to remain stone-faced.

He wasn't able to hide his reaction this time.

'What?' he bellowed. 'What the fuck are you talking about?'

'Haines was searching Claire Sanders out back of Patchett's one night. Used it as an excuse to give her one hell of a patdown. Scott saw it happen, threatened to report Haines — maybe to you — for assault. Every time he saw Haines around town, he referred to him as a pervert. Haines had it in for him.'

'Come on,' Augie said. 'Maybe Claire's making it up.'

'Scott actually told us this story, although he never said which cop it was. Looks like Scott was a constant thorn in Haines' side. One night, Haines had a chance to deal with it.'

Augie was slowly shaking his head. 'I still don't buy it.'

'You think it's just a coincidence that the night Scott goes off the roof of Ravelson Furniture, it just happens to be Haines who finds him? Haines wasn't answering a call. It wasn't someone else who found Scott. Haines found him. And then came to our door with the news. Something else that's bothered me. Haines must have known you were Scott's uncle. You'd think, if you've just found the body of your own chief's nephew, that you might put in a call to him. Maybe even bring him in to break the news to the family. But he didn't want to bring you in. Probably too rattled to do that.'

'Jesus,' Augie said.

'I might not have believed it before,' I said, 'but now I know what Ricky Haines is capable of. I think he murdered Hanna Rodomski. I know he murdered Dennis Mullavey, and tried to kill me and Claire. He planted tracking devices in my car so he could follow me to where Dennis and Claire had been hiding out. He wasn't expecting me to get picked up for threatening the Tapscott kid. He even offered to call my lawyer for me. He needed me free, to lead him to Claire and Dennis.'

Augie winced. 'It was Ricky who told me you were in custody. Just before I came and lied my ass off for you.'

'He and his mother have been keeping a prisoner in this house for seven years. You telling me someone capable of all that couldn't have thrown my son off that roof?'

That left him with nothing to say. I watched his cheeks grow red. 'The bastard,' he said finally. 'Why the hell didn't Claire Sanders come forward?'

'Seriously? With all the shit going down between you and her father? She figured she didn't need any part of that. She said if she'd reported it, you'd just say her father put her up to it to make you look bad.'

He sighed. 'Shit.' He pushed the chair back and stood. 'We've got to get Haines and his mother, bring them both in, sort all of this out. Believe me, if that fucker killed Scott . . . ' Augie made a fist at his side. 'I loved him, too, you know. He's my sister's boy.'

'I know,' I said.

'We'll get to the bottom of this. I swear to God.'

'Don't worry,' I said. 'I intend to.'

'Let's go find them,' he said, and started for the door.

My cell rang. I grabbed it from my jacket pocket, saw that it was home calling.

'Hey,' I said.

'Hi,' Donna said. Her voice was flat, lacking animation.

'What's going on?'

'I need you to come home.'

'I'm kind of — I'm with Augie, and we're right in the middle of something.'

'Still, I need you to come home,' she said. 'I've got a visitor.'

'A visitor? Donna, just tell me what's going on and — '

I heard the phone being jostled, then a different voice came on the line. 'Mr. Weaver? Phyllis Pearce here. We have some things we need to discuss. You're going to help me out, because if you don't, it's going to be your fault what happens to your wife.'

469

64

It wasn't as though Phyllis wanted to use a knife. She would have preferred a gun, but feared the noise would attract attention, certainly if she fired it outside the house. Her son may have a silencer for one of his weapons, but she certainly doesn't. And she has no expertise in poisons. She considered holding a pillow over his face, but she feared he'd put up too much of a struggle and she wouldn't be able to finish the job.

In the end, a knife seemed the way to go.

Now he's in the trunk, wrapped in the plastic. Later, she will get Richard to help her bury him in the woods. She knows she hasn't the strength to dig a grave. Richard is still a strapping lad, and it shouldn't be any trouble for him. She's already put a shovel in the car, and a pair of gardening gloves so he won't get blisters. And even though she didn't choose to use it on her husband, she has a gun in her handbag.

She just hopes Richard isn't too upset that she decided something had to be done with Harry. That it had to be done now. For seven years he's been burdened with the guilt of what he did, been so attentive to his stepfather. Phyllis knows he still loves him, that he remembers that there were good times among the bad, when Harry was a real father to him.

Richard's just going to have to get used to the idea.

Phyllis has one more stop to make.

She'll go to the Weaver house, hold the wife hostage, get him on the phone, tell him to bring her the book. Once she has it in her possession, she'll find out from the detective whether anyone else knows about Harry. If not, the killing can end with the Weavers.

You can't go around knocking off everyone. Have to draw the line somewhere. She'll be relieved to have it end with the Weavers. Then she and Richard can go on about their lives again.

It'll be good to have things back to normal.

She can feel the extra weight in the back of the car as she drives. Going around corners, she notices the back end is heavy, sways some. She's looked up Weaver's address, makes a call on her cell as she heads to that part of town.

'Yes, Mother?'

'Where are you now?' she asks her son.

'Almost home.'

'You know where Mr. Weaver lives?'

'Yeah.'

'That's where I'm going now. Go there, and park across the street and down a ways. Call me if you see anything suspicious.'

'What are you going to do?'

'Just let me handle things now.'

'What about Dad? Is he okay? Is he at the house?'

'Not anymore, child. I've moved him.'

'Moved him where?'

'I'll tell you all about it later. Just get to Weaver's house.'

471

Phyllis ends the call.

She finds the Weaver house, pulls up to the curb and parks on the street. Goes to the door and rings the bell. Seconds later, it is opened.

'Hello?'

'Mrs. Weaver?' Phyllis says.

'That's right.'

'I can't believe we've never actually met, and if we have, please forgive me for not remembering. I'm Phyllis Pearce. I own Patchett's.'

'Oh, of course, hello. What can I do for you?' Donna Weaver asks.

'May I come in?'

Donna opens the door wide and admits her. Donna is wearing a bulky, button-up-the-front, long-sleeved sweater, and feels the need to apologize for it. 'I just put this on. It's one of my husband's. It looks awful, but the house is chilly. There's something wonky with the thermostat.'

'I'm hardly a fashion plate myself,' Phyllis says. 'It looks very comfortable.'

'Excuse the mess,' Donna says, pointing to the coffee table in the living room. It is covered in sketches of the same person from different angles, all in differing stages of completion. Charcoal pencils, fixative spray, a thick book of sketch paper, a small pad of yellow sticky notes. One of the sketches has a yellow note stuck to it, a few words scribbled on it.

'What's this?' Phyllis asks.

'Just . . . drawings. Of our son.'

'Oh yes,' Phyllis says. 'I'm so sorry.'

Donna's attempt to smile turns into a jagged line. 'Thank you.'

'This has to have been such a difficult time for you. How long has it been now since he passed away?'

'Is there something I can help you with, Mrs. Pearce?'

'Phyllis, please.' The woman smiles. 'I understand your son died by misadventure. That he was under the influence of drugs when he fell off the roof.'

Donna puts a hand delicately to her chest, as though she has indigestion. 'I really don't want to talk about that.'

'I only mention it because we have something in common, in a way. I mean, your son must be a terrible disappointment to you. The things he could have done, all thrown away. Now, my Richard — you know him of course because you process his checks — is still alive, but I swear, if there's one thing he knows how to do, it's how to screw something up.'

'I think you should leave.'

'I need to see your husband,' Phyllis says.

'I'll be sure to tell him you were here.'

'He's been by a couple of times to talk to me. I think we kind of hit it off. I need you to call him now and get him over here right away.'

'I'm sorry,' Donna says. 'I'm not doing that. If you want to talk to him, call him yourself. And I repeat, I think you should leave.'

Phyllis sets her purse on the floor, opens it, and takes out a handgun. She points it at Donna and says, 'Call him.'

Donna struggles to remain calm, but she has never had a gun pointed at her before, and she feels as though her insides are about to melt. 'What do you want with him?'

'That's between him and me,' Phyllis says. 'Is the phone in the kitchen?'

'Yes.'

'Then we'd best go to the kitchen.'

Donna goes to the kitchen phone, puts the receiver to her ear, hits the memory button that will connect to her husband's cell. She talks to him briefly before Phyllis takes the phone from her.

'Mr. Weaver? Phyllis Pearce here. We have some things we need to discuss. You're going to help me out, because if you don't, it's going to be your fault what happens to your wife.'

'Leave her alone.'

'And you need to know, your house is being watched. You come here by yourself. If anyone else shows up, your wife will die. And bring the book.'

'What book?'

'Please don't do that. I'm sure you have it. The one my husband gave to that boy. I need to have that back.'

'Where's Harry?' Weaver asks.

'Excuse me?' Phyllis' eyes go wide.

'He's not in his room downstairs. Where've you got him?'

'Just get here,' Phyllis says, and replaces the receiver.

'Whatever's happened, whatever you've done,' Donna says, moving back into the living room, 'you should just turn yourself in. Get a lawyer. He can arrange a surrender for you. He can work something out.'

'I don't think so,' Phyllis says as Donna leans over the coffee table, shuffling her drawings. 'What are you doing?'

Donna, her back to the woman, continues to collect the pictures into a neat pile, slides them into a folder.

'I said, what are you doing?' Phyllis asks.

'I don't like you looking at pictures of my son.'

Phyllis comes around the other side of the coffee table, orders Donna to stop what she's doing and sit down. Phyllis goes to the window, pulls back the curtain an inch to get a look at the street.

Her son's black pickup is parked at the curb on the other side.

Phyllis sighs with relief. 'Richard is here.' She appears contemplative. 'I hope he understands what I've had to do.'

65

I'd waved Augie over so he could hear both sides of the conversation. He was huddled close to me, his ear close to mine, and when Phyllis ended the call we looked at each other and he said, 'Did you actually talk to Donna?'

He'd missed the first few seconds of the conversation. 'Yeah,' I said. 'She sounds okay, but she's scared.'

'She says the house is being watched. That'll be Ricky. What the hell does she want?'

'Me,' I said. 'And the book. Ricky must think he killed Claire, or she'd be asking for her, too.'

'What book?'

I patted my chest to reassure myself that it was still in my jacket pocket. 'A kind of diary Harry kept. It proves he's been alive all these years.'

I started moving toward the door.

'What are you doing?' Augie asked.

'Going for Donna.'

'What's the plan?' he asked as I kept walking.

'No idea, but hanging around here isn't part of it.'

He followed me all the way to my car, grabbing my arm as I was opening the door of the Subaru.

'Hold on,' he said. 'You think if you give her that book, that's going to be the end of it? Think about what you know. What she *knows* you know. You think she's just going to get in her car and drive off? You go off half-cocked, you'll end up getting you and Donna both killed.'

I stopped.

'Tell me how to handle it.'

'First,' Augie said, 'I'll take care of Ricky.'

'How you going to do that?'

'I'll figure that out,' he said. 'Give me a five-minute head start to see where he is, get in position.'

'Five minutes,' I said.

'I'll call you,' he said.

We decided we'd both drive to within a couple of blocks of my house, then I'd wait while Augie found a spot he could watch Ricky from. I'd give him five minutes to call me, then drive to my house.

When we were a quarter mile away, I pulled over. Augie rolled up alongside in his Suburban, held up all five fingers of one hand, then drove off.

I kept my eyes on the dashboard clock. Two minutes. Three minutes. It seemed more like three hours.

Hang in there, Donna.

I looked at the clock again. Four minutes.

I wasn't waiting any longer. I put the transmission into drive.

My phone rang.

'I'm ready.'

'Where are you?'

'I'm in a house. Looking out the living room at Ricky in his pickup. He's on the other side of the street from your place, two houses down.'

'How did you get in a — '

'I broke in. Go.'

I went.

A Ford Crown Vic was parked in front of our place. Just up the street, facing this way, Ricky's black pickup. Through the tinted windows, I could just make out someone behind the wheel. I turned into the driveway, got out, noticed a hand pulling back the living room curtain an inch.

Should I knock? It was my own house, and Phyllis could obviously see me coming. So when I got to the door, I turned the knob and entered.

Phyllis was waiting for me, standing ten feet away from the door, weapon drawn, held in both hands to try and keep it steady. Her face looked drawn and haggard, and she seemed to have aged ten years since I'd last seen her. Beads of sweat dotted her forehead, but it didn't feel all that warm in here.

I glanced into the living room, saw Donna sitting on the couch, her mouth a jagged line across her face.

'Take out your gun,' Phyllis said.

I reached around for my Glock, removed it from my holster.

'Put it there, right there,' she said, pointing to the table in the front hall where we set our keys and dropped the mail. I did as she asked. 'In there,' she said, pointing to the living room. I moved slowly.

'You okay?' I asked Donna. I thought it odd she didn't stand up. She sat there, holding her right wrist with her left hand.

'I'm okay,' she said quietly.

'She hurt you?' I said, looking at her wrist.

478

'No, I'm fine.'

'Sit down,' Phyllis said.

I took a seat that allowed me to see Phyllis and Donna, and catch a glimpse of the street through the sheers.

'Smartest thing for you to do, Phyllis,' I said, 'is walk out that door, hop in the truck with your son, and turn yourself in.'

'The book,' she said.

I reached, slowly, into my jacket and tossed it at Phyllis' feet. She knelt and picked it up.

'It's not very interesting reading,' I said as she stood, the gun still pointed at us.

'I'm sorry about all this,' she said. 'I am. But I have to do what I have to do.'

'You think you've just about got the well capped now?' I asked. 'What did Ricky tell you? That he got Dennis and Claire? That I'm the last one left who knows what happened? Now that you've got that piece of evidence in your hands, and you've taken care of Donna and me, you've got this under control?'

Her jaw trembled slightly. 'Something like that.'

'Claire's alive,' I told her. 'Ricky didn't hit her. And she's home now, with her father. So now Sanders knows. And I've talked to Augie, and he knows. You'll end up killing half of Griffon before you're done, Phyllis.'

The color was draining from her face. 'You're lying.'

'No,' I said calmly. 'I'm not.'

'We . . . we never wanted anyone to get hurt,' she said. 'It was that boy's fault. He had no

479

business coming into our house.'

'Ricky killed Hanna Rodomski, didn't he?' I asked. 'When he found out the girls had tricked him.'

'She wouldn't tell him where Claire went,' Phyllis said. 'Sometimes he gets angry. But most of the time he's a good boy. He's a *police* officer. He does good things all the time.'

I wanted to know whether Ricky had told her about what had happened between him and our son, but I couldn't bring that up, not now, with Donna present. What she was going through, at this moment, was traumatic enough without learning that everything we thought we knew about what had happened to Scott was wrong.

'I'm sure that'll be taken into account,' I said. 'Don't make things worse by hurting anyone else. Everything has to end here. You and Ricky will have to answer for the things you've done, and it's not going to be easy, but this can all come to an end quietly, or it can come to an end very badly.'

'You brought help, didn't you?' Phyllis asked.

'I'm all alone,' I said.

'You're lying!' she said, waving the gun. 'Someone else is out there.'

I got half out of my chair, pulled back the sheer so we had an unobstructed view of the street. 'You see anyone?'

Phyllis glanced out. 'I don't believe you.'

I sat back down, looked at Donna. Her face was rigid.

'Phyllis, give it up.'

'I could . . . we could take her with us,' she

said, waving the gun at Donna. 'Until we got somewhere safe.'

'Think it through, Phyllis. You have secret bank accounts somewhere? False identities in place? That doesn't strike me as your kind of thing.'

I looked out the window again. Something had caught my eye. Something to do with Phyllis' Crown Victoria.

'I'm somebody in this town,' Phyllis said. 'I'm Phyllis Pearce. I know things about people.'

I looked back at her. 'You think you know enough to get out from under this mess?'

This time, when I glanced out the window, I squinted. Something was dripping from below the trunk of the woman's car, close to the bumper. Enough that a small puddle was forming at the back of the car.

I said to Phyllis, 'Seems like a funny place for a car to be leaking oil.'

She said, 'What?'

She moved closer to the window and glanced out. 'Oh no,' she said quietly.

Phyllis was holding the gun, at that moment, down at her side, her back to both Donna and me. I was thinking: *This is my chance. Jump her now.*

I was getting ready to spring when I realized Donna was already on the move. Reaching up into the sleeve of my borrowed sweater, taking something out.

The small can of fixative spray.

She had her index finger on the nozzle, and as Phyllis turned back around, Donna pressed it.

481

66

Donna raised the canister to within six inches of Phyllis' startled face and let loose. The spray, which took my breath away when she sprayed it too close to me in the house, completely clouded Phyllis' mouth and nose and eyes.

She screamed, then gasped for air.

The gun was coming up, but before she could aim it anywhere, I was on my feet, grabbing her right forearm with both hands and slamming it against the windowsill.

Phyllis held on to the gun. I slammed her wrist again, much harder this time, against the sill, and the gun clattered out of her hand. Donna was still spraying. It was like her hand had gone into spasm, was frozen into position.

Phyllis coughed and hacked and clawed at her face with both her hands. But once her fingers touched her cheeks, they became adhered to them, and she struggled to pull them away.

I went for Donna's arm, steered it away from Phyllis' face. 'It's okay,' I said. 'Nice going.'

She threw the can to the floor and put her arms around my neck. 'Oh God oh God.'

As much as I wanted to hold her, I broke free to get Phyllis' gun before she dropped down and started patting around to find it. Something she might have been inclined to try the moment she got her hands unstuck from her face.

Phyllis was screeching.

Donna had moved to the window. 'Cal,' she said. 'Ricky's coming.'

I bolted out the front door, grabbing my Glock from the table in the hall along the way. The moment I was outside I glanced up the street.

Even if he couldn't make out exactly what he was seeing from where he was parked, Ricky must have noticed some commotion in the window as I struggled with his mother. Now he was out of the truck, coming our way, gun in hand.

The front door to the house that was closest to his truck flew open and Augie charged out.

'Haines!' he bellowed. 'Haines!'

Ricky glanced back, saw Augie, but kept on going. 'Freeze!' Augie shouted, but Ricky was not about to follow orders from his chief right now.

There was the sense that all hell was breaking loose.

Feeling exposed, I charged toward Phyllis' car for cover. I dropped to the ground near the rear bumper, my knee just missing the puddle that I now had little doubt was blood.

I had a pretty good idea what — who — was in that trunk.

There was screaming coming from the front door of my house. I glanced that way, saw Phyllis Pearce stumble out. Her hands were free but her face was streaked with blood where her fingers had pulled away skin. Donna appeared in the doorway behind her, still holding the gun, but

483

raising her arm in a gesture of futility, as if to say, 'I couldn't shoot her.'

Ricky was nearly to Phyllis' car. Still on one knee, I raised my weapon over the trunk and yelled at him: 'Stop!'

Ricky raised his gun and fired.

I dropped down behind the car. There was another shot. I couldn't be sure, but I guessed it was Augie, trying to stop Ricky.

Haines ran past the end of the car, turned the gun in my direction, fired wildly, missing me. Then he stopped, pivoted, aimed the gun back at Augie. I raised my head, saw my brother-in-law running this way.

Raised the Glock, aimed for the center of Ricky's body, and pulled the trigger.

Once.

Twice.

Ricky staggered back as though he'd been hit with an invisible sandbag. He dropped left, put out an arm to break his fall, but by the time his palm hit pavement it offered no resistance. He crumpled into a heap.

Augie was on him a second later, stomping on the hand that still clung to the gun. Haines didn't move.

Phyllis ran past me, screaming, fell to her knees at her son's side, threw her arms around him and began to weep. Augie bent over, pried the gun from Haines' dead fingers, and started to walk toward me.

He had a sudden look of alarm on his face. He was looking past me.

I spun around.

Donna was standing ten feet away, looking down, her hand pressed to her stomach, where there was a growing dark blotch.

Donna eyes met mine as she said, 'Something's wrong, Cal. I think something's wrong.'

TWO WEEKS LATER

67

Phyllis Pearce lived, and the story came out. About how one night her son had cracked a chair across Harry Pearce's back, then thrown him down the stairs. How they had covered up the crime, faked his death, and looked after him for seven years.

The rest we more or less knew.

Phyllis faced a raft of charges, including the unlawful confinement and murder of her husband, Harry Pearce. Even though she hadn't actually strangled Hanna Rodomski, or shot Dennis Mullavey, she was charged as an accessory in those crimes, too.

Patchett's was up for sale.

Augustus Perry submitted his resignation as Griffon's chief of police, and Bert Sanders accepted it. Augie believed the actions of Officer Ricky Haines reflected so badly on his own leadership that he had no moral authority to continue leading the department. He was talking about moving to Florida with Beryl.

He wanted to put Griffon behind him as much as I did. We both carried a heavy burden from this place.

We were damaged men.

Haines wasn't going to be facing a trial, of course. When they brought him into Emergency he had no vital signs. I think he may have been dead before he hit the pavement.

I'd never wanted to kill a man, but I was having a hard time working up any sense of remorse for what I'd done. First of all, I did it because Haines was firing at my brother-in-law.

So it was, as they say, justifiable.

But there was something else going through my head in the initial moments after I'd pulled the trigger twice.

This is for Scott.

What I didn't know, and wouldn't for another few seconds, was that it was for Donna, too.

It was that one wild round Haines got off when he ran past the end of the car. The bullet had ripped past me, past Phyllis Pearce, and found a home in Donna's stomach.

I'd told her to stay in the house.

I'd told her.

Things had been looking so good, minutes earlier. I thought Phyllis had done something to Donna's wrist, but she'd been holding it to keep the fixative from sliding out of the sleeve of my sweater.

Clever.

There have been some who've suggested, as horrible as it was, that maybe I should find some small comfort in the fact that Donna went quickly.

People say a lot of astonishingly stupid things when they're trying to console you, and it can be hard to accept that they mean well. I suppose they think, in the overall scheme of things, in the course of a lifetime, that five minutes is quick.

It's not.

Not when you are easing your wife gently

down to the ground, rolling up your jacket to put under her head for a pillow, applying pressure to the wound, telling her that things are going to be okay, waiting to hear the siren of an approaching ambulance, wondering what's taking it so long to get here, getting down on your knees and touching her hair and her face and telling her you love her and that she just has to hang in, that help is coming soon, putting your head close to her mouth so you can hear her whisper that she loves you, too, that she is scared, that she wants to know what it is you wanted to tell her, and you say you can't wait to ride the cable cars, that as soon as she's okay we're going to go away, and she says that sounds nice, but she still doesn't have anything to wear, and also doesn't feel too good, and you tell her she's going to be okay, that the ambulance is almost here even though you still don't hear it, and she finds the strength to raise one hand and touch it to your cheek, and she says now it doesn't even hurt that much, and that she's not all that scared after all, that things really are going to be okay, and you tell her again to be quiet, to just hang in, and her hand comes away from your cheek and falls to her breast and her eyes go glassy and you finally hear the ambulance coming but it doesn't matter anymore.

Five minutes. Long time.

68

More people turned out for the funeral than I might have expected. At least a hundred. Donna was more loved by her colleagues, and the entire Griffon Police Service, than she ever would have imagined.

I knew Augie would show up — it was his sister, after all — but I was still surprised when I saw him walk into the church with Beryl. I wasn't surprised by his attendance, but by how quickly the events of the past few days had worn on him. His wife was a sapling next to Augie's oaklike stature, but she seemed to be propping him up as they made their way to a pew.

It was blame and guilt eating us all up, like a cancer. Mayor Bert Sanders was feeling it, too. He had to be asking himself why he hadn't kept a closer eye on Claire, why he'd been so easily duped when she'd said she was going to see her mother in Canada.

Annette Ravelson showed up, too, along with her husband, Kent. She made a point of not sitting anywhere near Mayor Bert Sanders.

I was relieved when Sanders offered to say a few words about Donna. I knew I wouldn't be able to hold it together, and when I'd asked Augie if he wanted to say anything, he could only shake his head.

'Darkness has visited our town,' he said. 'It has touched us all, but it has touched some more than others, and we mourn for them.' He was speaking, of course, about Hanna as well.

But not Ricky.

Instead of offering up one of those 'insert name here' kind of eulogies, Sanders had asked around about Donna, particularly among her coworkers, and pulled together a brief, touching portrait of a woman who had already lost so much.

Besides the minister, there was one other speaker: a woman Donna'd kept in touch with over the years, and who'd gone all through public and high school with her. She uttered some nice platitudes. At least, I'm told they were nice. I'd stopped listening by that point. I was imagining being someplace else. Someplace with Donna and Scott. How I ached, sitting in that church, to believe in the tenets that had led to its construction. I had little expectation that I would find myself reunited with them one day.

The Skillings came. Sean, of course, had been released from jail, within twenty-four hours of Donna's death. His parents were threatening a massive lawsuit that included the town of Griffon and Augie personally. I was betting the Rodomskis would get in on that.

They'd do what they had to do.

Then the service was over, and people were filing out of church, offering their condolences.

I was surprised to see Fritz Brott, owner of the butcher shop. He took my hand in his and squeezed.

'Read about this in the paper,' he said. 'So sorry about your loss.'

'Thank you,' I said. 'I've been meaning to call

493

you. I made a promise to someone a few days ago.'

'Tony,' Fritz said.

'That's right. Tony Fisk. I found myself in a situation . . . and he helped me out. I promised him I'd speak to you, ask you to maybe reconsider, give him another chance. I didn't promise him I'd be successful, but that I'd at least make the pitch.'

Fritz nodded knowingly. 'He came to see me.'

'He did?'

'Came in, maybe the day after you saw him. Said you were going to come talk to me, that you were going to make me give him his job back.'

'No,' I said. 'That wasn't the deal.'

'I figured, and told him so. And then he took out a gun and started waving it around and called me a bunch of names and for a second there I thought he was going to shoot me.'

I felt my heart sinking. 'No.'

'After he left, I called the police. He's been arrested. Tony's in jail right now.'

You don't think you can feel any sadder. But you can.

Fritz moved on, and a few more people stopped and shook hands, but I couldn't tell you who they were or what they said. I believed Tony Fisk had some good in him, but not enough to keep him from being a hothead.

Then Sean stopped, along with his parents. They all shook hands with me, said the things people are supposed to say at a time like that, and moved on. But then Sean held back.

'Could I talk to you for a minute?' he asked.

'Sure.'

'I mean, private like?'

I put my hand on his shoulder and steered him back into the church, which was now empty.

'What's up?' I asked him.

'Well, first, I just want say thanks again,' he said. 'For getting me out of jail.'

'It wasn't really me,' I said.

'Yeah, well, I guess, but it was you, finding Claire and everything, that made it happen.'

I waited to hear what it was he really wanted to tell me. He was looking at his shoes, his hands stuffed into the pockets of his suit pants. The jacket was tight around his shoulders. The suit probably fit him six months ago, but he was at that age where he was having his final growth spurts.

'There's something I gotta say,' he said.

'Something you don't want to tell me in front of your parents.'

'Yeah, I guess. But maybe you're going to tell them anyway, and if you do, I guess I have to live with that. But you've been good to me, and I think I owe you the truth.'

'What is it, Sean?'

He licked his lips, then lifted up his head to look me in the eye. 'It was me. I did it.'

I leaned my head in closer to him and put a hand on each shoulder, as much to steady myself as anything. What the hell was he talking about? There was no doubt Haines had killed Hanna, that he'd planted Hanna's clothes in Sean's truck. Phyllis Pearce had confirmed those details since her arrest.

So what was Sean talking about?

'Sean, what are you saying? You killed Hanna?'

He shook his head violently and his eyes went wide. 'God, no, I didn't do that. No way. I loved Hanna. I just wish I'd gotten there in time, picked her up before . . . ' He shook his head sadly and looked down again.

'Then what are you — '

And then it hit me.

'Scott,' I said, dropping my hands from his shoulders.

He lifted his head slowly and nodded. Tears were welling up in his eyes. 'A couple of days before he, you know, I had some X. Sometimes, when Hanna and I would go around delivering beer and collecting money for it, you'd get the odd asshole who didn't have the cash. This one guy, he wanted to pay Hanna with a couple of tabs, and she let him, and got back in the car with the X, and I told her she was an idiot, that Roman wasn't going to take anything except cash and we were going to have to make up the difference, and I thought of Scott, because I knew it was his thing, and I got hold of him and he said, yeah, he'd take them off my hands.'

Sean looked at me, waiting for a reaction, but I was too numbed by the day to offer one.

So he continued, 'I don't even know if he was on the stuff I sold him when he jumped. I wasn't the only guy he got it from. But I know it's possible it was me.' A tear ran down each of his cheeks. 'I'm so sorry. If you want to hit me or something, like, I'm okay with that. I'll tell my parents why you had to do it. I've got it coming.

But I'm sorry, Mr. Weaver. God, I'm so sorry.'

'I'm not going to hit you,' I said.

'I just — I just, I don't know why I did it.' He sobbed quietly. 'I could have just made up the difference with my own money, you know? And thrown the shit out. I should have flushed it or something. But I was thinking . . . I don't know what I was thinking.'

His shoulders began to shake. I raised my arms tentatively, then put them around him and pulled the boy to me. I held him close, tightened my arms around him as he wept into my chest.

I felt Donna watching me as I did. Felt it was what she would want me to do.

'Everyone's done some pretty dumb things lately,' I said.

I felt him slip his arms around my back. 'I hate myself,' Scott said. 'I hate myself so much.'

We all hated ourselves these days.

Holding Sean, this boy about the same age and size as Scott, I could almost imagine he was my own. I remembered the feeling of taking him into my arms, of the father-son hugs we once shared.

If I forgave Sean, would I be forgiving Scott, too, for what he'd put us through? And wasn't there less to forgive Scott for, anyway, than what I'd once believed?

'It's okay,' I whispered again. 'It's okay.'

Because I no longer believed Scott jumped. I knew, in my heart, he was pushed.

Thrown.

And there was one person I was now ready to

talk to, in hopes that she might be able to shed some light on what happened that night.

★ ★ ★

Her name was Rhonda McIntyre.

I'd first heard it when I got a ride home with Annette Ravelson the night I'd found her in Bert Sanders' bedroom. Annette said she'd been one of the mayor's other flings, and she'd also been seeing a Griffon cop who didn't know she had a thing going on with Bert. I remembered Annette saying Rhonda had broken it off with the cop, that she'd found him kind of 'freaky.'

That cop had turned out to be Ricky Haines. Her name had come up as the Griffon police did a full investigation into his background. They'd found her e-mail address on his home computer, and in his phone.

When she broke things off with Haines, which was around the time she'd also stopped seeing the mayor, she quit her job at Ravelson and moved back in with her family in Erie.

I wanted to talk to her.

So I drove to Erie. I did the trip in just under an hour and a half. I'd gone back to Cayuga Lake one day, turned in my rented Subaru, and gotten my Honda back from the cottage where Dennis and Claire had been hiding out.

Rhonda McIntyre was living with her parents in a beautiful lakeside house on Saybrook Place, just west of the industrial city's downtown. I didn't call first. I had no idea whether she would want to talk to me, and I didn't want to give her a chance to disappear.

I knew it was a long shot, but I was hoping Haines might have told her something, if not actually confided in her, some of the details surrounding Scott's plunge off the roof of Ravelson Furniture.

Maybe, I thought, if she had some idea of what he'd done, it was the reason she'd broken things off with him and gone back to the safety of her family.

I found the house behind a tall, well-manicured hedge that shielded the McIntyres from the prying eyes of passersby. I drove up the long, paved drive and parked within steps of the front door.

A handsome woman in her fifties answered. 'Mrs. McIntyre?' I said. When she nodded, I told her who I was, and that I was here to speak with Rhonda.

'About all this sordid mess,' she said.

'Yes,' I said.

'I don't think that's such a good idea,' she said.

'It might be easier talking to me than the police,' I said. An implied threat that sometimes worked.

This time, it did the trick.

She led me through the house to a sunroom at the back that looked out over Lake Erie. The sky was overcast, and there was a north wind raising whitecaps. I could feel cold drafts of air sneaking their way around the windows.

'I'll get Rhonda,' she said.

Moments later, a small, wispy woman of twenty-five entered the room anxiously, her mother right behind her.

'Yes?'

'Hi, Rhonda,' I said. 'I need to ask you a few questions.'

'I'm sorry. I forgot your name,' the mother said.

'Weaver,' I said. 'Cal Weaver.'

Rhonda blinked. Her anxiety level appeared to have taken a jump. I thought it would be easier for her to talk to me without her mother present.

'Mrs. McIntyre, would you mind if your daughter and I spoke privately?'

'Well, I think I need to be here if — '

'It's okay, Mom,' Rhonda said. 'I'll be okay.'

The woman withdrew reluctantly. Rhonda and I sat in white wicker chairs with puffy yellow-flowered cushions.

'You should have called ahead,' she said.

'Rhonda, we know an awful lot now about Ricky, and his mother, and what they'd been up to for more than a decade. But there are still a few gaps in what we know — in what I would like to know — and I know that for a while there you were going out with Ricky.'

She became defensive. 'We went out a few times, but I could never . . . I was never really all that serious. There were things not right with him.'

I waited.

'First of all, this relationship with his mom, it was kind of sick, you know? He was always trying to please her, always rushing over to the house. Of course, I sort of get now why he was always there, because he was helping his mom look after his stepdad, in the basement there. I mean, that kind of explained a lot.'

'What do you mean?'

'He'd never take me to his mother's house. I mean, he wanted me to meet his mother once, but we did it at a coffee shop. We never went out to her place. One time, I was going by there and saw Ricky's pickup in the driveway, so I turned in and knocked on the door, just figuring I'd say hello, and he came out on the porch and went crazy on me.'

'They couldn't take a chance of anyone going inside,' I said.

'No kidding. But there was more. He was like two people. He could pretend to be all nice when it suited him, but underneath, he didn't really feel anything. Except maybe anger. Sometimes you could tell it was just simmering under the surface. I don't think he ever understood what it meant to be someone else.'

'What do you mean?'

'Like, to be in someone else's shoes. He had no, you know, empathy. Everything was about how it felt to him. He didn't care if he hurt you — like, your feelings, mostly — because he didn't feel the hurt himself. Except where his crazy mother was concerned. She could hurt him. Like I said, he was always worried about pleasing her.'

Rhonda looked out over Lake Erie.

'I really don't see how I can help you,' she said. 'That's really all I have to say.'

'The thing is,' I said, 'I'm not really here about any of that. I'm here about a more personal matter.'

Her head moved ever so slightly in my direction. 'What sort of personal matter?'

'My son. I had a son named Scott. A couple of months ago, he died. Maybe you heard about that.'

Rhonda nodded. 'Of course. I was still working at Ravelson Furniture then. Everybody felt just awful about it. He was a nice boy.'

Her voice started to get shaky. I leaned in closer to her.

'I drove down here today, hoping you might know something about what happened on the roof that night. For the longest time, I've believed Scott went off that roof because he was high on drugs. That's not what I believe anymore.'

Her face looked as though it might shatter.

'Why would I know anything?' she asked.

'Because of the man you were seeing at the time,' I said.

Rhonda put her hands over her face. 'Oh God, oh God,' she said. 'I knew you'd come. I knew you'd figure it out eventually.'

I reached out and gently pulled her hands away from her face. 'Tell me about it, Rhonda.'

'It was never supposed to happen,' she said. 'Never.'

'Did he do it because Scott had threatened him?'

She nodded, and I let go of her arms so that she could wipe her eyes. 'Your son, Scott, said he was going to tell. He was all, 'Hey, wait till everyone finds this out!' You know?'

Rhonda was describing the incident at Patchett's. Could she have been there? It seemed unlikely Ricky would tell her the story about his patdown of Claire.

'You saw that happen?' I said.

She nodded, reached for a tissue on a nearby table, dabbed her eyes and wiped her nose.

'You were at Patchett's?'

That startled her. 'What?'

Now I was startled.

'What's Patchett's have to do with this?' she asked.

My mind was struggling. 'Wait,' I said. I had a theory. 'Not Patchett's. You were on the roof.'

Her head went up and down. She grabbed another tissue.

'You were there when Scott got pushed off the roof?'

She dropped her head. In sorrow, or shame, I wasn't sure.

I pressed on. 'You saw Ricky do it?'

Her head shot up and her mouth opened. She looked as startled as if I'd slapped her.

'Ricky?' she said. 'You thought it was Ricky?'

69

It was dark. Half past ten. From atop Ravelson Furniture, I could see the Skylon Tower in the distance. It was quiet up here, the sounds from cars passing through downtown Griffon barely audible. I was standing with one foot on the ledge, one on the roof, in the very spot where Scott had to have gone off.

I'd called Kent, and he'd let me come up here. And he left a couple of doors unlocked so someone could join me.

I was expecting company any second now. Rhonda McIntyre had agreed to make a phone call for me to set up this meeting. I turned away from the view and looked at the door that led out onto the roof when I heard someone coming up the steps. I walked away from the edge so I could be closer to the door when it opened.

Seconds later, it did.

'Hello, Bert,' I said.

Bert Sanders stepped out onto the roof, his shoes crunching the gravel secured with tar.

'What — Cal, what are you doing here?'

'Waiting for you,' I said. 'But I guess you were expecting someone else.'

He started to turn for the door, but I got around him and blocked his path.

'You were expecting Rhonda McIntyre,' I said.

'I don't know what you're talking about,' Bert said.

504

'Bert, please. I went to see her, in Erie. We talked. I asked her to set this up.'

His eyes darted about, looking for an escape.

'Why don't you tell me your version of what happened?' I said.

'Whatever Rhonda told you,' he said, 'you have to understand where she's coming from. She's got an ax to grind. You've got to take what she says with a grain of salt. I was' — he looked around, to see whether anyone could possibly be listening — 'seeing Annette, and this thing with Rhonda just wasn't going anywhere. I mean, yes, there was the sex — '

'Which you had up here.'

Sanders nodded sheepishly. 'It's true. We met up here a few times. You know that kind of furtive, frantic sex you can have, where it seems all the more exciting because the location is so . . . different.' He tried an old boy's smile on me, like, hey, you know what it's like.

'So you came up here, the two of you, well after hours, and were getting into it,' I said. 'Rhonda had keys, just like Scott did. Was he already up here, or did he come up after?'

Sanders swallowed. 'After.'

'So lay it out for me. Where were you?'

There was a small structure that sat on the roof to accommodate the top of the stairwell and the door. Sanders pointed around the side. 'We were leaning up against that. And then, suddenly, we heard steps, and the door burst open.' He paused. 'And it was your son.'

'Go on,' I said.

'He was high as a kite, Cal. Skipping around,

with a bottle of something in his hand. He was feeling pretty good.' A slightly accusatory tone, the suggestion that Scott wouldn't have been up here if we'd kept better tabs on him.

'So he was high,' I said. 'What then?'

'Rhonda and I, we knew we had to get back downstairs without him seeing us. All we had to do was slip away, and we would have done it — we almost did it — but as we were coming around the corner there, Rhonda, one of her high heels got stuck for a second in the gravel, and she stumbled. That's when Scott turned around and saw us.'

'What did he say?'

'At first, nothing. He was as surprised to see us as we were to see him when he came out that door. It was like we'd caught each other being up to something we weren't supposed to be doing.'

He shook his head regretfully. 'But I guess, in his intoxicated state, he got over that worry pretty quickly and zeroed in on us. He knew Rhonda. He worked with her, saw her all the time. And he sure as hell knew who I was, too. He pointed a finger at us, like this, and he said something like, 'Holy shit.' He wasn't so high that he couldn't see that he'd caught us in something we didn't want to get out.'

'What happened then?' I said. There was a cool breeze, four stories above the street, but I felt hot.

'I said, 'Hey, Scott, it's not what it looks like.' And Rhonda said that too, that we'd just come up to see the stars. But the thing was, Rhonda's blouse was undone, and so was my belt, and

506

your son was no fool.'

Bert Sanders forced a smile. 'In fact, Cal, he was a good kid. You know, he got into some bad things, but he was a good kid. Everyone, everyone at Ravelson said that. Rhonda said so, too, that — '

'Shut up, Bert.'

I paced slowly back and forth in front of him, picturing it. Seeing it all in my head.

'So he didn't buy it,' I said. 'What happened then?'

'He was kind of rambling. He was saying he couldn't believe the two of us had something going on. Asking, wasn't I married? Which I told him I wasn't. And I don't think he knew Rhonda was seeing Ricky Haines — you know about that?'

'I do,' I said. And I thought he was probably right about that. Scott might have tempered his taunts where Haines was concerned if he knew he was going out with someone he worked with.

'I said to him, I said, 'Scott, you can't ever tell anyone you saw us together.' And he asked why, and I told him nothing good would come of it. And then Rhonda blurted out, she said if Ricky found out she was seeing me, he'd kill her. Scott says, 'Ricky?' He says, 'Do you mean Ricky Haines, the cop?' And Rhonda says yes. She says, 'Please don't say anything.' Because there was something not right about him. I mean, we all know that now, don't we? That Haines was sick in the head or something. Keeping his stepfather in the basement for almost a decade. He had to have a few screws loose.' He tapped his index finger to his temple twice.

'And there was more, you know. I mean, there I was, in the thick of it with Chief Perry, attacking him for how he runs his department, and I'm fooling around with one of his officers' girlfriends. The optics weren't good. Rhonda would be at risk, and I'd be compromised if it came out. The chief could have found a way to use it against me.'

'Scott,' I said. 'What happened with Scott?'

'I was worried that even if he promised not to tell, would he keep it? When he came down off his high, when the drugs wore off, would he remember what he'd seen, but not what he'd promised to do?'

Sanders tried to look as earnest as possible, like he still believed he could count on my vote in the next election.

'How did it happen, Bert? I need to hear it from you.'

He stammered. 'It — it was an accident. Really. He stumbled and — '

I closed in on him, grabbed his collar and propelled him closer to where Scott had gone off the building. He stumbled, but caught himself about ten feet shy of the edge.

'Cal,' he said. 'Please.'

'If you're honest with me, if you admit what you did, I won't throw you over,' I said.

'He just — he started shouting. He wasn't himself, you know. It was the drugs. But he was shouting our names. *Out loud.* If he'd kept it up, he was going to draw somebody up there. The police, a security company.'

I gave him another push and he tripped over his own feet, landing a little over a yard from the edge. I looked down at him, pulled back my jacket, and took out my Glock. I'd brought it along for tonight.

'Jesus, Cal, for the love of God.'

'What happened?'

'I — I tried to shut him up. I grabbed him, put my hand over his mouth. We struggled. We were fighting with each other. We were, we were right about here. I tried to get my hand over his mouth again and he — he bit me! He bit my hand. I drew my hand back and — I swear, it was just instinctive. It was a kind of defensive gesture — but I shoved him away.'

'You shoved him.'

'I swear to God, I never ... I never meant ... '

'Get up,' I ordered, waving the gun at him.

Sanders got to his feet, brushed some bits of gravel that had stuck to his dress pants.

'So you pushed him off right here,' I said.

Sanders nodded.

'Stand there.'

'Cal.'

'Stand there. On the edge.'

'I'm not good with heights,' he protested.

I gave him a shove. 'Was that how hard you pushed him? Must have been harder. You didn't go off.'

'Please, Cal. Please.'

'Step up.'

'I can't.'

'I'll shoot you. If you don't stand there, I'll

shoot you. I swear to God I will. I've already killed one person since this all began. Maybe it's easier the second time.'

He put his right foot on the raised edge.

'That's good. Now the other one.'

His left shoe dragged along the gravel. 'I don't — I don't think I can do it.'

'Don't look down,' I advised. 'Just look straight out. Look at the tower. It's pretty this time of night.'

Sanders stood there, his back to me, his arms out at his sides for balance. I raised the Glock and touched the barrel to the back of his head.

'Bang,' I said.

70

I'm not sure what I'll do. They say you shouldn't rush into these things. Take some time, then make your decisions.

But I can't see what's holding me up. There's nothing for me here in Griffon. I don't want to stay in this house, and I don't want to be in this town.

Augie and Beryl already have their house up for sale. I don't even know if they've decided where they're going. Still betting on Florida. Augie wasn't that far off from retirement, and they'd talked in the past about moving down to the Sarasota area. The trouble Augie will have is the same one I'm going to have to deal with. No matter where you go, your memories, and your regrets, move with you.

I'm thinking of going back to Promise Falls. Not to join the police. They wouldn't have me, and that's not what I want, anyway. I can keep making a living the way I've been doing it the last few years, but I think I'd rather do it in a place where I feel slightly more at home.

Not that I won't have to be coming back here. Sanders is going to go on trial. Rhonda McIntyre has cut a deal with the prosecutor to testify against him. I left him up there on that roof. Turned and walked away. I wanted to push him. Give him a little nudge with the end of the Glock. But in the end, I couldn't do it. I asked myself, in that millisecond when I had to make my decision, whether I believed I'd feel any better two seconds later when he hit the parking lot.

I decided I probably would.

But there was something that kept me from doing it. *Claire*. I couldn't do it to Claire. I couldn't kill her father. I could see him charged, I could see testifying against him, and I could see him going to prison. And I could see her having to deal with all of that, with the support of her mother.

But I couldn't see her dealing with her father's death.

There'd been too many deaths.

So now I'm figuring out what to do. It will almost certainly mean moving somewhere. If not Promise Falls, then Timbuktu for all I know. In the meantime, I have to start going through everything in the house. What to save, what to pitch.

I can't keep everything.

In the days after Donna's death, I didn't touch her things on the coffee table. I guess I avoided them. Looking at her drawings of Scott, it just hurt too much. It wasn't until after Sanders had been arrested that I had the time, and the strength, to sift through the items.

I picked up her folder of drawings, weighed it in my hand. So many sketches. I dropped it back on the coffee table, opened it up and a couple of pencils rolled out and landed on the floor.

There was a drawing on top. A sketch of Scott, of course, but with a yellow sticky note attached to it. I read the note, and looked at the sketch.

She'd gotten the nose right. I liked the way she'd captured the wisps of hair that fell across his forehead. At first I thought the lips were a bit too full, but the more I looked I realized I was wrong. Some shading had thrown me off.

I guess Donna was intending to leave this one out for me. Maybe when I'd come home after she'd gone to bed.

She had written on the sticky note, in pencil: 'Cal, I think this is the one. I'm done. What do you think?'

She'd always said she would stop when she believed she couldn't do another drawing that would be any better.

'It's perfect,' I said.

ACKNOWLEDGMENTS

Authors who do it all on their own are authors who don't sell books. I have a lot of support.

Thanks to Mark Streatfeild, Brad Martin, Alex Kingsmill, Spencer Barclay, David Young, Danielle Perez, Eva Kolcze, Valerie Gow, Kara Welsh, Malcolm Edwards, Bill Massey, Elia Morrison, Helen Heller, Juliet Ewers, Heather Connor, Gord Drennan, Cathy Paine, Kristin Cochrane, Susan Lamb, Nita Pronovost, Paige Barclay, Margot Szajbely Jenner, Duncan Shields, Ali Karim, Alan K. Sapp, Ken Bain and Lindsey Middleton.

And booksellers. Oh yeah, booksellers.

We do hope that you have enjoyed reading this large print book.

Did you know that all of our titles are available for purchase?

We publish a wide range of high quality large print books including:
Romances, Mysteries, Classics
General Fiction
Non Fiction and Westerns

Special interest titles available in large print are:
The Little Oxford Dictionary
Music Book
Song Book
Hymn Book
Service Book

Also available from us courtesy of Oxford University Press:
Young Readers' Dictionary
(large print edition)
Young Readers' Thesaurus
(large print edition)

For further information or a free brochure, please contact us at:
Ulverscroft Large Print Books Ltd.,
The Green, Bradgate Road, Anstey,
Leicester, LE7 7FU, England.
Tel: (00 44) 0116 236 4325
Fax: (00 44) 0116 234 0205

Other titles published by
The House of Ulverscroft:

NEVER SAW IT COMING

Linwood Barclay

Keisha Ceylon is a psychic. At least, that's what it says on her business card. The truth is, Keisha's real powers have more to do with separating troubled families from their money than seeing into other worlds. Keisha's latest mark is a man whose wife disappeared a week ago. She's seen him on TV, pleading for his wife to come home or for whoever took her to let her go — and right away, Keisha can see dollar signs. When she pays Wendell Garfield a visit and tells him about her visions, she knows she's got him hooked. The trouble is, unbeknownst to Keisha, her 'vision' is uncomfortably close to the truth. And advertising it may be the last thing she ought to do . . .

THE ACCIDENT

Linwood Barclay

Milford, Connecticut is a good place to bring up kids — but the recession sees even law-abiding folks getting a little creative to make ends meet. Glen Garber's construction business is hit hard, especially after a mysterious fire destroys one of his buildings. But Glen's troubles escalate dramatically. His wife, Sheila, responds to their financial jam with plans that seemingly involve a secret network of Milford's wives and they are about to pay off — big-time. And that's when the accident happens . . . Suddenly it seems that the neighbours' 'get rich quick' schemes are more likely to get you dead, and Glen — no longer able to trust even the people he loves — must risk everything to discover what's lurking behind the town's idyllic facade . . . before it's too late.

NEVER LOOK AWAY

Linwood Barclay

David Harwood is hoping that a carefree day taking a trip to Five Mountains amusement park with their four-year-old son Ethan, will help dispel his wife Jan's depression and frightening thoughts of suicide. But the day turns into a nightmare. When Jan and David become separated he goes to the police to report her missing — terrified that she's planning to take her own life — the nightmare reaches a new level. The police suspect that she might already be dead, murdered by her husband. To prove his innocence and keep his son from being taken away from him, David must face a terrifying possibility. That he's become the victim of a cold, calculating schemer prepared to destroy him and his family to keep a dreadful secret.

FEAR THE WORST

Linwood Barclay

It was the worst day of Tim Blake's life. His seventeen-year-old daughter, Sydney, was staying with him while she worked a summer job at the Just Inn Time hotel — father-daughter time to help with the after-effects of his divorce. Syd didn't arrive home at her usual time. Then, worryingly, she didn't answer her phone. And when the people at the Just Inn Time told him they'd no Sydney Blake working at the hotel, he was plunged into the abyss every parent dreads most. Where had she been every day, if not working at the Just Inn Time . . . ? To find his daughter Tim must discover who she really was, and what could have made her step out of her own life without leaving a trace.

TOO CLOSE TO HOME

Linwood Barclay

When the Cutter family's next-door-neighbours, the Langleys, are gunned down in their house one hot August night, the Cutters' world is turned upside down. That such brutal violence could be visited on an ordinary suburban family is as shocking as it is inexplicable — but at least the Cutters can comfort themselves with the thought that lightning is unlikely to strike twice in the same place. Unless, of course, the killers went to the wrong house . . .